A LITTLE CRUSH

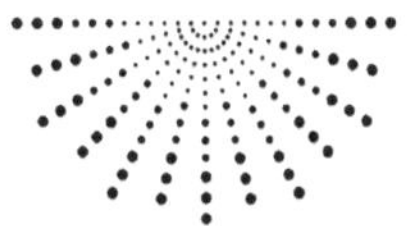

KELSIE RAE

To Stephanie, Allie, Marjorie, Taylor, and Shae...without your help, there's no way this book would've released on time :)

TRIGGER WARNING

Brief mention of miscarriage
Brief mention of cancer
Mention of losing a loved one
Main character has obsessive compulsive disorder

1

JAXON

I should probably be in a better mood. After all, one of my childhood friends is getting married and has been head over heels for the girl for years. I think all of us knew they'd tie the knot at one point or another. Add in everything they've been through to get here, and I'm pretty sure they're soulmates.

Guess I'm a little jaded after my own experience. It doesn't help that I just dropped off my daughter, Poppy, with my ex. A shiver runs up my spine from the memory alone as I reach for Maverick's parents' front door and walk inside without waiting for an invitation. To be honest, his parents would be offended if I did anything else.

It's quiet for what feels like the first time in months as I take in the empty foyer before walking further into the house. Ever since Maverick announced his proposal to Ophelia, the hinges have been working double-time to accommodate all the Sunday brunches as family and friends gathered to plan their big day.

The question is, where is everyone? I know I'm a few minutes early, but still. I take in the empty kitchen and large family room. A veggie tray, a bowl of fruit, and a basket of bagels sit on the kitchen counter as Maverick's mom appears from the opposite hallway. Her hair is the color of honey at the moment, though I've seen it range from black to silvery blonde over the years. I'm pretty sure this color suits her best. When she smiles, her eyes crinkle in the corners, and it never ceases to amaze me. The way she carries herself. So inviting and genuine. It reminds me of her daughter, Rory, though Archer, Maverick's twin, was the same way.

"Jax." Opening her inked arms, she strides toward me and pulls me into a hug. "Hey. You're early."

I return her grasp with a smile, wrapping my arms around her willowy frame. "Hey, Aunt Mia." The name rolls off my tongue with ease, despite the lack of actual blood relation. Even so, she's family, thanks to being one of my mom's best friends. Always has been, always will be. Letting her go, I explain, "I know I'm early, but I dropped Poppy off and figured, why head home only to turn back around and—"

My phone vibrates in my pocket, making my brows dip as I pull it out. "Shit, one sec." It's my ex, Iris. My stomach bottoms out at the four letters shining from my screen as I glance back at my Aunt Mia. "Sorry, I have to take this."

"No worries." She motions to the sliding glass doors off the kitchen. "People are going to be here in a few minutes if you want to use the balcony for some privacy."

"Thanks."

Heading toward the glass doors, I answer my phone, bringing it to my ear. "Hey, Iris—"

"You forgot her backup bottle."

My muscles seize as I register her words. Of course, that's why she's calling. It's not like she doesn't have a dozen bottles at her place. And I know I put it in the diaper bag. I fucking know it. It was in the side pocket, where I always put it. I also made sure to pack at least four extra diapers, two binkies, and diaper rash cream since the last time Iris watched her, she came back with a sore bum. So, no. I didn't forget the bottle. I know it, and so does Iris. She's calling to pick a fight.

Squeezing the bridge of my nose, I mutter, "Are you sure? I thought I—"

"I'm not an idiot, Jax. It's not here."

I grind my teeth and drop my hand to my side. "Never said you're an idiot, Iris. I'm sorry if I forgot to pack—"

"If?" she snaps.

Breathing in deeply through my nose, I pray for patience and step outside, hoping the fresh air will help ground me. It's warm and bright, making me squint as I offer, "I'm at Mav's right now, but I can swing by and drop off another bottle in a couple of hours."

A quiet splash from the pool echoes from beyond the wrought iron railing, distracting me. I walk toward the sound, confused. I thought I was early? Finley suggested a lazy pool party so all the ladies could soak in some sunshine and the kids could play in the water as everyone catches up. But if I'm early, who's in the pool now?

The warmth from the wrought iron seeps into my forearms while I listen to Iris berating me yet again and peer over the edge. The grass surrounding the pool is green but free of the dozen-plus bodies I have no doubt will be scattered across it within the next half hour. Mav, Ev, Reeves, Griffin. They'll be here soon with their families. The chairs surrounding the pool are empty, too, except for a stack of folded towels. Aunt Mia must've laid them out in preparation for the looming chaos.

Someone's in the pool, though I don't know who. Thanks to the light reflecting off the surface, I'm half-blind up here. Squinting, I try to collect clues as to who it might be. Baby blue bikini. Tan skin. No kids. No boyfriend or husband in sight. She's alone. A divot forms between my brows. Bending closer, I try to place the stranger beneath the water's rippling surface. She kicks her legs, stretching her arms in front of her as she swims from one end of the pool to the next, her head never fully breaking the surface. My dick stirs at the imagery. Her body rolling like a mermaid's. Her long hair trailing behind her. Her baby blue swimsuit outlining her tight ass.

Who the hell is this girl?

"Are you even listening to me?" Iris snaps. The venom dripping through the speaker is almost enough to convince me to drag my attention from the woman beneath me. But not quite.

"Yeah, sorry," I mutter. "I'm here."

Except I'm not. I'm still lost in the water. The fluid movements. The sun-kissed skin. The subtle curves. Fuck, thanks to the fallout with Iris earlier this year, I haven't wanted anything to do with the opposite sex in too fucking long until this very moment.

Nice to know I'm not dead.

When the stranger reaches the opposite end of the pool, her head fully breaks the surface, her long, ashy blonde hair floating around her. She flips onto her back, not bothering to open her eyes as she lazily soaks up the sun above us.

Gorgeous.

Fucking gorgeous.

And almost familiar.

Cocking my head, I take her in again from toe to head. The sun glistens on the water, painting her into a mirage. Long legs. Short torso. Oval-shaped face. Rosy cheeks.

Why do I recognize her?

As if she can feel my stare—as if she can read my fucking thoughts—the woman lowers her legs into the water. Brushing her wet hair away from her face, she peeks up at me on the balcony, the view threatening to knock me on my ass. Recognition sparks in her pretty gaze, and her pouty lips part as a stone falls in my gut, confirming what a small part of me already knew but didn't want to acknowledge.

Well, if it isn't the baby of the family, Rory Buchanan.

She's definitely not the little girl I remember.

Not even close.

And here I am, checking her out like she's a piece of meat, which is the last thing she needs and the last thing I should ever do, especially after the last time we saw each other.

"Fuck," I breathe out.

Iris gasps. "Excuse me?"

I hold Rory's gaze for another beat, my dick stiffening even more.

Shit.

She's... I thought she wasn't supposed to be here until tomorrow. Sure, I didn't blatantly ask Maverick when his little sister would be arriving for the wedding festivities. Considering our history, I had to beat around the bush, but I thought... It doesn't matter. Clearly, I was wrong. And clearly, she isn't the little girl she once was. Like an expensive bottle of wine, time has only made her sweeter but still as unattainable.

She's a kid, I remind myself, despite my subconscious calculating how old she must be now. Not that it matters.

It. Doesn't. Matter.

Holding my stare, she kicks her feet beneath the water's surface, keeping herself afloat, her small breasts bobbing in the glistening pool like a wet dream.

Snap the hell out of it! This is Rory! Sweet, innocent little Rory.

"Hello?" Iris snaps.

Giving Rory my back, I walk inside. "Sorry, there was a... bee. I'm here."

2

RORY

"**F**uck."

I watch Jaxon's lips move, forming the curse as the bane of my existence looks down on me from the balcony. I've imagined this moment. More times than I can count. And none of them—*none* of them—felt more like a kick to the ovaries than this one.

He looked…annoyed almost. Frustrated even. With my presence? I'm not entirely sure, but it sure seems that way.

I shouldn't be surprised, but it doesn't take away the sting.

Glancing up at the balcony again, I confirm I'm alone and climb out of the pool, reaching for one of the brightly-colored, folded towels as the sound of the sliding glass door from above causes a shiver of trepidation to race down my spine.

Is he gone? Is he back? Is one option worse than the other? Maybe he never left, and his wife joined him outside for the festivities. Wouldn't that just be a cherry on top of my day.

Yeah, I need to get out of here.

There's a reason I've kept a wide berth of all things Jaxon

Thorne since middle school. Trying to kiss a guy who's almost ten years older than you will do that to a girl. Yeah. Want to talk about a core memory? Pretty sure his rejection takes the cake. Don't get me wrong. I'm not stupid. I'm well aware I never should've crossed the line or put him in that position in the first place. But I was young and stupid and… in love.

I shove the reminder aside before I break out in hives when the short set of stairs from the balcony creak with footsteps.

Please don't be Jax, please don't be Jax, please don't—

My best friend, Tatum, comes into view with her boyfriend, Pax, and her sister, Ophelia, in tow. Relief washes over me. Although, now that I think about it, after the wedding, I guess she'll be my sister, too. Ophelia's engaged to my brother, Maverick, which means he isn't far behind, since the two are practically inseparable. Good. He can be a buffer between me and you-know-who. It's the only thing that convinced me to come home. The copious options for buffers, thanks to everyone being here to attend my brother's wedding.

It'll be fine.

Except for two minutes ago when it wasn't. But I digress.

When Tatum sees me, she grins. "Hey, Rore." Her eyes trail down my body. "You look hot."

I glance down at what little can be seen of my baby blue bikini, thanks to the towel wrapped around my shoulders, and grip the lime green and fluorescent orange terry-cloth a little tighter in my palms. "Gee, thanks."

She pulls me into a hug then passes me to Ophelia and Pax.

"Hey, Baby," Pax greets me. "Baby" is his nickname for me, thanks to the first time we met and how much younger I was than everyone else in the room. Then again, it seems not much has changed. I've always been the baby of the group. The caboose. It also doesn't help that the waterworks are always on standby, painting me as the fragile cry-baby everyone likes to dote on and comfort at the drop of a hat.

I shouldn't complain. At least he doesn't call me Squeaks. And honestly, I don't mind the nickname he's chosen for me. Pax is...Pax. Rockstar. Fighter. Sweetheart. He can call me whatever he wants as long as he keeps treating my best friend like gold.

"Hey, Pax," I return. "How was meeting the future in-laws?"

With a grin, Pax turns to Ophelia. "I don't know. What do you think, Lia? Do you think I passed your parents' test?"

Ophelia nods. "I think he knocked their socks off—"

"Careful," Tatum interrupts. She slips her swimsuit cover off, revealing a deep red bikini that makes my swimsuit look like it belongs to a nun. Tossing the extra material onto the closest pool chair, she warns, "Pretty sure Paxton's head is already big enough, thank you very much."

Pax chuckles dryly. "Pretty sure it's only getting bigger, thanks to the view." He whistles. "Damn, Birthday Girl."

As his eyes trail up Tatum's body, Ophelia scoffs and shoves him into the pool, causing a massive splash. With a squeal, I jump out of the splash zone while Tatum folds at the waist, cackling at the sight of her boyfriend drenched from head to toe. Paxton's head breaks the surface seconds later, and he shakes the water from his sandy-blonde hair, somehow managing to turn what would be an embarrassing moment into a sexy shampoo commercial for men. Not even bothering to hide her smirk, Ophelia pushes Tatum in right along with Pax, and I cover my mouth, laughing at the sight. I'm not going to lie. They've come a long way. Lia and Tate. For years, the two barely spoke to each other after my brother, Archer—Maverick's twin—passed away in a car accident. It was a rough time for all of us, but seeing the people I love begin healing from his absence is one of the most beautiful things in the world.

He'd love it.

The bittersweet thought flutters through my mind like a butterfly's wings, and I let out a slow breath, trying to keep the tears at bay. I'm not sure why I still bother. They come no matter how much I fight it, but I can't convince myself to stop. This whole event—the engagement dinner, the planning, the wedding—it's going to leave me emotionally spent, even if I couldn't be happier for Maverick and Ophelia.

The pitter-patter of feet distracts me from the impromptu water fight, and I look up in time to see a little boy in a shark-covered swimsuit and red floaties cannonball into the shallow end. Or at least, I think it's what he was trying to do. The kid can't be older than four, but he's an exact replica of his dad.

"Dude," Finley calls, juggling a three-month-old in her arms. "I said no running, remember?"

"I've got him." Pecking Finley's cheek, Griffin strides toward the edge of the pool, slips into the water, and tosses their little boy over his shoulder. As he pats the toddler's bum in a mock spanking, Griffin strides across the pool, introducing himself to Paxton while Tatum hangs around Paxton's neck like a little monkey.

"Seriously." Finley approaches us and grabs a folded towel, laying it out on one of the empty pool chairs while keeping her newborn pressed to her chest. "Whoever said the terrible twos are rough have never had to deal with that boy."

"Aw, come on. You know you love him," Ophelia quips.

"I do," she agrees. "I also love sleep. And between this little nugget"—she kisses her baby girl's head—"and Macky's decision to be done with naps, I'm running on empty." Her butt finds the edge of the pool chair. "Once training starts with the Lions and Griffin's gone for hockey, I'm screwed." She looks up at me and smiles, fiddling with the delicate necklace around her throat. "Hey, Squeaks. It's good to see you."

"Good to see you, too," I return. "And I believe this is…"

"Callie." Fin twists the newborn in her arms, then adjusts the too-big sunhat on her baby's head so I can see how adorable her little girl is.

"She's beautiful," I tell her. "And looks just like you."

"I know, right?" Finley grins. "Seems Griff got his mini-me with Macky, and now I have mine." Stealing a quick squeeze of Callie, she adds, "Do you want to hold her?"

"I'm all wet and don't want to make her uncomfortable. Later," I promise. And I mean it. I love kids. Always have. It's the grown ups who scare me.

With a smile, Finley returns, "I'll hold you to it."

"Well, if Rory won't take her, I will." Reaching for Callie, Ophelia cradles her against her chest and starts swaying back and forth as Raine and Everett traipse down the short set of stairs from the balcony. They stop by for a quick set of hugs before Everett reaches for the back of his T-shirt and pulls it over his head, revealing a canvas of Raine's artwork etched along his skin.

"Hey, is that a new tattoo?" Lia motions to a large piece on his side. A mean looking rhino blends in perfectly with the lion on his chest and the phoenix along his ribs.

Ev looks down. His mouth lifts. "Oh, yeah. That one. Raine did it a few weeks back. Gotta fit them in before the season starts."

Raine explains, "We don't want his pads to mess with the healing process. And sweat?" She tsks. "Yeah, not so great when it comes to fresh tattoos."

"Noted," I say. "I assume that means the new shop is going well?"

Raine smiles. "Yeah, it's kind of crazy, actually. We're

booked out for a solid two months. Seems Etch 'N' Ink's reputation precedes itself."

"That and your own work," Everett adds, wrapping his arm around his wife's waist before pulling her in for a playful kiss. "When Raine announced she was wrapping up at the new location, people lost their minds and caused their website to crash because of everyone trying to make an appointment before her last day."

After Raine joined her dad's team at Etch 'N' Ink, people started flying in from all over the country to book an appointment with anyone from the shop and—more specifically—Raine, herself. Because her dad's an excellent businessman as well as an artist, he suggested they expand to meet customer demand. Now, Raine travels to different places in the US, builds new tattoo parlors from the ground up, hires and trains different artists, and makes sure they live up to Etch 'N' Ink's brand before giving it her stamp of approval and doing it all over again at a new location. It's crazy and inspiring, and I couldn't be happier for them. But what's more? To help support his wife, Everett's put in multiple trade requests over the years so he can be wherever she is, watch his wife thrive, and maintain their rock-solid relationship. Seriously. It's incredible, but my favorite part is how they're finally settling back in Lockwood Heights so Everett can play for the Lions with Griffin and Reeves under Jaxon's supervision.

"So, what are you going to do when you run out of blank skin?" Ophelia chimes in. "Seems like you're already close to it."

Everett's smile widens. "There are still a few places she can mark."

Smacking his chest, Raine rolls her eyes. "And on that note, I'm going to take a dip in the pool. You coming?"

"Hell, yeah," Everett returns.

"Me, too," Finley decides, turning to Lia. "As long as you're good with holding Callie for a little longer?"

"Yeah, no problem," Lia answers.

"Thanks. You're the best." Standing up, Finley jumps in next to her husband, stealing Macky from Griffin's grasp. As her fingers dig into her toddler's sides, Macky squeals in delight.

"You comin', Rore?" Raine asks me.

I look at the cool blue water, then decide, "I'm going to use the restroom first, but I'll be back."

"Sounds good," Raine replies. "Don't be long. I've missed you. We need to catch up."

"Yeah, definitely," I return. And she's right. Living outside of Lockwood Heights when everyone else is very much inside Lockwood Heights—even if it's only metaphorically for certain individuals—has a way of keeping distance. Despite always saying it's for the best,—the less opportunities for uncomfortable encounters with Jaxon, the better—it does make gatherings like this feel a little like you're the third, er fifteenth, wheel sometimes.

Making my way up the steps, I run into a very pregnant Dylan, her husband, Reeves, and their two little boys, Eli and Parker. Trailing behind them are my mom, my dad, Aunt Kate and Uncle Macklin. Pretty sure hugs are like confetti at this point as I pass them around until finally reaching the blissfully empty kitchen. Resting my back against the closed sliding glass door, I take a deep breath, reminding myself this is only the beginning of a very jam-packed week.

I love everyone more than anything, but it's...a lot. Pretending like everything's okay. Like a simple run-in—hell, it wasn't even a run-in—with a certain someone isn't enough to knock me on my ass or leave me feeling completely off-kilter like I do right now despite my best attempts to act normal and unaffected. I wonder where he is now.

Don't think about him.

It doesn't matter.

Heading to the restroom, I do my business and wash up in the sink. The cool water feels good against my hands, and I bend forward, splashing it against my face.

I wonder if Tatum saw right through me. If she could feel how distracted I was after my little…whatever the hell it was with Jaxon before he disappeared. Was he upset to see me? Can I blame him if he was? Probably not. One thing is very clear. This is even harder than I thought it would be, which is kind of ridiculous, all things considered. Instead, here I am. Hiding in the bathroom. Terrified that, by the time I make it back to the pool, he'll be there. With his wife. And I'll be…I'll be the same pathetic girl who ran out of Lockwood Heights all those years ago.

Don't think about him.

With a deep breath, I pick up the soap bottle, rinse it under the faucet to get rid of any potential soap scum build-up, then set it back down. I shouldn't. I know it's a compulsion. But it's one of the few I don't fight, well aware that, in the big scheme of things, it ranks low on the totem pole in regards to my obsessive compulsive disorder. After drying my hands, I grab my swim towel from beside the sink and open the door, stopping short.

"Shit," I breathe out.

"Sorry." A shy Jaxon stands in front of me squeezing the back of his neck. "I needed to—"

"Yeah, of course." Stepping aside, I give him space to enter the bathroom, but he doesn't budge.

Of course, he doesn't.

He looks good. Really good. Older, yeah, but not in an old-man, the poor guy's let himself go kind of way. Nope. That would be way too convenient for me. Instead, he looks like a man who's finally grown into himself. His dark hair looks like he just ran his fingers through it, and his white T-shirt stretches across his chest and broad shoulders, proving his affinity for wellness and an active lifestyle wasn't a phase, rather a lifelong goal. One he's clearly committed to. Honestly, it isn't even fair.

"It's good seeing you again," Jax murmurs.

My attention snaps from his broad chest to his stupidly attractive, and as vibrantly dark green as I remember, eyes. Did he most definitely just catch me checking him out? Why, yes. Yes, he did.

As if he can feel my discomfort, Jax tacks on a smile that makes my knees weak.

And I hate him for it.

How, even now, even after all these years, the bastard still manages to affect me with a stupid off-hand comment. Is it good to see me? Has he thought about me even once since I left Lockwood Heights? Not in a romantic way or anything. I'm well aware he still looks at me like I'm a child, but in a *we used to talk all the time and then nothing* kind of way.

It makes me feel like I'm a little kid all over again. Like a fumbling preteen who's never had an attractive guy talk to her or look her in the eye. Then again, the assumption isn't completely off-base. Not really. A burn hits my eyes, and I dig my fingernails into my palms, fighting the urge to tap my thumb against the tips of my fingers, well aware it'll only feed my OCD.

"You look…" Hesitating, Jax looks me up and down, his attention gliding down my body as my heart gallops faster and faster with every passing second. The swim towel is in my limp hand at my side, leaving most of my skin available for easy perusal. It makes me feel even more like a child. Like with a single look, I'm dragged right back to my preteen years, and I now want to puke.

"Rore," someone calls.

My body tenses, and I look over my shoulder toward the culprit. In red board shorts, his tattooed chest on full display, Dodger Anders, Raine's older brother and Paxton's bandmate, strides toward me with a confidence I can't help but envy. "Hey. Raine told me you were up here."

Raising a shoulder, I offer, weakly, "Here I am."

"Here you are." His mouth curves up before his gaze shifts to Jax. If he's surprised, he doesn't show it. "Hey, man, I'm Dodge. I think we met at Everett's wedding a while back."

"Hey," Jax returns. "Jaxon. Good to see you again."

"Yeah, you, too." Satisfied he's performed the proper pleasantries, Dodger tilts his head, giving me his full attention again. "You good?"

Snapping myself out of whatever funk from Hell I've been in since coming face-to-face with Jax again, I answer, "Yeah. Hi. I was actually wondering when you were going to show up. I was getting a little lonely over here," I add, though I'm not sure who I'm trying to remind. Dodger and I are only friends, but after hearing about the engagement and commiserating over our own demons in Lockwood Heights, he offered to be my plus-one to the wedding, and I couldn't have been more grateful. Especially now. When my stupid body and emotions have already betrayed me after two seconds of being in Jaxon's presence.

Seriously. What is wrong with me? Did I honestly think I'd survive an entire week of this bullshit?

Forcing a smile, I lift my arms to hug Dodger before realizing he's half-naked and so am I. Is a swimsuit hug weird? I mean, it's a lot of skin, but would I care if Jaxon wasn't two feet away? Honestly, I have no idea. I *shouldn't* care. That much I know. But what about Dodge? If he's bothered, he doesn't show it. Then again, he's probably used to seeing skin. Thanks to him being the lead singer of IndieCent Vows,

I doubt he would've batted an eye even if I'd flashed him fully.

Without missing a beat, he opens his arms and pulls me into a hug, looping his hands around the small of my back and tugging me close. Dodger asks, "You ready to go to the pool?"

Nodding, I end the hug. "Yes, please."

"Perfect, I'll join you." He tosses his arm around my shoulders, preparing to guide me back to the party.

I should probably say something to Jax. Tell him I'll see him around or whatever, but I'm not sure I can do it. Force myself to pretend everything is exactly how it used to be when the elephant in the room is so much bigger than that. Than meaningless pleasantries. He has to see it, doesn't he? I mean, I can play nice. It's the least he deserves. But pretending our history is water under the bridge when you're known for wearing your heart on your sleeve? I'm not sure I can do it.

Literally.

It's like I'm physically incapable.

"We'll see you out there," Dodger says to Jax.

"Yeah, for sure," Jax replies.

Come on, Rore, I tell myself.

Acknowledge him. Show him you're not the bumbling idiot you once were. You're not drooling over him anymore. Not again. Not ever. You've matured, dammit. So prove it!

Peeking up at Jax, I murmur, "Good seeing you again."

Confusion swirls in his dark olive-colored eyes, but he gives a jerky nod. "Yeah, you, too."

3

JAXON

I don't like him. It's not personal, but it's true. Besides, he's way too old for her.

My gaze falls to Rory at the edge of the pool all over again. Tatum's on one side, Dodger's on the other, and Raine completes the Rory-Dodger sandwich as she chats with her brother.

I don't know much about him. I've never bothered to learn. He's a rockstar. Likes to travel. Fuck girls. Never had a serious relationship, or at least, not any I know of. And Rory? My brows knit as I search my memory for anything I should've picked up on over the years, but I come up empty. I'm not surprised. After our families found out about Rory attempting to kiss me when she was still a kid, everyone walked on eggshells around me when it came to all things Rory. I'm still not sure if she asked them to keep me in the dark, or if they decided some distance was needed on their own, but I never questioned it. Never felt like I had any right to. She's their daughter. Their sister.

I shove the memory aside as Maverick sidles up to me.

"Hey, man," he says.

Tearing my attention from Rory, I look one of my best friends in the eye. "Hey."

"Where's Poppy?"

"She's with her mom."

"I thought Lia said you were bringing her?" Mav questions.

"I was planning to, but it's Iris's week, so…" I let my words hang in the air, knowing Mav doesn't need any further explanation. Not when he had a front-row seat to the fallout of my marriage. And it's strange. How much a person can change. How little you can know someone despite being married to them for years. The woman I thought I loved—I thought existed—vanished into a wisp of smoke after Poppy was born. And when I finally caught her cheating on me and suggested we go our separate ways because of it? She flipped a switch and never looked back, choosing to paint me as the villain despite my best attempts to keep things civil for Poppy's benefit.

"Fuck," Mav grunts. "That sucks."

I give him a half-assed shrug, my gaze wandering to Rory all over again. "Yeah."

"How's all that going, anyway?"

Focus, I remind myself.

Folding my arms, I mutter, "About as good as can be expected."

"Did Chris move in with her yet?" he prods.

The name alone is enough to make my stomach curdle, but I keep my expression on lockdown. "A few weeks ago, yeah."

"Jax!" someone calls.

Twisting in the water, I find Reeves with his arm half-cocked and a rubber football in his hand. It flies through the air, and I open my palms to catch it. We spend the next twenty minutes tossing the ball across the pool. Each of us takes turns passing to Reeves' oldest, Eli. He's seven and the cutest little shit I've ever met.

Before I know it, everyone slowly trickles out for naptime, a shower, or dinner with the in-laws, leaving me in the fading sun with my dad, Colt, and Maverick's dad, Uncle Henry.

"You stayin' for dinner?" Uncle Henry asks.

"Of course," my dad returns. "You really think Ash is gonna let Rory out of her sight now that she finally gets to see her for a few minutes?" he challenges, mentioning my mom.

He's not wrong. My mom loves Rory. Everyone loves Rory. Maybe it's because she's the baby of the family. Maybe it's because she's always been sweet as honey. Actually, that's a lie. When she was little, she hated everyone but her parents. Well, her parents and me, but that ship sailed a long time ago.

Uncle Henry smiles. "Yeah, we've missed my baby girl, too. How 'bout you, Jax? You staying for dinner?"

For more reasons than one, I shake my head. "Probably not. Iris needs me to drop off another bottle."

The same sheen of understanding hits their faces, mirroring Maverick's from earlier.

My dad scratches his jaw. "Is she, uh, still giving you trouble?"

"Depends on the day," I return, despite how hard it is to take the high road after all the shit we've been through. Long story short? Yeah. She's giving me trouble. Hell, I'm not even sure she knows *how* to be pleasant anymore. At least, not when I'm around.

"Really wish she'd take Eleanor's route," my dad mutters, mentioning my birth mom. Yeah, I was quite the surprise when my dad found out about me after falling in love with Ashlyn. By some miracle, Ashlyn took it in stride, accepting a baby boy with his father's eyes and treating me like her own. And now that I'm in a similar situation, I'm finally starting to grasp how much of a miracle it really is. I wonder if Poppy will ever have that. A loving step-mom who treats her as her own. I wonder if I'll ever have that, too. Another chance with someone who accepts my past. The good, the bad, and a pretty fucking adorable little girl who will always come first.

"It's hard enough raising a kid when you're not together," my dad continues. "Add in the way Iris handles everything, and I don't get it. Why she keeps giving you such a hard time. Eleanor was…easy."

I chuckle dryly. "Yeah, if only Iris would move to another country, right?"

"Eleanor was easy before she married Phillip and moved to England when you were older," my dad clarifies. "She accepted Ash with open arms, shared the title of mom, and let us know we were a team. All of us. Considering everything Iris did to bring you two to this point, her behavior is…" He grits his teeth and takes a deep breath.

I don't bother defending Iris or her decisions that led us here. She fucked up, but I wasn't happy, either. Not really. Doesn't justify stepping out on me, but it is what it is. With a sigh, I grasp the lip of the pool, lift myself out of it, and rest my sorry ass on the concrete edge still warm from the afternoon sun. I appreciate my dad's restraint. His desire to not bad-mouth my ex no matter how big of a target she likes to paint on herself.

"Any chance she approved the latest list of nannies?" Uncle Henry interjects.

It's another sore subject, and my head rolls forward as I bite back my groan. "Not yet. It isn't easy finding someone Poppy doesn't hate, who's also willing to travel with the team for away games, then be left twiddling their thumbs with nothing to do anytime Poppy's with her mom."

"You gonna figure something out before training?" he prods.

Uncle Henry is the owner of the NHL Lions and my boss after offering me the position of head coach. It's funny. How excited Iris was when I received the offer. Now, I can't help but wonder if it had anything to do with all the extra travel I was signing up for and the free nights she knew she'd have to sneak around behind my back. The thought leaves a bitter taste in my mouth.

"The head coach needs to be at training," Uncle Henry reminds me.

I bite my lip to keep from saying, *Yeah, no shit*, and mutter, "You know I'll figure something out."

My dad scoffs. "I'm still not sure why she has any say in who you hire in the first place, but that's just me."

With a groan, I rest my elbows on my knees, giving my dad a pointed look. "If the roles were reversed, I'd want a say in who my baby's around."

"Then why is Chris living with her?" he demands.

It's a good question. One I've refused to analyze. "Chris isn't a bad guy." *Just an asshole who likes fucking married women,* I silently add before voicing aloud, "Not to Poppy."

"I still don't trust him," my dad grunts.

Slapping his shoulder, Uncle Henry interjects, "Cut your son some slack. He's figuring it out."

Says the man who felt the need to remind me that the head coach should probably be at training camp. To be clear, I love these guys, and I'm grateful for everything they do. But sometimes they make me feel like I'm still a kid instead of a full-grown adult with my own child to worry about.

Sensing how close I am to losing my shit, my dad caves. "I'll drop it. Just remember we're here for you, all right? Your mom even offered to fly with you for the first game if it'll convince Iris to let Poppy travel. All you gotta do is ask."

It would help if Iris liked my mom. It'd help if she liked anyone. After the divorce, she decided everyone related to me is of the devil and has no issue reminding me of her stance any time I pick up or drop off our daughter at her place.

"You know the staff will do their best to accommodate whatever you need," Uncle Henry adds.

If only the Lions' staff was the issue. If I'm being honest, Iris's desire for control and compulsive need to fuck with me is more than half the battle when it comes to this upcoming season. Keeping my concerns to myself, I reply, "I appreciate it. For now, I'll take it a day at a time. Enjoy the wedding. Keep searching for a nanny. One Poppy and Iris don't hate, but one I can trust, and if I have to ask Iris to switch weeks or…something during training, then we'll be good to go."

"Yeah." My dad nearly chokes on his snort. Placing his hands on the edge of the pool, he pushes himself onto the still-warm concrete surrounding the water and plops down beside me. "Sounds like a walk in the park."

I chuckle. "Exactly." Turning to Uncle Henry, I add, "Thanks again for today. This was great."

"Don't thank me," he deflects. "Thank Mia for putting this on and Finley for suggesting a pool party so the kids would be entertained instead of a dinner to celebrate the engagement."

"I'll be sure to do that," I return. "Anything else I need to know for this upcoming week?"

"I think we're gonna watch some childhood videos tomorrow night so we can choose which ones to play during the reception," Uncle Henry tells me. "I'm sure Mav would love to have you here."

"Yeah," I decide. "I'll be here."

4

RORY

"Hey!" Tatum's voice echoes through the Bluetooth speaker as I pull onto the main road. "So, how'd it go?"

I glance at Hades, my German Shepherd sitting pretty in the passenger seat after I picked him up from the groomer. "I mean, I think they did a pretty good job. He's nice and clean, and—"

"I meant the run-in with Jaxon," she clarifies. "Smart-ass."

My mouth lifts. "Oh. *That.*" Scrunching my nose, I debate whether or not opening this particular can of worms is worth the effort or if it'll only feed my obsessive tendencies. I'm an overthinker on a good day. Add in my best friend's two cents, and I could wind up spiraling for a week.

"Yes, *that,*" Tatum says. "How was it seeing Jaxon? I wanted to ask at the party, but I was being nice and biding my time, which is officially right now."

"It was very uneventful," I lie. "As it should've been, since he's married and all. How was the family dinner with Pax?"

"You already asked me that question at the pool party,

remember? And way to be subtle about the subject change, Rore. Spill."

Sometimes I hate how well my best friend knows me.

Tongue in cheek, I offer, "There's nothing to spill."

"Rory Buchanan, don't think I won't drive back to your house and smack you upside the head if you don't fill me in. I already pointed out how I was nice enough not to bring it up at the pool in front of Dodger and Raine, but this is like, ten years in the making, girlfriend. I repeat, *spill*."

Scratching behind Hades' ear with my free hand, I'm grateful for his presence in the passenger seat as I mutter, "He saw me at the pool before everyone else got there, said, '*Fuck,*' and disappeared back into the house. Later, I ran into him in the hallway when I went to pee. He said it was good to see me, I said it was good to see him, then Dodger found me and escorted me back to the pool. That's it. See? Nothing to spill."

She hesitates, and I know she's sorting through each and every minute detail I gave her during my short debrief. "Hmm."

"Told you," I say.

"I mean, he said *fuck* when he saw you in a bathing suit, so—"

"It wasn't like that," I argue.

"You sure?"

"A hundred percent certain, yes." I flick on my blinker and turn onto my childhood street. "Now, will you please let it go?"

"Fiiiine," she drags out, "but only because I can hear how testy you are right now. If there are any more updates, I expect full details, okay?"

Pulling into my parents' driveway, I mumble, "Sure thing."

"Perfect. PS, I'm actually on my way to your house right now."

"What? Why?"

"No idea. You're talking to amicable Tatum. She doesn't ask questions and only follows orders from the bride, and the bride just texted, asking if I could meet at your parents' house, so I'll see you in a few."

"See you then." I tell her, ending the call. After shoving my car into park, I turn off the ignition and open my door, calling for Hades to follow as I head inside.

It's kind of weird. Being home again. Don't get me wrong. I visited over the years. For holidays. Birthdays. Long breaks from school. Unlike Tatum, who avoided all things Lockwood Heights like the Plague until recently, I didn't mind coming home for short stints of time. But I've never had to field whether or not I'd run into Jaxon. Or maybe my parents fielded him for me. I wouldn't put it past them. It's not like I'm a hard person to read. But this trip is different. Jaxon is one of Maverick's closest friends, and I'm Maverick's little sister. Of course we're going to run into each other during all the festivities. But it doesn't matter how much I've tried to prepare myself, or how insignificant yesterday's encounter was. I'm still on edge. Still anxious. So much so, I can't help but scan the street one more time to be sure he isn't here.

So far, so good. Hades runs ahead, and I follow behind before opening the front door. In a flash, he gallops off with my parents' dog, Mufasa.

After Kovu died, they purchased another German Shepherd from the same breeder, continuing the lineage and tradition the same way I did after moving to school and realizing how ugly my obsessive compulsive disorder could be when I was away from home.

Yeah, Hades might not be as friendly as Kovu. Hell, he

flunked out of his training. But I needed him during those first few years of college more than I'd ever admit out loud.

"Hey, Hades." My mom's voice filters in from the kitchen. I follow it, finding her squatting next to the island as she pets my demon of a dog. "Don't you look handsome." Hearing my footsteps, she looks up and smiles. "So, what do you think of the groomer? Not too bad, right?"

"Yeah, I think he looks great. Thanks for the recommendation."

"He does look great," she agrees. "And you'll look so handsome at the wedding, won't you, Hades?" Her mouth curves up. "I think Fasa knows he's next."

"His appointment's tomorrow, right?"

"Yup," she confirms. "Poor guy. He hates the groomer."

"I don't know a dog who doesn't."

"Hey, Kovu didn't mind, and Nala was an angel," she adds, mentioning the puppy who started it all. The one my dad gifted her with when they first started dating.

"Yeah, well, they can't all be like Nala, now can they?"

She chuckles softly and stands. "I guess not. Are you hungry?"

"Yeah, but I can make something—"

"Don't even think about it. I'm your mom, and I haven't seen you in what feels like forever. Take a seat and tell me about your plans for after the wedding."

Slipping nto one of the bar stools tucked under the center island, I rest my elbows on the cool surface and ask, "Is it bad if I tell you I don't have any yet?"

"You? With no plans?" She rifles through the fridge, pulling out mayo, mustard, turkey, and a few more toppings for sandwiches. "Who are you, and what have you done with my daughter?"

I stick my tongue out at her for good measure, despite knowing she's not wrong. I'm a sucker for a plan. The problem is, plans mean commitment, and with the whirl-wind of graduation and traveling home for the wedding, I wasn't ready to jump into anything with both feet. "I mean, I have a couple feelers out," I tell her.

"There she is," my mom teases.

"Nothing concrete, though," I clarify. "It wasn't really worth applying anywhere when I knew I'd have to ask for a few weeks off for the wedding. Besides," I steal a pickle from the jar and pop it into my mouth, "I love Harden Heights, but if I accept a job there, I'm officially committing to stay there for at least a couple years, so I'm kind of playing things by ear."

"Well, if moving's on the table, I'm pretty sure your dad could find you a good deal at my old place."

Yeah, I'm pretty sure her *pretty sure* is an understatement. My family owns a few buildings around Lockwood Heights, one of which is an apartment complex by LAU's campus. He used to live in the penthouse, and my mom lived in the apartment beneath his. It also happens to be where my most embarrassing moment transpired. The thought of going back there, let alone living in those four walls, is enough to make me break out in hives.

Yeah, no thank you.

However, admitting that little tidbit to my mom is a different story, so I lie, "I'll be sure to keep it in mind."

"Mm-hmm." Giving me the side-eye, she pulls out a few pieces of bread and untwists the lids on the condiments. "So, I assume that means you aren't seeing anyone?"

Seeing anyone? The thought alone is laughable. If only it were so easy.

"I think we both know the answer to your question."

"You know, I thought I knew the answer until receiving your RSVP," she notes.

I peek up at her but stay quiet.

"You and Dodger, huh?"

So that's what this is about?

I fight the urge to snort. "We're just friends."

Her eyes thin. "Are you sure?"

"One hundred percent positive, yes."

"And Dodger?" she prods. "Does he know you're just friends?"

"I repeat, a hundred percent, yes."

"And you want it to stay that way?"

"Moooom," I drag out.

"I'm only asking."

Sure, she is.

"Yes, I want my friendship with Dodger to stay in the friend zone."

"Okay, because he's a good guy, and—"

"Seriously?" I give the woman a look daring her to push the subject more than she already has.

"I'm trying to make it clear that your father and I love and support you in every way. I know after the whole..." The sandwich making stops as she looks over my shoulder, confirming we're alone. "Jax incident—"

"Mom," I snap.

"Let me finish," she insists. "I know the experience made a huge impact on you, whether or not you want to admit it out loud, and I only want to let you know you're allowed to love whomever you want, and I mean that in every way possible. Older, younger, man, woman...whatever."

I've always loved my mom. Always. She might not be perfect, but I've never had to question whether or not her actions come from the right place. Reminding myself of this, I mutter, "Not gay, and not interested in Dodger, or anyone else for that matter. I'm choosing to focus on me and my future, and if, by some miracle, the stars align, and I find someone I'm interested in, then...good for me. But for now, I am blissfully single, and I have no problem keeping it that way. Happy now?"

"I mean, I wouldn't say I'm ecstatic," she says dryly. "But I guess this'll do." I give her a mock glare. "Just remember. I'm your mom, and I'm allowed to check in and receive updates every once in a while."

"And would you look at that? You just did," I quip. "Does this mean I'm off the hook from giving you updates for the next year?"

Lips pursed, she cuts a slice of cheese, adding it to my sandwich. "I'll give you six months."

I roll my eyes. "Gee, thanks."

"Don't mention it." Setting the freshly-made sandwich on a plate, my mom scoots it toward me as the front door opens.

"Honey, I'm home!" Tatum calls.

"Hey!" My mom wipes her hands on a dishtowel, then strides toward the entryway. "Come on in. Lia and the guys are already downstairs."

With a quick wave, Tatum disappears down the hall toward the stairs leading to the basement, followed by Pax, Aunt Blakely, and Uncle Theo.

"Thanks for having us," Aunt Blakely says.

"No problem at all. You guys hungry?"

"Already ate." Uncle Theo pats his stomach. "Thanks, though."

"We brought Mama Taylor's famous cookies," Aunt Blakely adds, lifting a plate of chocolate chip cookies into the air. "We'll take them downstairs."

"Sounds good," my mom returns.

Once they're out of earshot, I ask, "What are they doing here?"

"Everyone's looking at family videos for the wedding," my mom answers.

"The wedding's in a week," I remind her. "They didn't think to do that already?"

"They've already gone through the photos, smarty pants, but they figured a few videos might be fun, too. Come on." She rounds the edge of the counter. "You can sit by me."

Down the stairs we go as I balance my sandwich on a plate. Lia and her family are already scattered around the massive sectional, along with Maverick, my dad, and...Jaxon. He's wearing a pair of joggers, a T-shirt and running shoes. He must've run here, which is why his car wasn't in the driveway and why his wife and baby seem to be missing.

Perfect.

My pulse spikes as my heels dig into the ground. My mom gives me a funny look and moves past me, grabbing my dad's attention. When he sees us, he smiles, patting the cushion beside him.

I can feel Tate's stare as she cuddles up beside Pax on one of the side couches while a video of Maverick playing roller hockey with the rest of the guys in the circle outside our home plays on the television screen. Forcing my feet to move, I round the edge of the couch, keeping a wide berth from Jaxon, who's seated in one of the leather chairs on the opposite side of the room. Prickles break out along my arms, and I sit on the edge of the cushion.

"Hey, where's Hades?" my dad asks, leaning closer and stealing my attention.

"I think he went out back with Fasa," I answer.

He nods. "You just missed a good one. Kovu stole the ball, and Archer chased after him until he tripped on one of your Barbies in the grass." He laughs. "Then you came out, defending Kovu. What were you? Three?" He chuckles even more. "Hell on wheels, Rore."

"Whatever. I was an angel," I quip, refusing to give Jaxon

another ounce of my attention. Or at the least, die trying. Fake it 'til you make it and all that.

"A grumpy angel," Maverick adds. "Dad didn't mention the part where you were bawling your eyes out after you saw the Barbie's arm was bent out of place."

"Hey, it was one of my favorites," I argue when the sound of me crying in the video cuts me off.

Turning toward it, I find myself front and center, my eyes welling with tears and my hair a mess as I cry over…something. Not the Barbie, obviously. That was the last video. But I'm clearly upset in this one, too. On the screen, my mom rushes forward and dips down, asking me what's wrong, but my younger self is crying so hard I can't make out a single recognizable word. With a sigh, she looks over my head, and calls, "Jax?"

"Yeah?" A young Jaxon, who can't be more than fifteen, rollerblades toward me and my mom in the driveway, decked out in his hockey pads with a stick in one hand.

"Any chance you know why she's sad?" my mom asks him, well aware that the only person who could usually translate my emotions was Jax, even when I was little.

Setting his stick on the grass, he kneels in front of me and wipes at my cheeks with his thumbs. "Hey, Squeaks. Wanna tell me what's wrong?"

On the screen, I mumble a few more unrecognizable words, and a furrow forms between Jaxon's brows as he tries to decipher what the heck I'm saying. Coming up empty, he simply asks, "You want a hug?"

My head bobs up and down in the video while a fresh wave of tears drips down my bright red cheeks and off my quivering chin in one rivulet after another, making my heart crack in the process. I have no idea why I was so sad, and I don't think Jax knew, either. But the compassion and warmth in his teenage gaze makes it hard for me to breathe as I sit on the couch, motionless.

"Come here, Squeaks." He opens his arms and the younger me charges into them before my little legs give out. He holds me close, rubbing his hand up and down my tiny back as he looks at the camera and smiles, mouthing, "I have no idea."

Sometimes I tell myself I'm crazy. That it was only the hormones that made me fall for him. That my feelings had nothing to do with the man, er, *boy*, himself. But as I watch a younger Jaxon comfort a younger me, I can't help but feel it again. The sweet, innocent pull. The connection. The memory might be foggy at best, but the feelings it evokes? Those are as vivid as ever, and a not so small part of me hates myself for it.

"Any chance you know what had you all worked up?" my dad asks.

My head snaps toward him. "What?"

"Do you remember why you were sad?"

I pause before giving him a shrug. "No idea."

"Well, I think it's adorable," Tatum's mom, Blakely, interjects. "You were seriously so in love with Jax when you were little. It was the cutest thing ever."

Cute? I glance at the television again. Right now, it looks cute. I'm nothing more than a five-year-old little girl who worships an older boy. If only it would've ended there, then I wouldn't have had to battle years of dread and shame. I wouldn't have felt the need to hightail it out of Lockwood Heights out of fear of running into him again. I'm not stupid. I know I'm not a little girl anymore. I know trying to kiss Jaxon Thorne wasn't the end of the world. Not in the big scheme of things, and definitely not from a logical standpoint. But my heart? My gut? They have a harder time embracing the memo. And what's worse is the fact that the same man is in this very room. I can feel his gaze on the side of my face as my Aunt Blakely's words hang in the air.

You were seriously so in love with Jax when you were little. It was the cutest thing ever.

"Yeah, I was a needy little thing," I quip, hoping to lighten the mood, even if I'm the only one who feels the heaviness from it. Digging my fingernails into my palms, I force my lungs to exhale on a slow breath. Thankfully, the video ends, and another starts right after it. The respite gives me a moment to breathe. To get a handle on my warring thoughts and emotions as I try to stay in the present.

No one cares, I silently remind myself. *No. One. Cares.*

The new home video shows Lia pointing at Maverick. She can't be more than nine years old, and she's shouting that he pulled her hair. I tune out what's happening, force myself to act normal, and take a bite of food. It tastes like ash. My dad rubs my back, catching onto my discomfort like a seasoned pro. Then again, he's my dad. I guess he *is* a seasoned pro at reading my thoughts and feelings, especially since I'm shit at hiding them in the first place.

I'm not sure how much time passes. How many more videos are saved and filed away for the wedding. But now the hockey videos feature my brothers' time at Lockwood Ames University, while Lia's are set in high school.

As she reads her scholarship letter to the camera with a giant grin, I catch Maverick squeezing Ophelia's knee in our family room, appreciating the way their paths intertwined to bring them where they are today.

Engaged and happier than ever.

The video ends, and another replaces it.

It's me. With a big, dopey grin. I'm hiding in my bedroom after stealing my mom's phone. The memory tickles the back of my brain.

Shit.

I remember recording this, and I know exactly what's about to transpire on the screen if I don't stop the video as soon as possible.

My heart lodges in my throat, and I suggest, "Hey, maybe let's skip this one."

"Why?" my mom asks. "Look how cute you are!"

"I know, but we're looking for videos of Lia and Mav, so—"

The younger me from the video cuts me off as I grin at the camera. "Hi, my name is Rory Buchanan, and it's May fifteenth." I reach for the remote on the coffee table, attempting not to look like I'm seconds from puking while my younger self prattles on like a lovesick idiot. "I am eleven years old, and I'm calling it right now. One day, I'm going to marry Jaxon—" The screen goes black as I drop the remote onto the couch.

But it's too late.

Everyone heard it. My childish confession. I wish I could at least erase the bravado. The confidence I had. That a guy who's ten years older than me, a guy who only ever looked at me as a child—as he should have—would ever even think about dating me, let alone marrying me. Delusional. I was so fucking delusional. And no matter what I do, I can't erase it.

At least six sets of eyes pin me in place as they swivel toward me, one after another. And just like that, I'm brought back to Jaxon's couch in his penthouse. The flicker of the television as we watched a show. He was babysitting.

Baby. Fucking. Sitting.

And what did I do? I tried to kiss him.

Shame clogs my throat, and a familiar burn hits behind my eyes. I cannot believe this is happening. That even now, I can't run from my stupid crush or the fact that I spent years living in la-la land, believing it would ever be anything more than a stupid crush.

"Oh, boy. Would you look at that." I force a smile. "Talk about not understanding boundaries, am I right?" My facade cracks. "Anywho, I'm gonna…" I hook my thumb over my shoulder toward the stairs. "I'm gonna go check on Hades and make sure he didn't jump in the pool or start humping Fasa or…yeah."

Praying my legs don't give out, I push to my feet, keep my pace steady, and walk out of the theater room while the rest of my family stares at me without a word. Hell, it's so quiet I'm pretty sure you could hear a pin drop, and I don't mean it figuratively. Can they even hear my erratic heartbeat? Probably. I sure as hell can. Gripping the handrail, I stride up to the main floor, my pulse thumping in my ears with every deliberate step.

I hate it. How no matter what I do, no matter how I act or where I hide, I still can't get rid of it. The reminder that my entire personality as a kid was who I loved. Who I idolized. And how I handled it in the worst way possible.

When I reach my bedroom, I collapse onto my childhood bed, willing the floor to open up and swallow me whole if it'll get me out of this mess.

Knock. Knock.

The rap of knuckles against wood cuts through my inner spiral as I cradle a pillow to my chest.

Not now.

Knock. Knock.

Squeezing my eyes shut, I say, "Who is it?"

"It's me."

Jaxon.

Despite how much time has passed since we really used to talk, I'd recognize his voice anywhere.

Fan-freaking-tastic.

He's literally the last person I want to see right now. The last person I want to see, *ever*, actually.

Go away, I silently seethe. I really don't think I can handle dealing with him in this moment. Not now. Not after the front-row seats to my childhood lunacy we were both privy to downstairs. However, if I want to keep even a sliver of what's left of my pride, begging him to go away and leave me alone isn't the greatest way to handle this. So even though it kills me, I let out a slow breath and call out, "Can we talk later, please?"

"Let me in, Squeaks."

Squeaks.

I used to love when he called me that nickname. Not because it was a reminder of how much of a bawl-baby I am, but because he was the one who gifted me the nickname. He was the one who was clever enough to paint my most annoying trait as something cute and innocent instead of ridiculously annoying.

Now, it only makes me sad.

"Come on, Squeaks," he begs.

Pushing to my feet, I stride toward the closed door and press my forehead against the solid piece of wood, unsure what to say or do. "I'm serious, Jax. I'm not feeling well." It's a lie, and we both know it. "Just...we'll talk later, okay?"

"Listen, you have nothing to be ashamed of."

A pathetic laugh escapes me before I can stop it. Nothing to be ashamed of? He's kidding, right? I have everything to be ashamed of. But rehashing any of it with anyone, let alone the star of every embarrassing decision I've ever made, feels about as comfortable as scooping my eyeballs out with a spoon. So, yeah. I do have a few things to be ashamed of, but thanks for the bold-faced lie, buddy. Really appreciate it.

"Come on, Squeaks," he repeats. "Please?"

Tapping the outside of my thigh, I steel my shoulders and open the door.

When he sees me, he pulls back, surprised. "Oh. Hey. I kind of thought—"

"I wouldn't open the door?" I finish for him. "Yeah, well, color us both shocked." I paste on a fake smile. "As you can see, I'm totally fine. I'm just not feeling one hundred percent, so you should go back downstairs and give your two cents on all the videos. I'm sure there are plenty more to sort through, and…yeah. I'm good. Okay?"

I start to close the door, but he slaps his hand against it, preventing it from closing. "Yeah, I'm not gonna do that."

"Why not?" I demand.

Scrubbing his hand over his face, he mutters, "Listen, I know this isn't what you want to hear, but it was just a stupid video, all right?"

"Well, I'm glad we can agree on something," I tell him. "Definitely a stupid video that deserves zero attention. Now, if you'll excuse me…"

I start to shut the door again, but he slaps his hand against it like before. "Squeaks."

The nickname hits like a lash, and I peek up at him. "Please don't call me Squeaks."

His chest swells on a heavy breath, but he lifts his hands in surrender. "Rory." He takes another deep breath. "I know you're not a fan of confrontation or anything that makes you feel uncomfortable, but if either of us wants to survive this, we gotta air this shit out, okay?"

He's probably right. This week already feels like a decade long, and it's only been a couple days. How the hell am I supposed to survive with him hanging around?

It isn't his fault. I know that. It's mine. But giving in? Airing out my most embarrassing moment to one of the people whose opinions I actually care about? No, thank you. Tongue in cheek, I offer, "Or, we can simply avoid each other."

A ghost of a smile tugs at the corner of his mouth. "We're basically family."

Good point.

My body sags against the doorjamb in defeat. "Here's the thing. I appreciate you coming and trying to clear the air or whatever, but there's no need. We're good. I'm just tired."

"I thought you felt sick," he argues.

"Headache," I toss back at him. "Which can be from exhaustion or illness. Seriously. I'm fine."

He doesn't believe me. I can see it in his eyes. Feel it in what little space separates us. "If you were fine, you wouldn't be avoiding me like this."

"I'm not…" The lie falls flat on my tongue. I close my mouth and cross my arms, unsure what to say when we both know he won't buy it anyway.

"Look, I'm sorry, okay?" he offers.

My lips part as I register his words. Seriously, am I hallucinating? What the hell?

"*You're* sorry?"

"You're surprised?" He scoffs. "Yeah, Rore. Of course, I'm sorry—"

"Why?" My fingers dig into my folded arms. "Jax, you have no reason to be sorry."

"Rory, I rejected you—"

"I'm not mad at you for rejecting me." My shoulders sag even more as I fight the urge to tap my fingers against my outer thigh. Part of me wants to slam the door in his face and run in the opposite direction because this conversation is so freaking embarrassing. The other part? Well, I guess this is way past due, isn't it?

Fine.

"Of course you didn't kiss me back," I mumble. "Of course you shouldn't have kissed me back. You did the right thing, Jax. I was the one who screwed up."

"Rore—"

"Let me finish," I beg because if I don't, it'll continue haunting me like it has for years. "I was young, Jaxon. I was young and underage and stupid and reckless and head over heels in love with a guy who *would* never and *could* never love me back. A guy who looked at me like I was a little kid, which I was," I emphasize. "And now that I'm on the other side, I'm older and I see it, which…in all honesty, kind of sucks." A dry laugh lodges in my throat as I fight past my shame. "I get it, though. I completely understand, and that's why I came to my room tonight. Because I can't even watch home videos without being reminded of exactly how embarrassingly obsessed I was with you." Another pathetic laugh escapes me while I mentally replay the video from earlier tonight. "Jax, I was the one in the wrong—"

"You were a kid—"

"Yeah, but I'm not anymore," I argue. "And with every passing year, it only reinforces how…inappropriately I acted, and how stupid I feel about it."

"Rore…" His frown deepens. "I think you should cut yourself a little slack."

"Trust me. I've been working on it for years, but the good news is that I'm over it. Not the beating myself up part," I clarify, "but whatever weird childhood obsession I had with you." I wave my hand through the air. "Genuinely. It's over," I repeat, though I'm not entirely sure who I'm trying to convince. "So, there you go. We've now aired out the dirty laundry. You understand that you did nothing wrong, and I understand that I was nothing more than a babysitting gig and…we're good." I take a deep breath, grateful my hand is still clutched onto the edge of the door so I don't collapse into a ball right here and now. "Now, I really do have a headache," I mutter to myself, pinching the bridge of my nose. "Goodnight, Jaxon."

I close the door without waiting for his response and slide to my ass, pressing my knees to my chest.

There. I said it.

It's done.

So, why do I still feel so terrible?

I'm anxious. I shouldn't be, but I am. Ever since my chat with Rory, she's been on my mind. Okay, ever since I saw her in the pool, she's been on my mind, though I refuse to analyze why. Add in the disastrous video and the fallout afterward, and I feel…bad. The problem is I don't know how to make it right. How to tell her it was an innocent childhood crush. That I never looked at her like she was a babysitting gig. I think that part hurts the most. How she thinks I never cared about her.

She was my friend, too. My little side-kick. My shadow most days. One I enjoyed having around. Honestly, I've missed her over the years. More than I'd like to admit, especially with how things played out. I'd like to go back to being friends, if she's up to it. But she won't even give me a chance to express that. To tell her we're good. That I'd like to be friends again—real friends—and fuck knows I could use a few more of them. Instead, she closed the door in my face and has been absent ever since…until twenty minutes ago, when I arrived at the country club and saw her in a silky dress talking with Tatum. I'm still not sure if she noticed my arrival or if she chose to pretend I didn't exist. I'm not sure I want to know, either. Not that it matters. Clearly, that bridge is burned, and I don't know how to erect a new one.

With a sigh, I tug at the top button of my suit, unsure how much longer I can stand being here. Not that there's anything wrong with the country club Ophelia and Maverick chose for their wedding venue. The place is insane and a familiar backdrop for multiple Buchanan events, including the yearly B-Tech Enterprises company retreats. It's part country club and part hotel with a massive reception area perfect for hosting any event, including a wedding. Add in the polished marble floors, giant pillars, and pristine glass doors and windows allowing you to take in the rolling hills and expertly manicured foliage, and the place looks straight out of a storybook. So much so, I'm almost surprised they chose to have the actual wedding outside instead of in the main reception area. Not that it matters. Even the incredible backdrop isn't enough to make me want to stick around.

There's nothing wrong with weddings or love or rehearsal dinners. Honestly, I never minded them before. But after my own marriage burst into flames, it's hard pretending I still believe in happily-ever-afters and shit.

I roll my shoulders as Finley cuts off the wedding coordinator's instructions.

"Okay, so you need everyone to pair up, right?" Finley asks the wedding coordinator. Without waiting for her response, Finley rubs her hands together and does a quick headcount of the wedding party. "Perfect. Tatum, you're the maid of honor, and since Paxton's now in the wedding, you can pair up with him, then we'll go Dylan and Reeves—the best man—then Raine and Ev, Griff and me, and…" Clicking her tongue against the roof of her mouth, Finley looks at me like I'm nothing but a loose end. "You don't mind walking with Rory, do you?"

My attention cuts to the woman in question. The light, flowy dress reaches just above her knees, and her long, ashy-blonde hair is left straight down her back. She looks pretty today, even when she's staring at the ground.

Fuck, she won't even look at me.

"What about Dodger?" I ask.

"He's not in the wedding party," Finley explains, turning to Maverick's little sister. "Rore, are you okay with that? Being paired up with Jax?"

She says it like the idea of standing next to me and walking down an aisle is torture or something.

What am I, chopped liver?

"Sure thing," Rory squeaks. She looks about as comfortable as a woman purchasing a prescription for crabs—the STD, not the food. Despite her discomfort, she sidles up next to me and crosses her arms.

And yeah. This is awkward. I can feel the tension radiating off her. Like she's afraid to stand by me, let alone touch my arm or look me in the eye. Is this Rory's attempt at moving on from our past? Because it seems like she's shit at it. We're good, my ass. Then again, she's always been bad at hiding her emotions. Clearly, it hasn't changed over the years, unlike her hair, body, and height. I fight the urge to check her out and keep my eyes glued to the wedding coordinator in front of me.

"Okay, Groom, we need you up front," she starts, motioning to the front of the path lined with rows of wooden folding chairs. "And Bride, we need you at the very back with Mom and Dad. And then, the music starts, and once the bridesmaids and groomsmen have walked the path, you slowly walk toward your respective positions. Ready for a dry run? Perfect. In three, two, one."

The three-man orchestra set up on the north side begins playing as Tatum loops her arm through Paxton's, and they walk down the cobblestone aisle to a wooden arch covered in peach and white flowers. Dylan and Reeves follow behind, obeying Finley's suggested order, then the rest of the couples slowly traipse down the makeshift aisle as I look down at Rory, er, the top of her head, since she refuses to acknowledge me.

Keeping my voice low, I say, "You look nice."

Her chin drops to her chest, and a quiet huff of derision slips out of her. "Thanks."

Her sarcasm is as thick as molasses. I fight the urge to shake her.

"You ready?" I prod.

She forces herself to nod but doesn't look at me.

Why won't you look at me, Squeaks?

I offer my arm. She loops her own through it, raising her chin, though I don't miss the slight tremble of her body. The realization hits like a wrecking ball, and I glance down at her hand folded around my bicep. Wait. She isn't shaking. She's tapping.

One, two, three. Pause. *One, two, three.* Pause. *One, two, three.*

It's a compulsion. A subtle one, but a compulsion nonetheless.

She started this one after Archer's death. When she was nervous or overwhelmed or scared. I don't think anyone else noticed. Not at first. I did, though. Considering her degree, I assumed she'd be over these kinds of ticks. Clearly, I was wrong. Or maybe I wasn't. Maybe she's regressing.

Fuck, I hope that isn't the case. After she was diagnosed with OCD, I did a shit-ton of research, anxious to help any way I could, even if all I could offer was understanding. It helped that her dad was diagnosed with the same disorder after his best friend was arrested a few decades ago. Apparently, a traumatic experience can trigger it, and the death of a family member seems like a pretty solid traumatic experience to me. Then again, maybe Rory never stood a chance, since OCD's genetic and all. I guess we'll never know.

Tap, tap, tap. Pause. *Tap, tap, tap.* Pause.*Tap, tap, tap.*

The familiar rhythm seeps through my suit as I stare at her pale fingertips and light nail polish.

I thought she was getting better. And maybe she was. Maybe this is all too much, though I'm unsure if it's my presence or the lack of her brother's at an important event like this one that's triggering her. I'm not sure it really matters.

Before I can talk myself out of it, I squeeze her hand softly but don't call her out for giving in to her compulsion, well aware it won't help. Not in the big picture. Her manicured nails dig into my bicep, but the tapping stops as the wedding coordinator motions for us to start walking. So, we do. One step after another. Until we reach the end of the line. With a little too much enthusiasm, Rory lets me go, rushing toward the line of bridesmaids, so I take my place on the opposite side.

Yeah...we're not good, are we?

It's Ophelia's turn, or at least I assume. I'm too busy analyzing Rory from across the grassy lawn to check to see if the bride is walking down the aisle. Rory seems calmer now that she's not forced to hold my arm. Or maybe I'm only seeing what she wants me to see. What she wants *everyone* to see. A girl who's cool, calm, and collected.

Maybe she's harder to read than I initially gave her credit.

The realization stings. She's always been an open book. But now? Now, she's nothing but a prop on a bookshelf. No pages to be read. No pictures to be appreciated. Just a closed hunk of leather I've yet to access. Or maybe I'm incapable of it altogether.

A tender, sweet smile softens the divot between her brows. I follow her gaze in time to notice Dodger at the back of the area. He gives Rory a gentle wave as he sits down on one of the folding chairs, spreading his legs wide.

So, he's not in the wedding party, but he's here anyway?

Why? And who invited him?

"Perfect!" the wedding coordinator announces. I realize I've been blocking her out for at least a solid minute.

Shit. What'd I miss?

With a single but jarring clap of her hands, she adds, "Then the officiant performs the wedding, Ophelia says her vows, Maverick says his, he kisses the bride, and bam. The two live happily ever after, and we exit the way we came. Ready?" She claps her hands again. "Bride and groom, you two first. Then, you and you." She points to Tatum and Paxton, and they do as they're told, meeting at the center of the path before striding down it. Dylan and Reeves go next, then Everett and Raine, and Finley and Griffin.

And then, there were two.

Rory's gaze stays glued to the ground as she follows the procession, so I do the same, hating how forced it feels. Without a word, I raise my arm for Rory to take just like before. Her touch is light as a feather. Hell, I might as well be guiding a ghost. But it's the familiar silence that kills me, making me feel like I've lost my ever loving mind as I guide her back down the aisle.

"Lovely. Yes, lovely," the wedding coordinator croons from the back. "Everyone did amazing. Any questions before we wrap up?" She barely waits a second. "Perfect. I told you this would be relatively painless. There's a light dinner set up in the main building as a thank you for coming, and we'll see everyone on Saturday at 2:00 p.m."

As everyone disperses, Dodger pushes to his feet and tugs Rory from my grasp like I'm not even here.

"Look at you, stealing the show," he quips, pulling her into another hug until her feet are off the ground and her soft laugh filters through the air.

My brows wrinkle as I step away, giving them space to… do whatever the hell they're doing. But seriously? Who does this guy think he is? And why is everyone okay with him putting his hands on her?

"Hey, man." Maverick's voice distracts me from the view of his little sister spinning around in a rockstar's arms. "You good?"

"Yeah." I tear my attention from Rory and tuck my hands into the front pockets of my slacks. "Yeah, I'm good."

"You sure?" he prods. "You look—"

Distracted, I interrupt, "Can I ask you something?"

"Yeah, for sure."

Don't say it, don't say it, don't say it.

"What's up with Rory and Dodger?"

Looking over my shoulder, Mav takes in his little sister standing next to a fucking rockstar who's probably twice her age with the sun framing their silhouettes like they're the stars in some sappy rom-com. Oblivious, Mav shrugs. "No idea. Why?"

"Are they seeing each other?"

"No idea," he repeats. "Rory either doesn't have relationships or keeps them close to the chest, I'm not sure which."

Keeps them close to the chest? That's it? That's all he has to say? No offense, but Maverick's a terrible big brother if he's really this clueless when it comes to Rory's dating life. Actually, he's an excellent big brother, and I get that he's getting married and shit, but seriously? The rockstar's practically twice her age. Okay, that might be a bit of a stretch. Or is it? Hell, if I know, but I sure as shit am about to find out.

"So you're okay with it?" I challenge, trying not to sound like an interrogator, though I doubt I'm successful.

Giving me a weird look, Mav retorts, "Why wouldn't I be okay with it?"

"She's your little sister."

"So?" Mav laughs. "Rory's a big girl."

"Yeah, but Dodger's, what? Fifteen years older than she is?"

Hesitating, Maverick glances at Rory next to Dodger again and scratches his jaw. "Something like that."

"And you're good with it?" I push.

This doesn't bother him? Should it? Or is my conversation with Rory muddying the waters and fucking with my mind, leaving me less than unbiased after everything we've been through? The last time we spoke, she apologized for falling for a guy older than her. Hell, she even accused me of looking at her like she's nothing but a kid I used to babysit. But hooking up with a rockstar is appropriate? A rockstar who's older than I am? What the fuck? I had my assumptions after the pool party, but a hug like that? And the way she can't stop smiling at him? It's bullshit.

"Yeah," Mav grunts, lifting a shoulder in a half-assed shrug as he turns back to me. "I guess I am good with it."

"Why?"

Another laugh rumbles out of him. "Why not? She's over twenty-one and Dodger's a good guy."

I glance at Rory chatting with Dodger and the way her eyes crinkle in the corners. She looks…happy, and damn if it isn't fucking with my head. The girl can't even look at me, but she can smile at him like that? Something sharp digs against my ribcage, but I fight the urge to rub it away and clench my hands instead.

"If I've learned anything from this life, it's that you fall for who you fall for, you know?" Mav continues. "If we had any say in it, do you really think I would've fucked over Archer the way I did?"

I pull back, distracted by his candor. Because yeah. Falling for your twin's girlfriend is kind of a shit thing to do, isn't it? Add in Archer's death, and I'm pretty sure Mav could be painted as the villain in any retelling of his love story with Ophelia. He's spent years in therapy to let go of the staggering guilt of how things played out between him, Lia, and Archer. Clearly, it's worked, and I envy him for it.

My focus shifts to Rory again, taking in her silky peach dress, light makeup, and soft blonde hair. She curled it today. It looks nice. She's beautiful, objectively speaking, of course. I swallow back the knot in my throat. The same easy smile plays at the edge of her mouth as she peeks up at Dodger, attentively hanging onto his every word. And it's strange. Because even though it's been years, I'm pretty sure she used to look at me that way. With awe.

I don't like it.

And he sure as shit doesn't deserve it. Not that I ever did, either, but this isn't about me. What if he hurts her? He's a rockstar, for fuck's sake. A rockstar who couldn't even scrounge up a suit for the dress rehearsal. Instead, he's in a pair of ripped jeans and a T-shirt. How is no one else worried about this connection? Or maybe I'm projecting after my own relationship fell apart. Maybe not everyone's a cheater. Or maybe I'm right, and Rory will be hurt. None of the possibilities make me feel any better. None of them are in my control, either. That's why I'm frustrated. Because I don't want her to get hurt, is all. It's completely logical.

"Still protective of Squeaks, huh?" Maverick asks with a laugh. "Guess it's hard to turn off, even after all these years."

Dodger spins Rory around again, complimenting her dress as a blush hits her cheeks.

"I'm gonna get some more fresh air," I decide. Clapping Mav on the shoulder, I motion around the decorated space, adding, "Happy for you. This is gonna be epic."

"Thanks, man." He looks around the area and smiles, his expression clouding with pride and admiration. "Lia did a great job."

"Yeah, she did. I'll see you in a bit."

"Sounds good. Don't forget to grab some dinner inside."

"I will," I lie and make my way around the side of the grassy area instead of heading inside with the majority of the group. Call me an ass, but I'm not in the mood to face all the familiar faces I know are scattered inside the giant reception area. It's not that I don't want to see anyone. I just...really don't want to see anyone. The Buchanans rented out the entire country club, and thankfully, the place is big enough to find some quiet, so I stay outside, hoping if I spend enough time out here, the fresh air will clear my mind.

Mufasa lounges on the trimmed grass beneath a tree, and I veer toward him, not even the slightest bit surprised he's here. Besides, I'm anxious for a distraction. A compadre. I dunno. Something to help ease the tightness in my chest.

When the dog lifts its head, I stop short.

His dark chocolate eyes pin me in place as I stare back, curious to whom he belongs. His eyes are further apart than Fasa's, and his nose is a little shorter.

"You're not Fasa," I mutter.

He studies me the same way I study him. As if he's sizing me up. I keep my feet planted but shift my attention to the fresh-cut grass in an attempt to look less intimidating. I must pass his test because seconds later, he lays his head back on the green lawn. Slowly, I approach him and squat down, offering him a closed fist as an introduction. He lifts his head again, sniffs me, licks my knuckles, and nuzzles against my hand.

Satisfied I'm not gonna lose a finger, I say, "Hello to you, too, buddy." I scratch the side of his head, then reach for his collar and read the tag. *Hades.* "Hades, huh?" The dog grunts in response. "Nice to meet you. I'm Jax." I shift my attention to his chocolate brown chin, rubbing gently. "You're Rory's dog, aren't you?" I decide. "Yeah, I bet you are." I plop down beside him and stretch out my legs beneath the tall oak tree. "How's she doing?" I prod. Relaxing again, the dog rests his head in my lap. "You keeping a close eye on her?" His long sigh makes me smirk. "Yeah, I get it. Not always an easy job, am I right?" Patting his side, I smooth out the brown and black fur. It's soft and clean, proving he had a bath recently. My fingers thread through the thick coat, and I tug gently. It's thicker than Fasa's. He's a little meatier, too. I bet Rory spoils the shit out of him. "I'm glad you're looking out for her," I admit. And I am. The way things ended never sat well with me, and even though Rory and I have hashed it out since she's been home, it doesn't ease the guilt from our initial fallout. All the time we missed. It makes me curious, too. What she's been up to. Who she's been with. How long she's been seeing Dodger. "So tell me," I mutter. "What do we think of that guy? Dodger?" The dog lets out another grunt, nuzzling into my thigh. "That bad, huh? Yeah." I sigh, grateful at least *someone* feels the same way I do. "Figured as much—"

"What are you doing?" a feminine voice snaps.

Looking up, I find Rory marching toward me with a glare that could curdle milk. It isn't directed at me, though. No, she's glaring at her dog like he just got caught with his head in the garbage can or something.

"Is there a…problem?" I ask.

When she reaches us on the grass, she folds her arms. "Why are you touching my dog?"

Huh? This is what she's mad about?

My eyes widen as I take in the animosity in her voice. "I'm sorry?" I frown. "Am I not allowed to touch your dog?"

"That's not the point," she huffs. "You didn't know he was

mine, and going around touching random dogs is like, super stupid, Jax. What were you thinking?"

"I assumed he was Fasa until I got closer," I explain, defending myself. "Then, he asked if he could have a good scratch, and who was I to tell him no, you know?"

Her mouth twitches…barely. But it's enough to give me a glimpse of the less pissed version of herself I'm used to. She doesn't cave entirely, though. Instead, she pins Hades with her stare again. It's like she still can't decide whether or not he deserves to stay in the doghouse for *not* attacking me.

"I'm sorry I didn't ask permission before petting him," I add carefully. "It's not his fault. It's mine."

Uncrossing her arms, she laces her fingers in front of her and lets out a sigh. "Thanks for taking the fall."

"Anytime."

"I'm sorry I snapped," she adds. "It's just…Hades doesn't usually like people other than me, so I was a little surprised he let you touch him. That's all."

I glance down at my lap where Hades is still resting. "He seems to like me fine."

Eyes narrowing, she scrutinizes her dog like he's been swapped with an alien. "Surprisingly."

My brows hitch. "It's surprising that he likes me?"

"Not like that." She peeks up at me again. "It's just…he kind of failed out of service dog school, and like I said, he doesn't usually like people in general, but especially guys, which has actually been kind of categorized in the plus column, now that I think about it. Then again, you're Jaxon Thorne. I should've known he'd love you. You're a good guy, not some sleazy, random…" Her lips press into a thin line. "Come on, Hades." She turns around, not bothering to see if Hades follows.

Before he has a chance to clamor to his feet, I place my hand on Hades' side and call, "Wait." I don't know why. I shouldn't. She clearly wants nothing to do with me, but the cold shoulder? The awkward tension? Fuck me, it's messing with me, and I don't like it.

When she turns to face me, she tilts her head as if to say, "What do you want?" though she doesn't bother verbalizing shit. Now that I have her full attention again, I'm not sure what to do with it.

"It's, uh, it's interesting you went with a German Shepherd again. Did you get him from the same breeder as Kovu and Mufasa?"

She pauses, suspicious. "Why?"

"Just trying to make conversation, I guess," I ramble, determined to lower the walls she's clearly erected since… fuck, it feels like forever. I pat the dog's side one more time. "I see you stuck with the Disney trend," I continue. "I saw Hades' name on his tag. It fits him."

"Thanks."

"I'm really sorry about Kovu, too," I continue. "I know I never got to tell you, but…he was the best."

Her eyes well with tears before she sniffs and wipes under her nose. "Yeah. He really…he really was, wasn't he?"

Sensing her unease, Hades stands, trots toward her, and presses his side against her outer thigh in a show of camaraderie.

Rolling her watery eyes, she bends at her side and scratches his head, muttering, "Traitor."

"What was that?" I ask.

"Nothing." She sneaks another peek at me. "I really should get back. Come on, Hades."

"He can stay out here with me," I offer. "Unless it would make him a traitor."

Her unreadable gaze cuts to me again. "I'll see you around, Jax."

Turning on her heel, she walks off without another word.

All right, then.

6

RORY

I do not want to be here. It's selfish but true. If this was anyone else's bachelorette party, there isn't a chance in Hell I would've come, but it's Ophelia. My future sister-in-law. Add in the fact my best friend is the maid-of-honor who organized the whole thing, and it's not like I had much of a choice. Maybe it's a good thing. At least now I have distraction instead of being holed up in my room for the rest of the night.

"So what do you have planned?" I ask Tatum as she pulls up to the large cabin in the middle of the woods. It belongs to my Aunt Kate and Uncle Macklin. He built the place with his own two hands after a nasty divorce a few decades ago. The place is as picturesque as ever with a big balcony, large glass windows, and mature trees surrounding all sides. "And why did you make me bring Hades?" I add.

"That part's a secret." She winks. "First half is all of Lia's favorite's foods. Second half is a surprise."

My eyes thin.

"Don't worry. I'll make sure you're nice and lubricated before you have to face Jax again."

"Tatum!" I smack her shoulder, and she laughs.

"I meant with alcohol!" She wipes at the corner of her eyes as another burst of amusement escapes her. "But that's the best unintentional pun I might've ever made in my entire life."

Sure it is. I fight the urge to smack her all over again, distracted by her Jaxon comment and what it entails.

"Does this mean we're hanging out with the guys tonight?" I ask, searching the mountain road for any of the guys' cars. "Because I'm pretty sure a bachelorette party is supposed to be girls only."

"And in most circumstances, it would be. But this isn't about you or me. This is about Lia and Mav. And Lia and Mav?" She gives me a knowing look while opening the driver's side door. "They can barely be away from each other for thirty minutes, let alone an entire evening. Might as well give the people what they want, right?"

My shoulders sag. Because, yeah. She makes a good point. But also, the last thing I need is to be in the same room with Jaxon after how snappy I was after the rehearsal. Hell, the last two times we've been around each other, I've been an absolute brat. And for what? For my own ego? For my own shame? I don't even know anymore. All I know is that anytime I'm around him, my emotions are in overdrive. The good. The bad. And the ugly.

And boy, do I feel ugly lately.

Fighting the urge to curl into the backseat with Hades, I climb out of the car and open the back door, letting Hades explore the wooded area to his heart's content. And honestly, I'm jealous. Of how easy-going he is. Without a care in the world.

"Hey." Tatum grabs my forearm.

The simple touch is enough to snap me out of my funk.

I turn to her. "Yeah?"

"You good?" Her gaze narrows. "What aren't you telling me?" My expression must tell her everything she needs to know because her jaw drops. "Something happened. What is it?"

If only it was so easy. Where does she expect me to start?

"Rore?"

"Nothing really..." I lie. "Or at least not anything we didn't already know was going to happen."

"Rore," she pushes.

Say it.

"Jax confronted me the other night."

Her eyes widen. "And?"

"And instead of patching things up or...whatever,"—I shove my hair away from my face, starting toward the cabin —"I acted like a brat and told him how stupid I feel for falling in love with him all those years ago when everyone around us would agree how wrong it was." I squeeze my eyes shut, refusing to cry. "And then, at the rehearsal, I saw Jax petting Hades, which means I can't even trust my own dog not to betray me, and...and it's been a hard few days."

"Oh, Squeaks." Warm arms wrap around me, and she pulls me into a hug. "I'm so proud of you."

Proud of me?

"What?" I ask.

"I said I'm proud of you." She gives me one more squeeze before letting me go. "Even though your feelings weren't wrong, just misplaced, you're amazing. I know how hard that must've been to tell Jax how you feel, and I love the crap out of you."

"Thanks," I mutter. If only it was enough to get me out of tonight. "Also, who are you and what have you done with my best friend?"

She snorts. "What do you mean?"

"You're like, the queen of shoving down your feelings and

pretending like everything is absolutely perfect," I point out. "Since when do you compliment me for expressing my feelings to the last person who needs to hear them?"

"Uh, since I learned shoving down your feelings is a terrible way to handle things," she clarifies. "And I think you're wrong. Jax was the *first* person who needed to hear how you felt all those years ago, but I get why you might feel a little awkward now, even though you have no reason to be. Do you want to go back to your parents' house?" she suggests. "You can take my car. I'll tell them you're sick or something. I feel bad cancelling on the whole group bachelor-slash-bachelorette party, but—"

"I'm a big girl, Tate," I remind her. "I'll be fine. Promise."

"Good." She squeezes my arm, tacking on a grimace. "Because I kind of need Hades for the second part of the night. Speaking of which..." She looks around the wooded grounds. "Where is he?"

"Hades!" I call.

Branches break to my left before he darts into the clearing. His tongue lolls out on one side like he's on cloud nine.

Tatum smiles as she watches him. "That thing is a menace."

"But like, a cute menace," I retort.

"Sure, he is." She snorts before arching her brow. "But seriously? Hades didn't bite off his balls or anything?"

"The traitor was practically sleeping in his lap," I grumble as we make our way up the steps to the front door.

"I hope you make him at least sleep on the floor for a week as punishment."

My mouth lifts. "You forget who you're talking to, but I definitely should."

"Don't worry, Boo-Boo." She winks and tugs me closer to the front door. "We'll find you a backbone."

Sure, we will.

~

TATUM WASN'T WRONG. THE COUNTER IS LITTERED WITH SO many finger foods I feel like I won't need to eat for a week. Thanks to the warm weather, the massive fireplace stays unlit, and we wind up outside on the balcony. An hour later, drinks are poured, and the stars twinkle above us as we lounge on the cushioned patio furniture while Ophelia fiddles with her tiara. It's one you'd use for a princess costume. Tatum crowned her bride of the year as soon as she walked in. It's silly and ridiculous, and I've never been happier for her.

"To being engaged," Finley cheers. She lifts her bottle of Diet Coke with lime into the air.

Glasses clink as well all join in.

Repeating the gesture, I say, "To having the best sister-in-law ever."

"Amen to that!" Lia laughs.

Finley grins. "To losing the worst sister-in-law ever!"

"Here, here!" Dylan chimes in, holding her round belly as she cackles at their inside joke.

If only I could join in. My forehead scrunches, and I tilt my head. "Okay, what'd I miss? Because I'm pretty sure both your sisters-in-law are right here." I motion to Raine, Finley's brother's wife, and Dylan, her husband's baby sister.

When all eyes turn to me, I'm even more dumbfounded than before.

Seriously. What am I missing here?

"Iris?" Dylan offers. "Jaxon's ex?"

Ex? What the hell is she talking about?

"What?" I ask.

Finley exchanges a curious glance with Raine and Dylan. "You don't know?"

"Don't know what?" Tatum chimes in. She tucks her feet

under her butt on the couch, then leans forward, clearly invested in the gossip these girls are dangling in front of us like low hanging fruit.

"Jaxon's divorced," Raine explains.

Divorced. As in…not married. Wait, no. That can't be right.

"What?" I repeat, as confused as ever. I mean, yeah. I noticed Jaxon was mysteriously by himself at the wedding rehearsal, but I figured his wife stayed home to watch their baby or something, not that she wouldn't be coming to the wedding at all.

Why didn't I scope out his left hand for a ring?

"He's divorced," Dylan repeats for me.

Jaxon isn't married. Jaxon Thorne isn't freaking married. Feeling like the ground's opened beneath me, I clench the wine glass a little harder in my hand while trying not to lose my shit.

Finley nods. "And it was messy AF. She kept throwing fits about Jaxon coaching the women's team at LAU, so he applied for the head coaching position for the Lions, and your dad offered him a job. Six months later, he comes home to find her in bed with another guy. What was his name, anyway?"

Raine taps her chin, searching her memory. "Starts with a C, I think?"

"Chris," Dylan announces. "His name's Chris, and he's an ass."

"Good memory," Ophelia quips, adding, "Jaxon doesn't exactly like talking about it, like, at all, so…"

Dylan grimaces. "Ollie's overheard a conversation or two between Jax and his ex over the last few months. It's the only reason I remember."

"And of course your husband ran right to you to spill all the details," Finley quips dryly.

Resting her forearms on her round, pregnant belly, Dylan doesn't even bother denying it. "Exactly."

Raine steals another sip of her beverage and scoots closer to me on the couch, dropping her voice low. "But the real drama is whether or not Poppy is Jaxon's because the math is shady at best."

My lips part as I digest her words. Poppy must be Jaxon's daughter. I've never met her, but I don't need to, to know Jax treasures every tiny hair on her head. The idea of him dealing with that kind of betrayal and how much it must affect the other areas of his life has to be a hard pill to swallow. Hell, I can't even imagine it. The idea of being happily married with a baby on the way, only to have the reality ripped away, replaced with a mess of timelines and technicalities.

"That has to kill him," Tatum interjects.

"It does," Ophelia returns. "But honestly, he's been nothing but great about the whole thing. The way he looks at it is that if his mom, Ash, could step in and love him as much as she does despite them not being blood, then what's the point in finding out whether or not Poppy's actually his after already falling for her? He loves the crap out of that baby. He fell in love with her long before he found out he might not be the biological father, and it's not like Iris is going to say anything. Why would she? She'd lose all the child support."

My nose wrinkles in disgust despite knowing Ophelia makes a good point. What a greedy, selfish—

"Griff was the same way when I found out I was pregnant with Drew's baby," Finley confides. She plays with the simple gold necklace around her throat. "And even though I miscarried, he still looks at my first as *our* first."

I still remember hearing about it. Finley miscarrying at one of Griffin's games. She was a shell of a human for months after, though I don't blame her. My mom insists that without Griff, she would've never survived, and even though it's been years, I can see the way it still hurts her. The way she carries her baby's absence. It's similar to how I carry Archer's.

My fingers itch, and I force them into a fist, murmuring, "I think that's really sweet of Griff."

"He's kind of the best," Finley says.

"Speaking of which, are you ready for the second half of this evening?" Tatum asks.

Shifting the tiara on her head, Ophelia gives her sister a suspicious look. "And what's the second half of this evening?"

"Well," Tatum licks her lips, not even bothering to hide her Cheshire grin. "A little bird told me it's been a while since you've had a Game Night."

The rest of the girls hoot their approval, clapping their hands and lifting their drinks into the air.

"Shut up! You have no idea how much I've missed Game Nights," Ophelia gushes.

Raine shakes her head, peering around the shadowed forest beneath us. "And where are the boys?"

Pulling out her phone, Tatum checks the time, then grins. "They'll be here in two."

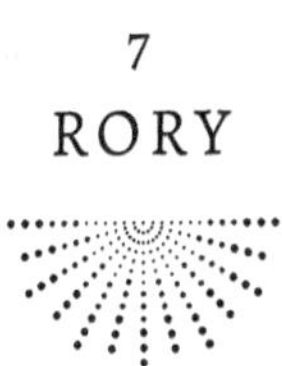

7

RORY

"Welcome, gentlemen," Tatum says as each of the respective men find their other halves scattered on the balcony. Griffin and Everett sandwich Dylan and Finley on the couch opposite me and Tatum while Ophelia sits propped on a wide chair like she's our very own queen of the evening.

When he sees me, Dodger moseys closer like this isn't his first time visiting Uncle Macklin and Aunt Kate's cabin even though it most definitely is. I smile up at him while pretending not to notice the *other* elephant in the room, Jaxon Thorne. The very single Jaxon Thorne. My face grows hot as the thought flutters through my mind despite my best attempt to keep it in check.

He hovers at the edge of the area after closing the sliding glass door behind him, leaning against it, and folding his arms. And it's strange. Feeling like my reality's been shattered. Last time I saw him, I thought he was married. Last time I saw him, I left in a huff and didn't look back. It's like I've been given a fresh perspective, and the truth is, it makes me kind of sad. Being on this side of things. Not that Dodger and I are a couple or anything, but at least we have each other to lean on during these social gatherings and in general. Jax? Apparently, Jax has no one. How can a guy like Jax have no one? I didn't see it before. The way he keeps himself just enough removed to keep his distance but not so far that he seems like an outcast. It's clear as day now. Until the girls informed me of his divorce, I would've never believed it. After all, he's a catch. Tall. Handsome. Well off. Has his life together. Or at least, he seems to.

Doesn't he?

I bite the inside of my cheek, my eyes trailing along his broad shoulders before taking in the scruff of his jaw, tousled hair, and olive-colored eyes that are so dark, they're almost black from this angle. Yeah, handsome doesn't even begin to describe the bastard, and it honestly isn't fair. Yet here he is, off to the side. You'd think he's a stranger when he grew up with almost everyone here.

As if he can feel my stare, Jaxon's eyes meet mine from across the balcony. I fight the urge to squirm before failing entirely. Shifting in my seat, I peek at Dodger in all his rock-star glory. See? Jaxon's not the only handsome guy in the vicinity.

Focus. On. Him.

"Hey, stranger," I say.

"Hey, Rore." Dodger glances down at Hades lying by my feet. "Hey, devil dog."

Hades growls back but doesn't bother lifting his head.

"Heeeey." I give Dodger a mock glare as if I'm personally offended by the new nickname, too, even if it isn't entirely inaccurate.

With a low chuckle, Dodger collapses onto the cushion beside me and says, "Blame Hades, not me." He cocks his head. "Or is it your fault for naming him after the devil himself?"

Okay, the man might have a point. Instead of arguing, my lips purse, and I look around the area, curious to see what's next on tonight's agenda because Game Night can mean anything under the sun, er, moon.

When everyone was little, and our families would get together, Aunt Blakely started teaching us kids different games. Things like Kick the Can and Spoons and Truth or Dare. Then, once we were good and distracted, the adults could have some time without the kids hovering. Not only did it stick, but the guys carried the tradition on to college and long after. Not going to lie. I'm kind of excited. I've only participated in a handful of Game Nights. Not because everyone was actively trying to exclude me and Tatum, but thanks to the age gap between us and everyone else, the stars rarely aligned for all of us to play together once the older kids moved on to college. The idea of participating tonight is enough to make my skin buzz with anticipation, and boy could I use a distraction.

In a dark T-shirt and jeans, Mav scoots around the edge of the balcony, approaching his fiancée. "You know about this?"

Ophelia shakes her head, her tiara wobbling. "Nope. You?"

"Not a clue." Straightening the ridiculous crown on her head, Maverick pulls her up, takes the newly-empty seat, and tugs her onto his lap.

"That's because Reeves and I are amazing," Tatum interrupts, giving the best man a wry grin as he places his hand on top of Dylan's round stomach. "You're welcome, by the way," Tatum adds, addressing Ophelia again. "I expect the same thoughtful treatment when I'm the bride."

Ophelia lifts a brow. "And when will that be?"

Finley laughs. "Pretty sure that's a Paxton question. Pax?"

Squeezing the back of his neck, the shameless guitarist answers her, "You're really asking me to tell all my secrets?"

"Ahem," Tatum interjects. "While I'm all for everyone grilling my boyfriend—"

"She said boyfriend," Dylan whispers beside Fin. "Boy. Friend."

Finley leans closer to Dylan as if sharing a secret despite all of us clearly being within earshot. "Who is this girl, and what has she done with Lia's little sister?"

Ignoring them, Tatum prods, "Reeves? Wanna take it from here before I smack your wife and her friend or…?"

"No bullying pregnant women," Reeves counters, though I don't miss the teasing lilt in his voice. "That's my job." Standing, he announces, "Aaaand tonight we'll be playing— uh, Rory?" He points to the corner of the balcony. "Your dog?"

I follow Reeves' finger in time to see Hades' front paws on top of one of the side tables as he scarfs down the last of the appetizers.

"Hades!" I screech. *When did he get over there?* "Off!"

He licks up what's left of Mama Taylor's cookies, then pushes off the table and plops down near the railing, his tail swishing back and forth in satisfaction.

"Devil dog," Dodger teases, as if Hades just proved his point from moments ago. Then again, I guess he did.

"You were saying?" Tatum prods.

Reeves clears his throat. "Tonight, we'll be playing Ghosts in the Graveyard. Rules are simple. Everyone takes a wine cork. Excellent work clearing out some bottles, by the way." He motions to the center table littered with empty bottles. "The cork with the heart written on the bottom is the *ghost*." Raising his hands, he does air quotes around the word ghost. "But don't tell anyone if you're it. After everyone's chosen a wine cork, we'll all spread out to go hunting, which means you walk around outside in the dark looking for the ghost. When the person who is the ghost finds an opening, they buckle down and hide. Everyone else? Your job is to try and figure out who the ghost is so you can be turned into one before Hades is let loose. If you find the ghost, you hide with them. But make sure you stay quiet. The last one to find the group of ghosts hiding has to tell a favorite memory with Ophelia or Mav or they get eaten by Rory's devil dog. Any questions?"

Dylan raises her hand. "You really expect a pregnant woman to traipse around the forest when it's pitch black outside?"

"You keep up with our boys just fine," Reeves quips. "I think you can handle this."

Folding her arms, she grumbles, "Sometimes, I really wish men could get pregnant."

"Here, here!" Finley agrees.

She raises her almost-empty bottle of Diet Coke into the air while Tatum passes around a plastic bowl filled with wine corks. Some are from tonight, but it's obvious she's saved a few more and brought them with her because there's no way we went through almost a dozen bottles in one night. As I take a cork from the bowl, I peek at the bottom. My stomach bottoms out.

There it is. A tiny heart drawn in black permanent marker.

Perfect.

When I said I wanted to participate in Game Night, I didn't mean I wanted to be front and center. If we don't get started in the next two minutes, everyone will be able to read my face and will know who the ghost is. I pull out my phone, clicking my tongue against the roof of my mouth in an attempt to look...I don't even know. Not guilty? Yeah, that would be great.

Impossible but great.

"Rore," Tatum calls. "Any advice for Reeves who's staying back with Hades?"

"Nope," I squeak. "When you want him to start searching, just say *tag*."

Lifting his head at my feet, Hades looks up at me. I show him my palm, silently motioning for him to chill. Satisfied, Hades lowers his snout back to the ground and relaxes. He learned this particular trick when I told my parents there was a not-so-small possibility that I'd be living alone at college. They wanted to feel confident I was safe, so they made sure Hades knew how to search for any unwanted lurkers in my house. Whenever I want Hades to sniff out any potential people hiding, I say tag, and he searches the premises. When Tatum came to visit, she found it hilarious and would hide in the bathroom or under the bed or... anywhere really, thus turning a nifty safety hack into a game of Hide and Seek. I've never used it in these exact circumstances, but I'm sure Hades will manage.

Reeves rubs his hands together. "Got it."

"Aaaand, let's go," Tatum announces.

Looking at my dog, I show him my palm. "Hades, stay."

Then, down the stairs we traipse until we're sprawled out beneath the balcony. Well, everyone but Reeves and Hades. With a flick of Reeves' finger, the cabin lights go out, blanketing the yard in darkness. My heartbeat ratchets up a notch as I look at my feet, but all I see is darkness. Thanks to the tall pines and balcony over my head, the stars and moon are shit at lighting up anything, which means I'm totally going to fall on my face out here.

I blame Tatum for this one. She's the only person who knows Hades' little hide-and-seek trick. Jokes on everyone else, though. Because Hades might know how to find people, but the only person he's going to look for is me. At least it means I won't be alone for long in this eerie ambiance.

"Let's go hunting!" Tatum announces to the dark night.

A branch snaps off to my left, and my pulse jumps.

I blink slowly, praying my eyes get their act together and adjust to the darkness. When they do, I find Dodger grinning at me. "You good?"

"Fine," I mutter as Ophelia and Maverick vanish behind the edge of the house.

Before I can stop myself, I scan the space for Jax, but he's already missing. Hell, maybe he stayed on the balcony. It wouldn't surprise me. He's never been a huge fan of Game Nights, or at least not that I know of. Not that I should be thinking about him.

Focus, Rory!

"Good luck," Dodger murmurs. He veers right, disappearing in the distance. Kate and Macklin's family cabin is up in the mountains about thirty minutes from town, surrounded by trees, boulders, and hidden trails. It's also surrounded by bears, cougars, snakes, mountain goats, and… well, if you name it, there's probably a story or two in their parents' repertoire starring one of the beasts. The reminder doesn't exactly settle my anxiety.

"Come on, Squeaks," Dylan urges. "Let's be partners."

"That's cheating!" Finley calls.

"Says the girl holding her husband's hand," Tatum quips. "No partners. Once you find the ghost, you'll have someone to hang out with, but not until then." She nudges Paxton's shoulder. "Come find me." She runs off while my feet stay planted where they are.

"Chop, chop, Squeaks," Reeves urges from above. "You too, Pickles."

"Fiiiine." Dylan trudges in the opposite direction, and I

force my feet to move, careful not to trip on any roots sticking up from the ground.

It'll be fine. I'll be fine. And everyone else will be fine. The last thought flutters through my mind, its presence more familiar than anything else. I guess that's what happens when someone you love passes away. A constant niggling in the back of your mind about safety for those around you. Most days, I simply push past it. Forcing myself to do exactly that, I peek over my shoulder, confirming I'm somewhat alone. Satisfied, I dip behind one of the large pine trees. Its trunk is easily as wide as I am, and the thick bark digs into my back as I lean against it, trying to quiet my breathing. Pretty sure I only made it a dozen paces from the house, but as long as Reeves doesn't send Hades to search for the ghost yet, I should be okay for a little while.

I'm not sure how much time passes when the familiar crunching of leaves, then a branch snapping on my left causes my heart to lodge in my throat.

Someone's close.

The question is…who?

8

RORY

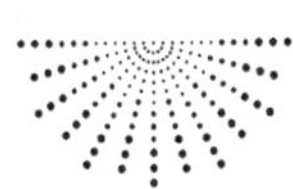

The temptation to peek around the trunk in hopes of getting a glimpse of whoever's coming closer is strong, but I fight it, pressing myself a little further into the tree until my skin screams in protest. I gotta hand it to Tatum and Reeves. This is definitely a good way to get the adrenaline pumping.

"Oh, ghost," someone sing-songs. Finley, maybe? It could be Lia. "Come out, come out, wherever you are."

Shit. Already? How did they find me so fast?

I seriously suck at this game.

Digging my fingers into the rough bark, I squeeze my eyes shut, praying it'll somehow prove the whole *if I can't see you, you can't see me* childhood assumption holds a semblance of accuracy when a hand wraps around my mouth.

A squeal of surprise crawls up my throat, muffled by a large palm. My body stiffens in response.

Someone else. Someone *else* found me. They snuck around from the opposite side, and I was so distracted by the rhino traipsing around the forest calling for me that I hadn't noticed. My eyes bulge, and my legs threaten to give out as a shadowed Jaxon slowly moves around me while keeping his hand on my mouth and my body pinned to the tree.

He found me.

Why did *he* have to be the one to find me?

I hold his stare, my pulse thumping in my ears as the previous footsteps fade into the distance as whoever is still searching continues on their merry way, leaving me alone in a dark forest with the one and only Jaxon Thorne. Slowly, he lowers his hand, brushing his fingertips against his full lips in a silent but effective "be quiet" order.

When I dip my chin in acknowledgement, his eyes fall to my mouth, and my lips part in response. This wasn't how I expected Game Night to go.

Not in the slightest.

It probably would've helped if I'd chosen a better hiding spot because right now, the only way to stay out of sight is to be pressed against each other, and boy oh boy is that a problem. He's close. Too close. *Way* too close. And without a buffer. A person or a dog or even a damn lightbulb would be nice right now. Nope. There's nothing but me and him and the dark trees surrounding us.

Unable to look him in the eye, I wipe my sweaty palms against my jeans and turn my head to the side. He smells the same.

The realization is…annoying. On a lot of levels. Because, yeah, he smells amazing, but memories are tied to smells. And just like that, I'm transported back to that night. It doesn't help that it's dark and eerie, and my senses feel like they're on overdrive. Like he's all around me when that little tidbit is the last thing I need, especially after the girls' gossip session earlier.

"You good?" Jax breathes out. The sound is so quiet, I barely hear it over my racing pulse.

I nod.

More rustling sounds nearby, and he pushes closer, caging me in on both sides. The moonlight dances across his silhouette, making him look damn near ethereal.

I want to ask about his ex. If he's okay. If he's still hung up on her. If he's had anyone to lean on. Anyone to open up to. Not that it should be me. It shouldn't. I burned that bridge a long time ago, but…I don't know. The idea of him carrying such a heavy weight all on his own is…heartbreaking.

"Surprised your boyfriend didn't find you first," Jax adds, his voice as hushed as before.

My brows crinkle.

Boyfriend?

Jaxon explains, "I thought for sure Dodger would've followed you out here."

I stay quiet, unsure what to say because Dodger? Yeah, he most definitely is *not* my boyfriend. But Jax thinks he is. I guess it makes sense. We've kind of clung to each other during all the gatherings so far. Dodger promised he wouldn't leave my side because he knew how uncomfortable I felt being home and around Jax. Yet here I am, chest to chest with the devil himself. The irony isn't lost on me. But the fact that Jaxon assumes my relationship with Dodger is more than platonic? It's…surprising, and I don't know if I should correct him. I mean, is his assumption entirely a bad thing? Maybe if Dodge is my fake boyfriend, Jaxon won't think I'm hung up on him anymore. And I'm not. So really, he might've just gifted me a huge favor, even if he didn't mean to, so who am I to question it? Right? Maybe?

It would help if Jax wasn't standing so close. If I couldn't feel his hips pressed against mine. Okay, hips is a stretch. Thighs, maybe? Is he really supposed to stand this close? Does it matter? Now that I know he's not married, at least I don't have to deal with the added guilt of still being attracted to the guy. Even so, he might not be married, but he sure as hell thinks I'm taken, so…

"I didn't mean to make it sound like Dodger would follow you out here to cheat and win," Jaxon adds as if my silence confirms his theory. "More like to cop a feel like the rest of the couples out here." He smirks, but it looks forced as he glances over his shoulder at the dark abyss surrounding us. "Nothing like a quickie when you might get caught, right?"

I wouldn't know, but it's not like I'm stupid enough to admit it out loud.

Turning back to me, he frowns, his gaze bouncing around my face like a ping pong ball. "Unless you're into that kind of thing. People watching or—"

"I'm not," I rush out.

"Oh." A divot forms between his brows. "Good." His head jerks back and forth. "I mean, not good. You're allowed to have your own preferences as long as you and your"—his throat constricts on a tight swallow—"partner are both in agreement. I guess I never pictured you as someone who, not that I picture you at all, but—"

"You guys are terrible ghosts," Tatum interrupts from my left, managing to scare the shit out of both of us. Clutching my chest, I give the tree the rest of my weight, both because my legs might give out and even a centimeter of added space between me and Jax is much needed for so many reasons.

I don't need any light to know Tatum's grinning from ear to ear, far too amused by whatever she heard during her not-so-accidental eavesdropping session to care that her best friend feels like her face is on fire.

Then again, maybe the lack of light is a good thing. At least they can't see how much I wish I could disappear in this moment.

"The demon has been released!" Reeves yells from some-where in the distance. The sound of muffled but rushed galloping footsteps mingles with squeals of laughter as people race to find the ghosts before the demon can rip them to shreds. But me? Well, call me a sucker, but I already feel pretty tattered after my awkward encounter with Jaxon. But what's worse? Is the reminder that Jaxon thinks I'm dating Dodger Anders, and I didn't correct him.

When Tatum finds out, she's going to have a field day. And so will my parents, considering how I literally told my mom earlier this week that I most definitely am not dating the guy.

Fantastic.

9

JAXON

"Hey, Mom," I answer the video call and sit on the edge of the couch. "I've got bad news."

She frowns. "No Poppy?"

I shake my head.

"Well, darn." She tucks her long hair behind her ear, jutting out her bottom lip for good measure. "I miss my grandbaby."

"She misses you, too." I check the time on my watch, confirming I have a few more minutes before I need to meet the rest of the guys at the gym. I could always take the day off, but after my encounter with Rory last night at the bachelor party, I could use the distraction. Hell, I'm desperate for it. I still don't know why I said what I did. Why I even tiptoed around Rory's sex life in the first place, when it's none of my business. All I know is, the sooner I get my shit together and get her out of my head, the better. And if it has to start with squeezing in a few more early morning gym sessions, then so be it.

"I thought it was your week to have Pops," my mom adds.

"Iris wanted to swap a few things around."

"Well, that stinks."

I give her a resigned smile. "Yeah, it does."

"How are you doing with it?" she prods. "The hand-off and everything?"

She's kind to ask. To show she cares. Even if the topic is less than comfortable. People never really talk about it. What it's like to share a kid with someone. To be a part-time parent. Getting a full night's rest is definitely something I appreciate, but otherwise? It's a bitch. She's a piece of me. A part of me. Handing her off to Iris every other week is a hard pill to swallow, let alone accept or embrace.

"That bad, huh?" my mom asks.

I clear my throat and shift forward on the couch, slipping my usual mask of indifference into place. I'd almost forgotten we're on a video chat. "I knew what I was getting into when I filed for divorce."

"Doesn't make it easy, though."

"No." I pause. "Not easy. Sometimes I wonder…" I scrub the edge of my jaw but can't force the words out.

"Wonder if you should've given her another chance?" she finishes for me.

I nod, well aware I hadn't even considered it before I saw Rory in the pool a few days ago. Guess I'm a glutton for punishment and figured if I was unavailable, she wouldn't have piqued my curiosity the way she did.

Or maybe she would've, and I'd feel even more like shit. Hell, she's dating someone, and I'm still fucked up enough to be interested. What's wrong with me? She's still a kid. Still the little girl who used to follow me around. But if that's the case, why is it so fucking hard to merge the two? Because lately? Lately, all I see is the woman from the pool who's burrowed her way under my skin in a far from healthy way.

"Trust me," my mom murmurs, "you made the right choice to end things. Iris is an unhappy person. And unhappy people have no issue dragging down the people around them. I should know, I was one."

She doesn't expand. She doesn't need to. I might not know all the dirty details when it comes to her history, but I do know she was cheating on her husband with my dad before my dad found out she was married. Not that they were ever actually dating, only hooking up here and there. Regardless, as soon as her infidelity came to light, my dad ended things, moved away, and enrolled at LAU. It took her years to clean up her life fully. To grow and become the amazing person she is today. Maybe there's hope for Iris, too? Honestly, I'm not sure.

"And even though I know this is hard on you," my mom continues, "it's really nice to know she isn't able to drag you down anymore. Not in the big scheme of things."

She's right. I know she is. Iris was miserable long before I caught her stepping out. Not in the beginning. But after a few years, I noticed the shift in our relationship, and even now, I can't help but wonder what triggered it. What infinitesimal event caused the cataclysmic fall out of everything we cared about. Everything we built together. Was it me? My obsession with work? The long days and nights spent on the road? Then again, does it even matter? I'm not sure it does. Not anymore.

"So how's Rory doing?" my mom asks.

The question is out of left field, though I know what she's trying to do. She's attempting to change the subject to something...safer. In reality, she just tossed a live grenade onto our conversation, and I really don't want to deal with it.

A few weeks ago, I opened up about everything that happened when Rory was a kid. How she didn't want to come home anymore, and how I could really use my mom's advice because I wanted to make sure Rory felt comfortable for the wedding. Now, I can't help but picture her naked, which is the last thing I want and the last thing she needs. Especially considering the fact that she has a boyfriend. Actually, fuck that. Even if she was single, I still wouldn't cross that line, and I doubt she'd even want me to. Whatever happened between us was years ago. Maybe even a decade at this point. And despite how much time has gone by, I'm still not comfortable dating someone so young. Add in being a single father, and she's my boss's daughter, and—

"Oh, come on," my mom pushes. " How was your first encounter? There's a reason you filled me in on everything that happened when she was a kid."

"Yeah, because you don't know her personally and are far enough removed from the situation that you could give me advice on how to handle everything without being too biased."

"Exactly." She grins. "Which is why you should give me an update now that you've officially seen her again."

An update? Well, she's not a little kid anymore. That much I know.

"Jax?"

"Not sure what you want me to say," I mutter. "She's here."

"And?" my mom pushes.

And what? She's still pushing me away, even though we've cleared the air as much as she'll let me. She got another dog, and the dog likes me. She's seeing someone, and I had no idea. Not that I should've known or should care in the first place. The most shocking part, though? The fact that her brother doesn't care, either. Doesn't care that Rory's seeing a guy who's almost twice her age. Doesn't care that he's a rockstar and could have a dozen STDs. That she's dating the last person I would've ever pegged her to date. To be with.

"Jax?" my mom prods.

I run my tongue along my upper teeth. "Sorry."

"You look frustrated," she notes. "Did something happen?"

Fuck video calls.

"Not frustrated," I lie, forcing my hand to unclench from my knee. "And nothing happened, really. I'm just confused, I guess." I pause, unsure if opening this can of worms is worth the effort or makes me look like a crazy person. It sure as hell makes me feel like I'm losing my mind.

"What's confusing?" she pushes.

"Nothing, it's just...Rory's seeing someone even older than I am, so I guess she's always had a thing for older men? I don't know. It's weird. Not that there's anything wrong with dating an older guy, but..."

Her eyes widen. "Wow. That's...news. Does this mean you guys are good again, at least? It's been, what? About ten years since you saw her last? Is she finally over her embarrassment and everything?"

"I think so," I mutter, though I'm not entirely sure. "She's, uh, she's still keeping her distance, but I don't know if it's because it's been so long and she feels like she doesn't know me anymore, or if it's because she doesn't want to make her boyfriend jealous, or if it's because..."

Because she still hates me.

The thought rears its ugly head in my mind before I can stop it.

Despite painting herself as nothing but a kid, I liked hanging out with Rory. I liked being the one to make her smile. The one to comfort her before and after Archer's death. The one she ran to when she scraped her knee as a kid or hated her new haircut. The one she could confide in. Hell, I was the first person who knew about her compulsive tendencies. And, despite what most people think, OCD doesn't necessarily have anything to do with being clean or liking things in order. It can be sticky thoughts or irrational fears that refuse to be brushed aside, not without a shit-ton of effort anyway.

And maybe that's all I ever was. A sticky thought. An excuse to call me or text me about her day because if she didn't, she believed something bad might happen.

Fuck, is that all I was? A compulsion?

"Well, I think it's good," my mom decides.

Her words cut through my thoughts like a hot knife through butter, and my focus sharpens on her kind smile and long, silvery hair, which she stopped dyeing about three years ago. "What's good?" I ask.

"That she's able to finally let you go and move on," she explains.

"Yeah." A pang hits between my ribs, shocking the hell out of me. Is that what happened? She let me go? And if that's the case, is it a bad thing? It shouldn't be. I want her to be happy, and she's happy, so why the hell am I struggling with it? I'm lonely. That's all. I'm lonely, and I miss our friendship. "Yeah, you're right. It is good."

If only I believed it.

10

RORY

I've been debating long and hard about whether or not I should have this conversation. Long. And. Hard. But even now, I can't decide if I'm making a mistake.

Clutching the coffee cup to my chest, I take another peek at the man across from me. I'm still not sure if it was a good idea to ask him if we could chat. But after replaying my conversation with Jaxon during Ghost in the Graveyard, I figured it couldn't hurt. Right? I probably should've ordered drinks for both of us, but since I didn't want this to feel like a date, I only ordered a coffee for myself. Now, I'm definitely second-guessing the decision. After all, I'm about to ask him for a favor, aren't I? Maybe I should wait for the barista to call his name before I bring everything up. Or maybe not. I don't know?

"You gonna tell me why we're here?" Dodger asks.

"Yeah of course," I rush out. "Should we wait for your order, first?"

"Nah, I'm good."

"Okay."

"Okay." He settles back in his chair and folds his strong

arms, letting me take the floor as the Bean Scene's customers hustle and bustle around us.

Now or never, Rore.

"So…" I start.

Dodger's mouth curves up. "So."

"I have a…" Something clogs my throat, and I clear it. "A situation."

He pulls back, surprised. "A situation?"

"Yeah."

Dropping his voice low, he murmurs, "Need me to ask my sister for a tampon or something?"

I fight the urge to laugh and cover my face. "Not that kind of situation. And also, your sister's not here, so…"

"Then, I'm glad it's not that kind of situation." Relief swallows his handsome features as he steals my coffee, taking a sip while waiting for his own order to be ready. "What's up?"

What's up? Well…where do I start?

Dodger's parents are my family's friends, but would I say we're particularly close? Not really. Not when he's like, fifteen years older than me and was touring the world with his band by the time I hit kindergarten. Okay, that might be a bit of a stretch, but not by much. We never even really spoke more than once a year until a little while ago when we wound up staying in the same town. It didn't hurt when Tatum started dating the guitarist in Dodger's band, either, but even so, close is definitely not a term I would've used to describe our relationship, or at least, not until recently. After the wedding announcement, Dodger could see how nervous I was to come back to Lockwood Heights, so he offered to be my safety blanket. And now, here we are.

Just say it.

"So…" I reach for my coffee, taking a long swig.

"Is it just me or are we going in circles?" he challenges, though I don't miss the mirth dancing in his kind eyes.

He's right. We are.

"Jaxon called you my boyfriend," I blurt out.

His brows kick up. "He did?"

"Yeah." I gulp. "And I can totally correct him or whatever, but I just…I guess I felt like I should give you a heads-up."

"So you can *totally correct him*," he volleys, mimicking my own words, "but you didn't when he first mentioned it?"

My nose wrinkles in shame. "Not exactly."

With a low laugh, he steals my coffee again but doesn't bring it to his mouth. "Are you coming onto me, Squeaks?"

"Not at all." My nose wrinkles even more. "No offense."

His smile grows like this is the most amusing conversation he's ever had.

That makes one of us, buddy.

"None taken," he retorts. "So, if you're not coming onto me, why didn't you correct him?"

"I don't know." Unable to look him in the eye, I pick at my cuticles instead. "I guess the idea of me looking like I moved on from my stupid, childish crush felt better than admitting I haven't even been on a date in over a year."

"A year?" He whistles. "That's quite a long time, Rore."

I roll my eyes. "Trust me, thanks to Tatum, I'm well aware."

"Okay, so what does it mean?"

It's a good question. One I've asked myself a hundred times since my encounter with Jaxon in the forest. "I don't know?"

"That's not an answer, or at least not one I'll accept." Reaching forward, he tucks my hair behind my ear, then urges my chin up until my gaze meets his. "Ask me, Rore."

"Ask you what?"

With a gentle shake of his head, he shifts closer but doesn't let go of my chin. "Ask. Me."

My lips part as I consider my options. I could back down.

I could turn around, head right back to Jaxon, and come clean, putting the kibosh on this entire thing. Or…or I could ask the rockstar in front of me to roll with it. To corroborate my little white lie until we're both on an airplane back to Harden Heights and as far away from here as possible.

I swallow thickly, let out a slow breath, and raise my gaze to his.

"There she is," Dodger mumbles. "Ask me."

"Will you…will you be my fake boyfriend for the rest of the time we're here?"

Dropping his hand, he lifts a shoulder. "Sorry, can't do—"

My look of terror cracks his facade, and he doubles over in amusement. "Kidding, Rore."

"Not funny!" I smack his shoulder.

"Kind of funny," he argues. "And yeah. Yeah, I got you."

"You sure?" I push. "Because if you're not—"

"It's not like the tabloids will catch me cheating on you or some shit. The band's on hiatus anyway. Besides, it's only a week or so. I can keep my dick in my pants for a week."

"You sure? Because when you put it that way…" My words trail off, letting my silence fill in the blanks while pulling another shameless grin from the man in front of me.

"All right, here's a caveat. If I feel the need to pull my dick out of my pants while I'm here, I promise to do it in private and away from Jaxon or anyone else you decide to lie to. Sound like a plan?" He snaps his fingers. "Wait, I have one more rule."

"And what's that?"

"No falling in love." He tacks on a wink. "It's Fake Relationship 101."

The man has a point, and in most chick flicks, I'd say he's onto something. But me and Dodger? He's like an older brother to me. No, he's even worse than that. He's like a… okay, I can't really think of something worse than the whole falling for your older brother example, but you get my point. Me and Dodger? No bueno. Not now. Not ever.

"No problem," I announce.

A cocky smirk tugs at his mouth. "That's what they all say."

"But you're okay with it?" I push.

"Yeah, what the hell? Go wild, Rore. Let's see what happens."

"Dodger?" the barista calls, interrupting us.

That same smirk teases me as he stands. "Be right back, *girlfriend*."

Yeah...this is going to be interesting.

RORY

She looks beautiful. Ophelia. My *almost* sister-in-law. And Maverick looks handsome as ever in his tux. It's dark and fitted and makes him look like a prince. Tears gather in my eyes as I imagine my other brother beside him. He'd be smiling, too. I know it. My mouth forms a small 'o', and I let out a quiet breath in an attempt not to lose my shit. It's hard, though. Almost impossible. I wasn't nicknamed Squeaks for nothing, and I'm pretty sure this moment would cue the waterworks even if you have a heart of stone, so cut me some slack.

"You ready?" Jax asks beside me.

I peek up at him, biting my bottom lip to keep from bawling like a baby because now is *not* the time.

We haven't spoken since the bachelorette party, and honestly, it's a good thing. I haven't even needed to lie to him about the whole *Dodger's my boyfriend* and stuff. Even the wedding preparations were enough to distract me from my impending—and much dreaded—walk down the aisle with Jax by my side. But now, here we are. And he looks good. Really good. His dark hair is pushed back, and his green eyes are lighter than normal. More of a forest green instead of a dark olive color. Or maybe it's the afternoon sunshine. Not that it matters. Honestly, it isn't fair. How, even when I close my eyes and pull up a perfect depiction of *the* Jaxon Thorne, he still manages to take my breath away. Annoyed, I pick at the edge of my cuticles and scan the crowd filled with familiar faces. The wedding coordinator quietly bustles around us at the back of the venue as the air fills with light anticipation while the audience quietly whispers in the main area. It's time to get this party started. And for the first time in who knows how long, instead of dreading Jaxon's presence, I'm almost grateful for it.

Almost.

My body trembles as I take his arm at the back of the venue, my fingertips tapping in a familiar pattern against his dark suit. I should stop, but I can't help myself.

I miss my brother.

The music begins, and just like at the rehearsal, everyone pairs with their partners, waiting for the moment they'll take their turn to walk down the aisle toward the husband-to-be, aka my big brother. Two by two, they start down the small path while the sun slips between the tree's full branches, dappling everyone in little polka dots of light.

I heard the photographer bitching about the contrast, but I like it. It's beautiful. And peaceful. And almost...cathartic, maybe. Like little kisses from heaven sent from Archer as he looks down from above.

"Rore?" Jax prods. "We're almost up."

With a slow nod, I turn my attention from the dappled light to the man beside me as he places his palm on top of my hand. I'm sure he can feel the way I'm shaking, but instead of asking if I'm okay—obviously, I'm a weeping mess—he gives my fingers a gentle squeeze and stands a little taller.

I'm grateful. For his strength. His stability. Both

metaphorically and literally, thanks to my legs feeling like willow branches.

"I got you, Squeaks," he promises, then guides me forward.

And in this moment? He does.

Three. Two. One.

Together, we step onto the path lined with friends and family. A few cast glances our way, but in general, we're nothing but props, an appetizer before the main course. There are benefits to not being the bride at a wedding. No one cares about you. You're just a body. And the lack of attention is much appreciated as I sniffle softly, using my free hand to dab at the corners of my eyes.

I really should've brought a tissue.

Keeping his hand on mine, Jaxon leads me toward the floral archway, squeezing me softly before removing his hand to dig in his pocket. My brows dip as I watch him pull something out. A crisp white hanky. Subtly, he sets it in my hand, then lets me go when we reach our destination.

I wonder what his wedding looked like. If his ex was a fan of flowers the same way Lia is. If he regrets proposing. I don't know why. Jax should be the last thing on my mind, but I can't help it.

"Canon in D Minor" plays, and everyone stands, turning their sights on a gorgeous Ophelia. Her lacy dress reaches the ground. It's a beautiful champagne color that makes her pale skin look flawless and highlights her strawberry blonde hair. With a bouquet of calla lilies, and her parents, Theo and Blakely, on either side, she walks down the aisle, one sure step after another.

My mom sniffles from the front row, and my dad wraps his arm around her. Leaning her head against his shoulder, she peeks up at Maverick before her gaze slides to me.

"I love you," she mouths.

Twisting the hanky in my hand, I mouth back, "Love you."

Then, she shifts her focus to Ophelia, her new daughter and my new sister.

It's a beautiful ceremony, somehow managing to make my heart feel heavier with grief yet light as air at the same time, and by the time they each say, "I do," I'm not the only one blubbering like a baby. Even so, I wouldn't have it any other away.

12

RORY

Is it hot in here? It feels hot in here. Scanning the venue, I fold my arms, unsure what to do or where to go. It seems everyone's on the dance floor with their significant others, and Dodger's MIA, which leaves me feeling like a fish out of water. When I spot my mom taking a breather at one of the tables near the back, I slip around a few white linen-covered tables, snatch a champagne flute from one of the caterers, and plop down on the closest seat.

"Hi."

She smiles back at me while patting her temples and chest with a linen napkin. "Hey, babes. How are ya?"

"Good," I return. "This is…" My gaze flutters around the crowded room. "Something else."

Her laugh is light and airy as she snatches my champagne and takes a sip. "Yes. Yes it is."

"You okay?" I ask.

"Yeah. Just took a break from dancing with your dad."

My eyes thin as I take in the haze hidden in her expression. "You sure?"

Her nod is slow but genuine. She reaches over, tucking my hair behind my ear. "Just missing your brother."

My bottom lip wobbles before I suck it between my teeth and bite down, fighting the urge to pull out the hanky Jaxon loaned me earlier from my clutch. "Me, too."

"He would've loved this," she continues. Her attention trails around the beautifully decorated space. "Would've been on the dance floor all night. Would've said an incredible best man's speech. Not that Reeves won't knock it out of the park." She sighs. "I don't know. I guess I'm all up in my feels today. The good, the bad, and the ugly."

Stealing another glass of champagne from a caterer's tray since my mom took mine, I let the bubbles fizz on my tongue, then rest my chin on my palm. "I think it's expected."

"Me, too," she admits. "Still bittersweet."

I nod my agreement. "Definitely."

"Have I told you how grateful I am for you lately?"

"Only about a thousand times," I tease. Giving in, I tug the hanky out and dab at the corner of my eye in hopes of not ruining my makeup, thanks to the oh so familiar burn behind my eyes. "I'm grateful for you, too."

"Hey, Rore," my Aunt Ashlyn interrupts.

I turn toward the familiar voice, finding one of her grandbabies on her hip. Scratch that. It isn't just any grandbaby. It's Jaxon's daughter. She's so little. Maybe six or seven months old. With a pair of dimples, baby blue eyes, and a pretty little bow on her head, she's probably the cutest baby I've ever seen. My stomach bottoms out as I stare at her. Her tiny hands. Her chubby cheeks. Her fancy little dress. We haven't been formally introduced, but I saw her on Uncle Macklin's lap during the ceremony. She looked grouchy then, and she doesn't look too happy now, either.

Tearing my attention from the adorably grumpy baby, I push the chair beside mine out from under the table and motion to it. "Hey, Aunt Ash. Take a seat." The baby's face scrunches with another soft cry, fanning my concern. "Is she okay?"

With the patience of a saint, Ashlyn simply smiles, patting the baby's back as she sits beside me. "Yeah, she's fine. Tired, but fine."

"Reminds us of you," my mom chimes in.

My brows pull. "What do you mean?"

"Poppy's a picky softie. Just like someone else we know," Aunt Ashlyn clarifies, though she's kind enough to soften the blow with another knowing smile. "The only person Poppy doesn't fuss around is Jax. Even her mom struggles to calm her down when she's really worked up."

"Just like someone else we know," my mom repeats, her eyes dancing with mirth. "Go figure, the only one to calm you down when you were this little was the very same Jaxon."

I force a smile, tossing her own words back at her. "Go figure."

"You look beautiful, by the way," Aunt Ash interjects.

I glance down at my dress and smooth out the silky fabric. "Thanks."

"Seriously," she gushes. "I swear it's like I'm looking at your mom from twenty years ago. Well, minus the tattoos."

With a laugh, I smooth out my dress again and deflect, "I don't know about that." My mom was and *is* quite the looker. Hell, she's drop-dead gorgeous even now. Maybe it's the willowy build. Maybe it's how she turns heads when she walks into a room and holds herself in conversations. Maybe it's her wide smile, thick but still silky hair, and charming personality. Honestly, it's probably the combination of all of that really makes my mom one of the most incredible women on the planet, and I have no idea how she birthed me. When I was in middle school, she used to joke that as soon as

I gained some confidence, I'd be able to wrap whoever I wanted around my finger. Instead, I curled in on myself, unable to look the opposite sex in the eye, let alone build a connection with them.

Fool me once and all that, I suppose. Not that it mattered.

I smooth out my dress once more, grateful for the distraction. Third time's the charm.

Shifting the fussy Poppy from one knee to the other, Aunt Ashlyn's expression sours. "Oof. I'm pretty sure this girl needs a bum change. Rory, will you hold her while I track down where her dad hid her diaper bag?"

She doesn't wait for my response. She simply hands me the fussy baby like Poppy isn't a ticking time bomb who could explode at any second. I take her in my arms, rub my hand along her little spine, and rock back and forth in my seat in hopes of calming her down. The same wrinkled forehead and pouty lips greet me as she squirms in my arms, unamused by the change to her new caregiver. "Sh, sh, sh," I coo. "It's okay, Baby Girl. It's okay."

Another cry slips out of her, and her tiny hands find my hair, gripping the strands. Instead of tugging like I expect, she tries to bring the fistful of hair to her mouth. I let out a quiet laugh before grasping her wrist to prevent her from gumming my hair to death. "What are you doin', silly girl? That's mine."

She coos back at me and curls closer, making me feel like I'm worth a million bucks. Seriously, she is the cutest thing ever.

"Well, would you look at that," my mom murmurs. "Seems karma's struck again."

My attention strays from Poppy for the shortest of seconds to give my mom a confused look. "What do you mean?"

"We always joked how you and Pops are alike." She smiles

softly and reaches closer, dragging her fingers along Poppy's cheek. "Very particular with your people."

I shy back slightly, unsure if the discomfort has anything to do with how closely she hit the nail on the head or how far off base she is. "I mean, I don't know if I'm that particular."

With a knowing look, my mom says, "Sure, you aren't." She glances back at Poppy. "This, however, I didn't see coming."

"What do you mean?"

"I've never seen this little girl calm down with anyone else but her daddy." Her gaze catches on someone behind me, and she beams. "Speaking of which. Hello, Jax."

My heart stalls in my chest as I look up and over my shoulder, finding Jaxon Thorne's sole focus pinned on me and *only* me. The look makes me squirm, and I can't decide if the twisting in the pit of my stomach is because I feel like I was just caught doing something I shouldn't, or if it's because I was just caught doing something I should. I'm not sure which option I prefer, either. Not when it makes the man look at me like this.

Despite the cotton filling my mouth, I whisper, "Hi."

Instead of replying, Jaxon's focus falls to the little girl in my arms.

"I know, right?" my mom quips. "It's a modern-day miracle."

As if only now realizing we aren't alone, Jaxon forces a smile, shifting the diaper bag he's holding to his opposite shoulder. Whatever I'd glimpsed in his handsome gaze is swallowed by a light, carefree expression as he turns to my mom. "Has my mom seen this? 'Cause she's about to be jealous as hell."

"It'll be our little secret," my mom returns, though I don't believe her in the slightest. Not when she's as close with her friends as I am with Tatum.

Normally, I wouldn't mind. And to be honest, I still shouldn't. But the more the spotlight hangs on me and Jax, the more I want to curl into a ball and disappear. Which is why I should leave. Right now.

Unsure what to do, I start shifting a curled-up Poppy away from my chest so I can get the hell out of here. "Here—"

"Don't." Jaxon's chest expands on a deep breath, and he takes the seat Aunt Ashlyn vacated. "She looks comfortable."

Without a word, I settle back in the chair, keeping Poppy against me as she sticks her hands in my mouth.

"I'm going to find your father," my mom announces. "Jax, keep my daughter company, okay?"

His stare holds mine as he dips his chin. "Sure thing, Aunt Mia."

When she leaves, my pulse gallops like a jackhammer. I swear it's so loud there's no way Jaxon can't hear it over the music playing.

"She's adorable," I murmur.

"Thanks."

"Looks like you," I add.

His mouth lifts. "You think?"

I nod. "I do."

"Hey." A buzzed Dodger plops down in the chair on my opposite side, interrupting us...or saving me from an awkward conversation. Honestly, I'm not sure which is more accurate.

"Who's this little nugget?" Dodge asks, grabbing my glass and tossing back what's left of my champagne.

Seriously, what is it with everyone stealing my drinks?

Jaxon shifts forward. "This is my daughter, Poppy."

"Hey, Poppy." Dodger's smile softens as he sets the empty champagne flute down and leans closer to the baby in my arms. "She's so small."

"Yeah, only in the third percentile at her last appointment," Jaxon returns.

"No shit?" Dodger's brows kick up. "That's tiny."

"Yeah," Jaxon mutters. Not in an angry way. It's more like he's…confused or dejected, though I don't know why.

"You look cute holding a baby," Dodger adds, pinning me with a knowing look there's no way Jaxon buys. "Any chance you wanna pass her off to her dad so we can sneak in a dance before the toasts start?"

With a slow nod, I hand Jaxon his daughter. He takes her without hesitation.

"Thanks again for keeping an eye on her," he says.

"Anytime." Poppy reaches for the hanky on the table, but I stop her from putting it in her mouth. "Trust me, Pops. You don't want to taste that." Keeping it fisted in my hand, I pause and glance at Jax. "Do you want to take it, or I can wash it and give it back later or—"

"Keep it," he insists.

"You sure?"

"Yeah, I'm sure he doesn't mind," Dodger interrupts. He stands and offers his tatted hand, waiting for me to take it. Once I do, he tugs me to my feet, leads me to the dance floor, and spins me into his chest like a seasoned dancing professional. To be fair, I wouldn't put it past him. With all the crazy things he's done in his life, learning how to dance is pretty believable.

Laughing, I say, "My hero."

"Professional cock blocker at your service," he quips while slowly swaying us from side to side.

"Is that what you're doing?" I challenge. "Cock blocking for me? 'Cause I thought we were dancing."

"Don't act like you don't know I just interrupted your little swoon fest over there."

I roll my eyes, refusing to look at the table in question. "I don't know what you're talking about."

"Let's say you don't," he decides. "Because you might honestly be as innocent as most give you credit for."

My lips purse. "Gee, thanks."

"Nothing wrong with it," he argues. "But let's say it's true, and you really haven't noticed the way he looks at you." He dips me over his arm, then pulls me back to a standing position, stealing the air from my lungs. "I have."

"Seems you don't know what you're talking about, either," I mutter.

"Nah." He chuckles. "I'm much less innocent than you are, Squeaks. I know what want looks like."

Want? As in Jax wants me? The idea is laughable at best, yet crippling in general.

With a slow shake of my head, I mutter, "He doesn't want me."

"Maybe not consciously," Dodger concedes. "Not yet. But I wouldn't write him off, either."

The urge to sneak a glance at a certain someone with his daughter is strong, but I fight it and lift my chin a little higher, refusing to give in. "I think you're being ridiculous, Dodger Anders."

With a flick of his wrist, Dodger spins me around again, then pulls me into him. "And I think you underestimate your feminine wiles, Rory Buchanan."

Feminine wiles, my ass.

If I had feminine wiles, I wouldn't be a virgin. I wouldn't be a crazy dog lady. And I sure as hell wouldn't be hung up on my childhood crush even after all these years. But instead of arguing with him, knowing it'll get me nowhere, I tear my attention from the top button on Dodger's dress shirt and let him lead me across the dance floor.

He's a good dancer. Confident. Sexy.

"Speaking of wiles," I murmur. "You never told me your reason for leaving Lockwood Heights."

His brow quirks. "Didn't I?"

"Nope."

"Then it looks like I wanna keep it that way," he quips, spinning me around once more.

I could fight him. I could pick. But I won't. Besides, we all have our secrets. Or at least most of us do. And if someone's lucky enough to keep theirs hidden from the world, who am I to reveal it out of jealousy?

Swaying to the slow, seductive beat, I peek at Jax, finding his gaze on me as he cradles a sleeping Poppy to his chest.

And it's strange. How a simple look has the power to knock me on my ass, and if Dodger's arms weren't wrapped around me, I might very well end up on the floor.

"Yeah, he's definitely jealous," Dodger muses.

My attention snaps back to my dance partner. "And I think you're too buzzed to make such an assumption."

"Never too buzzed to make an assumption. Especially a bad one." He winks. "But I'm not that buzzed, Rore, and this isn't a bad assumption. Even drunk Dodger can see the way he looks at you." His smirk widens. "Like he wants a taste."

"But only subconsciously."

"Don't knock our masculine urges, Rore. They're a powerful beast."

"And so is the alcohol coursing through your system," I argue.

Bending closer, he brushes his lips against the shell of my ear. "And so is the want coursing through your boy's over there."

I lean away from him, giving him the side-eye. "Careful, or you'll make our parents believe you're actually interested in me."

"Isn't that the point?" he asks. "I'm your plus-one and fake boyfriend until you decide to pull the plug on this."

The reminder doesn't exactly leave me with any warm fuzzies. I'm not a liar. Not usually. The thought alone is nearly enough to cause me to break out in hives—add it to the list-—but the thought of Jaxon assuming I've never moved past him, even if it is true, is enough to make my cheeks rival the color of a damn lobster.

But so is the possibility that Dodger's assumptions aren't completely off-base, and I don't know how I feel about it.

13

RORY

With a clink of her glass, Tatum stands tall at the table closest to the bar, waiting for everyone to quiet down. After a few seconds, everyone catches on and settles into their seats. "I've been instructed it's my job to start the toasts," she announces. "Ophelia," she turns to her sister, "You look hot as hell." Everyone laughs. "Maverick, you look pretty good, too." Another rumble of amusement echoes throughout the room. "As I was writing my speech or whatever, I thought about how many different directions I could take this toast. I could tell an embarrassing story, like the time Lia bled through her swimsuit when we were kids, and I called her sharkbait for the rest of the summer." I cover my mouth to keep from laughing. "Or I could go the sentimental route, and talk about how we've always had our struggles, but Lia's way too stubborn to give up on the people she cares about." She points at Mav. "Although, don't think I won't neuter you if you decide you have a free pass to treat my sister like shit." Her mouth lifts in a smirk. "But what I really think is the most important thing to tell all of you is that it was always Mav and Ophelia.

Always." A soft smile replaces her snarky one as she holds her flute of champagne to her chest. "And honestly, I think that's the most beautiful thing of all. Through thick and thin, it's always Mav and Lia, and I couldn't be happier for both of you to continue this life together. For better or worse. In sickness and in health." A slight quiver graces her bottom lip before she sucks it into her mouth. "You two are stuck together, and I think I can speak for most of the people in this room when I say, we wouldn't have it any other way." Raising her glass a few more inches into the air, she says, "To Ophelia and Mav."

"To Ophelia and Mav!" everyone repeats, each of us taking a sip of our drinks as Reeves clamors to his feet.

After clearing his throat, the crowd quiets and Reeves dives right in. "I'm not sure how I'm supposed to follow such an epic toast, but I'll do my best." He tugs at the collar on his dress-shirt. "Maverick is my best friend. Has been since we were at LAU. I still remember seeing the way he looked at you, Lia, and I couldn't help but poke the bear." My brother chuckles at his table. "Now, the story I'm about to tell happened before I ever met my Pickles, but, uh, I still remember the summer Ophelia moved in next door. We were at a fundraiser, and the bride was manning the kissing booth to help raise some money for the women's hockey team. Not gonna lie. I was a little bored and had a thing for getting under my buddy's skin, and what better way to get under his skin than to pay for a ticket and get in line to have his girl give me a kiss." His smirk widens. "I've never seen Mav move so fast as when I stood in front of Lia, waiting for the kiss I'd paid for."

The crowd laughs again, and I join in, imagining exactly how pissed Mav must've been. To see the love of his life lean in to kiss his best friend until he had no choice but to intervene.

Shifting closer, Ophelia kisses Maverick's cheek. He grins back at her with nothing but love and adoration in his navy blue eyes. It's so beautiful and sweet I can't help but feel a little jealous.

I've never had someone look at me like that. Like I'm their world. Their everything. My gaze drifts to Jaxon, and my heart pangs. I wonder if he's happy. If he misses his wife. If he mourned the life he was supposed to have with her the same way I would if I was in his shoes.

"So, here's to many more kisses and glimpses of the over-protective Maverick we all know and love. You two have always been endgame, and we're glad you finally got your shit together and made it official." He smirks. "To Opie and Maverick!"

Lia calls out, "Only my husband is allowed to call me Opie!"

But I don't miss her dopey grin as Maverick reaches over and tugs her into him, stealing a kiss while everyone repeats, "To Opie and Maverick!"

My dad is next, then it's Lia's dad's turn. Each toast grows a little more mushy, hitting me right in the feels while making me grateful Mav didn't ask me to say anything. Not sure I would've been able to say a single word before I'd inevitably turn into a blubbery mess. Actually, now that I think about it, I've only shed a dozen or so tears, which, for me, is kind of a miracle.

After Lia's dad, Uncle Theo, wishes them the happiest of lifetimes together, Maverick stands and raises his glass. "I, uh, I debated whether or not to do this. Didn't know if it was the right time or...I don't know." He rubs at his chest with his opposite hand, peering down at his bride. "But I think I'd regret it if I didn't, so, here it goes. All of these toasts are in celebration of me and Lia." He wipes beneath his nose with the back of his hand. "But I want to take a second to share my appreciation for my twin brother, who, uh, who can't be here tonight." His Adam's apple bobs in his throat. "For those who don't know, my brother, Archer, passed away around ten years ago."

My esophagus constricts, making it hard to breathe as I stare up at Maverick.

"It was, uh—" He sticks his tongue in his cheek, and a sheen hits his eyes. "It was the hardest thing I've ever been through and happened right after I was diagnosed with a rare heart disease." He sniffs, wiping beneath his nose again. "When I found out I would die if I couldn't get a new heart, I was…I was preparing to let go of everything I ever wanted. I was trying to wrap my head around…around what my doctors were saying, and the idea of not living for much longer." His chin drops to his chest, and Lia reaches up, tangling her fingers with Maverick's while staying in her seat. "And then my brother passed away in a car accident." He sniffs again. "Now, you might ask how my brother's death connects to my diagnosis, and honestly, I would've never guessed it either, but, uh," he forces out a slow breath, "I guess fate decided I needed to stick around a little while longer because I wound up receiving my twin brother's heart a few hours after we got the call about his accident."

My chest aches, the tears falling freely down my face and dripping off my chin as I relive the hardest night of my life. Unable to watch my big brother break in front of so many people, I stare at the small stain of tears on the linen tablecloth.

"Arch?" Maverick's voice cracks, and my heart crumbles with it. "Without you, I wouldn't be here. Period. I wouldn't have the opportunity to say I do to the most incredible woman on this earth. I wouldn't have been able to visit third world countries and bring them fresh water like you always hoped to do. I wouldn't be able to be a father and a friend and a son and a husband. I wouldn't be alive without you." He heaves a sigh, his knuckles turning white as he grips his wife's hand like it's a lifeline. "If you're out there somewhere, if you can hear me, I want you to know I still think about you every day. Still miss you every day. Love you, brother."

"To Archer," my dad announces.

"To Archer," the rest of the room repeats with a somberness that cuts me to my core.

Shakily, I bring the glass to my lips, but the bubbles fall flat on my taste buds as I force myself to toast my brother. And it's moments like this when I wish I could numb the pain. When I wish I could hide my emotions or at least stifle them until I'm alone. Until I'm not in a room full of people who are here to celebrate, not watch a bunch of people weep for a person who was taken too soon. But I'm not that person. Nope. Instead, I'm someone who feels and who cries and who wears her heart on her sleeve which makes this moment feel impossible. The pain is too much. Too real and sharp. With my heart thrumming in my ears, I push to my feet, ignoring the way my champagne trembles in my glass.

"Hey," Dodge murmurs from his seat beside me. "Hey, you okay?"

Head bobbing, I mutter, "Yeah. Yeah, I'm good. I just need to…" I set the glass back on the table so I don't spill it all over myself. "I need to use the restroom. I'll be back in a…I'll be back in a few."

My legs are wobbly at best as I stride out of the main area and down a dim hallway, stealing a tissue from a side table on the way. Afraid I won't make it to the bathroom, I collapse onto a small bench pressed against a random wall, cradling my head in my hands.

Tap, tap, tap. Pause. *Tap, tap, tap.* Pause. *Tap, tap, tap.* Pause.

The gentle tap-tap-tap sequence against my temples calms me, though I'm not stupid enough to believe it'll last.

No, giving in means the fallout will be even worse in the long run, but I can't help myself. Not after tonight.

"Hey," a low voice interrupts.

I jerk at the sound and wipe at my face with my crumpled tissue before peering up.

"I'm not in the"—I hiccup—"mood, Jax."

"I don't care if you're not in the mood, Rore," he growls. "You need…" He hesitates, and I swear he's going to say *me*, but instead he grits out, "someone."

Someone.

Not him. Of course not. Why would I need him, right?

His ambiguity only pisses me off more. "Well, since you clearly aren't that person, I think you should go."

He shakes his head. "I'm not going anywhere."

His stubbornness only breaks me more. Wiping the tears from my cheeks, I beg, "Leave. Me. Alone."

"I tried that," he mutters. "Didn't take." Without waiting for an invitation, he sits on the bench and offers me a fresh tissue. "All out of hankies. This'll have to do."

I take it and blow my nose, ignoring the deja vu accompanying it. When I found out about Archer's death, Jax was the only one I wanted. The only person I felt comfortable enough to break around without adding to their grief. Now here he is, watching me crumble all over again, and I can't decide if I should push him away for what feels like the hundredth time or give in and stop fighting it. The pull I've felt since the day I was born, or at least it's the story our parents tell. Not that it matters because the twinge in my chest has nothing to do with him. Not this time. Nope. Seems my brother's absence has stolen the spotlight once again, and I can't decide if I'm grateful for it or even more pissed.

It's funny. The way grief ebbs and flows. Not that someone's death is something you ever truly get over, but some days it's easier to stomach while others, it's full-blown crippling. Like right now.

I know myself well enough to know there's no way I'll be able to stop these alligator tears from flowing. I'm not that lucky. So, instead of pushing it, instead of pushing Jaxon away like I know I should, I crumble even more, too exhausted to do anything but give in. To my emotions. My feelings. My grief. Curling toward him, I let down my walls and simply *feel*. And it's painful. And messy. And consuming. But cathartic, too. Like a valve has been released, and the pressure can discharge the way it needs to. As my body wracks with silent sobs, Jaxon runs his hand up and down my spine.

"Sh, sh, sh," he coos. "I got you, Beautiful. I got you."

I always appreciated this about him. The way he doesn't lie or promise everything's going to be okay. The way he doesn't sugarcoat shit or rush me through my pathetic crying process I've perfected over the years.

"I miss him, too," Jaxon rasps. "I miss him so much."

Another sob wracks through me like a whip, and I lean into Jaxon's side. I shouldn't. I know I shouldn't. But I'm so tired. Tired of walking on eggshells. Of tiptoeing around each other or pretending like he hasn't seen the most vulnerable pieces of me. Even if it's been years, he knows it as well as I do. He knows what I've been through. Knows how hard I broke after seeing my brother's lifeless body attached to machines in the cold, sterile hospital room. Knows how torn apart I was when the doctor entered the room and told Maverick that Archer was brain dead but would be giving him one final gift before he'd be laid to rest. And when you share moments like that—like *this*—it's not exactly difficult to fall into the same rhythm. The same dance. The same trap.

"I miss you, too, you know," he rasps. "Fuck, Rore. What I wouldn't give to go back to before. Before you hated me."

Shaking my head, I burrow closer to his chest, stealing his warmth as well his words. I don't know how he does it. How he manages to read my mind and lasso my wants and needs before turning them into his own. It's as if he knows how to put my mind at ease. How to support and justify and give his stamp of approval no matter how unhinged I feel sometimes. Like right now. When I feel like I can't breathe, let alone voice my own thoughts. My own feelings. Or the fact that I've missed him, too. So damn much. Even platonically, he was my person. And in a way, I think I'm grieving that loss as well. The relationship we used to have until I screwed everything up.

I'm so sorry for screwing everything up.

My vision is blurred with tears as I peek up at him. His strong jaw. His long lashes. His slightly crooked nose after one too many fights on the ice in college. Swallowing past the knot in my throat, I whisper, "I don't hate you."

It's the first fully truthful thing I've said since being home. Without my guard up. Without the line I drew in the sand. Without my shame holding me back. Simply the truth in all its messy glory.

"I don't hate you," I repeat. It's surer this time but still as raw.

His gaze drops to my mouth, sparking the realization of exactly how close we are. Something flashes in his pretty eyes, though I can't place it. Maybe he's realizing the same thing. I can taste his breath. Mint and alcohol. Probably from the champagne. It brushes against my damp cheeks, proving our woven proximity since I've bawled all over his chest. But the funny thing is that if I didn't know any better, I'd say he's about to kiss me. Giving me a look like this. The thing is...I do. I do know better. Hell, I learned from the man himself.

And maybe it's the tears. Maybe it's the flashbacks of our past coming to haunt me. Maybe it's the exhaustion from tonight's experience. Honestly, I'm not sure, but I'm too tired to care. Instead, I stay curled beside him, letting his eyes take their time as they rove my tear-stained face when footsteps echo down the hall. They cut through the thick haze shrouding us in our little corner and bring me back to the present. To reality. Slowly, I pull away from Jaxon's side, turn toward the sound, and find Dodger striding down the hall. When he sees me, he stops short, his attention drifting to Jaxon before he clears his throat and tugs at the top button on his dress shirt. "Hey."

"Hey," I squeak.

"You didn't come back."

"I know." My tongue darts out between my lips as I wipe the never-ending tears from my face. "Sorry, I was having a…"—I wave my hand around my face—"a moment."

His mouth lifts on one side. "No worries. Just wanted to make sure you're okay?"

The question hangs in the air, so I take a moment to dissect it.

Am I okay? Yes and no. But it isn't any different than any other day of the week. My brother's gone. My best friend's been whisked away by the cutest rockstar ever, and the only man I ever relied on has been cut off from my life for years and is seated beside me with a tear-dampened shirt.

"I'm okay," I breathe out. Maybe it's a lie. Maybe it isn't. But it's a familiar reality. One I'm well-accustomed to. So, why hate it now?

"You sure you're okay?" Dodger prods.

"Yeah, Dodge, I'm good."

"Okay." Dodger rocks back on his heels, looking unsure. Hooking his thumb over his shoulder. "I'll, uh, I'll be inside if you need anything."

"Thanks."

With a deep, shuddered breath, I crumple the well-used

tissue in my palm, adding it to the first while I watch him leave. I'm not ready to follow yet. I should probably freshen up in the bathroom first, but I can't find the willpower to do anything but sit in a dim hallway next to a man who's impossible to read. Even so, his words whisper in the back of my mind.

I missed you, too, you know.

Did he?

Even after all these years, did he miss me? Our friendship? Our talks? Or is he simply trying to make me feel better after watching me break down outside my brother's reception?

"He seems like a good guy," Jaxon tells me.

He. As in…Dodger. Right.

"He's actually really great," I admit. And it's true. Dodger's been nothing but a saint throughout this entire ordeal. Letting me take the lead. Going with the flow. I'm not sure I would've survived this trip without him, though I keep that to myself.

"Glad you're happy," he mutters.

"Thanks." It's forced. Awkward. And brings us right back to square one, making me miss the old Jaxon more than ever. "I, uh, I heard about the divorce. I'm sorry."

"Don't be." He hesitates, but I don't miss the way he shuts down even more, proving it's a touchier subject than he'd like it to be. "I should probably check on Poppy," he adds.

Another beat of silence hits, knocking me harder than I want to admit. How can I already miss him when he hasn't even left me yet? I've survived without him for years. Hell, around a decade now, and the idea of going back to silence and awkward looks and stilted conversations feels…empty.

I feel empty.

Wiping his hands on his slacks, Jax begins to stand, but I grab the sleeve of his shirt to stop him. "Jax?"

His eyes stay glued to my grip on him. It makes me way more self-conscious than I want to acknowledge. But the really surprising part? He doesn't pull away.

"Yeah, Squeaks?" he rasps.

I force my fingers to loosen from his sleeve and link them in my lap. "For what it's worth, I, uh, I've missed you, too."

With a shallow but sharp inhale through flared nostrils, he stands to his full height and stares down at me, leaving me desperate to read his mind. To know what he's thinking. How he's feeling. If I crossed another line like I did all those years ago.

"It's worth a lot, Rore." The same raspy tone rolls over me, leaving prickles of awareness along my bare arms.

"I know we're not the same people we once were, but..." My words get lost in my throat, though I know I'm too far gone to turn back now.

"But what, Squeaks?"

"But do you think you'd want to try being friends again?" I sniff, refusing to lose my nerve. "I don't know. I just...after Maverick's toast, I was reminded how...how frail life can be, and I feel like I've already lost enough people I care about, you know?"

Those dark green eyes threaten to swallow me whole as he stands motionless, towering over me the way he used to when I was a kid. And maybe it's the alcohol, maybe it's the defenses he managed to barrel over with one simple conversation and an offered shoulder to cry on, but I swear I see interest swirling in those vibrant eyes. It's enough to leave me off-balance, and I open my mouth to rescind my suggestion, but he cuts me off.

"Not gonna lose me." Folding at the waist, he kisses my forehead, but I tamp down the butterflies left in its wake, refusing to entertain them when they're not important. Not in the big picture. What's important is this. This friendship.

This connection. I've ignored it for so long, misconstruing it into something it isn't, and therefore, avoiding it like it's something ugly, when what I feel for Jaxon is the furthest thing from it. And as long as I can keep the romantic meter in check, what's wrong with moving forward and letting our past go in an attempt to salvage our platonic connection—one I've only ever felt with him?

Nothing. Nothing at all.

Right?

14

JAXON

I've never been a fan of small talk, but I'd give anything
to discuss the weather instead of drowning in Iris's
ramblings. I used to find it cute. The thought is laughable now. Or maybe there was less venom before. Less
nitpicking on her end, and less tongue-biting on mine. By
some miracle, she let me keep Poppy overnight after the
wedding. We stayed in one of the rooms at the country club
with the majority of the wedding party, though I left the
reception earlier than most, grateful it was Poppy's bedtime
and I had a solid excuse to hide away. After my conversation
with Rory, I appreciated the quiet. The time to think. If only
Iris hadn't ruined it with an early morning phone call,
demanding Poppy be ready in ten minutes despite our orig-
inal plan.

Scrubbing my hand over my face, I buckle Poppy's car
seat into the back of Iris's Land Rover while she prattles on
about how it would've been nice if she'd received an invitation to the wedding.

We've had this conversation at least a dozen times, and
even though Mav gave me the final call as to whether my life

would've been made easier or even more of a shit show than it normally is if Iris was invited, I'm not sure what path would've made Iris less nasty.

"I told you I would've been happy to drop Poppy off at the house this afternoon like we planned," I remind her before giving my daughter one more kiss on the forehead.

"It's not your week," she snaps. "Remember?"

Not anymore, I want to clarify, but I swallow my comment. After all, Iris is the one who asked if we could switch weeks despite the wedding being on the calendar for over a month. The change gave Iris two weeks back-to-back, along with free ammunition for her allowing me to steal Poppy for one night thanks to the big event. The irony isn't lost on me, since I was the first to accommodate the switch, even if it messed with my own plans. It'd be nice if she didn't throw my generosity in my face, but here I am. The bad guy all over again.

Too tired to put up a fight, I mutter, "My mistake," and unfold myself from the back of her car, closing the door behind me.

"Speaking of mistakes," she continues, "Have you found a nanny yet?" She crosses her arms. "Because I will not let some stranger stay with my baby while you traipse around the world."

Continent, I silently correct. And no, I haven't found a nanny yet because anyone who even comes close is shot down as soon as I forward Iris the resume. Not that it matters. It's not like Poppy likes anyone but me, and the idea of her bawling for hours on end anytime I'm coaching is almost enough to make me draw up my resignation papers right here, right now. It's not like the weeks when I don't have her are much better, though. I hate it. Being away from her. Feeling like she's leverage Iris can use anytime we're apart.

Fuck.

I don't even know what to do anymore.

"You know, you could always leave her with me full time," Iris continues. "Although we'd have to take it into account when it comes to child support, but I'm sure my lawyer would be happy to send you his revisions."

Of course, he would.

"That's a very generous offer, but I'm taking care of it," I reply.

"Oh, you are, are you?" She cocks her head. "How so? Because it looks to me like you're doing nothing but procrastinate. The team's training camp is in three days, Jaxon. Three. Days. Have you even asked if I can cover your week and watch her?" She scoffs. "No. You haven't. Because you don't think about anyone but yourself."

Bullshit. The last person I think about is myself, and if Iris hadn't asked me to swap weeks a little while ago, I wouldn't have had to find a nanny to drag to training camp with me, *and* I would've had more time to find someone. My mom, who also happens to be my lawyer, warned me about this. About Iris weaponizing her time with Poppy so she could ask for more child support despite my initial generosity during mediation. Yeah, my mom warned me about that, too. How I should've fought harder instead of giving in to Iris's every whim. Not that it matters anymore. If I don't find someone to watch Poppy while I travel, Iris will be my only option. Sure, my parents can step in here and there, but that isn't a long term solution. Hell, it's the furthest from it.

So where does it leave me? Fucked. Absolutely fucked. My molars grind as I stare at Poppy's profile through the back window. Her button nose. Pouty lips. The way they wobble ever so slightly, like she's dreaming of her bottle or some shit. My mouth lifts at the view.

Reaching for my bicep, Iris twists me to face her. "Are you ignoring me, Jaxon?"

My patience thins even more, but I mutter, "Not ignoring you."

"Then why won't you answer me? Hmm?"

Because right now, you're trying to poke the bear, and I'm not in the mood. The thought flickers through my mind, but I clear my throat, preparing to answer when someone calls out, "Hi!"

My head twists toward the sound as a barefoot Rory strides across the lawn.

"Hi," she repeats. Offering her hand to my ex, Rory waits for her to take it.

Instead, Iris stares at Rory's extended arm. "Who's this?" she asks me.

"I'm the new nanny," Rory answers. "My name's Rory. Hi."

"You're the nanny?"

"Yes. Hi," Rory repeats for what, the third time? Fourth? Honestly, I've lost count already. It's way too early for this shit.

"Hey, Rore," I offer. The words come out more accusatory than I mean them to, but also, what the hell is she doing?

Rory's attention flicks to me. "Hi." But the look in her eyes? It screams, *trust me.*

And I want to. Fuck, do I want to. Seeing Rory with Poppy last night messed with my head on a level even I don't understand. My daughter looked happy. Content. In someone else's arms other than mine. And the spark of hope that filtered through me was only slightly tainted by resignation. Because…go figure. The one person my daughter likes is the one person who wants nothing to do with me. Or at least, she didn't. So, why is she saving me now?

Ignoring Rory's presence, Iris folds her arms, giving me a pointed look. "I thought you said you were working on it."

Shit, she's right.

"Just finalized the paperwork this morning," Rory interjects. "Last night was a test run to see if I was a good fit with Poppy, and…"

"And I offered her the job after seeing how well they got along," I finish for her. "I was just waiting…"

"For my official acceptance, which…here it is." Rory steps forward. "I'll take the job. Obviously. By the way, Poppy looks so much like you," Rory adds, giving Iris the warmest, kindest, most genuine smile. And honestly, I shouldn't expect anything less. It's Rory. "Anyway, I know if the roles were reversed, I'd be super anxious to let my brand new baby hang out with just anyone, so if you ever want to chat or… anything at all, I am open to whatever you need, and, uh, I'll be sure to send pictures if…" she peeks over at me. "If that's what my employer wants. Um, I'll leave you two to it." Still facing us, she takes a step back toward the main building where the rest of her family are probably still tucked in their beds. "Nice to have met you. Have a good day." Then, she turns on her bare feet and strides away, leaving me in a whirlwind of confusion.

Did that really just happen?

And is it a bad thing?

A good thing?

I don't even know.

Is she serious? There's no way. She doesn't even live in Lockwood Heights anymore. This is only a…a short term solution, but at least I have a few more days to come up with an actual game plan. It's more than I had two minutes ago.

"Rory, huh?" Iris clicks her tongue against the roof of her mouth, giving me an icy stare that could curdle milk. "As in *the* Rory?"

My jaw clenches, and I tear my attention from Rory entering the country club, turning back to Iris. I've never talked about her. Not really. Not because Rory or I have anything to be ashamed of, but because...I don't know. Maybe a small piece of me always knew Iris would never understand any of it. How close we were. The way Rory always looked up to me. The way I always looked out for her. Like a brother. That's all.

"She just graduated," I tell her. "Came home for the wedding and hit it off with Poppy so I...I offered her the job."

"Hmm." Iris purses her lips. "She's young."

"She's in her twenties and more than capable."

"And young," Iris repeats.

My shoulder lifts. "Poppy likes her."

"I don't give a shit if Poppy likes her, Jaxon, I—"

"I'm not required to give you a say in who watches our baby, Iris," I remind her. "Not when she's with me. Just like I have no say in how you let Chris move in with you."

"Are you saying you're interested in her?" she seethes, jumping to non-existent conclusions so fast my head spins. My patience threatens to snap.

"She's an employee and a family friend. Nothing more. And if you knew Rory at all, you'd know Poppy couldn't be in better hands."

The same purse of her lips swallows her expression, making me wonder how I ever fell for her in the first place.

I'm not sure why I'm pushing this. Why I'm committing to this insane idea when there's no way in hell Rory was serious. She was being impulsive. Rushing in to save the day without thinking of any actual consequences or long-term effects. Hell, we don't even live in the same state. It would never work. But at least it buys me a few more days. I can come up with a solution by then. Can't I? Not sure I have a choice. Not anymore.

"Do you need anything else, Iris?" I ask.

She glares up at me. "You need to forward me her background check."

I nod. "I'll have it for you as soon as possible."

It's another boldfaced lie. What she'll have is my actual gameplan, once I come up with one.

The woman's Jimmy Choo taps against the pavement, her nostrils flaring. I know she wants to lose her shit. Wants to curse me. Call me names. Do whatever it takes to spread her frustration until it brands my skin, leaving me blistered and angry. She's always been this way. Unafraid of hurting feelings or hitting below the belt if it'll leave her the victor. When we were married, she'd cool down and apologize, but now that we're divorced? Well, I'm pretty sure sorry has left her vocabulary. I lift my chin and wait for the blow.

Instead, she seethes, "Fine." With nothing left to say, she climbs into the driver's side of her SUV and slams the door, rousing a sleepy Poppy in the back before she peels out of the parking lot.

A sigh reverberates through my chest as the taillights disappear around the corner, and I turn back to the main building.

Now what do I do?

Rory's pacing in the front of the massive windows. I wonder if she knows I can see her. If she cares. If she regrets her decision to butt into my life without an invitation. If she's serious about being my nanny until I find a long-term solution. She wouldn't put her life on hold for me, would she? An image of Poppy on Rory's lap rises to the surface all over again, and my steps falter as I head past the valet desk and into the main area.

A small part of me wonders if I'll regret this, too. But there's no turning back now. Not if I can help it. What I really want to know is the reason why she intervened in the first place. I guess it's time I find out.

The main doors sliding open is nothing but a whisper but cuts through my racing thoughts like a fog horn as I step inside the quiet lobby area.

Rushing forward, Rory blurts out, "I am so sorry—"

"Sorry?" I frown and guide her toward the edge of the large open space in search of privacy. Not that there's really anyone here. It's not even six in the morning, and everyone's still asleep, just like how Rory should be. "Why are you sorry?"

"I didn't mean to eavesdrop, I swear. It just happened. I was coming around from the back after an early morning walk because I couldn't sleep, and then I heard what your ex was saying, and it kind of pissed me off, because like, who talks like that? And then, before I even knew what was happening, I opened my big fat mouth and my feet were moving like they had a mind of their own and..." She shoves her hair away from her face. "I'm so sorry. If I caused any trouble. If I rocked the boat. If I...I don't even know. I'm just sorry."

With a low laugh, I grab her hands to stop her from fidgeting. "You have nothing to apologize for."

She peeks up at me and rolls her eyes. "Liar."

"I'm serious, Squeaks. If anything, I should be thanking you for stepping in." I gulp, realizing how close we're standing before forcing my grasp to loosen from around her wrists. Shifting back, I murmur, "The question is...what now?"

"Yeah," she breathes out. "That is, uh, that is the question, isn't it."

"At least I have a few extra days to figure out a game plan."

"Yeah, that's something." She looks down at her bare toes. "You don't think...you don't think it's too late to back out?"

I scrub my hand over my face. "Not sure what my other options are."

Her nod is slow as she lifts her hand, nibbling on the edge of her thumb before tapping it against her lips.

One, two, three. Pause. *One, two, three.*

"What is it, Rore?" I ask.

She shakes her head but doesn't answer.

"Tell me," I push.

"How…" A sigh slips out of her, and she lowers her hand. "How long have you been looking for a nanny?"

"A couple months now."

"And no luck." Her gaze meets mine. "Right?"

"Not yet." I wipe at the corner of my eye, defeat settling over me. "I know it makes me look like an ass who dropped the ball, but it isn't easy."

"I'm not criticizing you. I'm just saying…" She sighs again, like this conversation is the last one she wants to have. "If you've been looking for a while now and haven't had any luck, who's to say the next few days will be any different?"

"Not sure I have much of a choice in the matter, Rore."

"I know," she says. "I just feel bad."

"Not your problem," I remind her. "Even if you were nice enough to stick your neck out for me this morning."

"Anytime." She forces a smile. "You know that."

I do. I do know it. Rory's the most selfless person I've ever met. Honestly, I shouldn't have been surprised in the first place.

"Well, thank you," I tell her. "I'm gonna head upstairs and see if I can get some more sleep."

She nods but doesn't say anything else.

I turn toward the elevator when she stops me.

"What if…what if I don't back out?"

Convinced I misheard her, I face Rory again. "What?"

"I mean, I graduated with a psychology degree and a minor in child development. It's not like I don't know how to take care of a baby." She twists her fingers in front of her. "At least, for the short term."

I blink, trying to piece together what she's talking about.

"What are you saying, Rore?"

"What if, for the short-term and until you find someone stable, I help out? Clearly, you need more time to find someone solid, especially if you've already been looking for a while." She glances up at me, answering my unspoken question. "I know you. You aren't someone to leave something like this to the last minute. How many people have you interviewed?"

"At least a dozen," I mutter. "Maybe more."

"Which is the right thing," she says. "Finding someone you trust to watch over your baby isn't the same as picking out a candy bar at the store." She pauses. "If I help, you'll have time to interview twice as many prospects until you find the perfect fit. Maybe I can even sort through some of the applications, since I'm sure you'll be busy once training starts." A crease forms between her brows. "Except I didn't think about Hades." She grimaces. "Do you think he can come?"

"Another German Shepherd on the Lions' roster?" I offer, not missing a beat. "Pretty sure the fans would go wild."

I'm right, too. The first year the Lions became a professional team, Henry bought Rory's mom a puppy to be the mascot for the organization. She even had her own social media page Mia ran for her. Nala. The most chill German Shepherd I've ever met. I was old enough to remember her, though she died before Rory was born.

"Seriously," I add. "The long-time fans will love it."

"Well, then. I guess it's settled," Rory murmurs. "I'm in until you find a replacement."

Part of me wants to jump for joy like a kid on Christmas. The other part? Well, I guess I can't help but acknowledge the guilt spreading through my marrow. "You sure you're up for this, Rore?"

She rolls her eyes. "Jax—"

"Trust me. I don't want to be the voice of reason right now," I admit dryly. "But agreeing to watch a kid while also traveling across the US and Canada is a lot. It's gonna be long nights. Long days. Long flights. Long stints in the hotel with nothing to do while Poppy naps." Another punch of guilt spreads through my chest as I consider giving her an out even if I don't want to. Does it make me selfish? Yeah. Yeah, I guess it does. "Shit," I mutter as another snag filters through my mind.

"What?"

"What about Dodger?"

Her brows pull. "What about him?"

"You really think your boyfriend is okay with us traveling together?" I challenge.

Understanding hits her pretty eyes, and her body relaxes. "Oh. Yeah, it's not a problem. Honestly, he's the least of my —" She clears her throat. "Sorry. Uh, yeah. No. That's. It's fine. Dodger is…fine."

"You sure?"

"Yup." She paints on a fake smile, though I don't miss the way she refuses to look me in the eye. "One quick phone call and…he trusts me, so. We're good."

"Okay." I tilt my head, studying her. "You sure you're up for this?"

"I already said yes."

"Well, I'm gonna need your answer one more time." I fight the urge to tilt her chin up and force her attention. I tuck my hands into my pockets instead. "You sure you're up for this, Rore?"

Nibbling on the edge of her lip, she peeks up at me. "What are friends for?"

"Friends?"

"I meant what I said last night." She tucks her hair behind her ear. "I want us to be friends again, Jaxon. And clearly, you're a friend who could use a helping hand."

The organ in my chest skips like a broken record, constricting as I stare down at her. She's always been selfless. And even though we agreed to try the friendship route again last night, I never would've expected this. She's giving me a lifeline. A much needed lifeline. And I couldn't be more grateful for it.

"One month," I decide. "Give me one month, and I promise I'll find a replacement."

Something hits her baby blue eyes, though it's gone in an instant.

"Yeah, Jax." She smiles. "Whatever you need."

15

RORY

"What am I doing, what am I doing, what am I doing?" I pace my childhood bedroom as Hades watches my mental breakdown from my bed. I thought if I slept on my manic offer to nanny Poppy, the nerves would go away. Pretty sure they've multiplied.

I'm supposed to go home today. My bags are already packed, and I had no intention of doing anything but escaping back to Harden Heights as soon as Mav and Lia said "I do." Instead, I opened my big, fat mouth and offered to help Jax out of a bind. And not just a little bind. Oh, no. It's a big, fat one. My big, fat mouth got me into a big, fat doozy, and now I don't know what to do about it. Is there anything I can do about it? I mean, I could always back out. But that's a terrible idea. Not only is it selfish, but it also screws over Jaxon. He'll look untrustworthy to his ex and will probably be distracted during the first weeks of coaching the Lions. It might even set them up for a bad season, which will hurt my dad's wallet, might even put stress on their relationship, not to mention affect my cousins' livelihoods, which would be absolutely terrible and—

"Knock, knock!"

Flinching at the sound, I press my hand to my chest as the door handle twists and Tatum steps inside.

As soon as she sees me, her brows clash. "Okay, what happened?"

With a fake smile, I force my feet to stay in place and stop tapping my outer thigh. "Hi."

"Hi?"

"Hi," I repeat.

I'm still not sure why I called Tatum. Okay, that's a lie. She's my confidante. My other half. My sister from another mister, even when she's a pain in the ass. Although, now that she's here, I'm kind of regretting my decision. Why? Because there's no way I'll be able to tell her my impromptu job opportunity without her flying off the handle or calling me out for losing my mind. And the worst part? She'll be right. I have lost my mind.

Completely. Fully. Lost. My. Mind.

With a laugh, Tatum collapses onto my bed, causing an unamused Hades to move to the floor. She ignores him, crossing her legs in front of her. "Okay, now that the totally not awkward pleasantries are out of the way, what's up?"

What's up? It's a simple question. It deserves a simple answer. Come on, Rore. Just say it.

"Uh. Well? I, uh." My face scrunches. "I'm not going home."

"What?" Her eyes bulge. "Rory, I thought we were catching the same flight—"

"I know, but there was a change of plans," I blurt out as another wave of queasiness washes over me.

Tatum shakes her head. "What kind of change of plans?"

Come on, Rore. You've already come this far.

Grabbing the collar of my T-shirt, I tug it away from my skin in search of a light breeze because…is it hot in here or is it just me?

"Rore?" she prods.

"I, uh, I'm staying…for…a little while."

Her forehead wrinkles. "Why?"

"Well, it's actually a really funny story," I ramble. "I, uh, I found a job, so…"

If it were another situation, I'd find Tatum's deer in the headlights expression amusing, but it only makes me want to puke more.

"You found a job?" she repeats.

"Yeah. I found a job." I gulp, refusing to dab at my hairline despite the perspiration I can literally feel accumulating under my best friend's knowing stare. "It's only temporary, but still."

"Well, that's great," she returns. "I'm just a little surprised. I didn't even know you were looking."

"I mean, technically I wasn't," I mumble.

"So, what is it?"

Blah, why does it feel like I'm being interrogated right now?

"It's, uh, it's in childcare," I answer.

"Childcare?" She leans back on her elbows, her gaze narrowing. "Childcare psychology? Or…?"

"Just childcare," I answer. "I'm, uh, I'm gonna be nannying for a little while."

"Nannying?" She laughs. "For who?"

I fight the urge to cringe, preparing for the onslaught of questions and assumptions I have no doubt will follow as soon as I fill her in. "Well." Acid fills my mouth, but I choke it down. "I overheard Jaxon talking to his ex, and it came out that he doesn't have anyone to watch Poppy while he has her, and I kind of blurted out that I was the new nanny, and—"

"You what?" she screeches. Jumping to her feet, Tatum grabs my biceps and stops me from pacing. Not sure when I started up again, but here I am. "Okay, enough fun and games," she announces. "Watching you freak out was kind of funny, but I'm over it. Rory, spill. And I mean everything."

Fisting my hands at my sides, I repeat, "I already told you. I'm Poppy's new nanny."

"Rory—"

"I know," I rush out. "I know what you're going to say, but it's only for like a month or two, and it'll be totally fine."

"Totally fine." She gives me a look like I've grown a second head. "Are you serious right now?"

"I mean, it's not that big of a deal—"

"Rory, sit down." She tugs me to the bed and forces me to sit. "Okay, you know I love you, and I think we can both agree that you've always been the one with the brains in this friendship, but do you have any idea how insane this plan is?"

Yes. Yes, I do. But it's too late. I've already considered my options and none of them leave Jaxon unscathed. Besides, I'm the one who butted my head into his already precarious situation. No one made me do it. It was all me. And it isn't fair for him to take the fall or to come out looking like a liar. Right?

"Rory, please tell me why you would agree to this," my best friend begs.

"Tatum, he needed me—"

"So?" She snorts. "Look, I know you think you're capable of handling being around Jaxon again, but you have to cut me some slack for being the voice of reason here. I really don't want to see you get hurt."

"I won't," I promise.

"You don't know that."

"I think I know myself pretty well, Tate," I argue.

"Rore." She squeezes my hands softly. "Look, I know you

think you're over him, and maybe you are, but do you really think it's a good idea to travel with this guy for an entire month when you've barely come around to the idea of being in the same room with him without wanting the ground to open up and swallow you whole?"

The girl knows me too well.

"I mean, technically it's only two weeks," I argue. "When Poppy's with her mom, I'll be home with my family and helping Jaxon interview my replacement."

She drops her head back, looking up at the ceiling. "Yeah, because that makes it better."

"It'll be fine."

"Fine," she repeats, looking less than convinced.

"Yeah. Fine."

Her head rolls forward, and she eyes me warily. "Are there no take backs? No other options?"

She thinks I haven't already asked that question?

Resting my elbows on my knees, I thread my fingers through the hair on top of my head and tug gently. "Not without his ex holding it over his head."

The mattress dips beside me before Tatum rubs my back. "Which is the last thing you want."

"And the last thing he deserves."

"So you're stuck."

I nod in my hands. "I'm stuck."

"Shit."

A dry laugh escapes me. "Pretty much."

"You need to promise me something," she decides.

"What?"

"Promise me if you catch feelings, you'll leave. You'll put yourself first, and you'll get out of there."

"I won't—"

"Rory." She gives me a look that would make both our mamas proud.

"It's not even an issue," I retort. "Besides, Jaxon thinks I'm with Dodger, and I'm sure if I ask Dodge to continue our little ruse, he'll be up for it as long as not too many people find out, and any potential awkward encounters will be mitigated because Jaxon will know I'm not interested. Because I can't be. Because I have a boyfriend."

Giving me the side-eye, Tatum argues, "Yeah, that was really convincing."

I shove her shoulder and lay down on the bed, staring up at the ceiling. "It'll be fine."

"You're right. It will be. And the moment it isn't, you'll call me and Pax, and I will fly to where you are, and we'll pick you up. We promise."

She would, too. I know it. Even though I want to tell her there's no need and she's being ridiculous. The truth is, I'm grateful. That she has my back even when I don't necessarily deserve it. After all, I'm willingly putting my fragile heart in a very difficult position, and I can say I'm fine all I want, but if I'm honest with myself, I'm not entirely sure. I want to be. I want to be over him. I want to be solid with my stance on our friendship and my own feelings. But wanting something doesn't make it true. Not really. Only my sheer determination will get me through this, and even that wavers from time to time.

Don't think like that, I silently remind myself.

Rolling onto my side, I face my best friend. "Thanks, Tate."

"You know I've got you."

And she's right. I do. It's my favorite thing about the girl. Tatum might be a mess in some areas of her life—hell, before she met Pax, she was a mess in all areas of her life—but when it comes to her relationships, when it comes to me and our friendship, she's as solid as stone, and I've never been more grateful for it.

As Tatum lays beside me, I ask, "So, how are you and—"
My phone buzzes with a text, interrupting me.

JAXON

Hey. Is this still Rory's number?

My heart surges into my throat as I scan the message. Even if I didn't have his number saved in my phone, I'd still recognize it even after all these years. Whether or not it's a good thing is debatable, though.

"Who is it?" Tatum asks.

I gulp. "Jax."

Curious, she rolls onto her stomach and props her head on her hands. "What'd he say?"

Showing her my phone so I won't have to relay the entire conversation, I type my response.

ME

Hey, Jax. Yes, it's me. Hi.

JAXON

Hey. I was thinking, would you be interested in grabbing a drink with me tonight so we can talk?

Talk? Talk about what? My palms sweat at the thought alone as I fight the urge to dissect every single word like it holds the answer to world peace despite the other half of my brain screaming at me that it isn't a loaded question. He wants to meet up to talk. Simple. Straightforward. And very Jaxon Thorne. I shouldn't expect anything less. But if that's the case, why is the thought of sitting down alone with the guy so nerve-wracking?

"He wants to buy you a drink?" Tatum asks.

I glance at her. "I mean, it's logical. Right?"

"Coffee's logical. Drinks?" Tatum whistles. "Drinks are dangerous."

"His mornings are probably full," I argue. "The guy's busy."

"Yeah, busy sending you mixed signals—"

My buzzing phone cuts her off.

JAXON

I'd love to discuss a game plan for this arrangement. Thoughts?

Her lips press into a thin line as she reads the message over my shoulder.

"See?" I offer. "Completely platonic."

"And boring," she decides before kissing my cheek. "You two are perfect for each other."

"I thought I was supposed to run in the opposite direction if I catch feelings," I argue.

"Semantics." She waves her hand around and climbs off the bed, reaching for my already packed bag and unzipping it. "The question is, what will you wear?"

I ignore her, turning back to my phone.

ME

Sounds great! Just tell me when and where.

16

JAXON

What the hell was I thinking? Seabird? Really? I debated whether to invite Rory to dinner at Butter and Grace or even Rowdy's but decided buying her food felt a little too much like a date. However, now that I'm inside the infamous bar, I'm second guessing myself. The low lights, the live band on the raised stage, the flowing alcohol.

Yeah, I fucked up.

Rory isn't someone who shows up late to anything, which is why I'm fifteen minutes early to make sure I have a spot for us to sit, well aware she'll show up any minute now. Finding a booth as far from the stage and dance floor as possible, I set my beer on the table and glance at the heavy door, waiting for a glimpse of my new nanny. Instead, all I see is a pretty blonde with the sweetest eyes and poutiest mouth I've ever laid eyes on.

Rory.

I check the time on my watch, confirming my assumption. My mouth lifts. She's five minutes early.

Of course, she is.

Standing, I wave my arm over my head to get her attention as she hikes her purse strap a little higher onto her shoulder. She looks nervous. Small. Beautiful. Nervous. When she sees me, her mouth curves in an anxious smile before her gaze falls to the ground, and she weaves her way toward me.

"Hey, Rore." I motion to the opposite side of the booth. "Wanna sit?"

"Yes, thank you."

As she slides into the seat, I do the same and reach for my beer. "I didn't know what to order for you, but I warned the waitress to keep an eye out for when you got here, and"—movement in my periphery steals my attention, so I toss the approaching waitress a smile—"here she is."

"Hi," the waitress greets Rory. "Can I get you anything to drink?"

"Lemon drop martini, please."

"Perfect." The waitress turns her attention to me. "You still good here?"

"Yeah," I return. "Thank you."

"Of course."

It isn't long before a lemon drop martini is set in front of a fidgeting Rory, and she takes a long sip. Her expression puckers at the taste. "Mmm." She smacks her lips together. "It's good."

"Should've known," I quip.

"Hmm?"

"Still a fan of Sour Patch Kids, too?"

"Always," she returns. "Why do you ask?"

"I debated whether to order for you before realizing we've never had a drink together, so I didn't know what you'd like, but I should've known," I repeat.

"I mean, I'm not exactly the little girl you used to know, so you were probably smart not to assume."

Yeah, she's hardly a little girl anymore, is she? The thought hits out of nowhere, and I catch myself checking her out. I clear my throat and reach for my beer. After chugging a quarter of it, I offer, "Thanks for meeting me."

"Thanks for the invitation."

"How's your day been?" I prod.

"Good." She plays with the thin stem of her glass while eyeing me carefully. "Yours?"

"Good."

"You gonna tell me why you wanted to meet?" she questions.

"I already told you."

"Ironing out logistics," she finishes. "Okay, let's hear it."

My mouth lifts. "Actually, I'm more curious if you have any questions for me."

Surprised, she pulls back. "Me?"

"Yeah." My amusement spreads. "I know you're a go-getter who gets shit done without asking questions, but you're doing me a pretty big favor. I figured the least I could do is buy you a few drinks and answer any questions you might've thought of over the last twenty-four hours."

Her gaze falls to her glass, and she steals another sip. "Let's see," she whispers, though I have feeling she's talking to herself more so than to me. She focuses on me again and sits up a little straighter. "What does the average day look like when you're traveling? Am I on duty twenty-four-seven? Do I get days off? Am I supposed to bring Poppy to the games? That kind of thing."

"As far as a daily schedule goes, it depends on the day, but I'll share my calendar with you and have my assistant write up an itinerary before every week I have custody. Poppy's just a baby, so she can't watch the games, but you have a reserved seat so you're welcome to sit with her in the family section whenever you're up for it." I hesitate. "I'd love to see her as often as I can, even if it's only in the stands some of the time."

"Well, I'm sure she'd love to see her daddy as much as she can, too, so we'll make it happen."

"Thanks. There's another thing." Pulling out my wallet, I hand Rory a credit card. "When you're on duty, all expenses go on here for both of you."

"I think I can afford—"

"It's non-negotiable," I order. "Use the card, Squeaks. I already feel guilty enough as it is. Speaking of which, I know we haven't talked salary, but I emailed you an official offer earlier today."

"Yeah, I saw it," she mutters. "And you're way too generous, Jax. I don't need that much—"

"You're worth it. Trust me."

She finishes her drink and orders another round, so I do the same, grateful for the liquid courage. Not that I need it. It's just…yeah, okay, I guess I could use it, and clearly, so can she.

"Well, I think you answered all my questions," she says. "Any more logistics that need ironing?"

"Let's see, uh, my assistant was able to add you to all of our flights for the next month."

"That's good."

"Yeah," I agree, "but I wanted to ask how you feel about the room situation."

Her forehead wrinkles. "I'm sorry?"

"There are some nights when I won't arrive at the hotel until it's late, and Poppy will already be asleep," I explain. "Not to mention nap times, downtime when I'm at a press conference. I guess my question is, would you prefer to put her down in my room and wait until I get back to the hotel before you can go to your own room or would a suite with separate bedrooms suffice or…?" My voice trails off, and I reach for my drink, finishing another third as a silent Rory stares at me. Her unreadable expression only leaves me more on edge. Did I go too far? "I want whatever makes you feel comfortable," I rush out. "Obviously, you're welcome to talk to Dodger and see what you both feel comfortable with before making a decision."

She shakes her head, her boyfriend's name seemingly snapping her out of whatever train of thought she'd been on. "Dodger's fine, and, uh, I think the suite is a good idea. Then we only have to deal with one crib, and I can go to bed if you're late, and you can just let yourself in and…" She taps her forefinger against the lacquered table. *One, two, three.* Pause. *One, two, three.* "Yeah. Yeah, that's fine."

"You sure?" I question, my attention zeroing in on her fingertips.

She makes a fist, and her hand disappears beneath the edge of the table as she rests it in her lap. "Yeah, I mean, it's definitely the logical solution."

I could call her out on it. Draw attention to her subtle compulsion. And maybe if this were ten years ago, I would. Instead, I clear my throat, muttering, "Good."

"Okay, then."

"And I promise to be on my best behavior—"

"Yeah, that much is guaranteed. I wouldn't expect anything less from you," she teases, though I don't miss the glimpse of tension peeking through before she covers it with another smile.

I don't know why it feels off-putting, but it does. The way she says it. That she wouldn't expect anything less than for me to be on my best behavior. Like it's impossible for me to be anything less than perfect.

Sensing my annoyance, she asks, "What did I say?"

"Nothing." I bring the glass to my lips then set it back

down on the cardboard coaster. "Actually, no, I wanna know why you said it."

"Said what?"

"That you wouldn't expect anything less from me."

Confused, she shakes her head. "What?"

"You said you wouldn't expect anything less than me being on my best behavior," I repeat, tossing her own words back at her. "Why?"

I shouldn't put her on the spot like this, and maybe it's the beer talking, but I want to know. Fuck me, I wanna know real bad.

Peering over the rim of her cup, she takes another sip of her drink as the waitress reappears. Without asking Rory, I order another round for both of us, then turn to my new nanny, waiting for her answer.

The clink of the glass against the table is followed by a soft sigh as she drags her fingers along the thin handle as if memorizing the shape of it. "For starters, I didn't mean it in a bad way."

"Of course you didn't. You don't mean anything in a bad way. You're too nice to be mean," I point out. "But I don't want to hear what you didn't mean. I want to hear what you *did* mean."

"I just meant you've always been the good guy, Jax. The one with his head on straight. The gentleman. The knight. Just like Archer. The good one through and through, you know? And hitting on your nanny or putting her in an uncomfortable situation is so ridiculously far from your MO that even the possibility of you crossing a line is laughable. That's all."

She thinks I'd never hit on her? I mean, I wouldn't, but it isn't because she isn't attractive. It's because we have boundaries. And history. So much history, it makes my head spin sometimes. Add in her rockstar boyfriend, and I'd be an ass to cross the line. Even so, the way she relates me to a gentleman or knight is…okay, offensive might be the wrong word, but clearly she doesn't know me as well as she thinks she does.

"You know I'm not perfect," I point out.

She scoffs into her third drink. "Of course not."

"I'm not," I repeat.

A sheen of mirth hits her big doe eyes as she meets my gaze over the rim of her glass. "I didn't say you were."

"Maybe not the words, but your eyes say it all."

"And what do my eyes say?" she challenges.

My cock stirs in my jeans as I hold her gaze.

Yeah. Drinks were a very bad idea.

"Cat got your tongue, Coach Thorne?" she quips.

The sass makes my dick harden even more, and I shift forward, resting my elbows on the table separating us. "It says you trust me."

"I do trust you."

And maybe you shouldn't, a small voice whispers in the back of my mind. Somehow, it manages to cut through the light buzz from the alcohol, though it's not enough to sober me. Instead, it only spurs me on.

Oblivious, she takes another sip of her drink, adding, "Actually, I trust you won't touch me so much that I'd bet a thousand dollars I could be lying on this table, naked, and you wouldn't even steal a peek." She takes a long pull of her drink then licks the moisture clinging to her lips. "Isn't that right, Mr. Goody Two-shoes?"

"Pretty sure your boyfriend would kill me if I did anything else."

"Pretty sure you're using him as an excuse, but don't worry. My ego's already been battered by you before."

Frustration surges through me at the reminder of that fucked up night. She's never gonna let either of us live it down despite already admitting I did the right thing. I guess it doesn't take away the sting of rejection. If only she knew how disconnected the little kid she used to be is to the woman sitting in front of me. Hell, sometimes I forget they're the same person until she orders a lemon drop martini and I'm reminded of how much she was obsessed with all things sour. Maybe that's the problem. Maybe she still sees herself the same way. As a shy, innocent little girl who simply wanted to share her first kiss with someone she trusted. Someone she loved.

"Pretty sure you're not an innocent kid anymore," I tell her.

"Pretty sure you'll always see me as a kid."

"Pretty sure I haven't seen you as a kid since the moment I recognized you in the swimming pool." I don't mean to say it. Fuck, I shouldn't have said it. Shouldn't have blurred the line between friends and...how fucking gorgeous I think she is now that she's all grown up. But it's too late. The confession hangs heavy between us as her eyes fall to my mouth. The air charges, leaving the hair along my arms standing on end. I could backpedal. Say it was a joke. Say anything at all to break the tension.

"Pretty sure I've had enough to drink for one night." Clearing her throat, she tucks her hair behind her ear. "I'm going to, uh, I'm going to hire a Lift, and, uh, if you could make sure your assistant sends me your itinerary, that would be great. I'll be where you need me to be." She stands but loses her balance at the last second before her hand grapples for the edge of the table. Once her footing is solid again, she slips her purse back onto her shoulder and rubs her lips together, forcing herself to give me a final look. "Thanks again for the drinks."

Then, she walks away.

17

RORY

So, Poppy is adorable, and watching Jaxon in his element is strangely…hot. I don't bother trying to tell myself any different as he crosses his arms at the bench, ordering Reeves to cut sharper. They've been doing drills for at least the past thirty minutes. At first, Poppy was somewhat invested, though she fell asleep a few minutes ago and is curled up in my arms while Hades rests his head on the top of my foot, proving he's as equally exhausted as Poppy. I guess a long walk through the park will do that to a dog. Sweat drips down the players' temples, and one of them lifts the hem of his jersey to wipe at his face, showcasing one of the most toned sets of abs I've ever seen in my entire life. Hell, they're chiseled enough to rival Dodger's, which is saying something.

"Seems you're a little out of shape, Crowther," Jax calls, but the rest of the team only laughs.

Crowther's a rookie this year, brought up from the AHL. My dad's gushed more than once about how excited he is to see what the guy brings to the Lions' roster this year. And from a completely unbiased yet feminine viewpoint, I have no doubt his pretty face will fill more than a few seats this season. Seeing him mesh well with the rest of the team is an added bonus.

"All right, hit the showers," Jaxon announces. "Good work today."

As most of the team heads down to the locker room, Jaxon opens the glass partition and takes the stairs two at a time up to where I'm sitting with Poppy and Hades in the stands.

Hades lifts his head, keeping himself between me and whoever's approaching, though when he sees who the footsteps belong to, he swishes his tail and lies back down.

"Hey, Hades," Jaxon murmurs before he takes the open seat next to me. "How is she?"

Tilting the sleeping baby in my arms toward him, I answer, "Out like a light."

With a soft smile, he drags his fingertips along the swell of her cheek, then looks at me. "And how are you?"

"Good. And impressed," I add, motioning toward the ice. "You guys are not quiet, and Poppy still managed to fall asleep with all the chaos."

"Yeah, she's a pretty heavy sleeper so far."

I smile down at the baby in my arms, taking in her pouty lips as she lets out a quiet sigh. "I hope it's all right we came. I know I didn't give you a heads-up—"

"You know you're always welcome." He leans closer and peeks at his baby girl again. "Besides, it's probably good to keep exposing her to the chaos, don't you think?"

"It's why we're here." I grin. "My mom says they did the same thing with me, brought me to all the games and even some practices whenever my dad was checking in. Although from the horror stories my mom tells me, I never learned to sleep like the dead, unlike this little one."

"Nah, you bawled the whole time unless your mom was holding you," Jaxon offers.

Or if he was.

I push the thought aside. "Do you want to…" I start to lift Poppy toward him, but he stops me.

"Nah, she looks comfortable. How was the park?"

"Good," I answer. "Hades and I both got in a good workout, and I think Poppy liked the sunshine. She also loved sitting on my lap on the swing. I sent you some pictures."

"I saw," he returns. "And I appreciate them. It makes me feel like I'm not such a bad dad for missing it."

"You're not a bad dad, Jax."

"I just don't want to miss anything," he says with a dash of longing that hits me straight in the chest. "But, uh, seriously, thanks for coming. I kind of figured you'd spend all your time hiding in the hotel. It's good to see you out and—"

"Hey, Coach!" Crowther calls from the base of the steps.

Hades lifts his head again, but I reach down and pat his side.

"Yeah?" Jax answers.

Realizing his coach isn't alone, Crowther tacks on a shy smile and slowly walks up the stairs so he doesn't need to yell. "Hey, sorry for interrupting."

"No problem." Jax motions to me. "Crowther, this is Rory, my…nanny, and my baby, Poppy. She's asleep."

"Nanny?" Crowther's grin stretches. "Figured you were the wife." Moving closer, he drops his voice low as if sharing a secret. "If I wasn't so distracted by your pretty eyes, I would've checked for a ring."

My cheeks heat, and I force myself to maintain eye contact instead of giving in and blushing like a schoolgirl. Yeah, this man is going to be great at selling tickets to games. I'd heard rumors about the young rookie being a flirt, but I never expected I'd be on the other end of it.

"No ring," I murmur. "And yes, just the nanny," I give Jaxon the side-eye. "Apparently."

"She's a family friend," Jaxon clarifies as his attention shifts from Crowther to me and back again. "And one of my favorite people. But what can I do for you, Crowther?"

"A few of the guys are saying we're supposed to bring a plus-one to the banquet before the first home game. That true?"

"It's voluntary, but yes, you're allowed to bring a plus-one."

"Good to know." He tosses another smirk at me. "Nice to meet you, Rory."

"Nice to meet you, too."

As Crowther jogs down the stairs again, I find Jaxon staring at me. His expression is unreadable, but it makes me want to squirm nonetheless.

Shifting an inch in his opposite direction, I ask, "What?"

"Nice to meet you, too," he says, mimicking me. "What's that about?"

My cheeks flame as he stares at me. Mirth dances in his eyes, but there's something beneath it. Something I can't quite place. "What's *what* about?"

"Nothing, it's just...what would Dodger say?"

"To me being polite to a stranger?" I counter. "He would say nothing. Because there's nothing to say."

"Yeah, but there's a difference between being polite and being flirty," he argues.

Flirty? He thinks I was being flirty? What the hell is he talking about? If that's flirty, I've been reading the wrong playbook my entire life. Okay, scratch that. Now that I think about it, I probably have been reading the wrong playbook my entire life. The realization doesn't exactly make me feel any better. Was I flirting? It's not like I have any game or feminine wiles as Dodger likes to call it. I've never even really kissed anyone. Not after my first disaster of an experience. But still. I replay the short conversation with Crowther again, then shake my head. No, I'm not crazy. There was zero flirting going on.

"Exactly," Jaxon says, as if he's already won. "Like I said, there's a difference between being polite and being flirty."

"Says the guy who took me out for drinks a few nights ago," I point out.

He pulls back, surprised. "That was…work related."

"And in a way, so was my polite conversation with Crowther." Shifting Poppy in my arms, I throw Jaxon a bone and change the subject because let's be honest, he isn't the only one who would prefer to keep our little get-together at SeaBird in the past. "So, what's the plan for the rest of the evening?"

"They're bringing in food, then they're probably going to have a movie night or something and hit the weight room in the morning."

"Got it. And where do you want me and Pops?"

"I was gonna go back to the hotel and look over some tapes from last year. Do you want to come?" He hesitates. "You can leave Pops with me and go out or…stay in and order room service. Whatever you want."

Go out? I'd laugh if the idea alone wasn't so ludicrous. If anything, I'd take Hades on another walk which would take an hour, tops. Other than that? I got nothing.

"Room service sounds great," I tell him.

"Well, then." He stands. "Let's get outta here."

18

RORY

Just like we discussed, Jaxon's assistant booked us a suite. It has two separate rooms, a small kitchenette, and a shared living area with a television and pull out couch. Poppy woke up by the time we got to the room. While I ordered room service, Jaxon changed her diaper on the bed in his room. It's kind of strange. Knowing only a wall separates us. The familiar buzz of the television cuts through the silence, and a few minutes after, the smell of Jaxon's steak hits my nostrils. I opted for a Cobb Salad, though regret swells in my stomach as I enter the main living area, finding Jax balancing Poppy on one knee while shoving a bite of steak into his mouth.

He lifts his chin toward the second tray, and I take the lid off, my expression falling. I mean, it's a fine salad. All the usual fixings. But it's not a thick, juicy steak.

Chuckling, Jax offers, "Wanna split?"

I collapse onto the chair beside his and shake my head. "No, I'm good."

"Liar." He reaches for my plate and scoops half the salad

onto his before cutting the steak in two and sliding the bigger half onto my own. "Here."

"Jax—"

"Veggies are good for me."

I give the broccoli that came with his meal a pointed stare.

"Eat up, smart-ass."

So, I do because who likes cold steak, anyway?

Once I'm finished with my meal, I twist my fingers in my lap, unsure what to do or where to go. See? This is the part that's weird. The part where I don't know if I'm still on call or if I have the rest of the night off or if—

"Stop tapping," Jaxon orders.

I frown. "What?"

He sets his fork down and reaches beneath the table, stopping me from tapping my fingers against my thigh.

Shit. When did I start doing that?

My muscles freeze, and he squeezes my hand softly. Sometimes I forget how well he knows me. My quirks. My anxiety. My history.

"Hey, Rore," he says. It's like a welcome back but not in a condescending way, more like he knows I was lost in my own head and needed a push back to reality. He's not wrong.

Forcing a smile, I reply, "Hi."

"What are you thinking about?"

"Nothing—"

He squeezes my hand again.

The locked and loaded excuse dies on my tongue, and my mouth bunches to one side. Sometimes I really hate how well he knows me, and it doesn't help that his hand is still on my thigh, burning a hole through my jeans. It doesn't help that we're sitting close. Maybe a little too close, considering I have a fake boyfriend and all. As if only now realizing he's still touching me, his fingertips press into me one more time before he oh so slowly lifts his hand and presses his palm onto the table. His nails are trimmed short, and there's a light dusting of hair along the back of his hand, his veins popping and his fingers spread wide. I never thought hands were sexy. And maybe they aren't. Maybe it's because they're connected to Jaxon. My family friend. The reminder of how he introduced me to Crowther shatters my daydream of what it would feel like to have his hands on me, roaming my skin, leaving me hot and tingly and wanting.

Ooookay. Down, girl.

"You don't have to tell me if you don't want to," he mutters.

"It's really nothing," I say. "I was only thinking about whether or not I'm officially off the clock or..."

"I got Poppy for the rest of the night."

"You're sure?"

"Yeah, Squeaks, er, Rore." He hesitates. "Sorry, I know you don't want me calling you Squeaks. It's a hard habit to break."

Caving, I say, "It's okay if you call me Squeaks."

"Nah, you asked me not to—"

"I was angry and overreacted."

"Yeah, and that's usually the only time you speak your mind," he argues dryly. "When you've been pushed over the edge. *Rory.*" His mouth lifts, softening the blow of his assessment. "Can I ask you something, though?"

"What?"

"How long have you hated the nickname?"

If only he knew how complicated the question is.

Avoiding his gaze, I mumble, "I don't hate it. I actually really love it, all things considered."

"Just not when I say it," he assumes.

I shake my head. "That's not it, either."

"Then, what is it?"

"I don't know. I guess, it made me feel like, after everything we'd been through, you were able to just sweep every-thing under the rug, and I wasn't able to, you know?"

"Never wanted to sweep everything under the rug," he murmurs. "I only wanted to make you feel comfortable, and if *not* addressing the fallout was the best way to do it, I was game."

My mouth quirks. "And you say you're not perfect."

He rolls his eyes. "Don't start that again."

"Just so you know, now that we've talked everything out and we're friends again, I'm okay with the nickname every once in a while."

"All right, *Squeaks*," he emphasizes. "Enjoy your night off. I've got Poppy."

"You're sure?" I ask.

"I'm sure."

"Like, totally positive?"

"She's my kid, and I'm done working for the night, so yes. I'm positive." His lips quirk up on one side. "Go. Read a book. Call Dodge. Take a bath. If your tub is anything like the one in my room, it looks nice."

I preen at the options I hadn't even considered. "A bath, huh?"

"Unless you're not a fan of baths anymore." His brow arches.

Damn. The man knows me too well.

I love baths. Give me the bubbles, the heat, the constant trickle of water against my toes from the faucet. It's cleansing and cathartic in a way I can't explain and sounds like the perfect way to end my night.

"The rest of the night's yours," he adds, "but I'll be out by six a.m., so you'll have the morning with Poppy. Is that okay?"

I check the time on my phone. "Yeah, just leave your bedroom door open so I can hear her when she wakes up."

"Sure thing."

"Good."

The chair legs scrape against the tile floor as I force myself to stand. "I'll see you in the morning."

"See you."

Hades follows me into our room, and I search through my bag for my book and pajamas because there's nothing worse than being dripping wet while searching for clothes. Once I find everything I need, I tuck my things under my arm and step into the bathroom when my shoulders fall. Sink. Toilet. Shower. No bath.

Well, that sucks.

And it's not like I can read in the shower. Hmm. Tiptoeing back into the bedroom, I peek through the cracked door finding Jaxon with Poppy again. They're snuggled on the couch as Jaxon reads her a pop-up book. My heart melts a little more. Why does he have to be so cute with her? I mean, I want him to be. Obviously. But still. It almost feels... unfair. Like, when we were away from each other, I could pretend he wasn't as perfect as my memory made him out to be. As if the younger lens I viewed him through had somehow magically created the guy I thought he was, but now that time has moved on, I could see the real, uninteresting and completely less than perfect Jaxon Thorne in all his boring glory. Instead, I'm left with this. A good guy with a sexy smirk and a big heart. Perfect? No, despite how much I love teasing him. Yet even more enigmatic and genuine than I remember.

As if he can feel my gaze, Jax looks up, catching me watching him like a Peeping Tom.

"There a problem?" he asks.

"No, I was just..." *Please don't blush, please don't blush, please don't blush.* I lift my book into the air. "Putting this away."

He frowns. "Why?"

"Change of plans. I'm going to shower instead."

"No bath?"

"No bath," I confirm. "Literally."

Realizing what I'm talking about, Jaxon offers, "You can use mine if you want."

"No, no, no, I don't want to impose—"

"You're not imposing," he argues. "Poppy and I are hanging out in here. She had a late nap, so it's not like she's going to bed for the next hour or so. That should be plenty of time for you to enjoy a bath and read a book. After watching Poppy all day, I'd say you've earned it."

"You're sure?" I ask.

He nods. "Yeah, no worries."

"Okay."

Clutching my pajamas and book to my chest, I stride past them with Hades trudging behind.

Once the water is close to boiling, I strip down and set my clothes on the edge of the bath, placing my book on top so it's within reach before dipping my toe into the pool of heat. With a groan of appreciation, I slip inside, letting the scalding water kiss my skin. Seriously. There's nothing better than a hot bath.

I'm not sure how long I spend in the achingly delicious water, but I've officially enjoyed at least three chapters, and my fingers are pruney. It's nice. Escaping into a book for a little while. Letting my problems drift away until all that's left is me and a few dragons. Alas, I should probably get out and give Jaxon his bathroom back. I reach for a folded towel tucked under the sink, but it's out of reach. Stretching a little further, I try to snag the top one when my feet slip out from under me.

Shit!

As if in slow motion, I tumble over the edge of the tub and splay my arms out to catch myself while Hades darts out of the way. With a crack, pain shoots along my shoulder and down my arms, and a scream of agony rips through me. "Ah!"

I cling my hurt arm to my chest and squeeze my eyes shut.

Yup.

Yup, yup, yup.

This does not feel good. This does not feel good. At. All.

"Squeaks?" Jaxon calls from outside the door. Concern laces his raspy voice.

I squeeze my eyes shut even tighter, caught between shame and pain as I lie on the wet tile, naked as the day I was born. "Yeah?"

"You okay?"

My bottom lip wobbles as I keep my arm to my chest while trying to ignore the way it feels like it's literally been ripped from its socket. Add in needing to shove a worried Hades from licking the side of my face, and I'm seconds from having a full-blown panic attack. What am I supposed to do? I can't freaking move! I try to piece together a game plan or something, but the agonizing pain is too much. I can't think straight, let alone piece together a course of action.

I look down at my naked body and zero in on where the pain is sharpest. My shoulder. "Ouch, ouch, ouch," I whimper.

"Rory?" Jaxon calls. He sounds even more anxious than before. "Answer me. I heard a crash. Are you okay?"

Tears well in my eyes, and I shove Hades' muzzle from my face again. "I mean, I've been better."

"What happened? Can I come in?"

I reach for one of the towels as a pathetic laugh slips out of me, but it turns into a whimper when another sharp pain shoots up my collarbone. Okay, no towel. I didn't need it anyway. It's fine. I'm fine. Everything's fine. Shit this hurts.

"Squeaks, I'm coming in—"

"I'm naked." I let out a slow breath, trying to rein in the excruciating pain. "I'm naked, and I'm pretty sure I broke my arm or my shoulder or my collarbone or…something." A tear slides down my cheek. "It hurts really bad, Jax."

"I won't look," he promises.

Another pathetic laugh escapes me as I remember our conversation at the bar. How I could be laid out naked in front of him and he still wouldn't look. The reminder makes my heart pang and my head roll forward in defeat. "Of course, you won't."

"What was that?" Jaxon calls.

I bite my tongue to keep from repeating myself, well aware my emotions are all over the place, and there's no need to add fuel to the fire.

Praying he didn't hear me, I choke out, "Okay." *Breathe.* "You can…you can come in."

19

JAXON

The hinges squeak as I push the bathroom door open, unsure what's waiting for me on the other side. As soon as I see her, my cock swells in my joggers. Wet skin. Crossed legs. Her breasts pushed up as she holds one arm in front of her. The sight hits like a wrecking ball. I know I said I wouldn't look, and I hadn't planned to, but...fuck. I tilt my head up at the ceiling, willing my erection to calm the hell down for more reasons than one. This is not the time. Not that there would ever be a time with Rory Buchanan when my hard cock is needed, but when she's in pain and sprawled on the tile floor? What the fuck is wrong with me?

Blindly, I reach for a folded towel I know is tucked beneath the sink. Terry cloth in hand, I sweep it over her bare body.

Keeping my eyes glued on the textured ceiling, I ask, "You covered?"

"Y-yes."

Satisfied, I take her in again, but the added towel does shit to erase what I now know is underneath.

Still as gorgeous as ever.

Not. The. Time.

"Put Hades in my room," Rory begs. "He's worried about me and won't stop licking my face."

"Come on, Hades," I order, only half-surprised he actually listens. Apparently, he really does like me. Once he's locked on the opposite side of the suite, I return to the bathroom and try to keep my head on straight and my fear in check. There's something about seeing someone you care about in pain, causing unease to swim in my gut. Rory hasn't moved an inch, so I crouch beside her. "Let's take a look, Squeaks." Gently, I grasp her good arm and help her stand.

A whimper of pain slips out of her, and she digs her teeth into her bottom lip as she gives me her weight, leaning against me. "Ouch."

"You'll be all right," I promise, refusing to acknowledge that my hand slipped beneath the towel when she decided walking without help was a no-go. Now, all I feel is warm skin beneath my palm as I keep my arm around her waist.

"Where's Poppy?" she asks.

"She's in her crib. Put her to sleep about ten minutes ago," I tell her, keeping my voice quiet so she doesn't wake up, though if she could sleep through practice, I have no doubt she'll sleep through my conversation with Rory. "Let's…let's get you some clothes, then I'll find someone to hang out in the room with Poppy while I drive you to the hospital."

Rory's eyes widen with panic. "The hospital?"

"I mean, yeah." My mouth lifts. "You're gonna need an X-ray."

"I don't want to go to the hospital." She shakes her head, another wave of panic rolling through her before she yelps in pain from the sudden movement.

"Careful," I tell her, tightening my hold on her waist so she doesn't collapse to the floor.

"Please, Jax," she begs. "Please don't take me to the hospital."

I want to tell her it'll be fine but stop at the last second when I notice the fear swallowing her pretty gaze. When was the last time Rory was in a hospital? Was it the night Archer died? Maybe. But fuck, I hope not.

I still remember that night like it was yesterday. Still have nightmares over it, too. She only wanted me. Not even her parents could stop her breakdown as she stared at her brother's broken body in the hospital bed. I'd never felt more helpless in my life as I held her to me, watching her fall apart, knowing there wasn't anything I could do to stop it. To take away her pain. It reminds me of right now. What I wouldn't give to trade places. To be clutching my arm to my chest instead of watching the tears stream down her face and drip off her chin. I search my memory for any breadcrumbs of conversation with her family over the years. Conversations where they might've mentioned a broken bone or an allergic reaction or...something that might hint Rory's had another visit to a hospital since her brother's death, but nothing stands out.

Tearing my attention from her glassy eyes, I look down at her arm still pressed to her chest and frown. "You sure you don't want me to take you to the hospital?"

"Please no," she begs.

My chin hits my chest and resignation settles over me. "Let me...let me call Uncle Mack," I offer, mentioning Everett's dad and one of the Lions' medics who travels with the team.

She looks down at her barely covered body. "I can't let him see me like this."

With a slow nod, I guide her past my sleeping baby and into the main area, making sure she has her bearings on the couch before I let her go. "I'm gonna grab one of my shirts.

You should wear something baggy and easy to slip into," I clarify. "The less we jostle your arm, the better."

Her head jerks up and down and she wipes at her damp cheeks with her good hand. "Okay."

Tiptoeing back into my room, I rummage through my luggage, find a large T-shirt, and return to the family room. After bunching the fabric the best I can, I slip it over Rory's head, careful not to jostle her too much, just like we planned. Tears well in her eyes as I guide her arms through the sleeves, watching her face twist in agony until her hurt arm is pinned back to her chest. And dammit, I hate it. Seeing her like this. Before I can stop it, my lips brush against her forehead, and she inhales sharply, as surprised as I am at the gesture.

I shouldn't have done that. Honestly, I'm not sure why I did. I should apologize, but apologizing means addressing the kiss in the first place, and I don't have it in me. Because I don't want to take it back.

"It's, uh, it's gonna be okay," I murmur. "I think it's only dislocated, which is an easy fix compared to the alternative."

"Easy." She smirks, her tears slipping freely down her face and already staining my T-shirt. "Right."

"I'll, uh...let me call Uncle Mack. If he agrees, we won't go to the hospital, all right?"

Her head bobs again before her expression constricts in discomfort, and she lets out a slow, controlled breath. My hands clench at my sides as I fight the helplessness raging inside of me. Trying to maintain some semblance of a clear head, I pull my phone out and dial Macklin. He answers on the third ring. After telling him what happened, he promises to meet us in our room, and I find some baggy sweats, helping Rory get a little more covered so she isn't uncomfortable with someone else around. Or me. So she isn't uncomfortable with me around, either.

When a knock echoes from the hotel door two minutes

later, Hades barks from behind the closed door, and Rory calls, "Hades, hush."

He quiets instantly, and I go to let Macklin into the suite. Brows stitched in concern, he examines Rory's injury while I watch from the edge of the room. This is its own kind of torture. Seeing her discomfort. The stilted breathing. The glassy eyes. When he encourages her to straighten her arm, she hisses under her breath, and I fight the urge to throw Macklin out on his ass, knowing he has no choice but to cause discomfort as he pinpoints the real issue.

"You're right," he mutters, barely casting me a glance as he keeps his focus on Rory's arm. "It's dislocated."

"That's good," Rory returns. "It means no hospital, right?"

His eyes meet mine again from across the room, coming to the same realization I had when she freaked out the first time I mentioned a hospital. I give him a subtle nod, and he gives Rory his attention. "I don't think anything's torn, so technically, no. We don't need to go to the hospital unless there are any complications with recovery. You want me to reset it?"

I can sense her hesitation as Rory licks her lips then forces out, "Yes. Yes, whatever you have to do so I don't need to go to the hospital."

"Okay," he mutters. "On the count of three—"

"Wait." Rory turns her watery gaze back to me and reaches for me with her good hand. It shouldn't surprise me, her request, but it does. Fuck me, it shocks me with the force of a live wire, and I stride toward them without hesitation.

The couch dips as I sit beside her. "I'm here, Squeaks. You got this. I'm here."

Burrowing her head into the crook of my neck, she squeezes my fingers as hard as she can, and her head moves up and down against my skin as if to say she's ready.

"One. Two." Macklin snaps the joint back into place.

With a sharp gasp, Rory's body tenses against me, and a cry wracks through her. I wrap my arms around her back, holding onto her waist and keeping her pressed against me as wetness seeps through the collar of my shirt, making my heart crack in response. I've never liked seeing her hurt. Never liked seeing anyone hurt, but especially Rory. Outside of my baby girl, Rory's the last person I want to witness go through something like this. She's too sweet. Too perfect. Too vulnerable. I pull her closer, rubbing my hand up and down her spine as her fingers twist in my T-shirt and she silently cries against me, though I'm not sure if her tears are from relief or if she's still feeling the aftereffects. Probably both.

"Gonna need some painkillers," Macklin adds. "I'm also gonna insist you wear the sling I brought after Jax told me what happened on the phone." He digs through his bag and helps fit it into place before handing her some pills to take. "Here. Take these. They'll help with the pain." Once she swallows them, he nods in satisfaction and turns to me. "Jax, you good doing neuro checks every hour tonight?"

"Yeah, I got it," I say, way too familiar with what to look out for thanks to my profession.

"Good." He hesitates. "I'm also gonna walk you through some PT exercises in the morning."

"Okay," she whispers before dropping her head back to my chest as if it weighs a thousand pounds.

"Gonna need you to promise me something," he adds. "If you have any complications, no matter how slight, you gotta promise you'll let Jaxon take you to the hospital. We clear?"

She gives him a jerky nod but doesn't lift her head to look at him.

Holding my stare, I read Macklin's unspoken question. *Do you need anything else?*

I shake my head. "I'll keep an eye on her. Thanks."

"Anytime." He pats her back gently. "Glad you're okay, Squeaks."

"Mm-hmm," she squeaks, earning the nickname for the thousandth time. "Yup. Thanks." Her words are broken and forced, proving that, despite her tears, this is her best attempt to keep her shit together. It's endearing as hell.

Realizing the same thing, Macklin's mouth lifts in a tender smile. "Love you, Rore. I'll see you tomorrow."

"See you," I call. "Thanks again."

He stands and heads toward the door. Once it's closed, I kiss the top of Rory's head again, refusing to overthink shit. "Let me see you," I urge so I can examine her expression and make sure she's okay.

Her bottom lip wobbles, but she lifts her head, letting me have my fill of her pathetically adorable expression. Grasping either side of her face, I brush my fingers along the trail of tears in hopes of erasing them. She leans into my grasp.

Fuck, she's beautiful. Even like this. Her eyes swollen and bloodshot. Her hair in a lopsided messy bun with half the strands sticking out in every direction. Messy and unkempt and natural and…gorgeous.

"Sorry," she whispers.

"For what?"

She juts out her bottom lip even more. "For being a big baby."

"Not a baby," I rasp, though my amusement gets the best of me as I'm reminded of how cute the girl looks when she pouts. Shoving the thought aside, I remind her, "You just had your shoulder dislocated. Pretty sure it's a solid excuse to shed a few tears."

She sniffles but gives me a watery smile. "And what's my excuse for all the other times?"

"Nothing wrong with crying, Rory." I go to kiss her forehead again but stop myself at the last second. No need to create a bad habit. "We'll, uh, we'll make sure you'll be okay. You should get some rest."

Her head bobs on another nod. "You're right." Pulling away from me, she glances down at my T-shirt swallowing her body whole. "And, uh, thanks. For taking care of me and…everything."

"Anytime, Squeaks."

And fuck, do I mean it.

We don't talk about my shoulder. We don't talk about the forehead kisses, either, despite them being tattooed onto my memory for the rest of my measly existence. Instead, I've kept a wide berth, spending my nights in my room, as far from any potentially intimate situations as possible. I also got a week and a half off, so I could have some time to recover from my injury. Thanks to painkillers and constant check-ins from Uncle Mack and Jaxon, I'd say I'm healing quite nicely and have been cleared to lose the sling after wearing it religiously up until this morning.

I didn't return his shirt, though.

It's not the brightest thing I've ever done, but I've never been particularly bright when it comes to all things Jaxon Thorne, so why start now, right?

Thankfully, Poppy is still light enough that, as long as I'm careful, I'm able to hold her without any issues despite my still-healing shoulder. She's babbling more and more every day and loves when Hades kisses her toes. I love it, too. Seeing them together.

As I sit in the stands with Hades at my feet and Poppy on my knee, Jaxon whistles for the team to gather around. It's been a good practice. Lots of drills. Lots of plays. Lots of goals. He's in his element again. Driven. Focused. A little bit of a hard-ass, but in the best way possible. Or maybe it has something to do with those forehead kisses that makes him seem so perfect. I'd rather not think about it.

"Excellent work today!" Jax announces to the team. "The Grizzlies aren't gonna know what hit 'em at our opening game."

The guys cheer, and Crowther lifts his stick into the air. "Here, here!"

"Don't forget the banquet before the home opener. It's a black-tie event. And as always, yes. You're welcome to bring a date, and yes, it's an open bar."

"Here, here!" Crowther repeats, as jovial as before, pulling a round of low chuckles from his teammates.

"All right, that's it," Jaxon announces. "Hit the showers. We'll ride the bus back to Lockwood Heights in the morning. Ev, come talk with me for a minute."

Ev skates toward the bench without missing a beat. While they're chatting, part of the team makes their way back through the tunnel while the other half stays near the blue line. Reeves, Crowther, Griffin, and a few other players. Most have been on the team forever as they all talk back and forth, not ready to head to the locker room quite yet. When Reeves looks up at me in the stands and gives me a wink, I squirm in my seat. Why does it feel like they're talking about me? I peek down at them again in time to find Griffin glancing at me.

When our gazes connect, he waves me down, calling, "Rore, come here!"

Crap.

I called it.

Balancing Poppy on my hip, I walk down the concrete steps. Hades trails behind while Crowther, Reeves, and Griffin meet me halfway.

With only the half-wall separating us, Reeves asks, "Hey, are you going to the banquet?"

I shift Poppy a little further up on my hip and peek at Jaxon still chatting with Everett a few feet away. "Uh, I'm not sure?" I hesitate. "I guess it depends on if Jax needs me to watch Poppy."

"You should ask for the night off," Griffin interjects. "My brother's a big boy. He can find another sitter for the night."

"You talking shit about your big brother, Griff?" Jaxon asks, clearly distracted from his own conversation after hearing his name mentioned across the ice.

"Give the woman a night off," Griffin volleys back at him. "Ask Mom and Dad or something. You know they've got you covered."

I rock back on my heels, unsure what to say. "Then I guess I'm not going?" It comes out as a question more than anything else because…since when does Griff or Reeves care what I do on a Saturday night?

Griff shares a knowing look with Reeves. It makes me uneasy.

"Actually," Reeves starts. He skates around Crowther and slaps his hands on his shoulders, pushing him closer to me. "Our boy here needs a date."

My eyes widen. "I'm sorry?"

"Crowther needs a date for the banquet," Griffin explains.

"And since he thinks you're cute and all…" Reeves chimes in.

"What are you? Twelve?" Jaxon interrupts, completely ignoring Everett beside him.

Reeves' head snaps in Jaxon's direction. "Nothing wrong with trying to help the rookie out, Coach."

"I'm like five years older than you," I point out.

"One," Griffin corrects. "But close."

"Besides, age is just a number, baby," Crowther returns with a smirk that somehow rides the line between making me want to laugh and run in the opposite direction at the same time. Seriously, though. Who is this guy?

"You forget Rory's dating someone," Jaxon growls.

Surprise paints Reeves' and Griffin's expressions as they turn back to me. "You're dating someone?"

"See? I knew she was too good to be true," Crowther chimes in.

My jaw drops as my attention shifts from one person to the next. But seriously. What is happening right now?

"Who are you dating, Squeaks?" Griffin asks me.

Okay, this is bad. Very bad. It's not like I honestly thought there was zero a percent chance of everyone finding out about my little white lie. But after the wedding ended and everyone went on their merry way, I guess I assumed I'd gotten away with it scot free. Now here I am. Hello, rock. Hello, hard place.

Shifting Poppy to face me, I stutter, "Well, I mean, uh—"

"She's dating Dodger," Jaxon answers for me. Clearly, he's given up on his conversation with Everett and is fully invested in outing me to the rest of the world as he moves closer to where I'm still standing.

Griffin's eyes pop. "You're dating Dodge?"

Panic spreads through me like a virus, making me feel like my tongue's grown ten times its normal size despite knowing it's from my own stupid lie. The problem is that the more people who know, the more people who can ask questions, and it's not like I can keep Dodger locked into a fake relationship forever. The longer it goes on, the higher the odds of my lie unraveling. But how the hell do I backpedal now?

Wiping my sweaty palm against my thigh, I stutter, "Well, no, I—"

"Wait, you're *not* dating Dodger?" Jaxon interrupts. His face is red, and his brows are pulled low as he folds his arms over his broad chest, scrutinizing me.

"Hold up." Ice sprays against the half wall separating me from everyone as Everett stops short in front of me. "Since when are you dating Dodger? Does Raine know about this?"

Raine? Right. Dodger's sister and Everett's wife. Yup. It would definitely make sense for her to know about this.

"Maybe there's hope for me after all," Crowther quips.

Everyone's attention turns to me as I stand on numb legs, playing out every potential scenario without finding a single one that won't blow up in my face. Don't get me wrong. I've never been one for the spotlight, but this? This is an entirely new level of torture, and I have no idea how to get it out of it. Besides, Dodger promised me a week of fake dating, not a lifetime. What if the paparazzi take a photo of Dodger and his flavor of the day? Then, the guys will all come out swinging, and he'll be painted as a cheater, and I didn't even think about Dodger keeping Raine in the dark on our fake relationship. There's no way he'd do that, would he? What if he—

"Rory?" Jaxon pushes.

Okay, this is bad. This is very, very, very bad.

Is he onto me? I think he's onto me. Actually, I think they're all onto me.

Abort! Abort!

"I, uh, Dodger and I broke up," I lie. "It wasn't super serious anyway, and he's a rockstar, so...yeah. We're just friends."

Pinning me with a stare I can feel in my bones, Jaxon demands, "Since when?"

"So, what do you say?" Crowther asks, ignoring his coach's interrogation. "Want to be my date?"

My attention ping-pongs from one person to the next. "I, uh…"

"What if I take you out for a drink tonight and then you can see how you feel?" Crowther offers.

But I don't answer. I'm too busy trying not to crumble under Jaxon Thorne's impenetrable gaze.

"She's working," he snaps.

"Come on," Griff prods. Either he's oblivious to the frustration rolling off his older brother's shoulders, or he simply doesn't give a shit. "Give Rory the night off. We all know you'll just be in the hotel hanging out with Poppy anyway."

He's right. That's exactly what Jaxon will be doing. And meanwhile, I'll be hiding in my own room in hopes of keeping some distance between us while reminding myself exactly how stupid it would be to fall for Jaxon Thorne all over again. Not that I am. Not that I've even thought about it.

Okay, I've totally thought about it. But not seriously. Not legitimately. I'm not *that* stupid.

Am I?

"What do you say, Rore?" Crowther questions. Skating closer, he cuts off my line of sight with Jaxon and rests his elbows on the half-wall separating us. "One drink. My treat."

I'm not *that* stupid.

"Sure," I whisper. "I'd, uh, I'd love to."

21

JAXON

I should go into my room. I should put some space between us. I should watch a movie or a game or shit, I don't know. I should do anything but what I'm doing right now. My gaze drifts to Rory's closed bedroom door as the faint sound of her footsteps slips through the small gap along the bottom.

Poppy's favorite elephant blanket is spread out on the floor, and she gums a boardbook, oblivious to my inner turmoil. Good. She should be oblivious. Daddy issues is *not* the thing I want to pass on to her, despite my many fuck ups. In hopes of focusing on what really matters, I slide onto the ground and spread my legs wide, rolling a plastic ball toward my little Pops. When it hits her chubby little thigh, she turns to me and smiles, giving me exactly what I need.

This. This is what matters. This is what I should be focused on. Spending some quality time with my baby girl instead of overanalyzing a hundred potential outcomes between my nanny and a rookie hockey player.

Seriously. What the hell does she see in him? And since when does she hop from one guy to the next? She just broke up with Dodger. Now, she's already jumping into bed with a known player? I dunno, I guess I thought I knew her better than this. Clearly, I don't know her at all. Not really. Not anymore. Or maybe I never knew her. Honestly, I'm not sure what's worse. Not that it matters. It doesn't. She can do what she wants, and my brother was right. It's not like I couldn't give her the night off. Ever since her shoulder, she's been hiding in her room after dinner like some kind of a prisoner. A night off is the least she deserves.

Was it the forehead kisses? Did I piss her off? Did I cross a line?

Shit, I don't know, and I have no idea how to ask her, either.

My body jerks upright as Rory opens her bedroom door, revealing a baby blue sundress that hits just above her knees. Before I can stop myself, I scan her up and down, taking in every inch of silky smooth skin. It isn't sexy. Or at least, it isn't meant to be. But fuck, does the girl pull it off. My mouth waters at the sight, and I clench my fists in my lap.

"How do I..." Rory's voice trails off as I finally meet her gaze. "I didn't exactly pack for a date with a guy like Crowther, or any guy in general, actually," she clarifies, smoothing down the front of the dress.

"Makes sense, considering the fact you had a boyfriend earlier this week," I point out.

Her lips curve down. "My relationship with Dodger wasn't exactly serious—"

"I sure as hell hope not."

Surprised by my animosity, she asks, "What's that supposed to mean?"

"Nothing," I deflect. "It's just...kind of a weird move, don't you think? Saying yes to Crowther, who's known for being a player right after you get out of a relationship with a rockstar? I dunno, I guess I just never pegged you for being interested in those kinds of guys."

Dammit, I really shouldn't have said that.

"And what kind of guy should I be interested in?" she challenges.

I lift a shoulder and reach for Poppy's ball, rolling it toward her all over again in hopes of looking…I don't know. Unaffected, I guess?

"Okay, well, um,"—she takes a step toward the door but stops and faces me again—"do you not want me to go?"

The question catches me off guard, and I cock my head. "What?"

"I said, do you not want me to go?" She hesitates. "You're acting…weird."

Guilt twists my insides, and I lean my back against the couch, trying to get my shit together. What the hell am I doing? What am I saying? She's a big girl. She can do what she wants. I know it. She knows it. And if some asshole said to my little sister, Dylan, what I just said to Rory, I'd be pissed. Yeah. That's the problem. I still see her as someone I need to protect. To keep safe. Not that it justifies my asshole behavior, but…

"Jax?"

Her hushed voice shoots straight to my cock, so I bend at the knee and hike my legs up to hide the evidence. "Sorry," I mutter. "And you're right. I'm acting weird. I guess I still see you as a little kid, you know? And I want to make sure you're being careful and don't get hurt."

Her lips pull into a thin line. "I'm an adult, Jax."

"No, I know—"

"I'm not a kid."

"I know," I repeat.

"Do you?" she whispers.

I hold her stare, unsure what to say as my Adam's apple

bobs in my throat. Part of me wants to prove it. To push her up against the nearest door and show her exactly how little I've thought about her age since the moment I saw her in her parents' pool. The other part? The other part knows how wrong it would be to cross that line with her. There are enough intersecting relationships within our found-family group already. No use adding another one. Right? It would muddy the waters. It would mess things up. It would throw off dynamics. I tear my attention from her pretty eyes, taking in her dusty blue dress all over again. What I wouldn't give to hike it up around her waist and cup her ass.

"What do you think?" she whispers.

"Huh?"

"Of the dress," she clarifies. "You never answered, and I'd love your honest opinion." Swishing her hips back and forth, she lets the light fabric rustle around her thighs as she twists her fingers in front of her.

"Beautiful," I rasp.

"You sure?"

"Yeah." I swallow thickly. "Yeah, he'll love it."

"And it's not too childish?" she pushes.

The girl has no fucking clue. Childish? No. Innocent? A hundred percent yes, and I've never wanted to dirty anything more.

"What time will you be back?" I ask.

She shrugs. "I mean, it's one drink, and I'm pretty sure we aren't even leaving the lobby, so…"

"Do you want me to wait up?"

Her mouth twitches. "I think I'm okay. Thanks again for the night off."

"Anytime."

22

RORY

Crowther—who's first name is Eric, by the way—is…great. He's sweet, kind, attentive. And I feel absolutely no spark. I push the thought aside and give him a smile as we step out of the elevator onto my hotel room's floor.

"Thanks again for the drink," I tell him. "And for walking me back to my room."

"Thanks for saying yes even though your friends cornered you," he jokes.

I look down at my flats, trying not to die from embarrassment. "You felt it, too, huh?"

"Guess you could say that."

We reach my room, and I fold my arms, unsure what to do or say now that we're here. Despite Tatum's insistence that I'm a prude, I've tried dating. Really, I have. But there's a saying about how the definition of insanity is doing the same thing over and over again and expecting different results. So, I stopped. I got sick and tired of driving myself to insanity and threw in the towel on dating. Tatum might hate me for it, but I've never regretted the decision.

Honestly, if we're talking regrets, I'm pretty sure it's exactly what I'm feeling as we stand awkwardly in front of the door to my room. Seriously. What now? His hand falls from my waist, and he rocks back on his heels, looking about as nervous as I am. The realization soothes my nerves.

He really has been sweet tonight and is nothing like the playboy persona he puts on for the media. Then again, neither is Dodger despite the copious rumors and nefarious footage the paparazzi have gathered over the years.

The comparison eases my anxiety even more, and I peek up at him. "You're a good guy, Crowther. Thanks again."

"Anytime," he replies. "I had fun tonight."

"Me, too."

It's mostly true.

"Can I…" He squeezes the back of his neck. "Can I have your number by chance?"

With a slow nod, I rattle off my number, and he types it into his phone, tucking his cell into his back pocket as I rub my lips together. Where do we go from here?

Hooking my thumb toward the closed door, I tell him, "I should…"

"Yeah, of course." He shifts forward, and I swear he's going to kiss me, but I turn my head, letting his lips skate across my cheek instead.

Nothing.

Zip.

Zero.

Zilch.

It only confirms what a small part of me already knows.

I'm still not over my stupid crush on the stupid man on the opposite side of this door, no matter how much time has passed.

It's the only possible explanation as to why my knees aren't buckling from Crowther's charm. And he is charming.

He is. And attractive. And kind. And…I really need to get my shit together.

If Crowther is disappointed I gave him the cheek, he doesn't show it. Leaning back, he gives me another glimpse of his boyish grin as I stare back at him, feeling like a fish out of water.

"I'm sorry—"

"Never apologize. For anything, but especially for making a guy work for it." He winks.

I nod and tuck my hair behind my ear. "Sorry."

With a low chuckle, "There it is again."

I cringe. "Sorry."

The same low chuckle greets me. "Seems you have a bad habit, Rory."

My mouth lifts with a shy smile. "I'll work on it."

Rocking back on his heels, he leans closer and murmurs, "I think this is the part when you head inside."

"Oh. Right." I dig into my purse, pull out the keycard, and tap it against the door. Once it's unlocked, I push the heavy door open, giving him a small wave. "See ya."

"See you around, Rory."

The lights are off. So is the television in the main room. My gaze wanders to Jaxon's bedroom door before I can stop myself. It's closed. As it should be. It's not like I expected anything less. I even explicitly told him not to wait up. So why am I disappointed? Realizing disappointment is indeed the emotion twisting inside me, I tuck my room key back into my purse, head into my room, and close the door behind me.

If only I could do the same to my bleeding heart. Instead, it seems the stupid thing is a glutton for punishment no matter what I do. It's annoying. I don't like it. Honestly, I'm exhausted from it. And so, instead of sleeping, I pull up the

Google Drive Jaxon's assistant sent me and begin sorting through nanny resumes until my eyelids droop and my exhaustion is so consuming, I can't help but fall asleep.

23

RORY

"So?" Tate asks as soon as I answer my cell.

"So?"

"How was everything?" she prods. "I know I've been a little MIA over the last few weeks. Things have been a little crazy over here, but I want to know everything."

Everything, huh? Where do I start?

"It was…good?" I set my luggage onto the edge of my childhood bed. I'd barely made it through my parents' door when my phone started ringing. But it feels good to be home. To have some…distance.

"Come on, I need more than it was good," Tatum pushes, distracting me from a certain person I'd rather not think about.

"Let's see." I pause. Choosing the safest subject, I tell her, "I dislocated my shoulder—"

"What?"

"Yeah." I laugh, caught off guard by how surreal the memory is. "Uncle Macklin had to pop it back into place."

"How?"

"I mean, he pretty much just grabbed my arm as Jaxon held me against his chest, and—"

"I meant how did you dislocate your shoulder," she clarifies. "Although, the whole Jaxon holding you against his chest is quite the carrot you just dangled, my squeaky friend."

Ignoring the Freudian slip of Jaxon's involvement, I snort. "Don't ever call me your squeaky friend. It makes me feel like a dog toy."

"One I'm sure Hades would love. Now, spill. Tell me all the things."

"There's not much to tell," I lie. "I slipped in the bathtub, Jaxon called Uncle Mack, and he held me as Macklin popped my shoulder back into place. See? That's it."

"Yeah, but you keep brushing over the whole, *he held me to his chest* part," she repeats. "How did that happen?"

I puff out my cheeks. "Well, he wrapped his arms around me, and—"

"Stop being a smart-ass. That's my job," she snaps.

I unzip my bag and begin sorting my clothes so I can start a load of laundry. "You know, you're a lot more nosy now that you're in a happy relationship," I note.

"Guilty," she sings.

I can hear the mirth in her voice, and my lips curve up.

"So were things…platonic?" she prods. "Did you still feel the connection? How's your heart?"

"My heart's fine."

"It doesn't sound fine," she mutters.

Giving up on unpacking, I collapse onto my bed and stare up at the ceiling. "It's just weird. Realizing that the stupid crush you've had on a guy doesn't really go away even after a ton of time. It's probably because he's my first or whatever, but…I don't know. I thought my date with one of the players would've helped me move past everything, especially when I saw how much it helped when you met Pax, but...I don't know. I guess he just isn't the right guy."

"You dated someone?" Tatum asks.

"One date," I clarify. "But, yes. He asked me if I wanted to go out for a drink, and I said yes, even though I kind of felt pressured into it by the rest of the team, but the butterflies? Yeah, they were nothing compared to when Jaxon kissed me."

"Jaxon kissed you?" she squeals.

Dammit! I had no intention of ever revealing that particular tidbit to anyone, let alone my best friend who, like we've already discussed, is way too nosy for her own good.

"Rory Buchanan," Tatum scolds, sounding way too much like my mother. "Did Jaxon kiss you?"

"My forehead," I rush out. "I probably should've clarified that."

"You think? But also, uh, when did he kiss you, and why didn't you immediately call me afterward?"

"Fore. Head," I emphasize. "And it was after Uncle Mack popped my shoulder back in, and I was crying and he was trying to comfort me, and...it was purely platonic." I toss my arm over my eyes in an attempt to block out this conversation entirely, but it doesn't work.

"You sure about that?" Tatum retorts.

"Positive. I mean, it's Jax. What else would it be?"

"Hmm. How did he react when you went out with the hockey player?"

"Fine?" My nose scrunches as I replay our stilted conversation before I left to meet Crowther like a bad horror movie. "Even said that he still looked at me like I'm a kid, so..."

"Ouch."

I swallow past the bitter taste in my mouth. "Exactly."

"Well, I'm proud of you," she decides. "You've officially spent a copious amount of time with your childhood crush, and not only did you keep it in your pants despite drowning in his schmexy pheromones while watching his adorable daughter, you also accepted a guy's offer to buy you a drink, which we both know you've only done like ten times in your entire life. To me, that's a win."

"Is it?" I challenge.

"Yup. And that's worth celebrating, Squeaks."

I want to call her out for her bullshit, but I don't. Mainly because she's so deliriously happy that I'm pretty sure she can't even help it at this point. Her overly enthusiastic positivity, even when it's not warranted. "Thanks, Tater Tot," I mutter.

"Anytime," she quips. "So what's the plan? Are you going back?"

"I mean, yeah?" I pause. "Poppy's with her mom this week, so I'm hanging out at home and sorting through some resumes. Jax gets her again next Monday, then we fly out for the first game of the season."

"Well, that's exciting."

I hesitate, nibbling on the edge of my thumb before deciding to focus on the less tender parts of last week's adventure. "Yeah, I think it will be an entertaining game. The team's really good."

"I believe it. Now that Reeves, Griffin, and Everett are back on the same team and have the infamous Jaxon Thorne at the helm, people are stoked to see how the season plays out. I bet he's nervous."

"Who?"

"Jaxon," she clarifies. "It's gotta be a lot of pressure, don't you think?"

I drop my hand to my side. "Probably."

"He'll be fine," she decides. "I mean, it's Jax."

"Yeah, totally," I agree. "The man's a rock."

24

RORY

He isn't fine.

And for being a rock, Jax sure knows how to… crumble. Throwing his iPad against the bench, he curses as the final buzzer sounds in the arena. Grizzlies win three to one. I left Hades at the hotel, unsure if I wanted to juggle the public chaos of an NHL hockey game, a baby, and a dog who hates humans. As the Grizzlies' fans cheer around me, I decide I made the right decision. One by one, they each funnel into the main aisle before filing up the stairs until only the cleaning crew is scattered around the seats, sweeping up spilled popcorn and empty candy wrappers. It sucks. Witnessing the first loss of the season. But the really crappy part? It's the fact that I can't do anything about it. It might only be a game to most people. But to my family? It's work. It's passion. It's life. And I hate to see them hurting or stressed.

Balancing Poppy on one knee, I keep my arm wrapped around her little belly and send out a handful of texts. To my dad. To Reeves, Ev, and Griff. To Crowther. And last, to

Jaxon. I hover over his name, unsure what to say or how to help while knowing the silence will only make it worse.

Keep it simple, I decide.

ME

I'm sorry about the loss.

There. It isn't much, but at least it's something. My phone buzzes with his response.

JAX

Yeah, it's a bitch.

ME

The agenda your assistant sent says you have a few interviews. Do you want me to wait?

JAX

I'll meet you at the hotel.

ME

Okay.

I snap a quick photo of Poppy in a gold and black Lions onesie and send it.

ME

She's still your biggest fan.

Blue dots appear almost instantly.

JAX

Needed that. Thanks, Rore.

I'll be late tonight. Don't wait up.

Text me when you get to the hotel.

"Always thinking of others," I mumble under my breath.

As I wait for his response, I balance Poppy on my knee, bouncing her up and down in a gentle rhythm. "Your daddy's gonna be okay," I tell her. "He's just a little bummed."

I check my phone again, but there aren't any notifications.

With a sigh, I slip my phone into one of the diaper bag's pockets. "He'll be fine."

My lips curve toward the ground, but I slip the diaper bag strap over my shoulder and head outside with Poppy. After grabbing us dinner, I head back to the hotel room, ready for some downtime. Thanks to the flight and the late game, Jaxon's still-packed bags sit next to mine just inside the door. After laying out Poppy's elephant blankie in the main area, I grab their things and place them in the larger bedroom before sending a quick follow up text to Jaxon, telling him we made it to the hotel. He doesn't reply.

I like hanging out with Poppy. I like her smell, her little coos, the way she flaps her arms when she's excited, and how her eyes light up anytime I'm in the room. Honestly, she's the best distraction I could hope for after tonight's loss, and I'm almost sorry she's stuck with me when she should be working her adorable magic on her daddy. I bet she could make him feel better.

A crib is set up next to the king-sized bed, and after a few stories, Poppy rubs at her tired eyes.

"You tired, Little Miss?" I brush my lips against the crown of her head, and she squirms in my lap, letting out a quiet fuss. "I'll take that as a yes," I add with a smile. Tossing the book onto the coffee table, I start her bedtime routine. Jaxon walked me through it when he first hired me. Change

Poppy's bum, feed her a bottle, zip up her sleepsack, then lay her in the crib so she can get some sleep. It should be easy, and on paper it is, but this is the trigger I've yet to voice aloud. The seemingly ordinary routine that leaves me anxious and on edge.

Scanning her up and down, I do one more run-through of my mental checklist. Changed bum? Check. Clean jammies? Check. Bottle on the nightstand and *not* in her crib where she could possibly choke? Check. Baby monitor pointed directly at the crib but out of arm's reach? Check. Sleepsack fully zipped and buttoned so she can't wiggle out of it and possibly get it wrapped around her neck or cover her face or become a hazard? I crouch down and drag my hand along the zipper and snap one more time. Check.

"Check," I repeat under my breath, hoping the verbal acknowledgement will keep my OCD from triggering. It's funny that way. The way it manages to weave itself into the things we care about most. Like taking care of an innocent little girl. An innocent little girl whose life is in my hands. All it takes is one minor slip-up, one minor mistake, and—

Stop!

Forcing my body to move, I walk out of the bedroom and close the door behind me, ignoring the itching beneath my skin at the prospect of closing the door entirely on the off-chance it's locked or gets blocked and I'm not able open it if I need to.

Yeah, OCD's a bitch, and it doesn't matter how much childhood therapy I endured, or how many hours I spent learning about the disorder, or the fact that my degree is literally in child psychology. It's always there. Always. Some days it's stronger, and some days it's so quiet I'm almost convinced I finally managed to get rid of the beast forever. But ever since my first night watching Poppy—the weight of her safety entirely on my shoulders—the intrusive thoughts have reached a new pitch, proving to be louder than they've been in a very long time.

Did I leave the bottle in her crib?

No, I don't think so, but maybe I set it too close to the edge of the nightstand and it could fall in?

Stop.

With a deep breath, I lean my forehead against the door-frame, well aware that if I don't walk away and find a distraction, I'll repeat the checklist and will likely wind up pulling Poppy from her crib, change her bum, top her off with another ounce of milk, and—

"Stop," I whisper before twisting the door handle and closing the door with a quiet click, despite the insistent screaming in my mind to go inside and check on her again.

There. She's safe. Fed. Clean. I'm sure she'll be out like a light within minutes.

Stretching my arms over my head, I yawn, then check the time on my phone. My fingers itch to unlock my cell so I can check the baby monitor, but I force myself to slip it back into my pocket.

Jax hasn't responded to my text yet. It's been hours. Is he okay? Of course, he's okay. The interviews should be over by now, but he probably needs some more time to calm down. Maybe watch tonight's footage and come up with a game plan for the rematch? Maybe. Probably. He's fine.

Yeah, I definitely need a solid distraction tonight, especially when I know I'll be up before 5:00 a.m. just like every other morning.

Unsure what else to do, I head to my side of the suite, brush my teeth, and climb beneath the thick white comforter. I must check my phone a dozen more times as the television plays a mindless sitcom before I finally give in and shut it off. Checking on Poppy one more time through my phone's app, I fall asleep to thoughts of all things Jaxon with a sprinkling of a certain little girl's safety in the other room.

THE BED DIPS, AND I JOLT AWAKE. BUT IT'S THE SMELL THAT gets me. Alcohol. *A lot* of alcohol. Hell, it practically punches me in the face. My nose wrinkles, and I blink the sleep from my eyes, finding a hot, shirtless body slipping under the sheets.

"What are you—"

A drunk Jaxon cuts me off. "Fuck, what are you doin' here, Rore?"

What am I doing here? Is the guy delusional?

"Uh, sleeping?" I offer. I can't decide if I'm more amused or confused as my eyes trail down Jaxon's bare chest before I can stop myself.

Uh, why is he shirtless?

"Sleeping?" He chuckles loudly. "What are you doin' sleeping in *my* bed?"

My hand finds his very naked pectorals in an attempt to stop his movements, but his massive body collapses onto the mattress, jostling me beside him and rendering my effort useless. Yup. I am officially sharing a bed with Jaxon Thorne. A very drunk Jaxon Thorne. I stare at the man beside me, unsure what to do. Do I leave? Go to his bed? Do I kick him out? He scoots a little closer, and I shouldn't like it. Feeling his bare skin against me. The light dusting of hair. The steady beat of his heart. The heat of his body. Seriously, is this guy a furnace? He sure as hell feels like one.

He shouldn't be here.

"Jax, this is my bed," I point out.

"Your bed?" he mumbles.

"Yes?"

Can't he tell it's a queen-sized bed and not the king-sized one on his side of the suite?

Finding my waist, he tugs me toward him, using me as his own body pillow. "Sorry about that." His body melts into me even more, molding to mine. I stay on my back and stare up at the ceiling while trying to ignore how easily we fit. "Sorry about a lot of things," he slurs before his words turn into a defeated sigh. "Can't believe I fucked up tonight."

Fucked up? How did he fuck up? By climbing into my bed or pulling me closer or…oh. Hockey. Right. Because some people care about more than their messed-up libido.

Get your head out of the gutter, Rory!

"I fucked up so bad, Squeaks," he rasps.

"It was only a game." I know it's a lie. It's so much more than a game. This is his job. His livelihood. And not only is this his first year as a head coach, but he's a young head coach. A young head coach who, despite his potential, never played a day of professional hockey in his life. Someone my dad had to fight tooth and nail for with the Lions' board in order to offer him the position. No wonder this is killing him. He must be feeling so much pressure. "It was only *one* game," I clarify. "You'll get them next time. Besides, it takes a little while for a new coach to click with the team."

"Tell that to ESPN and the board." His low laugh is sardonic at best as he nuzzles into my neck, his upper body blanketed over mine. "It's always the coach's fault." He exhales. "*My* fault."

It shouldn't surprise me. The way he's carrying tonight's loss like it all belongs to him and only him. Not the players. Not his staff. Not the refs. It's his fault and only his fault. Or at least that's the way he sees it. He's always been like this, though. Always hard on himself. Always holding himself to impossible standards. Always determined and stubborn and unyielding even when it comes to the unreasonable expectations he's placed on his own shoulders. A small part of me has wondered if it has anything to do with the fact that he's the oldest, or that he has a different birth mom than the rest of his siblings, or if it's because his dad is such a great guy—and a hockey legend—that Jaxon wants nothing more than to make him proud and to make his own mark in the industry. Then again, I'm not sure the reason matters. The outcome is still the same, tainting a pretty-close-to-perfect man's perception of himself while labeling tonight's loss as an epic failure all because of him.

Determined to take away the self-loathing radiating from him, I run my hands through his hair and along the back of his neck, hoping some rest will ease the sting of tonight's loss.

With a soft sigh, Jax relaxes against me even more. "That feels good."

My mouth quirks up as I continue tickling the back of his shoulders, neck, and scalp. "Glad I can be of service."

His breathing evens a little more, and he's quiet for so long, I swear he's fallen asleep. Good. He needs it. And so do I. I've never been a great sleeper. Add in a way-too-early-in-the-morning phone call about Archer's death all those years ago, and it was basically the final nail in the coffin, preventing me from a good night's sleep from then until eternity. Well, with the exception of that first week, anyway. When Jaxon refused to leave my side. The only time I slept was when I was in his arms and felt safe enough to let go and actually rest. After that first week, though? Yeah, I'm not sure I even remember what it's like to feel energized in the morning. Which means I need to stop overthinking so I can get some decent shut-eye before my inevitable early morning wake-up call.

I begin counting sheep in my head when Jaxon's raspy voice cuts through the quiet room. "Did you kiss him?"

My brows dip. "What?"

"Crowther. On your...date or whatever," he mumbles against me.

He sounds sleepy. And buzzed. Part of me wants to ask why he wants to know, but the idea of drawing any more attention to my dating life feels like a terrible idea considering all the lies I've woven, so I let it go, answering, "No, I didn't kiss him."

"That's good."

That's good?

What in the world is that supposed to mean?

Unable to fight my curiosity, I ask, "Is it?"

"Mm-hmm." He shifts down and nuzzles into my boobs as if they're pillows, and hell, with how drunk the guy is, he might very well think they are because there's no way he'd be doing this if he wasn't three sheets to the wind. Seriously, am I dreaming? I've never been felt up before, and I sure as hell never thought I'd be in this position with anyone, let alone the only guy I've ever even considered being in this position with.

"Real good," he rumbles, though I don't know if he's talking about my boobs or the fact that I did not, in fact, kiss Eric Crowther. I'm not sure which option I'm more comfortable with, either. Why is he here? Why is he acting like this? It's not like I've never been drunk before. A person doesn't turn into a complete stranger all because of a few drinks. So what does it mean? Has he wanted to do this before? Touch me like this? Ask me these kinds of questions?

His hot breath brands my chest, and his light scruff scrapes against my skin as he nuzzles closer, making my nipples peak. I wonder if he can hear my racing heart. If he notices my stilted breathing. If he feels my thighs pressing together as he pins me to the mattress. This shouldn't be a turn on. This shouldn't. Be. A. Turn on.

So why do I like it so much?

"And why is it real good?" I ask, continuing to gently tickle his bare shoulders, neck, and scalp. I know this is a one time thing. That tomorrow, he'll pretend this didn't happen. That he didn't climb into my bed or say things I've wanted to hear for as long as I can remember. I know I'll never get another opportunity like this. To feel him against me. Without our past or our own defenses hanging between us. Even if it's all a fluke. Even if it'll all be gone tomorrow. It's still nice. To pretend that it could be like this. And in another world, maybe it would've been. If I hadn't put him in an uncomfortable position all those years ago. If I hadn't been born ten years too late. Maybe.

Lifting his head from my chest, Jaxon fully rolls on top of me and stares down, propping himself up on his elbows as they cage me in on both sides. His eyes are glassy, and alcohol lingers on his breath as it fans across my cheeks, reminding me of exactly how far gone the guy really is.

"Fuck, I could kiss you right now."

"What?" My heart stalls in my chest, and I swear I misheard him because there's no way he's serious.

Right? *Right?*

"Let me kiss you." He lowers his head and presses a gentle kiss to my lips without waiting for my approval, though I would've given it to him. I'd give him anything he asks for. It's a scary thought, but not a new one. No, even when I was a little girl, I knew Jaxon Thorne had a hold on me. I didn't mind. I still don't. Because he'd never take advantage. He's too selfless. Which is why I'm so confused. Does he want to kiss me because he wants to kiss me or does he want to kiss me because he thinks it's what I want? And yes, I want to kiss him, but not if the feeling isn't mutual. So, is it? Is it mutual? Or is it something he'll regret in the morning? When we aren't blanketed by darkness? When he isn't inebriated and vulnerable?

"Let me kiss you," he repeats, his voice even raspier.

"Jax," I whisper, too caught up in the feel of him pressed against me to think straight, let alone be the voice of reason.

What should I do?

Keeping most of his weight on his forearm along the side of my head, he shifts closer, dragging his lips along the edge of my mouth before cupping my cheek with his opposite hand. It's messy and far from innocent, and my heart pounds faster and faster as he presses the tip of his tongue along the seam of my lips. I open for him. Scared. And excited. And knocked so far off-kilter I can do nothing but follow his lead.

Taking full advantage, Jaxon explores my mouth, tasting like whiskey and beer. And it's fast. Too fast. I might be as sober as a nun, but the room is still spinning. Jaxon Thorne is in my bed. Jaxon Thorne is laying on top of me. Jaxon Thorne is kissing me. *The* Jaxon Thorne. His hand slides down the side of my throat before moving lower, and my breath hitches as I zero in on his blazing touch skating across my collarbone. When he finally palms my breast, I squirm beneath him, surprised by the pressure building at my core from a simple touch.

Holy shit.

Holy. Freaking. Shit.

I've never felt like this before. So hot and bothered and on edge. It's like my body isn't my own. No, right now, I'm nothing but a puppet, and Jaxon Thorne is the one pulling the strings.

"Tell me you want me," he rasps, shifting lower and resting his forehead between my breasts.

My pulse stalls in my chest as I register his words. But even then, I don't believe them. *Can't* believe them. "What?" I whisper.

He breathes in deep, relaxing into me even more. "You smell incredible."

With a light laugh, I drag my fingertips along the back of his skull like before and try not to lose my ever-loving mind.

"Fuck, that feels good," he adds. Turning his head to one side, he collapses onto me again, giving me all of his weight. And honestly, I'm grateful. If he kept kissing me, if he kept touching my boob, I'm pretty sure he would've tried taking things even further, and there's no way I could've let that happen. Not when he's like this. There are only so many firsts a girl can cross off the list in one night. I also don't know how I would've told him to stop.

His breathing turns deeper and deeper, slowly transitioning to a light snore while I keep dragging my fingers along his hairline. Up and down. Up and down. Up and down. And all the while, my mind spins.

Jaxon Thorne just kissed me.

Jaxon Thorne is literally asleep on top of me. In my bed. After touching my boobs and turning me on in a way I've never been before. It's scary. And confusing. And addictive. I never really understood Tatum's desire to hook up with random guys before she settled down with Paxton. But now that I've felt it? What actual attraction and chemistry feel like? Okay, I definitely see the appeal. And if Jaxon hadn't stopped kissing me—and wasn't drunk—would I have let him go further? The answer's yes. Hands down, no questions asked, one hundred and ten percent yes.

And that? That's a terrifying thought. The uneven pitter-patter in my chest only feeds my anxiety. But it isn't fear behind it. It's hope. And anticipation. And maybe even a little excitement mixed with trepidation as I memorize the feel of his silky strands between my fingers.

He kissed me.

He kissed *me*.

Is this it? Is this the moment I've never even hoped to dream about? Is it possible? Does Jaxon Thorne have feelings for me, too? I shouldn't get my hopes up. I know this. But I can't help it. This entire night might not mean anything in the morning, but if it does...

Stop, I silently reprimand.

But I don't. Instead, I spend the rest of the night soaking up every single second with the man on top of me, praying this isn't a dream, and he finally wants me for real.

25

JAXON

I wipe at my tired eyes, my skull throbbing like I took a baseball bat to the head at some point after the game. Hell, with how fuzzy last night feels, I just might've. Stretching across the bed, I cover my yawn with my forearm and force one eye open. Light filters in through the hotel window, proving it's well past my usual wake up time.

Where's Poppy?

Sitting up, I search the room for her crib, but it's missing.

What the hell?

Babbling sounds from the main area, and I wipe at the corner of my eye, attempting to piece together what happened last night. We lost. It sucked. I gave my two cents during the post-game interviews, fought the urge to throw a chair at one of the reporters, then went to the bar with a few of the players. After that, it's fuzzy at best. I scrub my hand over my face, trying to piece shit together. What happened after the bar? Let's see. I came back to the room, and…shit. Nausea swirls in my stomach and I pinch the bridge of my nose. I kissed Rory. I climbed into her bed, rambled for who the fuck knows how long, kissed her, felt her up, then fell asleep on top of her.

Shit!

My body feels like I was hit with a truck, but I force it to move anyway. Rolling out of Rory's bed, I pad to the doorway and lean against the doorjamb when Rory and Poppy come into view. They're on the couch, reading a book about all the animals on a farm when Hades lifts his head from the ground, triggering Rory to look up at me.

"Oh." She smiles at me. "Hey. Good morning."

Good morning? That's all she has to say? Did I dream it? Last night? No, I literally woke up in her bed, so it's not possible I dreamt it. Not this time, anyway. But she's acting... normal. I think? Shit, I don't know.

"How are you feeling?" she prods.

Confused as shit is how I'm feeling. And guilty, and hung over, and...

I pinch the bridge of my nose again in hopes of easing the pounding behind my eyes, but it doesn't do shit.

"I'm gonna brush my teeth," I mutter before striding into my side of the suite without a backward glance. Grabbing my toiletries from my bag, I squeeze some toothpaste onto the brush and start brushing while trying not to lose my shit. I can't believe I screwed up like this. I've done stupid shit before. A lot. But nothing compares to this. I'm her employer for shit's sake. And her family friend. And her dad is my boss. And she just got out of a relationship. And she's kind of dating one of my players. Or maybe not, since she confirmed they never kissed. Or did I imagine that part? Fuck, I dunno. Not that it matters. What the hell was I thinking? I lean over the sink, spit the minty foam into the swirling water, and rinse my mouth one more time in hopes of eradicating last night's alcohol still lingering on my tongue.

Can't believe I kissed her with this mouth. I probably

tasted like ass to her. How could I be so stupid? Scrubbing my hand over my face, I force myself to turn off the bathroom light, well aware I can't hide in here forever, not when my baby girl's in the other room.

They haven't moved from the couch. When Poppy notices my presence, her arms bob in the air as she reaches for me, so I close the distance and pick her up, kissing her forehead. I can't believe I slept so late. That I didn't hear her when she woke up. Add it to the long list of mistakes I've made in the last twenty-four hours. How could I mess up so badly? And how do I make it right?

Shoving aside my self-loathing, I murmur, "Thanks for waking up with her."

"No problem," Rory answers. "I was awake anyway and figured you could use the rest."

A huff of amusement escapes me, and I kiss Poppy's nose. "Guess you could say that."

"I ordered room service a little while ago," she adds, pointing to the small kitchenette. "It's over there."

"Thanks."

"Mm-hmm."

"Listen." Shifting Poppy to my other side, I take a deep breath, refusing to sweep last night under the rug no matter how much I want to. "I want to apologize."

An adorable furrow forms between Rory's brows as she peeks up at me from the couch. "Apologize?"

"I fucked—messed up," I say, correcting my shitty language in front of Poppy, despite knowing it doesn't quite matter. Not yet, anyway.

Rory's lips press together, but she doesn't reply. It only feeds my guilt.

"I shouldn't have climbed into your bed, let alone kissed you. That was messed up. I don't know what I was thinking.

Actually, I wasn't thinking," I clarify. "I was drunk and pissed over the loss and…I crossed a line, and I'm sorry."

"Sorry," she repeats, though it isn't a question. No, she's processing.

"I don't want to lose you as a nanny, not yet—"

"Wait." She lifts her hand to stop me. "Are you sorry you kissed me because you're afraid I'm going to quit before the month is over or are you sorry you kissed me at all?"

I frown, unsure how to respond. Why do I feel like I'm walking on eggshells? Why do I feel like one wrong move will make or break this conversation and all the progress we've made since the wedding?

"Uh," I lay Poppy on her elephant blanket and hand her a small stuffed animal from beside Hades. "I don't know what you want me to say."

"Got it." Rory's nod is slow and jilted. "I'm going to… shower." She pushes to her feet, refusing to look me in the eye.

It only makes me feel guiltier. Clearly, I fucked up. Again. Though I can't figure out how. I apologized. I didn't sweep it under the rug. I owned up to my mistake. I didn't justify it or pretend it never happened. So, why is there a shift in the air? She seemed fine before I brushed my teeth. She seemed fine when I grabbed Poppy from her. What did I do?

As she moves past me, I grab her arm, preventing her retreat. "Look, I really am sorry—"

"So you already said."

"Yeah, but clearly not enough," I argue. "You're mad at me."

Tearing her attention from where I'm touching her, she glares up at me. "Are you seriously this dense?"

I pull back, surprised by the animosity in her voice. "What?"

"I'm not mad at you for kissing me. I'm mad at you for apologizing for it."

Letting her go, I rest my hand on top of my head in hopes of stopping myself from reaching out for her again. "What?"

She scoffs and starts to move past me again. "Forget it."

"Rore," I beg.

Turning on her heel, she faces me. "Explain to me why I am so undesirable that not only do you have to get drunk to kiss me in the first place, but you also feel the need to apologize afterward."

What?

Like, seriously. *What?*

There are so many things I want to address in her statement, but one of them stands out more than the others. It consumes me completely as I tilt my head, studying the woman in front of me. "You think you're undesirable?"

She shakes her head, but the blood drains from her face, proving she let something slip that she had no intention of revealing. "That's not the point—"

"Rory, you were dating a rockstar less than a month ago, and you think you're undesirable?" I push.

Rubbing her hands up and down her bare arms, she mutters, "You don't know what you're talking about."

"Oh, I don't?" I laugh, though there isn't any humor in it. "Because I'm pretty sure there are hundreds if not thousands of women who would kill to be dating a rockstar, but you're just gonna brush it aside?" Jealousy knots my gut, but I push forward. "Bullshit, Rore. I'm not gonna let you play the pity card or ignore the evidence right in front of your nose. Clearly, you're desirable—"

"You don't know what you're talking about—"

"Oh I don't?"

"No," she snaps, "You don't."

"Pretty sure the evidence proves—"

"We were never dating, Jax."

"What?"

Her mouth clamps closed, and she stares at the ground, proving she let something *else* she had no intention of telling me slip past her lips, all because she's fired up. But it's too late. The cat's out of the bag. Even so, I swear I misheard her. There's no way.

Is there?

Moving forward, I push, "What did you say, Rore?"

"I said…" Her tongue darts out between her lips, moistening them. "I said we were never dating."

Blindsided, I step even closer and cock my head as I stare at the woman in front of me. The woman who lied to me about dating a rockstar. So I *didn't* mishear her. The realization doesn't make the truth any less murky. It makes no sense. Why lie about something like this? Especially when none of her family cares. Not really. All they want is for her to be happy. No one even batted an eye. No one but me, though I'm taking it to my grave.

"Why'd you tell everyone you were dating Dodger if you weren't?" I demand.

"Because…"

Her bottom lip trembles, and I nudge her chin with the edge of my knuckle, forcing her to look at me. "Because what, Squeaks?"

Animosity shines back at me in her pretty gaze, proving I've pushed her too far. She spits, "Because the idea of seeing you again without a boyfriend or really any dating history in general felt about as pleasant as what you clearly experienced last night."

My brows wrinkle, and I swear I'm still drunk because the woman's talking in riddles. "What?"

"If the first words out of a guy's mouth after he kisses you are, *I'm sorry, that was a mistake*, it probably wasn't a very pleasant experience, am I right?"

Yeah, the girl's definitely talking in riddles.

"Are we talking about the one—as in singular—instance between you and me, or are you saying that's a consistent response when someone kisses you?" I challenge.

Staring at her fluffy socks, she folds her arms, her body deflating like a balloon. "Well, since you're the first and *only*, I guess I don't have much to go off, now do I."

Only?

"What?" I repeat for what feels like the hundredth time since I rolled out of Rory's bed.

"Nothing," she snaps. "Now, will you please let me go shower?"

But I don't move. I don't back away. And I sure as shit don't step aside so she can slip past me and hide in her room the way I know she wants. "Rory, was last night your first kiss?" Her nostrils flare, and she shifts to her left, but I mirror her movements, blocking her. "Answer the question."

"Let me go, Jaxon—"

"Answer the question," I growl. Because she has to be lying. She has to. There's no way a woman like Rory, a woman who looks like her and acts like her and has a heart of gold like her would be a virgin, let alone so innocent she hasn't even experienced an actual kiss until the sloppy one I planted on her while I was blackout drunk.

Fuck! I screwed up even more than I thought.

"Tell me I'm wrong," I beg. My chest heaves with restraint. "Tell me it was a shitty kiss and nothing compared to Dodger's or Crowther's or any other guy who was lucky enough to have a chance with you over the years. But don't, for the love of everything good in this world, tell me that I stole your first kiss and can barely remember it."

Peeking up at me, her thick, dark lashes somehow

managing to make her already pretty eyes brighter than any I've ever seen, Rory whispers, "Don't make me say it."

Like a punch to the gut, the air whooshes from my lungs, and I shake my head. "Rore."

"Please."

My attention falls to her lips, her perfectly pouty lips, causing my guilt to reach an all-time high. She's never been kissed? And I fucking took it from her? Just like that? How do I fix this? I need to fix this. "I'm not gonna lie to you," I rasp. "I don't remember much after I slipped into your bed, but…" I swallow, sorting through last night's memory, though it's just as fuzzy as before. Not much sticks out other than the realization of how soft and sweet she felt beneath me. My dick twitches in my sweats, and I fight for control. Of the situation. Of my own visceral reaction. Of my not-so-innocent thoughts. All of it.

"It was an honest mistake," she says numbly.

"Let me finish," I beg as determination floods my system. "I don't remember much, okay? It's messed up, and I wish it wasn't true, but I'll tell you what I do remember, all right?"

"Jax, don't—"

"Rory, these were the sweetest lips I've ever tasted."

Her expression falls as if my admission hurts her when I was trying to do the opposite.

"You don't need to flatter me, Jax."

"Not flattering you," I growl, desperate to make her understand.

"Of course not." She swallows and reaches up, patting my chest. "I'm going to…I'm going to shower. Do you have Pops?"

I glance at my daughter on her tummy a few feet away. Her arms and legs flap back and forth as she pulls Hades' tail, oblivious to just how badly her father's fucking up this morning. With a huff, Hades raises his head, licks her fingers, then rests back on the ground, giving her the side-eye but not bothering to move from his spot next to the couch.

I give Rory a subtle nod, confirming I'll keep an eye on my baby girl, even though it means Rory's only obligation for standing in the same room with me is null and void. At least for the time being.

Without a word, Rory steps around me, and this time, I let her, watching as she disappears into her room and closes the door behind her.

I fucked up. The problem is, I don't know how to fix it. I scrub my hand over my face, reeling. How the hell was that her first kiss? Her first *real* kiss?

I always knew that moment all those years ago would've affected her, hitting her self-esteem harder than I ever could've imagined while knowing I had no choice. But even then, I never would've guessed she'd shy away from intimacy completely. It's like she took that one experience of rejection and carried it with her, convinced it was the standard for every potential encounter from there on out, so why bother opening up with anyone ever again? It's like she's still stuck in middle school on my couch. Her eyes brimming with tears and her cheeks flushed pink with embarrassment when I turned her down after realizing what she wanted from me.

It's why she's still hurting.

Why my apology this morning cut her so deeply.

Because last night, I gave her hope. I let her believe that a kiss doesn't have to suck or be followed by shame. And what did I do? I proved how fucking wrong she was all over again.

I never minded silence. Not until now. Unless we're discussing Poppy, Rory's barely said two words to me. Not since she admitted I was her first and only kiss. Hell, even getting her to look at me feels like an uphill battle. I might as well be a ghost. But the worst part? I can't even blame her for it.

I messed up.

I took something that didn't belong to me.

Or maybe it did belong to me, and I messed it up anyway.

Neither option makes me feel any better.

She deserves more than a sloppy, drunken kiss from a guy who couldn't speak without slurring his words, let alone throw together a decent kiss that doesn't taste like ass. And then to apologize for it afterward? Yeah, I get why she feels like a discarded piece of trash, when my intention was to prove the opposite. She's so much better than an asshole like me. But I get it. I get it, and I want to make it better. I just don't know how.

After we land, Iris meets me outside the airport for the usual Poppy hand-off. It's pouring rain. I shouldn't expect anything less after the shitty forty-eight hours I've endured, but it still manages to crawl under my skin, leaving me testy at best. At least there's an awning covering us for now, though the trek to the parking garage is a different story. Yeah, we'll be soaked in seconds. As I buckle Poppy into her car seat in the back of the SUV, Iris makes sure to throw in a few digs about the loss while Rory hangs back, her nose glued to her phone and her dog sitting at her feet.

I drove us to the airport for our flight out, but I have no doubt she's trying to hire an Uber so she isn't stuck in the car with me on the ride home. I'm sure the flight was miserable enough for her. Even so, I can't let Rory disappear without smoothing things over. I can't.

"Are you even listening to me?" Iris snaps from the front seat.

I wasn't, and she knows it as well as I do. Ignoring her glare from the rearview mirror, I drag my hand along Poppy's light blonde hair and lean in for one more forehead kiss before unfolding myself from the back of the SUV. "I'll see you in a week," I tell her before closing the door.

Tires squeal as my ex pulls away from the curb, leaving me alone with a woman who wants nothing to do with me. Perfect.

Tucking my hands into my pockets, I stare at the side of Rory's face and wait for her to look at me. She doesn't. She's pretending I don't exist. Like I can't tell she's ignoring me or that I *know* she can feel my stare despite her best attempt to prove the opposite. She's so damn stubborn, and so damn determined to act like everything's normal, when it clearly isn't. I want to smack her ass for it.

"Cancel the Uber," I announce.

Rory's gaze cuts to me, her lips gnashing together in annoyance. I know she wants to tell me no, or even lie about the whole thing altogether, saying she didn't hire a someone to pick her up when we both know she's far too calculating to have not taken advantage of the last two minutes in order to create a game plan that'll take her away from me as fast as possible.

"Let me give you a ride, Squeaks." I soften my tone, hoping it'll be enough to sway her into complying.

"Not necessary."

"Please?"

Maybe I shouldn't push it. Maybe we could both use the space. But I can't help myself. Seeing her like this? Feeling the distance she's created both emotionally and physically after I finally got her back? It's too much.

"Please?" I repeat. My tone is even softer but just as desperate. I keep my feet planted where they are on the pavement, watching as she debates whether or not to give in.

Nostrils flaring, she opens her phone and jabs at the screen with a little too much force before shoving it back into her pocket. "Fine. I cancelled it."

"Thank you."

Moving closer, I reach for her luggage, but she tugs it closer to her. "I've got it," she tells me. "Hades, come."

I want to push it. To tell her my dad raised me better than to let her carry her own shit, but I don't. It won't get me anywhere, anyway. With a wave of my hand, I motion toward the crosswalk, and she leads the way with Hades trailing behind.

As soon as Hades is in the back with Rory's luggage and I'm behind the wheel, Rory tucks her headphones into her ears, squashing any hopes I had of us talking shit out. We drive in silence, neither of us uttering a word as the water pelts against the windshield. It's more tense than the flight. Without any buffers. Only me and Rore and a snoring German Shepherd in the back. Fucking perfect.

Honestly, I didn't even think it was possible, but with

every passing mile, the tension grows and grows. It reaches a feverish pitch, making me so damn aware of every movement, every fucking flutter of her lashes or twitch of her fingers, that I swear I'm losing my mind. I'm not sure how much more I can stand without breaking from the pressure.

When we reach her parents' house, she takes out her headphones, twisting toward me in the passenger seat, and surprising the hell out of me. I figured she wouldn't wait for the car to stop before climbing out of it like the devil himself is sitting in the driver's seat.

"Just so we're...clear, or whatever, we're good," she announces, though I don't miss the way she's staring at my hairline instead of looking me in the eye. "You. Me. Poppy. The rest of the month. Everything's fine, I'd just prefer to-—"

"How come you haven't kissed anyone?" I interrupt. I shouldn't have, but the question's been plaguing me ever since that morning, and after wracking my brain for the last few days, as well as the entire flight, I want to know why. She's beautiful. Kind. Sweet. She's like a flame, and every sorry sucker out there is the moth, myself included, despite my best intentions to keep my distance. So, how has she never kissed anyone? It doesn't make any sense, but I don't think she's lying, either. Not about her innocence. Not when I could see the shame and embarrassment swirling in her pretty gaze as she admitted the truth about Dodger. "How come you haven't kissed anyone, Squeaks?" I repeat, though I know the odds of her giving me an answer aren't exactly in my favor. Not when considering our history together. "Tell me. Please?"

Her silence feels heavier than a damn elephant as she runs her tongue along her front teeth, staring at me before coming to some kind of conclusion. One I'm not sure I'll like.

"And on that note, I'm going inside," she announces. "I'll see you...next week." Reaching for the door handle, she exits the passenger side as the rain pours from the dark, angry clouds above us. With a squeak, she yanks open the door to the backseat and retrieves her luggage as Hades darts toward the covered porch without any instruction from his owner.

Rotating on the black leather so I can still see her, I push, "Rory."

"You're not stupid, Jax," she snaps. "Stubborn, pigheaded, and a little holier than thou sometimes but not stupid." Her icy gaze cuts me to the core before she slams the door and marches toward her childhood home without a backward glance.

And fuck, I've never hated myself more.

I knew it was possible. I knew there was a small chance that the reason behind her innocence had something to do with me. Whether it was my initial rejection from all those years ago or her long-standing crush I'm not entirely sure has dissipated. Hell, maybe it's a combination of the two. But what's worse is the way it messes with my head.

Am I the reason she never kissed anyone?

Squeezing the steering wheel, I watch her take three steps through the angry storm before I'm out the door. The rain pelts my T-shirt, soaking me as soon as I climb out of the car. "Dammit, Rory!" I yell, praying she can hear me over the pounding rain. "Let me talk to you—"

"Why?" She twists around to face me and shoves her wet hair away from her face. "Why should I let you talk to me when there's nothing to talk about in the first place?"

"Because there *is* shit to talk about!" I march toward her as water splashes off the concrete pathway. "I screwed up—"

"Was it really so bad?" The question comes out as a squeak, and her angry facade slips to reveal a hefty dose of confusion and exasperation when she finally looks me in the eye. I don't know how it's possible, but she's more gorgeous than ever. Her wet blonde hair clings to the side of her face as her tongue slips between her lips to catch the rainwater. "You keep apologizing," she murmurs, "like it was…like it was this terrible experience. And don't get me wrong. It was…sloppy, but I didn't think," her chest heaves, "I didn't think it was this absolutely disgusting moment like you keep painting it to be every single time you open your stupid mouth and apologize—"

"Not apologizing because it was disgusting," I growl. "I'm apologizing because…" My nostrils flare and I try to reel in my temper. "I want to make it right."

"What?"

"I said, I want to make it right." Rain droplets stream down our faces as she stands motionless in front of me. "I had no right to your first kiss," I continue. "Not all those years ago, and I sure as shit had no right to it when I was drunk off my ass and couldn't give you what you deserved."

She rolls her eyes and shakes her head. "Drop it, Jax—"

"Not gonna drop it, Squeaks." I reach for her, and by some miracle, she doesn't pull away. "Not after everything I've put you through."

A clap of thunder makes her flinch, and she squeezes her eyes shut. "Stop making yourself a martyr," she begs.

"So you're saying I haven't put you through shit?" I counter, ignoring the raging storm around us as I inch closer. "You said so yourself. It was sloppy, and you deserve a hell of a lot more than a drunken kiss as your first."

She wipes the rain from her forehead with the back of her hand, though more droplets replace them in an instant. "So what's your solution?" she asks. "Obviously, the apology didn't get you anywhere."

"Give me a redo."

Her brows dip. "What?"

"Give me a redo," I repeat. "If you've waited this long for the perfect first kiss, let me give it another try." I move closer, not even giving a shit that we're both soaked from head to toe. Not giving a shit that I'm crossing a line I have no right to cross. Not giving a shit that the odds of this fixing anything are slim to none. But even then, I can't convince myself to stop. Because I can't do it again. Can't let her waste another ten years building walls and convincing herself that she deserves anything less than being tasted and savored and appreciated like a fine fucking wine. "Let me give you the first kiss you deserved before I went and fucked it up."

With a shaky breath, she parts her lips, and I raise my hands, cupping her cheeks and slipping my fingers along the back of her head before slowly descending. She lifts her chin and waits. Not pushing me away. Not telling me to stop. Instead, her eyelids flutter, her innocence driving me forward and making me feel like I've lost my damn mind.

I press my mouth to hers, softly framing her bottom lip with mine before lifting her head another inch and tilting my own for better access. She's soft. Supple. Fucking perfect. Forcing myself to make this the best damn kiss she'll ever have, I skate my mouth along her bottom lip again, using the lightest suction before dipping my tongue along the plump flesh. The taste of fresh rain mixes with our kiss. It slips between our parted lips as I drag my thumb along her wet cheeks, committing her taste to memory.

Perfect. Fucking *perfect*.

Reaching up, she grabs onto my wrist and opens her mouth. Barely. Hell, the movement is so subtle, I would've missed it if I wasn't so wrapped up in all things Rory that I'm pretty sure I could get struck by lightning right here, right now, and I'd die a happy man. I kiss her harder, deepening the kiss and invading her sweet little mouth so I can taste her more fully. Her breath hitches at the intrusion before she meets me halfway, dragging the tip of her tongue against mine. Cautiously. Carefully. The subtle touch shoots straight to my cock and steals the oxygen from my lungs. I knew she'd taste incredible. I knew her innocence would be a turn on, but this? This is more than I bargained for, and more than my self-control can handle.

Fucking perfect. The same thought filters through my mind, and I doubt it'll be the last time. My fingers dig into the back of her scalp with the slightest pressure before I force my hands to relax and tear my mouth from hers. The things I could do to her. The things I could show her. Teach her. My jaw locks as I try to get ahold of myself, but it's hard, and I mean that literally. If I don't stop now, I'll ask her if I can come inside—also in the literal sense. My dick pulses at the possibility, and I press my forehead to hers, willing myself to calm the hell down.

Get a grip, asshole!

"Any better than last night?" I ask.

Her lips curve in a shy smile as she peeks up at me, the rain clinging to her lashes. "I mean, I kind of liked the whole boob grab thing you had going, but—"

"Don't tempt me," I growl.

"Why?" Her voice is breathy and quiet and hot as hell. "Are you tempted?"

The woman has no clue.

She has no clue about a lot of things. She's young and innocent and works for me and is a family friend, and if I screw this up, her dad will never forgive me. Neither will her brother or her mom or my mom or...anyone. My eyes trail to the camera attached to the door. Did Henry see this? Did Mia? It's cloudy and pouring rain and we're far from the lens, but is it enough?

What the hell am I doing?

I'm a divorced single father who travels for work. She's an incredible, recently graduated woman with her entire life ahead of her. No baggage. No hang ups. She deserves more than being caught up with a guy like me. And that's if I can commit in the first place. I need to think this through. She needs to think this through.

Slow the hell down.

"You should..." My throat constricts, but I force the words out anyway. "You should go inside. I don't want you to catch a cold."

Something hits her eyes as the rain slides down her face, but she doesn't open up. Doesn't talk to me the way she used to. The way a small part of me still wants her to, even if I'd never admit it out loud. It'll only mess things up even more.

"Of course not," she murmurs, licking the moisture from her swollen bottom lip. "That kiss was, uh, was definitely a memorable one, so...I guess your job here is done." Turning toward the door, she walks slowly up the steps, and I can't help but notice the way her clothes cling to her skin, leaving little to the imagination. I fist my hands at my sides to keep from chasing after her and pushing her tight little body against the door, but fuck, do I want to. When she peeks over her shoulder at me at the last moment, the last of my restraint threatens to snap, but instead of inviting me inside, she says, "And don't worry. I'll, uh, I'll delete the footage. My parents never check the camera anyway unless something weird happens. See you later, Jax."

Like a punch to the gut, I take the hit and keep my expression in check. "See you later, Squeaks."

She doesn't hear me. The sound of water hitting the pavement drowns me out. If only it had the power to quiet my racing thoughts, too.

RORY

I thought a hot shower would be enough to erase the feel of Jaxon's hands on me. It doesn't work. Then again, maybe I should blame the panty-melting video footage I deleted because that kiss was one for the books. After drying the shampoo and conditioner bottles so there isn't any potential soap scum on the little shelf, I towel myself off, then slip into some sweats and a T-shirt before finding a text from Tatum.

TATUM

Hey! How was your flight? I'm ready for an update.

With a quiet groan, I dial Tate's number and bring my cell to my ear, figuring it'll be easier to word vomit the entire ordeal instead of telling her everything over text. There's no way I'm keeping this mess to myself.

It rings a handful of times before my best friend's voice echoes through the speaker. "Hey, Rore!"

"Hey," I return. "I figured a call might be easier. How are you?"

"Good. Just hanging out. How are you? How was the flight? I'm sorry about the Lions' loss."

"You watched the first game?" I flick off the bathroom light and enter my bedroom. "You never watch—"

"Technically, Lia told me."

"Ah, makes sense."

"Yeah, just because I've decided I don't hate all things Lockwood Heights anymore doesn't mean I'm willing to sit through an *entire* hockey game."

A spark of amusement manages to break through my mopiness. "Of course not."

"So?" she pushes. "Was this trip as uneventful as the last one? How's Crowther and Poppy and Jax and-—"

"He kissed me," I blurt out. There. I said it. And maybe I shouldn't have, but I don't know. I guess I could really use my best friend after whatever the hell happened outside. Honestly, I'm still spinning. My lips still tingle. My heartbeat is still erratic and unsteady, and…I can't believe he kissed me.

"Crowther?" Tatum asks.

"Nope." It comes out as a squeak, and a burn hits my eyes at the memory as I press my fingertips to my lips.

"Wait, *Jaxon* kissed you?" Her voice cracks on his name like she's just as blindsided as I was before the sound of her phone clattering to the ground greets my ears. "Sorry," she adds. "But seriously. *Jaxon* kissed you?"

"Mm-hmm," I choke out. My butt finds the edge of my bed. "Yup. Twice, actually. He also touched my boobs, but he was drunk that time, so I'm not sure if—"

"Hold up," she orders. "Rory, slow down and start from the beginning."

So I do. And just like I expected, it comes out like word vomit, one confession after another until the dam is broken and tears trickle down my face like the rain did outside thirty minutes ago.

How was that only thirty minutes ago?

When I'm finished, I wipe at my cheeks, drowning in my best friend's silence as she processes everything. "Okay now it's your turn," I tell her. "Say something."

"Uh, well?" Tatum hesitates. "That's…a lot."

With a pathetic laugh, I reach for a tissue on my nightstand, blow my nose, and reply, "Yeah, no shit, Sherlock."

"I'm debating on buying a plane ticket and giving you a hug because you sound like you need one."

She's right. I do. Even knowing it won't fix anything. Not really.

Twisting the tissue between my fingers, I mutter, "What I really need is a Jaxon translator."

"Did he ask to come inside after the kiss?"

"I already told you, all he said was that I should go inside because he doesn't want me to catch a cold," I repeat.

"And that's it?"

"Yup." I puff out my cheeks and lay down on the mattress, my exhaustion getting the best of me. "That's it."

"Maybe he didn't want to pressure you," she offers. "Maybe he thought that if he came inside, it might lead to something…more. Like him *coming* inside, if you know what I mean."

Is that it? The real reason why he left me hot and bothered? I mean, it's possible. The guy's as straightlaced as they come. Or at least, I thought that was the case until he climbed into my bed and felt me up. Now, I'm not so sure.

"Maybe," I murmur, but I'm not entirely convinced. He's so hot and cold. So hard to read. I know he wouldn't use me. But I gave him multiple opportunities to drop the whole drunken kiss debacle, and what did he do? He followed me out into the rain and ruined me with a single brush of his lips. So what the hell am I supposed to do now?

"Wait, does he think you cheated on Dodger with him?" she rushes out. "Maybe that's why—"

"Nope." I stare up at the ceiling and crumple the tissue in my hand, letting out a long, dejected sigh. "He already knew Dodger and I were never real, thanks to the whole *never been kissed* thing."

"Oh, right. Hmm." She pauses. "Well, are you still going to nanny for him, or what?"

"I said I would." I sigh again.

"Yeah, you sound super convincing," she notes.

Rolling onto my side, I pull my knees to my chest, imagining what it'll be like to see him again. Will he pretend like the last few days never happened? Will *I* pretend like the last few days never happened? I'm not good at pretending. The idea alone is enough to make my stomach eat its own lining. But so is the idea of leaving him high and dry without a nanny. I'm not that kind of person.

"Rore?" Tatum prods.

"I don't know if I can be around him, let alone share a hotel room with him if I don't know where we stand."

"And where would you like to stand?" Tatum pushes. "I know you've dreamed about being with Jaxon since you were a little girl, but now that it might be an actual possibility, how do you feel?"

It's a good question. And if I'm being completely honest, it isn't something I've entertained. Not since I was a kid and would write Mrs. Jaxon Thorne on my notebooks. And that's if it's an actual possibility in the first place. We shared a kiss. Okay, two kisses, but still. Technically, it doesn't have to mean anything, and it might *not* mean anything. Not to Jax. Maybe he really did mean it in a transactional way. Like he was doing me a favor by giving me the kiss he felt he owed me. Maybe he was hoping that if he could make up for stealing my first kiss, I'd let things go and stop pouting and giving him the silent treatment. Or maybe that's all bullshit and he finally sees me the way I've always seen him? Or at least, the way I always *thought* I saw him.

It's kind of strange. Ever since the wedding, his perfect persona has started to crack, giving me glimpses of the real, flawed human he really is. But instead of it turning me off or stalling my attraction to the guy, it's only fed my interest, transforming my stupid childhood crush into something... more. Something deeper and scarier and genuine. Or at least, it could be if I knew he felt the same way. I don't know, and I'll never know if he keeps pushing me away like he has been.

"You still there?" Tatum asks.

"I'm here."

"So? How do you feel? Do you want to explore a relationship with Jax if it's on the menu?"

I rub at the corner of my tired eyes. "I'm still not convinced that being with Jax is an actual possibility, even after the recent events."

"Well, let's pretend it is," she argues. "Let's say that the reason he ran isn't because he's not interested—"

"Then why would he run?" I snap before pressing my lips into a thin line, hating my overreaction. "Sorry."

"No need to apologize. You're good, and you know I love you," she assures me. "But maybe he ran because he knows a commitment between you and him in this family isn't something you can brush aside or take slow. If it doesn't work out, it could get...messy. I mean, he works for your dad. And yeah, it worked out for Griff and Fin, and Mav and Lia, but when you add in Poppy and Iris and everything else, jumping into a relationship isn't something you should take lightly. And from the sound of things, it isn't something Jaxon's taking lightly, either."

I didn't think about it that way. The way Iris and Poppy and our families play into everything. And it's frustrating.

Because I'm not sure I should need to consider everyone else. Isn't a relationship supposed to be between two people?

A huff of frustration makes my nostrils flare as I mumble, "So, it's a bad idea."

"I didn't say that," she argues. "I'm just saying be patient with Jax. He's always been an overthinker, and to be fair, you have, too. He's probably taking some time to really consider every angle of the situation instead of jumping into bed with his boss's daughter at his boss's house."

I snort and toss my forearm over my eyes because, well, when she puts it that way, she might be onto something. "Okay, that's kind of a good point."

"Definitely," she argues. "Actually, as I was talking, I was even convincing myself that it has to be the reason why he left instead of screwing your brains out—"

"Tatum!"

"Rory," she volleys back, using my same tone. "Damn your best friend's a genius."

"And humble."

"Don't you forget it," she quips. "Now, do you need me to fly out so we can have a girl's night or...?"

"I'm good," I tell her, though I'm too tired to analyze whether or not it's true. I'm a big girl, and it doesn't matter how much I miss my best friend, I'm not about to make her jump on a plane all because I could use a hug. Besides, I have a mom for that. "Thank you for talking me off a ledge, though," I add. "I needed it."

"Anytime, Squeaks. You know I love you."

"Love you, too. And tell Paxton hi for me, okay?"

"Only if you promise to keep me updated," she counters.

"I promise."

After ending the call, I finish unpacking, throw in a load of laundry, find a snack in the kitchen, then head to the theater room. It doesn't take long until the *Gilmore Girls* theme song echoes through the sound system, and I settle into the couch cushions, preparing for a marathon in my favorite small town, Stars Hollow. Apparently, my mom's friends made her watch it for years, and, grudgingly, she slowly fell in love with the characters, too, before continuing the tradition with me. And even though it's dated in more ways than one, it's also my comfort show. Maybe it's because I share the same name as the mother-daughter duo. Maybe it's because I'm also awkward and nerdy and don't always know how to be in my own skin. If only there was an adorable German Shepherd in the mix, it would officially be the perfect show. Even then, it comes pretty close in my book.

I'm not sure how much time passes when my mom calls, "Hey, babe! Oo, what episode?"

Peeking over the edge of the couch, I answer, "the one where Rory's introduced to the Life and Death Brigade."

"Aww, that's a good one. '*You jump, I jump, Jack,*'" she adds, quoting one of my favorite scenes in the episode with Logan and Rory. She plops down on the cushion next to me and steals some popcorn from the bowl in my lap.

"Hey!" I start to pull the bowl from her, but she only tosses the stolen piece to Hades who's curled up on my opposite side.

As he catches it, she dives in for another handful, munching on a few buttery kernels. "You know he's not supposed to be on the couch."

Stroking Hades' soft fur, I argue, "I needed snuggles."

She nods her understanding and caves instantly. "Long flight?"

"Guess you could say that."

"I bet it was extra fun after they lost the first game of the season," she adds. "How's the team?"

"Gloomy except Reeves."

She chuckles. "Do you think anything could make that man have a bad day?"

"I doubt it," I offer dryly. Pretty sure the only thing that could dampen Oliver Reeves' mood is if his wife stubbed her toe and he wasn't there to kiss it better.

"What about Jax?" my mom prods. I don't miss the knowing glint on her eye. "Your dad's worried he's putting too much pressure on himself."

Is he that obvious? Why, yes. Yes, he is.

I pick at my cuticles, debating how many details I should give before deciding on a broader approach instead of getting into the nitty gritty. You know, like Jaxon climbing into my bed without an invitation. Not that he wouldn't have gotten one with a simple request. But I digress.

"Yeah, Jaxon likes to put a lot of pressure on himself," I admit, "but it isn't Dad's fault."

"I know, but it's still hard to see someone you care about beating themselves up."

"True."

"Speaking of which." She tilts her head toward the show. "You sure you're okay? I know this is your comfort show."

Apparently, Jax isn't the only one who's obvious.

Barely casting the television a glance, I pick up another popcorn piece and nibble on the edge, lying, "I'm good." Or maybe it isn't a lie. Honestly, I'm not sure.

I can feel my mom's gaze bouncing around my face as if she can't decide, either, but I don't bother looking up. The less help I give so she can read me like an open book, the better.

"How's watching Poppy?" she asks.

"Good." I smile, and this time it's more genuine. "She's the cutest thing ever."

"She really is." My mom shifts on the cushion, trying to make herself comfortable. "You know, when we had Mav and

Archer, it was a pretty big trigger for your dad. How are you on that front?"

My lips bunch on one side as I realize why she was shifting on the couch. Because she was uncomfortable. Not physically, but by the topic she was about to bring up.

Sneaky, Mom. Very sneaky.

We don't usually talk about it. My OCD. Not that it's taboo or anything. But the more attention you give OCD, the louder it can be, and since my dad has the same not-so-awesome disorder, they're well-versed in the do's and don'ts accompanying it.

"I'm handling it," I answer.

"You're sure?"

I nod. "Yeah. I mean, I can feel when I want to question things or when I want to act on my compulsions, but overall, I'm able to keep it in check."

"That's good."

"Why do you ask?"

"No reason in particular." She tucks my hair behind my ear. "I just worry about you sometimes. I know you have your fancy psychology degree and that you know how to take care of yourself, but it's okay if you need a tune-up, you know?"

She's right. It is. And it's not uncommon, either. Experiencing new things or routine shifts are known triggers for a lot of disorders, including my own. Add in twenty-four-seven access to an attractive hockey coach I've been in love with for decades, and the responsibility of a helpless child I adore, and I'm not sure I ever really stood a chance.

"Don't worry," I say. "I'm not above asking for help if I need it."

"Good." She steals another handful of popcorn before patting her shoulder. "Now, get over here. Hades isn't the only snuggler in this house."

Scooting closer, I rest my temple on her shoulder and sigh, grateful for my mom and the relationship we have. That I can talk to her. Commiserate with her. Share everything with her. Okay, maybe I didn't share everything, but it isn't because I can't. I'm just...not ready. And after decades of conversations with my mom, I know she's okay with that part, too. The waiting game. The open door and open arms I know are ready to catch me whenever I'm ready to let her. She's my rock. My confidante. My best friend.

"Missed you," I tell her.

"Missed you, too." She kisses the top of my head, then rests her own against me while *Gilmore Girls* plays on the screen in front of us. Two episodes later, the popcorn's gone, and an almost empty pint of Ben & Jerry's sits on the coffee table beside the empty bowl when my phone buzzes with a text.

DODGER

So...I heard we broke up.

With a laugh, I unlock my phone so I can respond.

"Who is it?" my mom asks.

"It's Dodger."

"Aww, how is he?"

"Good." Giving her the side-eye, I add, "We broke up."

"That was quick," she muses, but I don't miss the cocky lilt in her voice. It's the same one she uses when talking about Santa and the Tooth Fairy with all the grandbabies.

Twisting toward her, I say, "You knew, didn't you?"

"I'm your mother. Of course I knew." She lifts her chin toward my phone. "You gonna answer him?"

Oh. Right.

"Yup." I reread the message, then type my response.

ME

Seems word travels fast.

DODGER

Apparently. How are you doing?

ME

Good. Watching a show with my mom. Why
do you ask?

DODGER

Just checking in. Wanted to make sure
you're okay.

ME

How very sweet of you.

DODGER

I'm an excellent fake boyfriend.

I grin even wider.
"What did he say?" my mom prods.
"That he's an excellent fake boyfriend."
"*Ex* fake boyfriend, right?" she counters.
Good point.
I type exactly that and hit send.

ME

Ex fake boyfriend.

DODGER

Right. EX fake boyfriend. How could I forget?

ME

So, how are things with you and the band?

DODGER

Still on hiatus for now. Judge's nephews are
a pain in the ass.

ME

That bad, huh?

I don't know why I ask. We went to the same university together, and yes. His assessment is spot on. Jagger, Hawke, and Ford are menaces. They're cocky, athletic, reckless. And okay, yeah, they're good-looking and wealthy and charismatic when they want to be. But they also have no issue reminding the rest of the town that, as far as their father's concerned, they're closer to kings than regular people and should be treated as such. Or maybe that's only their public persona, and they're really gentlemen with big hearts and a penchant for community service in the form of fight nights, gambling, and underground deals. Who the hell knows? They don't let anyone get close, especially not a Goody Two-shoes like me.

My phone buzzes with another text.

DODGER

You have no idea. Speaking of, I just got a text from Judge, but I'm glad things are going well and we're on the same page. I'll talk to you later, yeah?

ME

Of course. :) Thanks again for your help, and good luck with the nephews!

DODGER

Thanks, we're gonna need it.

"Oo, who are Judge's nephews?" my mom chimes in.

"Mom!" I tuck my phone to my chest, but she only laughs.

"I'm only asking."

"You were reading over my shoulder," I argue.

"Yes, yes, I was, and I don't feel bad about it in the slightest."

"Talk about an invasion of privacy—"

"Are you going to answer my question or not?" she prods. "Who are Judge's nephews?"

My eyes thin, but I answer her anyway. "Just some boys who are troublemakers."

"Troublemakers, huh?"

"Yup," I answer.

"Good." She grins. "You could learn a thing or two from them."

"Excuse me?" I elbow her playfully. "You know, most moms would love having a perfect daughter like me."

"I do love having you," she argues. "And you're definitely pretty close to perfect. All I'm saying is, there's nothing wrong with not taking life too seriously or making sure that every second is planned out. Some of the best things in life are the things you never expect. You really think I planned on sleeping with my boss when I worked for your dad?"

My nose scrunches. "Ew!"

"I'm just saying." She kisses the top of my head again. "You're allowed to make mistakes and be impulsive and have fun before you settle down and start your career. I think traveling and nannying is a great start. Now, if we could just convince you to have an actual fling or two instead of a fake one with a rockstar, then I'd be really impressed."

I snort. Count on my mom to call me out like this.

Giving her a mock glare, I mutter, "Gee, thanks."

"Mm-hmm." She tosses her arm around my shoulders. "Now, come here. I'm ready for more snuggles."

"But only if I don't overthink it, right?"

Her light, airy laugh wraps around me like a warm hug, and she squeezes me tighter. Now that I think about it, she might be onto something. The whole, don't take life so seriously and have a fling or two. There's nothing wrong with it, right?

Keeping this in mind, I open another conversation on my phone, though I've been avoiding this one for days.

ERIC

Hey! Any chance you'd be interested in being my plus-one for the banquet this weekend?

Before I can talk myself out of it, I type my response.

ME

Hey! Sorry I haven't responded. But, yes. If the offer is still on the table, I'd love to go with you.

I hit send and flip my phone upside down in my lap, tapping the edge against my leg.

One, two, three. Pause. *One, two, three.*

It vibrates.

ERIC

Sounds great! I'll pick you up at seven. See you then!

JAXON

Scratching my temple, I try to keep my attention on what David Hoffman is rambling on about, but he isn't making it easy. He's on the Lions' board with a few other men and insists that if I considered trading one of the players on the roster for his grandson, we'd be in much better shape this season. It doesn't help that I have nothing to do with trades, or that his grandson's stats are about as extraordinary as an average, middle-aged man who plays recreationally on the weekends.

Not that I'd ever point it out to Mr. Hoffman, though.

It's not his fault I'm distracted. I haven't been able to form a coherent thought since kissing Rory. Hell, if I'm being honest, my mind's been fucked since long before then. Ever since Rory showed up for Mav's wedding.

Looking for an excuse to get the hell out of this conversation, or at the very least a solid distraction, I take in the crowded room. A long banquet table is set up on one side. It's covered in a black tablecloth and littered with different foods. There's also a dance floor, a live band, and waiters in tuxes balancing trays of champagne. Members of the Lions' organization mingle with players and their families while cameras flash here and there, documenting the event.

Iris has Poppy, which means it's Rory's night off. You'd think it would be a good thing. The space and time apart. But it's been driving me even more insane. I haven't seen her since our kiss in the rain. Is she pissed? Scared? Offended? Does it matter?

"As I was saying," Hoffman continues.

I nod as he prattles on about how biased the NHL can be when Crowther's loud laugh echoes across the large hall. Glancing over Hoffman's shoulder, I fight the urge to double over as the oxygen catches in my chest. Rory Buchanan in an emerald green dress.

She's here.

She said yes.

She's Crowther's plus-one for the night despite her mouth on mine.

What the fuck?

"Coach Thorne?"

I tear my gaze from Rory and turn back to Mr. Hoffman, my blood boiling. "I apologize. There's someone I've been meaning to chat with. Make sure to bring up your grandson at the next board meeting. I'm sure they'd love to see what they can do." With a friendly hand on his shoulder, I move around Hoffman before any logic has a chance to grab hold. She's here. And she's here with Crowther. Fucking Crowther. Of course, she is. I stride toward the shit show in front of me, ready to demand answers when the man of the hour leads Rory onto the dance floor, effectively preventing me from approaching without looking like a moron. I jolt to a halt on the edge of the dance area, my hands fisted at my sides.

Snap the hell out of it!

I take a deep breath through flared nostrils in an attempt

to get my head out of my ass. I don't know what I was thinking. Approaching them like this. When it doesn't matter. When I can barely think straight, let alone form a coherent sentence, after witnessing them together. But you can't blame a guy for wanting an answer or two. What the hell is she doing here? Was it always the plan? Or did she reach out to Crowther after our kiss?

"Hey, Jax," Henry greets me. I jerk at the sound, and he grins. "Did I scare you?"

"Sorry, uh, no, you didn't scare me, and hey," I add. "The place looks great."

"Thanks," he returns. "My assistant's thrown a few of these together over the years. Seems she hasn't lost her touch."

"Not at all. Erika did an incredible job."

"I'll be sure to mention it at her next one-on-one," he says.

I steal another glance of Rory and Crowther, just in time to catch him dipping her on the dance floor. She laughs as he spins her around before flicking his wrist and pulling her back into him. Since when does every asshole know how to dance? First, Dodger, now this guy? What, they're all required to take lessons or something?

"So, where's Pops?" Henry questions.

Unable to tear my attention from the train wreck in front of me, I answer, "She's with Iris."

He nods slowly, then realizes what I'm staring at. "Wanna tell me about the rookie?"

Tugging at the front of my tux, I lift a shoulder, unsure what to say as I attempt to focus on the conversation instead of the mess unfolding on the dance floor. "Who? Crowther?"

"Yeah," Henry says. "The guy dancing with my daughter. Is he a good guy?"

Does it matter? I want to shout. *He's touching her.*

"Don't know much about him," I reply, trying to keep my

expression indifferent no matter how impossible it feels. "Unless you mean when he's on the ice."

Henry smiles around the rim of his scotch. "Your little brother says he's all right."

"That's 'cause Griff was the mastermind behind..." I tilt my head toward the couple in question. "Whatever this is."

"It was probably his wife's idea," Henry mutters dryly.

The corner of my mouth curves up, surprising the hell out of me, all things considered. Yeah, this has Finley written all over it. "Probably."

"It's strange," Henry continues. "Seeing your daughter grow up. Not sure it's something I'll ever get used to." He sighs and looks at me instead of Rory across the room. "You'll get it when Pops grows up. The way you have to fight the urge to be overprotective and let them...be who they want to be. Live how they wanna live. Love who they wanna love."

Love.

My gut twists as I steal another glance at Rory on the dance floor with Crowther. Could she love him? Not yet, obviously. It's way too soon. But, one day? Could she fall for him? It's like a fucked up game of deja vu. Not only the dance, but the added love interest. First Dodger, now this? And am I so wrong for not liking it? For questioning my own damn sanity after knowing what she tastes like?

Talk about moving too fucking fast. Is she trying to get back at me? Is that what this is about? Or am I so self-absorbed that I can't even consider the possibility that she made plans with Crowther before the kiss? Does the timeline matter? Did the kiss matter? My hand thrums at my side as I spiral more and more, the same thoughts echoing in a carousel of jealousy and unease.

Dodger. The wedding. The break up. Crowther. The date.

The loss. Our kiss. Another fucking kiss. Then she walks in with him?

"I thought she was with Dodger, though," I say. It's a lie. I know the truth. But does Henry?

With a subtle shake of his head, Henry brings the scotch to his mouth. "Nah. He might've been Rory's plus-one, but I know Dodge."

His sagely tone makes me pause. "What does that mean?"

"You'd understand if you knew him," he explains. "Let me know if you hear anything unsavory about Crowther, though. Just 'cause I want my daughter to be able to make her own decisions and feel free to do what she wants to do doesn't mean we should feed her to the wolves."

Maintaining the facade of indifference, I nod. "Will do."

The song ends seconds later, and Crowther snakes his arm around Rory's waist, guiding her off the dance floor when Rory's eyes light up.

"Hey, Dad!" she rushes toward him and gives him a hug.

"Hey, Squeaks," Henry returns before letting her go and tilting his head toward the man beside her. "You gonna give me an official introduction?"

"Dad, this is Eric Crowther, as I'm sure you know. Eric, this is my dad, Henry Buchanan."

Crowther's eyes bulge as they dart from Rory, to the owner of the NHL Lions, then back again. "I thought you were my boss's nanny, not my boss's *boss's* daughter."

"Rory Buchanan," she says, proudly, and offers her hand. "Nice to meet you."

With a low laugh, he takes her hand, kissing the back of it like they've been transported to some 1500's bullshit ball or something. "Should I call you princess, or…?"

She stifles a sweet giggle that makes my throat knot and pulls her fingers from his grasp. "Lady Rory's fine."

He laughs even harder. "I'll keep that in mind."

"You know, I think I like where this is going. Every man wants his daughter treated like a princess," Henry notes. It makes my mind reel even more. He likes where this is going? He likes the idea of Crowther and Rory together? The man's a womanizer. Henry has to see—

"So, Coach," Crowther says, addressing me. "Tell me something. How did you win over Rory's dog?"

Rory laughs. "Eric—"

"The thing almost bit me in the ass when I picked up our Rory here," Crowther continues, speaking over her. "And she mentioned the only guy Hades has ever approved of is you."

The world feels like it's spinning as I process Crowther's words. First of all, since when is Rory *our* Rory? Yeah, that pisses me off. But the idea of Hades nearly biting Crowther in the ass is almost enough to stifle the emotion. And the reminder that I'm the only man Hades approves of? Call me a sucker, but it's like music to my fuckin' ears.

I open my mouth to tell him to fuck off, but Rory chimes in, cutting me off.

"I never said he's the *only* guy Hades approves of," she defends. "He likes my brother and dad, too."

Henry's giant hand lands on Rory's shoulder. "Hate to break it to you, but yesterday, your dog growled at me for kissing your mom goodbye."

She rolls her eyes. "That's only because I hadn't let him outside yet."

"Sure it is." With a smirk, Henry gives his attention to Crowther. "I've tried peanut butter and beef jerky as bribery, and neither of them got me anywhere. If you figure out something that works, let me know. And you." He turns to me. "Should've known you'd be the one to crack the code with Hades. Did the same with Rore from day one." He kisses his daughter's cheek. "I'll see you at home, Rore."

"Bye, Dad."

As he leaves, an awkward blanket settles over our little threesome, and I tuck my hands into my pockets, rocking back on my heels. What the hell am I supposed to do now?

"You bring a date tonight?" Crowther asks me.

The asshole probably means well, and it only pisses me off more. The way he's trying to be inclusive.

I shake my head. "Nah, I'm not seeing anyone."

Rory's gaze drops to the ground as she gives a single dip of her chin before giving Crowther her full focus. "Hey, we should get a drink. Or three."

"Anything for you, princess." He touches her back again, then leads her to the bar. With every step she takes, my frustration grows. It clouds my judgment, threatening to blind me completely until all I'm left with is jealousy.

She's not mine. I know it. Fuck, do I know it. But now that I know what she tastes like, I can't help but wonder if I should do something about it.

Yeah, I need a drink.

29

RORY

"You sure you don't want to come?" my mom asks. A cute little painted lion sits on her left cheek as she slips on a light jacket.

The sight only confirms my decision. "Yeah, I'm sure. You guys have fun, though."

I've been vegging out in the basement all day. Okay, hiding out is probably a more fitting term, but is it my fault I can't stop reliving my kiss in the rain with a certain someone I'd rather not think about?

"It's the opening game," my dad chimes in from the stairs.

"I'm aware."

"And you don't want to come?" he prods. "We have the suite—"

"We always have the suite," I remind him dryly. It's one of the perks of him owning the team. "But seriously, I'm okay," I continue. "I have a lot to catch up on anyway."

My dad gives me an unimpressed look. "Like what? Poppy's with her mom this week—"

"Rory, you're fine," my mom interjects, defending me. "We

just love you, that's all. Mind if we leave Mufasa with you and Hades?"

"Not at all." I pat the empty cushions on both sides of me. "Plenty of room for snuggles. And don't worry, Dad. I'll make sure to cheer the team on from here. Promise."

His expression doesn't budge. If anything, it deepens, causing a slight wrinkle between his brows and a subtle tilt of his head that only the people who know him best would notice. "Mm-hmm," he grunts. "First Mav and Lia bail, and now you. It's like you guys don't even like hockey anymore."

"Laying on the guilt trip pretty thick, don't you think?" my mom quips.

He gives her a pointed look. "Who's side are you on, anyway?"

With a smirk, she kisses his cheek. "Yours, obviously."

"Mm-hmm," he repeats as if he doesn't believe her.

Bringing the focus back on the conversation instead of how annoyingly adorable my parents act with each other even after all these years, I point out, "To be fair, Mav and Lia are on their honeymoon for like the next twenty weeks—"

"Six," my mom clarifies. "It's six weeks, and only two are for their honeymoon. The other four are being spent in Haiti. But your daughter's right, Professor." She slips her arm around his bicep, stealing his attention and covering for me by handling him like a pro. "I'm pretty sure they'd love to be here if they could. Now, give your daughter a break. She's allowed to have some downtime on her week off."

Too stubborn to give in right away, he quirks his brow, then drops a quick kiss to his wife's forehead. "You're right."

"I'm always right," she teases.

With a subtle shake of his head, he steals his arm back and moves closer to where I'm planted on the couch like a bump on a log. "Love you, Squeaks."

He kisses my forehead the same way he did my mom's,

and I preen like a little girl. "Love you, too. Wish the team luck for me."

"We will."

As they retreat, I reach for the remote on the coffee table and turn the television to ESPN, keeping my promise to watch the entire game even if it kills me. It's not that I don't like hockey. I love hockey. And if I wasn't still reeling from my kiss with Jaxon, I would've had my mom paint my face just like when I was little, so I could be front and center, cheering the Lions on. But alas. Here I am. Hiding. And annoyed that I'm hiding. With a huff, I grab my laptop, determined to distract myself. It only stays open for about ten minutes before I give up and snuggle with the pups instead.

It's a good game.

Crowther scores once in the first period, and Reeves scores twice in the third. Neither goal would've happened without Everett's assistance. Add in a couple solid fights and a crazy call on Griff with four minutes on the clock, and I'm on the edge of my seat the entire time. I even manage to not drool over a certain coach anytime his stupid face comes on the screen.

Maybe I have a backbone after all.

As soon as the thought filters through me, a flashback from the banquet rears its ugly head, and I'm left reeling all over again.

"You bring a date tonight?" Eric asks.

Jaxon shakes his head. "Nah, I'm not seeing anyone."

Not. Seeing. Anyone.

I heard it from the man himself. He's not seeing anyone. Just slipping into my bed and kissing me in the rain, but hey. He's definitely still single.

Gah!

I turn off the television and toss the remote onto the

coffee table. Why is it so impossible to get this man out of my head?

30

RORY

The next two days go by in a blur while also managing to move at a snail's pace. Other than my somewhat awkward night at the banquet, I spend most of my time watching movies, swimming, and walking Hades. By some miracle, I even manage to refrain from texting my congratulations on a good game to Jaxon. Pathetic? Maybe a little, but it is what it is, and at this point, I'm determined to celebrate every win, no matter how infinitesimal. My parents left for a B-Tech Enterprises retreat yesterday, and the quiet's been nice. It's given me time to think. And overthink. And go through the stack of nanny resumes. I'm sure at least one of them would willingly start before the month I promised Jax is up, but the idea of leaving Poppy creates a pit in my stomach, so I haven't bothered asking any of the potential hires if they'd be interested.

Reaching out in general, though, feels pretty necessary since I promised a certain someone I'd tackle the process during my week off. I puff out my cheeks and drag the resume into the maybe folder on my iPad when Hades grumbles at my feet.

I glance down, finding his dark chocolate eyes staring up at me.

"Is there a problem, sir?"

Sitting up, he gives me another grunt and pushes his head against my calf. He's bored. Or restless. Or both. Then again, so am I.

"Fiiiine." I shut off my iPad. "We'll play in the backyard. But only for a minute," I add, as if the beast has the power to understand time constraints. "Where's your ball?"

Barreling out of the office, Hades rushes toward the laundry room where his things are kept, his cumbersome footsteps echoing down the hall. When we meet at the back-door, his neon green ball peeks out from beneath his chocolate colored snout, proving he understands a lot more than most give him credit for.

With a twist of the handle, I open the door. The sun is high in the sky, seeping through my threadbare T-shirt and cotton sleep shorts as I skip down the stairs to the grass. Wrenching my arm back, I throw the ball across the lawn, and Hades darts after it before bringing it back to me so I can repeat the process all over again. I don't mind, though. He's my boy. My only boy, it seems. *Which is all right*, I remind myself. I don't need a guy. Especially one who has a habit of running in the opposite direction every chance he gets.

As the ball rolls off the tip of my fingers for the tenth time, something catches Hades' attention, and he lifts his head, choosing to stare at the edge of the house instead of the ball soaring through the air. Following his gaze, I find an unsure Jaxon rounding the corner with his hands in his pockets.

A gasp catches in my throat, and I try to cover my surprise, though I doubt I'm successful.

What the hell is he doing here?

Hades looks up at me, checking in, so I smooth my features and give him a nod. "Go say hi."

Like a flash, he dashes across the lawn, and Jaxon's mouth lifts before he squats down to scratch Hades behind the ear. Unease spreads through my chest as I watch their interaction. I'll never understand it. Why my dog, who hates everyone, seems to accept Jaxon without any reservations. Considering how many people are on his shit list for no reason at all, it makes zero sense. And also kind of makes me want to withhold his treats for the next week or something. Not that I want him to hate anyone—including Jaxon—but it's like saying the sky is green instead of blue. It just...it doesn't make sense.

Then again, I guess I can't blame my furry beast since— like my dad so eloquently pointed out during the banquet— I've always felt the same pull with the same person despite the lack of logic. Maybe it's what makes Hades such a good companion for me. We're the same terrible judge of character despite our best intentions. Okay, that's probably not fair. Jaxon has great character. And great kissing abilities. But I digress.

Standing to his full height, Jax tucks his hands in his front pockets again and glances at me on the opposite side of the yard. "Hey."

The single syllable lacks any real or phony enthusiasm. Quite the opposite, actually. It's like he still can't decide whether or not he's welcome despite Hades' all-too-welcoming response. Then again, neither can I.

Why are you here?

His footsteps are slow and calculated as Hades dives for the forgotten ball and gallops toward me, dropping it at my feet. Tearing my attention from Jax, I crouch down, pick up the ball, and toss it through the air in an attempt to act unaffected by his unplanned visit.

"Hey," Jax repeats when he's close enough. I steal another peek at him despite my best intentions. I shouldn't notice how cute he looks with his hands tucked in his front pockets, but I do. He looks really handsome. Nervous. And handsome. The man's usually so sure of himself, it's strange to see him like this. Like he doesn't know what to do with himself or how to act around me. The combination hits harder than it should, and I fight the urge to reach out to him. To make it better. To smooth the crease in his brow when he's the reason it's there in the first place.

"Is Poppy okay?" I ask because it's the only explanation as to why he's here.

Why are you here?

"She's fine," he murmurs. "With her mom still."

Pressing my lips together, I give him a short nod but don't say anything else. Honestly, I refuse to. Why should I be the one to break the silence, to bail him out, when he's the one who tracked me down in the first place?

"How was the banquet?" Jax asks.

Seriously? He wants to talk about the banquet?

I grit my teeth and answer, "You tell me. You were there, too."

"I meant with Crowther," he clarifies.

No shit, Sherlock.

My teeth dig into the inside of my cheek to keep from lashing out, but boy, is he making it difficult, so I settle on, "It was fine."

"Glad he got you home safely."

"Yup." I cross my arms when the slobbery ball rolls near my feet, bringing me back to the present. Picking it up, I throw the ball again, ignoring the way I want to crawl out of my own skin if the awkward silence continues much longer.

"Are you guys...together now?" he asks.

Part of me wants to lie. To tell him that we are. We're

dating, and he fucked my brains out, and I've never been happier. Then I remember how we've already played this game, and where did it get me? Nowhere. Absolutely nowhere.

But before I have a chance to tell him the truth, he moves on, saying, "You, uh, you weren't at the game."

"I was busy," I lie. When his head dips in acknowledgement, I run my tongue along the inside of my cheek, unsure what the hell I'm supposed to say right now. "Why are you here?'

He scrubs at his jaw, unable to look me in the eye. "I've been asking myself the same question."

My eyes pop. "Wow. Thanks—"

"Iris and I weren't a good fit," Jax announces.

Iris? He wants to talk about his ex right now?

"Figured as much," I mutter. "What with the divorce and all."

He lets out a soft chuckle and squeezes the back of his neck. "Yeah."

Okay?

"Didn't always feel that way, though," he adds. "I thought I loved her."

"Figured as much," I repeat. "What with the marriage and baby and all."

He smiles before letting it fall. "Yeah. The marriage and baby." His attention falls to the grass beneath his Nikes as he shifts from one foot to the other. "I thought I had it all, Rore."

A pang of jealousy hits my sternum, but I stay quiet. To be honest, I don't know what he wants me to say in the first place. You loved someone? Good for you. If only it was that easy for everyone. To fall in love and be accepted and wanted and appreciated. And yeah, it didn't work out, but at least you had something. Right?

"Which is why I now have a hard time trusting my gut,"

he adds. "Because I thought I really did love her. And then, I caught her cheating on me with one of the parents of the players I was coaching when Pops was a couple months old."

My eyes widen all over again. Only this time, I'm even more blindsided.

"Talk about a mindfuck, right? And before you ask, no, I didn't get a paternity test. I don't want one, either, and neither does the man my ex was hooking up with. Poppy's mine."

"She is," I agree, praying he knows how much I mean it. How often I look into her pretty, round eyes and see her father staring back.

"Still a bit of a mindfuck, though," he adds dryly, not even bothering to hide the familiar disgust in his tone. I don't blame him. Experiencing a betrayal like that would be rough for anyone, and coming back from it? Feels like one in a million.

"I can imagine," I murmur. "Having an experience like that would mess with anyone, I think."

"You're probably right. I just…I feel like you should know that I…I don't know what I'm doing."

He doesn't know what he's doing?

Try being on this side of things, buddy.

I'm annoyed. Maybe I shouldn't be. Maybe I should cut him some slack after his crappy ex cheated on him, but I refuse to skirt around the subject since he's the one who chose to bring it up by coming here. "You don't know what you're doing about what?"

"About…" He tears his attention from the blue sky above us, meeting my gaze. "This."

This? Me and him? He wants to talk about me and him? Confusion, curiosity, and want all swirl in my veins as I stare back at him, unsure what to say, let alone how to read the man in front of me.

"Is there a…" I wiggle my fingers between us. "This?" My nose wrinkles, and I drop my hand to my side. "Because no offense, Jaxon, but you haven't exactly been very upfront about anything."

"I know," he rushes out. "And that's on me. It's why I'm here."

"To be up front?" My arms fold. "Yeah, that would be nice."

"I'm trying," he admits, "but it's complicated."

"Of course it is."

"I've known you forever, Rore," he argues. "I feel like I just got you back."

I bite back my scoff because the truth is a hell of a lot more pathetic. Despite my best intentions, he's always had me. I'm just…not running from him anymore, and whether or not that's a smart decision is on me.

"What if I screw it up?" he continues. "What if we decide we're better as friends? And I know you've been looking at the resumes online. What happens when the month is up? Do you leave?"

I open my mouth, preparing to ask if he wants me to leave, but he barrels on, proving his thoughts are even more sporadic than his actions lately, which is saying something.

Pacing through the grass, he says, "Fuck, I travel a shit ton, Rore. Your dad's my boss. Your brother's one of my best friends. You work for me. Not to mention Crowther and the rest of the team or what my ex would think. I just—"

"Whoa, there," I mumble, catching us both off-guard before I snap my mouth closed.

His pacing ceases, and his chest heaves with a sigh as he gives me his full attention again. "What is it?"

"Nothing," I deflect. "It's just…whoa."

"Whoa?"

"I, uh, I get it now."

He frowns.

Giving in, I explain, "Tatum's always complaining that I overthink things way too much, and now that I'm talking to you, I finally understand what she's saying, and…" I grimace. "Whoa."

"Is that what I'm doing?" he asks. "Overthinking shit?"

He isn't offended. Isn't frustrated with me calling him out like this. No, he's genuinely curious. Like, the idea of me throwing him a bone and hashing this out or clearing this up isn't a want. It's a need. For him, at least. The question is, what do I want? What do I need?

"Don't answer that," he decides.

Hades screeches to a halt in front of him and drops the ball at his feet. As if he's grateful for the distraction, Jaxon retrieves it, gently tossing the ball from one hand to the other. Hades swishes his tail back and forth in preparation for a quick dash, though it seems Jax is too distracted to share in my dog's not-so-subtle show of anticipation. "I just…I can't stop picturing the look on our family's faces if they find out I can't help picturing you naked."

A snort escapes me before I can stop it, and I press my hand to my lips. "Sorry. Uh, but I'm pretty sure they don't need to know that kind of information regardless of whatever does or doesn't happen between us."

"So I keep it from them?" He cocks his arm back, and the ball arches through the pale blue sky. "We keep this from them?"

What this? I want to scream.

I could let it go. I could leave the proverbial can of worms untouched. Or I could grab the rusty can-opener at the very back of the drawer, dust it off, and wrench this baby wide-open. Isn't it past time? For me, yeah. For him, though? I peek at Jaxon again and twist my fingers in front of me.

"Here's the thing," I say. "I know you recently got out of a serious relationship. I know you probably think that you need the answer to everything if you're even going to consider pursuing...something with anyone, let alone me. Or at least I think that's what you're saying," I clarify. "And maybe it's my degree talking here, but I don't think requiring the answers to every single question before even considering pursuing this is the healthiest way to deal with the situation."

"So you admit there's a this?" he challenges, tossing my own words back at me from moments ago.

My mouth lifts despite the cloud of melancholy hanging over me. I need to tell him the truth. The truth that's weighed on me for as long as I can remember, despite my best attempt to brush it aside. "I think we both know there's been a this for me a lot longer than there's been a this for you, Jax."

He sobers, his reaction causing heat to unfurl in my chest. "I know."

Does he, though? I doubt it. Even I don't fully understand the pull I've always felt with him. It's...exhausting. And consuming. And scary as hell.

As if he can read my thoughts, Jax murmurs, "That's why I didn't ask to come inside before, Squeaks."

"Because I'm a crazy stalker?" I retort.

"Considering all the thoughts I've had about you lately, I'm pretty sure it's the other way around." He steps closer. Slowly. And with a weight of calculation that's both sexy and annoying. Because it makes me feel like he feels the need to treat me with kid gloves, and that's the last thing I want.

"I've always cared about you, all right?" he says. "Even after you left, I always thought about you. Always hoped you were getting everything you wanted in life."

Everything I wanted but you, a quiet voice whispers in the back of my mind. With the game of fetch forgotten, I wrap my arms around myself. I'm unsure what to say or how to even process the conversation we're having, let alone the kiss we shared on my front lawn in the pouring rain.

With a sigh, Jaxon narrows his gaze and tilts his head, considering me. "But the thing is, ever since you came back, things have felt…different."

"Different," I repeat.

"Yeah. Different. The things you do to me are new." His gaze dips to my mouth. "Very new. I'm still processing it."

"Guess that makes two of us." I take in a soft breath, hoping the additional oxygen will keep me from jumping to conclusions. Like if he's thinking what I'm thinking, or if I'm reading him wrong—again—like I did all those years ago.

"So, what do we do?" he asks.

What do we do? He's leaving this to me?

"Well, I'm not expecting a marriage proposal or anything," I mutter. "I think it's okay to take a breather and figure things out without announcing them to the world." I tuck my hair behind my ear. "What if we don't make this complicated? What if we both admit we enjoyed that kiss, and what if we both admit we're curious about what it would be like if we kissed again. Maybe we could stop overthinking and start testing the waters to see if we're both interested in it." *To see if you're interested*, I silently clarify because I'm not stupid, and I know what I want. *Him.*

"Testing the waters, huh?" he questions, towering over me until I'm left with no choice but to raise my chin and tilt my head back so I can hold his gaze. This is it. The look. The one I've dreamt about for years and have only seen a handful of times—the first being in that hotel room last week.

"Mm-hmm," I hum in an attempt to keep my mind in check when I'm seconds from spiraling into a fit of likely misread interest.

He lifts his hand from his side as if he wants to touch me, but he doesn't. He lets his hand hover an inch from my waist, the lack of touch branding me more than if he'd grabbed my hip. "I don't want to hurt you."

"I'm a big girl," I remind him. "And I'm not asking for a commitment. I'm only asking for you to be honest and open and straightforward with what you want."

Something flashes in his gaze, but it's gone too fast for me to place it.

"What I want?" he challenges.

"Yes." My skin prickles with awareness as I metaphorically twist the handle on the stupid can opener, well aware there's no going back. Not after this conversation. Steeling my shoulders, I ask, "What do you want, Jaxon?"

RORY

I'm not sure who this girl is. The one confidently standing in front of the only guy she's ever had feelings for, asking him what he wants. Yet, here I am. In the flesh. Six inches from the infamous Jaxon Thorne with only my very blunt question hanging between us. Honestly, I blame Tatum. It's clear she's rubbing off on me, but I'm too determined to hear Jaxon out to care.

"What do you want, Jaxon?" I repeat.

His lips tug toward the ground as he considers my question. "No one asks me what I want."

"I believe I just did," I counter. "And that's not an answer."

The tendons along his jaw flex. "What if…what if what I want hurts you in the long run?"

Hurts me? He's afraid of hurting me in the long run? Doesn't he get it? Not being with him hurts me. Over-thinking the push and pull he's been putting me through hurts me. Living in denial and not knowing what he wants hurts me.

Playing with the hem of his shirt, I counter, "Maybe, for

once in your life, you should stop thinking about other people's feelings and be selfish."

"Selfish, huh?" His fingers graze my waist, leaving a hot trail along my skin as he gives in and touches me.

"Yes," I whisper. "Be selfish. Stop thinking of me or your ex or our families. What do you *want*, Jax?"

"I want to kiss you again."

I lift my chin another centimeter and press my trembling hand to his chest, soaking in the familiar *thump-thump* against my palm as I silently beg my legs to not give out. "No one's stopping you."

"But what if—"

"Don't you dare finish that sentence." Fisting the fabric of his T-shirt, I tug him toward me, daring him to push me away, to hit the final nail in the coffin and end things once and for all. But he doesn't. Instead, his lips meet mine as he captures my mouth in a kiss. And it feels good. Really good. My own what-ifs threaten to rise to the surface, but I push them down, refusing to let my insecurities ruin this moment. Because despite my faux confidence in the situation, he isn't the only one who's scared. Who's unsure. Who doesn't know what they're doing. He isn't the only one who doesn't want to hurt anyone in the process of giving in to what they want for the first time…ever.

And, yes. I want this. I want this so much it hurts.

"Fuck, Squeaks," he rasps against me. "This is such a bad idea, isn't it?"

"Probably one of the worst," I agree before diving in for another kiss. His fingers tickle my skin as he drags them across the hem of my sleep shorts before pressing his knee to the apex of my thighs. On instinct, my muscles tighten, and my core throbs.

Yeah, I'm ready. I don't even know what I'm ready for, not personally, but I can feel it. The desperation as it spreads through me. It's not like I don't know how sex works or what an orgasm feels like. But experiencing it with someone is very different than on your own in a quiet room with nothing but your imagination to spur you on. Having Jaxon up close and personal? His warm, woodsy scent washing over me? His hands on my skin? His tongue dragging against mine? It's an entirely different concoction and puts any fantasy of what I thought it would be like to be with him to shame.

"Fuck," he rasps. "The things I could do to you."

"So do them," I whisper, rolling my hips against his thigh.

"The cameras—"

"I'll wipe the footage before my parents even think about checking them," I reply, daring him to come up with another excuse as to why we can't keep this interaction on its current trajectory because, uh, yes, please.

Sucking on the sensitive patch of skin beneath my ear, he murmurs, "You should go out with me."

Go out with him? He wants to talk about going out when it's clear I'd rather have him come inside? And I mean it in the literal sense, just like Tatum suggested during our phone call a couple days ago.

Fighting the urge to roll my eyes, I squeeze them shut instead and tilt my head, giving him better access to whatever the hell he wants from me. "And you should not be a wet blanket and let me enjoy this."

"Rore—"

"Come inside," I beg. "I want to see what this is like without you pushing me away before we get to the good part."

A low groan slips out of him as he dives in for another kiss, hitching his knee a little higher until all I can do is rub myself against him.

"Tell me your parents aren't home," he growls.

"My parents aren't home."

Bending down, he grabs the back of my thighs and scoops me into arms, making me squeal in surprise. "Spread your legs," he orders.

So I do, wrapping them around his waist as he carries me toward one of the pool chairs that's lying flat and sets me down. I reach for his shoulders, praying he won't pull away, and by some miracle, he doesn't. Instead, he climbs on top of me, shifting between my thighs until he's cradled between them when his mouth meets mine again. Liquid heat pools at my core as the ridge of his cock presses against me, leaving me lightheaded and needier than I've ever been.

A small part of me wonders if I'm moving too fast, but the other part? The other part is screaming that this has never felt more right, and if we really consider the timeline of my crush on the guy, he's basically put me through the slowest burn ever. It's not like I've kept my distance from the opposite sex because of fear or because I want to keep my virginity intact. It's because no one has ever made me feel the way I feel right now. No one has ever made me want to be touched like this. Like how Jaxon is touching me in this moment. Arching my back against him, I let out a soft whimper, savoring the feel of his mouth on my sensitive skin.

"You a virgin, Beautiful?" he rasps against me.

My body oozes with need as I force my head to nod. But the feel of his hands on me, his breath against the column of my throat, it's too much. He's too much. My eyelids flutter, and I tilt my head a little more, giving him better access as he breathes me in before planting an open-mouth kiss against my neck.

"Gonna take things slow," he promises, though I'm not sure if it's for me or for him. "Gonna worship every inch of you." *Kiss.* "Gonna drive you so crazy, you'll be begging me to push into this tight little body with my cock. But first?" His mouth reaches my ear, and he nips at the lobe. "First, I'm gonna give you my fingers, then my mouth. You all right with that, Beautiful?"

My head bobs on another nod despite the lust fogging all my senses and turning me into a puddle of goo. Okay, the lust and the feel of his calloused fingertips trailing along my stomach. I want him.

"Please." The word barely makes it past my lips.

"I got you, Rore," he promises, letting me grind against him as his fingers find the edge of my sleep shorts before he slides them into my underwear. "Fuck, you're soaked."

"Seems you have that effect on me." My words are breathless as he sweeps his fingers along my clit.

His mouth lifts, and he repeats the motion, gathering moisture from my slit and bringing it to the little bundle of nerves. "So sensitive."

"Mm-hmm." I grab his wrist and rock my hips. And it's strange. Caught between wanting to push him away and pull him closer. Like it's too much, yet not enough.

My eyelids flutter, and he folds forward, pressing a kiss to the edge of my mouth. "So fucking beautiful."

Dipping into my slit, he plays with my entrance before giving me one finger, then two. My lips part, and my breathing staggers at the intrusion. It's tight, and a little uncomfortable, but he pulls out seconds later, giving the same addictive attention to my clit until my hips are shifting toward him all over again.

"Gonna need to get rid of these shorts," he murmurs.

I nod my approval, and he tugs on them until I'm left bare from the waist down. The warm sun kisses my skin, making me feel even more exposed before Jaxon's mouth is on mine all over again. It's like he knows. When my stupid insecurities are about to rear their ugly heads. And he knows the best way to quiet them. So I give in, focusing on the feel of his hands and mouth as he explores my body, using his own to block most of me from view. Peppering kisses down my body, he sucks the skin beneath my bellybutton into his mouth before scooting lower.

"Jax," I whisper.

He stops immediately.

"Tell me what you want," he begs. "If you want me to stop—"

"I don't," I rush out.

A patient smile graces his lips. "You sure?"

"Yeah, it's just…new and scary, and…" I run my fingertips along the side of his face as his mouth hovers a few inches above my pubic bone. And it's strange. Seeing him like this. With me. Right here. It's hazy like a dream, yet so acute and sharp, I'm afraid I'll be left flayed open and raw if we finish what we've started.

"Rory," he breathes out. Indecision taints my name. Like he can't decide whether or not this is a good idea.

"I'm fine."

That same warm smile broadens before he sobers. "You're a terrible liar."

"I want this," I whisper.

"You say stop, I stop," he promises.

The word rests on the tip of my tongue, but I close my mouth instead, my chin dipping in another subtle nod. Satisfied, Jaxon settles between my knees and kisses the little divot between my thighs and pussy. My body jolts at the contact, pulling another smile from the man in front of me. "You're gonna love this, Beautiful."

He presses his mouth to my core, and I arch my back, ignoring the stars behind my eyelids. "And you?" I gasp. "I don't want to do this if—" Sensation cuts me off as he sticks the tip of his tongue inside of me.

Holy hell.

"Jax," I plead. "Jax—"

"You taste fucking incredible, Rory." Fingering me, he kisses my clit. "And if you threaten to take away my new favorite snack, I'm gonna lose my mind. We clear?"

Nodding, I let my eyes roll back and grab onto his head as he sucks at my folds, kissing and nibbling and licking every inch of my sex. And it feels incredible. And scary. And also incredible. And really fucking scary. And—

"I got you, Rory," Jaxon rasps.

I lift my head and look down, finding his eyes on me and his mouth hovering above my sex.

"I got you," he repeats. "Take your time. Breathe."

"I'm breathing."

With a smirk, he lowers his mouth, using the flat of his tongue to give me the perfect amount of pressure.

"Breathe," he orders against my sensitive skin before diving in again.

Closing my eyes once more, I lower my head to the pool chair and take a slow, controlled breath. Part of me hates how well he knows me. How easily he could see I was getting lost in my own head. The other part? I guess I'm flattered. That he knows me so well. What I like and don't like. How much I could use an anchor in this moment.

My thighs quiver as he drags his fingers along my slit, pushing them deeper inside of me while rolling the tip of his tongue against my clit.

Uh-huh.

Uh-huh, that's…that's perfect, actually.

I lift my hips slightly, letting him take control while angling my body and giving him better access to…whatever he needs. Whatever he knows will make me come, and boy, do I want to come. Another low groan rumbles against my core as he spreads me wider, eating me like he was put on this earth to do exactly this. Bring me pleasure. And maybe he was because there sure as hell has never been anyone else who makes me feel this way.

I run my fingers through his hair as something builds inside of me. A deep pressure and a strong ache. I can feel it. It's close. So fucking close I can almost taste it. The perfect pressure of his mouth and the perfect rhythm of his fingers. They push me closer and closer to the edge until tingles spread from my pussy and my muscles constrict, shocking the hell out of me. With one last brush of his tongue, I tumble over the edge, coming against Jaxon's mouth until I'm spent beneath him.

Holy shit.

I actually came.

I came on Jaxon's mouth.

Head swimming, I try to catch my breath before realizing how much I've been pulling his hair. Forcing my hold on his head to loosen, I whimper, "Sorry." With a laugh, he rubs at the top of his scalp with his clean hand. You know, the one that *wasn't* inside of me for the last ten minutes. My face floods with embarrassment. "Seriously, I am so sorry."

"Are you kidding me, Beautiful? You could smother me with this pussy, and I'd die a happy man." He licks some of the evidence of my orgasm from his mouth and grins.

"Jaxon!" I squeal, both surprised by and hella attracted to the more carefree side he's showing me. But I guess it makes sense. Orgasming in front of someone does have a way of lowering a few walls and all. "Speaking of dying a happy man, does this mean it's my turn to return the favor?" I reach for him, but he grabs my hands, kissing my knuckles softly.

"Nah. Gotta bask in the afterglow, Beautiful."

"Yeah, but what about your afterglow?" I challenge.

"Trust me, with your taste on my tongue, I'm living the dream." He kisses my knuckles again. "Besides, I want to take things slow."

"Slow, huh?"

"Yeah. I think the real question is, *now*, will you go out with me?"

I fight the urge to cover my face, forcing myself to look him in the eye, even after what we just did. He wants to go out with me? Like, for real?

Praying I don't come off as insecure as I feel, I ask, "You're serious?"

"Of course, I am. I want to take you on a date. Just me and you and…a chance to test the waters."

"Without our families finding out," I add.

He glances around my family's empty backyard. "Not unless they already have."

"They're out of town," I tell him, but it doesn't stop the pink from hitting my cheeks at the possibility of my family witnessing my first steamy encounter with the opposite sex, let alone the man in front of me. "You're, uh, you're safe."

Relief washes over him like the possibility is enough to freak him out, too. With a quiet sigh, he tucks my hair behind my ear. "Good. Because even though I don't regret what we just did, having your family witness it isn't exactly on my bucket list."

I snort, grateful for the way it quiets my insecurities. "Mine either."

Climbing up my body, his smile softens and he kisses my forehead. "Go out with me."

Four words I've dreamed of him using for as long as I can remember, but as they hang in the quiet air between us, I can't help but ask, "You sure?"

"Are you kidding? I've never been more sure of anything in my life."

"That's not what you were saying before we…" I wave my hand toward my still very bare lower half, pulling another low chuckle from him.

"You're not a random hookup, Rore," he promises. "Even if what we did was hot as hell. I wouldn't have crossed this line if I wasn't willing to play things out and see where they lead. What do you think?"

"So, we don't tell anyone." It isn't a question. It's an assumption. A conclusion. Because I get it. The desire to keep things under wraps to soften the fallout if there is one. And considering how closely our lives are tied together, it's probably a wise choice, even if it's a little disappointing.

"For now," he clarifies. It's as if he can taste my reservations and knows they match his own. "This is complicated enough with only two people's opinions and views. Add in our families, and…"

I mimic an explosion with my hands. "Boom."

"Exactly." Taking my fingers again, he entwines them with his. "I don't want to overthink. I want to just…be. Me and you and good food and the possibility of this turning out to be what I think it can."

He wants me. He actually wants me. I don't have to question whether or not the feeling is mutual. I've always been obsessed with him. And I get it. His reasoning. His motive. His desire to see things play out while keeping too many cooks out of the proverbial kitchen.

"Okay," I whisper. "Let's see what happens."

Rory looks beautiful. So much so, it's hard to keep my eyes off her as the host guides us toward a quiet booth at the back of Butter and Grace. She chose a simple sundress that reaches just above her knees and seems to pour gasoline on her already innocent persona. It's different than the dress she chose when she met up with Crowther. A little more fitted and white instead of blue. Fucking perfect. Add in her loose waves, light makeup, and glossy lips, and I'm a goner.

Seriously, should I put myself out of my misery now and kiss the shit out of her before we even make it to the table, or do I let her torture me for a few more hours?

I'm still not sure what we're thinking. Coming here. It's not like I'm a celebrity or have an entourage or some shit. But thanks to the relatively small town vibe and coaching Lockwood Ames University's women's team for years before accepting the Lions' offer, it's not like I fly under the radar. I also don't give a shit. Besides, family friends are allowed to grab a meal together, aren't they?

Fuck, I don't even know anymore.

"I haven't been here in forever," Rory tells me. "Excellent choice, Jax. Thanks for bringing me here."

"No problem."

I debated what we should do for our date for way too fucking long before deciding to take Rory's advice. I'm gonna *not* overthink shit, and we're gonna go with what's comfortable. Butter and Grace is a long time favorite for most of our families, though I'm not very worried about running into them. Maybe I should be. Maybe it's a bad idea. But as long as we don't run into my ex, it should be fine. If she finds out I'm dating anyone, even casually, she'll lose her damn mind. But if our families see us? We can brush it off as a friendly night out, one we'd entertain with any one in our families.

I glance at Rory again. The hem of her dress has me playing peekaboo with her silky thighs as it hikes up a few inches when she scoots into the booth.

Yeah, I definitely wouldn't entertain these kinds of thoughts with any of our other friends. My jaw locks, and I clench my hand to keep from reaching out to smooth out the cotton fabric.

We both order our drinks, and the waitress sets them in front of us minutes later, leaving me alone with Rory and a charged silence I don't know what to do with.

It's not awkward but still holds an unfamiliar weight.

Placing the linen napkin on her lap, Rory peeks up at me, asking, "Is this weird?"

"Not weird."

"You're being quiet," she notes.

She's right. I am, but fuck me, I can't help myself. I'm too distracted, too caught up in the woman across from me. Hell, I can barely think straight, let alone form a coherent sentence.

Get your head out of your ass, I remind myself. She's not a piece of meat.

"You're right." I scratch my jaw. "Sorry, you just look really beautiful tonight."

She hides her shy smile by picking up her glass and stealing a sip of her drink.

"Tell me where you've been the last ten years," I prod, determined to reconcile the woman across from me with the sidekick I grew up with while also hoping the innocent line of questioning will help make her feel comfortable.

She raises a shoulder. "I don't know? Hanging out. Earning my degree. Staying as far away from Lockwood Heights as possible."

"I noticed the last one." I snort. "At least you're honest."

Brow quirked, she licks her pouty lips. "I'm always honest."

"Up front, then," I clarify. "Usually you're one to beat around the bush."

She caves instantly. "Good point."

"What made you choose child psychology?" I ask.

"Oof. Let's see." She hesitates, playing with the straw in her glass. "After everything with Archer and Mav, it almost felt like a no-brainer. I spent years in therapy trying to understand the way my brain works and how to handle my compulsions and my anxiety and...the list goes on and on and on because it's not something that can be fixed, you know?" Her smile turns rueful. "And then one day, I realized I could take all of the time I've spent in therapy and all of the things I've learned to help others with it. Add in how old I was when Archer died, and how different my experience was compared to Mav's or Lia's or yours, and I'm hoping it'll help me relate to kids who have been through trauma in a way that would be beneficial to them. And then, like I said, add in my OCD and anxiety and...I guess it just made sense."

My nod is slow as I process her response. "How are your OCD and anxiety?"

"As good as they can be," she answers. "Neither are ever going away, which I know, but overall, I think I have a pretty good handle on them. Except when I'm lying naked on the bathroom tile with a throbbing shoulder while refusing to go to the hospital, but you know. Pretty good."

I fight my amusement as I take a sip of my drink. The way she owns her shit even when it's hard or could make others feel uncomfortable. I envy it. "I think you're doing great, Rore."

"Thanks." She takes a deep breath, "Since we're broaching the awkward subjects with the whole, *how's your OCD and anxiety going*, I have one."

"Hit me."

"How's your unrealistic desire to be perfect?"

A burst of laughter escapes me, and I reach for my water, chugging down half of it before setting it on the linen-covered table. "Still thriving, I guess."

"And I wouldn't expect anything else from you," she quips. "But for real." Her expression turns cautious. "You doing okay?"

"Is my friend asking or my potential therapist?"

Her mouth twitches. "I saw you crumble from the pressure after the first game of the season. I just want to be sure you're taking care of yourself."

Ever the caregiver. I shouldn't expect anything less.

Swirling the ice in my glass, I answer, "I'm doing my best."

"Of course you are. You never give anything but your best." She reaches beneath the table and touches my knee. "And that's the scary part."

My lungs expand as I fight to hold her gaze. "Trying my best is scary?"

"No, but running at full-throttle without ever taking a second to rest is a recipe for burnout. Do you know what that means?"

Despite feeling like I'm being scolded by my mom, I appreciate her candor and how she feels safe enough to tell me something I don't want to hear. Leaning forward, I lace my fingers in front of me. "What does it mean, Rore?"

"It means your best stops being your best, and there's a reason greatness is treasured instead of tossed around like little pieces of candy."

"Pretty sure you're jumping around with the metaphors," I note.

"Pretty sure I'm allowed since it's my degree and all."

I snort. "Cop-out."

"A hundred percent," she agrees with a grin. "What do you like to do for fun?"

"Fun?"

"Oh, come on, don't act like you never have any fun."

I squeeze the back of my neck, playing shy. "I mean, since it's been so long and all…"

Her grin widens as she swirls the straw in her glass. "Care if I take a stab at it?"

"Go ahead."

"When I was young, you'd take me miniature golfing, like, all the time. Are you still a fan?"

Miniature golf? I search my memory for the last time I went to the local putt-putt course before realizing the truth, no matter how pathetic it is. "Damn, I'm pretty sure I haven't been golfing since I was with you."

"Really?" She sits a little taller and rests her chin in her hands, though I don't miss the slight tinge of pink in her cheeks.

Does she like that? Knowing my last experience of something—no matter how many years it's been—was with her? Fuck, if the roles were reversed, I'd be happy as hell.

"Yeah, really," I confirm, sobering. "Didn't feel like going after how everything ended. What about you?"

She shakes her head. "Haven't been since then, either."

My brows raise, and my chest puffs up with satisfaction. "No shit?"

She nods. "One guy tried to take me my freshman year of college, but I couldn't pick the right putter without feeling like I was going to have a panic attack, so he dropped it and took me home."

Ignoring my unfounded jealousy at the idea of a guy taking her out years ago, I force a laugh and ask, "What was wrong with all the putters?"

"I don't know?" She laughs. "That's the funny part. They didn't feel...right." She grimaces. "They were either too long or the grip was torn or the color was wrong or..."

"Still got a thing for colors, huh?" I conclude.

Gaze narrowing, she flicks the straw wrapper at me. "Maybe."

"You know all putters are the same size if you're using the miniature-golf owned ones," I point out, unable to help myself as I pour more salt in the wound. It's only because I know she'd rather put up with my teasing than pretend like her OCD doesn't exist at all.

"Whatever." Flipping her long, ash-blonde hair over her shoulder, she rolls her eyes. "They were different, and I stand by that."

"Of course you do," I chuckle again. "So, what do you say? Wanna play nine holes?"

"Of miniature golf?"

"Yeah."

Taking a sip of her fruity cocktail, she eyes me over the rim before licking her lips and setting it down. "All right. I'm in," she decides.

"Really?"

"Yeah? What's the worst that can happen?"

"The putters are too long or the grips have holes or the color is wrong?" I offer.

She reaches across the table, smacking my shoulder. "Keep it up, and I'll shove my putter up your ass."

"Ouch." My amusement reaches a new pitch, and I settle back into my side of the booth. "I thought I was the one filling your holes, not the other way around."

"Jax!" Her hand connects with my shoulder again, though the mirth dancing in her eyes, only eggs me on even more.

And honestly, it's refreshing. Being able to joke with someone who understands my sense of humor. Hell, it's freeing. And addictive. So much so I can't help but add, "Unless you're a fan of filling other men's holes. And hey, I'm not one to judge. Guess I just figured that since you're a..."

My mouth snaps closed as I realize exactly what I was about to let slip before searching for a way to backpedal. The last thing I would ever want is for someone to feel stupid about their experience, or lack thereof.

The unease I was hoping to prevent swallows her amusement as she stares at me, her drink forgotten. "Since I'm a... *what*, Jax?"

"Nothing." I clear my throat. "We should probably order."

"No deal." Reaching for my hand, she keeps me from opening the menu. Her hand looks so small compared to mine. I could pull away with ease. But I won't. Because I like the way she touches me. The way I feel it everywhere. Hell, it's like she knows how to reach right into my chest and squeeze.

"Tell me," she says.

Tearing my attention from her hand, I hold her gaze. "You said you're a virgin, Rore. And there's nothing wrong with it. Honestly, I feel bad for even insinuating that being innocent is something to be ashamed of, okay? I was teasing, but it still came out wrong, and that's on me. I screwed up."

She tilts her head, watching me but not saying anything. And her silence? It only feeds my regret.

"Rore—"

"I feel like I should make something clear."

"You don't have to—"

"Just because I'm innocent doesn't mean I want to stay that way."

Then how the hell does a girl like her still have her v-card if she hasn't been determined to keep it?

The question sits on the tip of my tongue, but I stop myself from voicing it aloud. Why fuck up twice in less than five minutes? I'm an idiot, but I'm not *that* dense.

Even so, it's like she can read my mind because she explains, "I never found a guy who made me want to be… curious enough to be…scandalous or whatever." The tip of her tongue plays peekaboo as she wets her lips. "They weren't you."

Her words, her expression, the brightening tinge of pink as it spreads along her neck. It all mingles together, making my dick harden and my mind run wild with fantasies. Of me and her and this table. All of it. Add in her lack of experience, and I'm pretty sure I could blow a load in my pants right here. Right now.

"Did I just make things awkward?" she whispers. Her attention drifts around the crowded restaurant as if each and every other customer knows exactly what we're talking about. "I'm sorry—"

"Never apologize for telling a guy you're interested in that they make you curious about your sexuality. Never."

She licks her lips again but forces herself to nod.

"That's my girl. Now, let's order some dinner, because after?" I smirk. "We have a game to play."

∿

SHE WASN'T KIDDING. CLEARLY, THE WOMAN HASN'T PLAYED A game of miniature golf in years. Her stance is all wrong, she's hit the ball completely off the green at least three times, and she insisted we stop keeping score after one too many triple bogeys. Honestly? I've never felt happier.

The ease of not keeping score. The lackadaisical response to every screw up. The banter and flirty looks and easy conversation. It's both familiar and new in a way I can't even explain. All I know is I like it. I like it a lot.

When we head toward the last hole, a bathroom comes into view and Rory announces, "I need to use the restroom. Give me two seconds."

"Take your time," I return.

Waving on two more couples to play through, I pull out my phone to see if Iris felt like sending any photos of our daughter—she didn't—when a pair of panties drops on my screen. Jerking back, I look up and find Rory grinning at me. The same familiar twitch in my jeans manages to catch me off guard as I grab the underwear, shoving them into my pocket before anyone notices. It doesn't matter how quickly I try to make the evidence of Rory's lack of clothing beneath her sundress disappear. I still feel the dampness of her curiosity on my palm.

She was wet. She's still wet.

I tilt my head. "What are you doing?"

"Being curious." Clutching her fingers behind her back, she rises onto her tiptoes and waits. The combination somehow manages to make her look even more tempting and innocent than before as her breasts strain against the thin cotton of her dress. "Is that a problem, Mr. Thorne?"

"Rory…" I look around the crowded course, then back to the woman in front of me. She's seriously testing my self-control, and if I'm not careful, I just might out our…whatever this is to everyone in the vicinity before we've even had a chance to thoroughly test the waters. The question is, how do I play this? How does she want me to play this?

As if she can read my questioning gaze, she adds, "Just to be clear. There's only one right answer. If you give me the wrong one, I'll run out of this place, call a cab, and never talk to you again."

Yeah, like my restraint has anything to do with me not wanting her. The idea alone is laughable. She's gorgeous. Sweet. And ripe for the picking.

Shifting closer, I murmur, "The path on the other side of this hole leads to an abandoned ice cream stand where we might be able find some—"

"Jaxon?" someone calls.

Rory's eyes bulge as the blood drains from her face. Hell, it probably matches my own expression, all things considered. I glance over my shoulder, confirming my suspicion.

Shit.

I knew I recognized that voice.

Pressing my hand to my pocket and what I know is tucked inside, I face my dad and give him a smile. "Hey, Dad. What are you doing here?"

"Thought we'd give Griffin and Finley a date night," my mom answers for him while rocking side to side with a baby strapped to her chest. If the plume of dark hair is anything to go by, I'd say it's a sleeping Callie. A few feet away stands my nephew who's wielding his putter like it's a lightsaber.

"Charge!" he yells.

My dad blocks a potential blow to his shin. "What are you guys doing here?"

Macky swings the putter again. "Gonna get you!"

"Why don't you go get your uncle instead?" my dad suggests.

Macky's eyes light up, and he rushes toward me, his putter held high above his head. "Expelliarmust!" he yells.

I manage to dart out of his path at the last second before grabbing his little wrist and lifting him into the air, swinging him around.

"Wrong franchise, young Padawan," my dad jokes, rolling his eyes at Rory. "Dylan's boys have been rubbing off on him. Can you tell?"

With a light laugh, Rory smooths down the edge of her white dress, probably trying to make sure her bare ass stays covered, and replies, "Yeah, if it's a Harry Potter reference, then it's definitely Reeves' family's fault."

"Don't I know it," my mom quips. "So? What are you guys doing here? You don't have Poppy, do you?"

"Not this week," I answer, praying there are no follow-up questions because I have no idea what to say if either of my parents point out that I'm here with a certain someone who's wanted nothing to do with me for around a decade. Yeah, most people in this town would buy the whole family friend excuse. But our families? Not so much.

"Oh." My mom's attention darts from me to Rory and back again. "Okay?"

All right, maybe a follow-up question or two would've been more appropriate. Because the awkward silence enveloping us? Yeah, it's something else. Why would I be here with Rory? Why would I be here *alone* with Rory? What the fuck are we supposed to say? I knew it was a risk to take her on a date, but I didn't think—

"Actually." Rory clears her throat. "We were interviewing a few potential nannies and wanted to see if they knew how to have fun, so we brought them to play miniature golf, but then they bailed, and we figured, why not play a round ourselves for old time's sake, right?"

My teeth dig into the inside of my cheek to keep from laughing or admitting defeat right here and now. Is she serious? She really went with interviewing nannies as our reason for being here? At a miniature golf place? Before they *bailed*? She might as well tattoo her forehead with, *Liar, liar, pants on fire*, at this point. Then again, she is missing her panties. No wonder she's spooked. Even so, the woman can't think my parents are this delusional. Can she?

"Interviewing *here*?" my dad asks. He looks about as confused as Tatum is whenever hockey is a topic of conversation. "Why would you—"

"She's kidding," I interrupt.

Rory squeaks beside me, and it takes everything inside of me to keep from shooting her a warning look to stop being so damn obvious.

"Crowther has a thing for miniature golf," I continue, "and Rory asked if I could coach her on a few holes so she doesn't get her ass handed to her."

"Ass is a bad word," my nephew chimes in, still resting on my hip while eavesdropping like a pro.

Shit, despite holding him, I'd almost forgotten he's here.

I set the little tyke back on the ground, and he rushes off to his grandpa with his putter pointed directly at the man's crotch. It seems the light saber slash wizard wand is now a lance, and my dad's junk is about to be impaled by the damn thing in an impromptu jousting session.

My dad blocks the attempt before Macky does any real damage and shakes his head. "Aaaand, no more knight books for you," he announces. "Anyway, Crowther's a good guy. I heard about his mom, though. It's a shame."

"His mom?" Rory interjects.

"Your dad was telling me they just found out her cancer's back," my dad explains. "I think he's taking a leave of absence for a few games so he can be with her?"

Macky wiggles in my dad's arms. "Potty now. Potty now."

"And that's our cue," he tells me. "Come on, little man. Let's use the restroom so we can finish the game, yeah?"

Grasping Macky's shoulders, my dad turns my nephew around and begins guiding him toward the bathroom. "Have fun, you two!"

"Wait! Let me hold the golf equipment while you go in," my mom adds, trailing after them.

"It was good seeing you," Rory calls.

My mom gives her a quick smile over shoulder while patting Callie's bottom through the carrier. "Good seeing you, too, Rore. Love the dress. Nice and breezy in this warm weather."

Rory's cheeks redden even more as she crosses one ankle in front of the other. "Thanks. Bye!"

Once they've rounded the corner, she snatches my hand and drags me as far away from the course as possible. And even though I don't blame her for wanting to get the hell out of dodge, I can't hide my rumble of amusement as she tugs at the hem of her dress, confirming the breeze isn't getting out of hand.

33

RORY

"So…" A pebble skitters across the asphalt as we make our way back to Jaxon's truck. I shouldn't replay the conversation. I *really* shouldn't replay the conversation. But I can't help it. I love Aunt Ashlyn and Uncle Colt. Seeing them always brightens my day, but apparently, lack of undergarments will put a damper on even the lightest of situations. The real question is…how the hell am I supposed to ever face them again after a stunt like this?

"You good, Rore?" Jaxon asks beside me.

"Do you think they bought it?" I grimace. "The lie?"

"Which one?" Jaxon teases.

With a groan, I cover my eyes with my hand as if I wield the power to shut out the world in its entirety. "Don't remind me."

We both lied tonight. Both tried to cover our tracks, thanks to the agreement we made in my backyard before he went down on me. Bloody hell, I still can't believe he went down on me. Or that he asked me on a date afterward. It shouldn't have surprised me, but it did. The idea of him wanting to spend time with me and not only my body.

He's right for wanting to take things slow, though. To keep this quiet until we're both sure what we feel is more than physical attraction. And yes, I might love the guy both inside and out, but when my sexual experience can be counted on one hand with one person, I don't want to rush into anything, either. Not unless we're both sure. I've been connecting with him emotionally for years. But for Jaxon? I'm afraid this is new. So new, it'll freak him out, and he'll run in the opposite direction.

"I always knew you were a terrible liar," Jaxon adds.

"I knoooow." I drag out the word and tilt my head toward the darkening sky. "I cannot believe I honestly said we were there to interview a nanny. For a baby. At a miniature golf course."

Jaxon chuckles dryly. "Yeah, I'm not gonna lie. Not your best work, Beautiful."

Beautiful.

It isn't the first time he's used the term with me, but I'm not sure I'll ever get used to it. Hearing Jaxon Thorne call me beautiful.

Heat builds in my cheeks as I replay the sexy way it rolls off his tongue before attempting to focus on the shit show we just experienced.

"I kind of feel bad," I admit. "You know, how we lied and all. Not that I want to come out and tell everyone we're having fun together, but…"

"I get it," he returns. "I feel bad, too."

"Yeah." My face scrunches. "Add in that I'm a terrible liar, and I feel like this is a recipe for disaster."

"Nah, you did good."

"Now who's the liar?"

With a smirk, he tosses back at me, "Now who's the over-thinker?"

My eyes thin, but I don't bother responding, knowing he's

not wrong. I am an overthinker. Always have been. Probably always will be. Especially when it comes to all things Jaxon Thorne. Am I crazy to think things were going well before his family showed up? I felt like we were…connecting. It was almost like the good ol' days, except for when I'd catch him staring at my legs or mouth. Yeah, those parts are new. I like them, though.

When we reach his truck, he opens the passenger door for me like it's second nature. "Here you go."

Peeking up at him, I whisper, "Thanks."

"Anytime." He offers his hand, and I take it, using it as leverage before sliding into the passenger seat, and holy hell, could I get lost in those eyes.

Tucking my hair behind my ear while trying to keep my libido in check, I add, "And I feel bad about Eric."

"Me, too. Your dad sent me a text earlier. Crowther's gonna miss a few games but promised to keep the higher-ups in the loop."

"That's good."

He nods. "Yeah."

"You're not going to be too hard on him, right?" I add. "What with the whole banquet thing."

"Depends." He looks around the parking lot, then leans in and kisses my cheek. "You gonna tell him you're just friends?"

With a laugh, I roll my eyes and shove him playfully. "Depends. Are you gonna keep treating me like a yo-yo every time we kiss, Mr. Hot-and-Cold?"

"Ouch." He backs away, but before the door closes fully, he tosses something between the gap. It lands on my lap, feeling lighter than a feather. My face flames even more when I realize what it is. My. Freaking. Underwear. This is what I get for trying to be spontaneous and sexy. Enough shame to last me a lifetime. As I tuck the flimsy material under my thigh, Jaxon climbs into the driver's seat, giving me a smirk that makes me want to turn into a puddle.

"I'm not sure why you find this so hilarious," I point out. "One small breeze, and your family would've seen a lot more than they should."

"You mean, the breeze my mom pointed out?" Mirth dances in his eyes as he rests his forearm along the top of the steering wheel. "It'd almost be worth it just to see how you'd react."

"You're so funny." I give him a mock glare. "You wanna know who else is funny, though? Eric. Maybe I should give him another call. See when he wants to go on the miniature golf date you mentioned to your parents."

The curve of his mouth shoots straight toward the ground. "Now look who's being funny." Reaching over the center console, he squeezes my bare thigh.

I jolt in response. "Don't you dare tickle me—"

His laugh cuts me off as he squeezes me again. "I forgot how ticklish you can be."

The sound of my hand smacking his rings through the air. "So help me, Jaxon—"

"I'll play nice," he promises.

"Liar!"

"Don't you trust me?" He stops squeezing but keeps his hand planted on my leg. It's a dare. A game. A test.

My eyes narrow in suspicion, but I don't pull away. Not yet. Not unless he betrays me.

"See?" Slowly, he glides his thumb up and down along my inner thigh. "Nice."

And it's crazy. How a simple touch manages to burrow deep and drive me insane, making me oh-so-aware of all things Jaxon. Including the invisible string seemingly tied around his thumb, connected straight to my libido. And here he is, tugging on it with an easy brush of his fingertips.

As I shift in the seat, my attention darts to the windshield. "We're still in the parking lot," I breathe out.

"And you're still not wearing underwear." His fingers dance along my outer thigh, bringing the light fabric of my dress with them.

Inch after not-so-innocent inch, I stare at his calloused hand on my leg as he moves it higher and higher. "Jaxon." It's a warning.

"Tell me to stop."

Heat builds in my core as I consider the man himself instead of what he's doing to me. The subtle clench of his jaw. The slight part of his lips. The dark sheen of his eyes trailing from my own gaze to my mouth. He's right. I could tell him to stop. I could remind him that his parents are less than a football field away and could catch us. I could beg him to take me home where we have a semblance of privacy. But the idea of ending it. Of letting whatever's in this truck fizzle into nothing. It feels like a waste. A waste of perfectly good, and achingly promising, curiosity. And damn, am I curious.

Pressing my lips together, I lean my head against the headrest, my gaze never wavering.

"Part your thighs," he rasps.

I shift my hips forward and do as I'm told, spreading them ever so slightly. His chest heaves in appreciation, and his fingers dig into my thigh before dancing along my skin, and disappearing beneath the hem of my dress. I'm not stupid. I knew I wouldn't wake up the morning after he went down on me, suddenly immune to the way he makes me feel. But I figured I'd at least be a little more familiar with what to expect and how to react. I was wrong. Very wrong. Instead, I feel just as on edge and curious as before. It's still so new. Still makes every touch feel like it's the first time, even if it's the second. I think a not-so-small part of me knows I'll feel the rush no matter how many times we play this game and explore each other. How many times we touch or kiss or feel. The realization is a scary thing, but I'm too turned on to analyze it.

With his knuckles, Jaxon brushes along my entrance.

A gasp escapes me.

"So fuckin' sensitive." He glances out the window, then shifts a little closer in his seat.

"Jax—"

"Love it when you say my name." His lips bruise mine as he kisses me hard. But his fingers? His fingers maintain their gentle teasing until I'm restless and needy.

"Jax," I repeat. It's a plea. Not for him to stop, but for him to keep going. To touch me the way I know he can. And I know he hears it, too. The neediness in my voice.

His dark lashes flutter as he presses his forehead to mine. "You want my fingers, Beautiful?"

I nod. "Please."

His hand cups my sex as I spread myself even more in the front seat, rotating my hips against him. Then, he dips his finger between my folds. Drawing a slow circle along my entrance, he pushes inside. With another quiet gasp, I dig my fingers into his forearm, unsure if I want to push him away or pull him closer.

"That's it, Beautiful." He adds a second finger, stretching me a little more.

It burns, but only a little. Or maybe I'm so distracted by the gentle pressure against my clit that the slight pain doesn't even matter as I shift against his hand. I'm not sure, and honestly, I don't care. I just want...more. More of this. Me and him and his hands and his mouth. Seriously, his mouth was the hottest thing ever. The things he can do to me with that thing are—

"You should see yourself right now," he murmurs. "The way your cheeks are flushed. The way I can almost hear your moans, though you're too stubborn to let them loose."

"We're in public," I remind him, though it comes out as a whimper.

He smirks and goes in for another kiss. "We could be surrounded by people, and I still wouldn't stop."

Why is that so hot? The idea of people watching what he does to me. How he makes me feel. Maybe it's because I spent so much time watching him from afar. That I always wondered what it would be like to be the center of his attention. To know that others can look from the outside in, the same way I did for years, but no one... No. One. Can do what he does to me.

Please let the feeling be mutual.

"Jaxon." I squeeze my eyes shut in an attempt to block out the world until there's only me and him, even if it's just for a little while.

"Don't worry." He circles my entrance, then presses his thumb against my clit. "The only person who gets to see you like this is me. *Ever*," he growls as his fingers continue thrusting in and out of me.

And maybe it's his words. The idea of him wanting to be the only person who ever sees me like this. The idea of him being the only person to ever make me feel this way. It's enough to make me shatter into a million pieces, well aware he's the only one who can make me feel this way. Act this way. Be this way. Wanton and careless. Reckless. Needy.

I can feel it. The need. With every sweep of his touch, it builds at my core, bringing me higher and higher until I squeeze my eyes shut even tighter and push into his hold, not giving a shit about what's going on outside this car. Only the way he's making me feel in this moment. Seen. Appreciated.

"That's it, Beautiful. I can feel how tight you are. How

much you want this. My fingers inside of you." He bends closer over the center console. "Want to know a secret? Just wait 'til it's my cock."

Falling apart at his words, I come against his fingers as he swallows my moans with his mouth, kissing me with so much fervor I could come again if he keeps doing this. Sweat beads along my hairline, and my breath comes out in unsteady pants as I slowly force my eyes open, fighting against the embarrassment threatening to take hold.

I cannot believe we did that. In his freaking truck.

With a small smile, he pulls his fingers from between my thighs and brings them to his mouth. "Told you I could be nice."

A laugh slips out of me before I can stop it. I playfully shove him back to his side of the truck. "You're ridiculous." My head hits the headrest again, and I sigh. "And also really good at that finger thing."

His low chuckle is raspy and light, and I swear I can feel him looking at me, but I don't open my eyes to check. I'm too busy basking in the afterglow of a seriously good orgasm.

"Mmm," I hum. "You know, if I smoked, I'd say this is a perfect time to light up." I peel my eyes open and roll my head toward him. "Isn't that what they do in the movies? Either that or..." I hesitate, sneaking a peek at his groin area where a massive bulge is outlined. "Return the favor? Because I'm pretty sure I owe you two times now."

He shifts forward in the seat, blocking my clear view of his arousal. "You don't owe me anything."

"Jax—"

"The opportunity to touch you already makes me feel like the luckiest bastard on the planet."

It's a compliment, but it's also only a half-truth. I can see it in his eyes. "But I'm not allowed to touch you?" I challenge.

"You can touch me anytime you want, though I have a feeling we've already pushed our luck in the parking lot."

I glance around the area, grateful it's still relatively empty even if the man makes a good point. "Then you should take me somewhere," I decide.

"Rore."

"Jax."

"I don't want to pressure you."

"You're not."

"I'm not?"

"No, you're not, I promise."

He doesn't look convinced, but he does cave, muttering, "Good."

"Good," I toss back at him.

"So, now that we both agree I'm not pressuring you..." His lips curve up on one side as if he's fighting back his smirk. "I believe you mentioned you're a terrible liar."

Fighting my blush—because I most definitely am a terrible liar—I hold onto my sass and say, "And?"

"And it got me curious...have you told anyone? About me and you?"

I shake my head.

"Not a soul?" he pushes. "Not even...Tatum?"

Tatum? Did he really have to call me out so blatantly? I mean, it's Tatum. Of course, I told her. Unable to hide the truth, my face bunches, and I roll my head forward, letting my light hair block me from his view.

With a bellow of laughter, he says, "I knew it!"

I smack his chest. "Oh, shush. You know nothing—"

He grasps my wrist. "I know I like you."

He likes me?

He *likes* me.

He likes *me*.

My stupid heart skips a beat as his confession hangs

between us, and I fight to hold his gaze. Because I get it now. The difference. When I was younger, he never looked at me like this. I mean, he looked at me. But before, it was so… platonic, I guess? Genuine, definitely. But now, there's a sprinkle of something else. Something more. Something that turns the butterflies into a giant albatross, and I can't help but feel…lucky. Lucky that, even though it was a bumpy as hell ride, we still somehow found ourselves here. Like this. Now, I'm not stupid enough to believe he's going to propose next week or something. We haven't even voiced our wants and needs for whatever this is. But that sprinkling of actual *intimate* interest? The fact it matches my own thoughts and feelings that I've kept buried for as long as I can remember? I like it. I like it a lot.

"Nothing to say, Beautiful?" Jaxon prods. "Do I need to go back on the whole not pressuring you part? Am I coming on too strong?"

"Not at all," I rush out. "Just trying to piece together past Jaxon and current Jaxon and the way you're looking at me right now."

His gaze softens even more. "And how am I looking at you?"

"Like you like me," I answer.

The same curve of his lips spreads over his handsome features. "I mean, I did just tell you I like you."

"I know." I take a deep breath. "And I, uh, I like you, too. Which you already knew, but…"

"It's nice to hear it out loud every once in a while," he murmurs. A warmth hits his gaze, making it hard to breathe.

"And I'm sorry I told Tate," I add.

"Don't be." He brings my hand to his mouth and kisses my knuckles just like when he touched me in my parents' back-yard. "I like that you have someone to tell. Someone you trust."

"What about you?" I prod. "Do you have someone you trust?"

He lifts a shoulder and pulls out of the parking spot. "To be honest, the only person I've ever fully trusted with something like this is…" His eyes cut to mine. "You."

And damn, if it isn't the sweetest thing he's ever said.

I haven't seen Jax since he dropped me off after our date. Despite asking him to take me somewhere else so I could return the favor, he took me home, announcing that he had to be up early the next morning for a flight. And even though I knew it was the truth, it didn't ease my disappointment. This whole sexual awakening is kind of fun, and I've been dying to get my hands on him the same way he's had his hands—and mouth—on me.

The downtime has been weird, too. Staying home while he travels with the team. But since it was still Iris's week with Poppy, I had no choice but to stay in Lockwood Heights and twiddle my thumbs, watching Jaxon in action through the television instead of in person. Now that we're kind of seeing each other, and I'm not mad at him anymore like I was during the first home game, I've learned I definitely prefer being at the arena.

He's texted me though. A lot, actually. And it's been fun. Reconnecting and flirting and being open in a way we've never been before. Tatum told me it's probably a good thing. That we've had some distance. We can test the waters while still connecting and taking the physical side of things a little slower than I'd probably like and he probably needs.

She might be onto something, though I refuse to admit it to her. The woman's head is already big enough, thank you very much.

He got back yesterday, though I haven't seen him yet. Thanks to Jaxon's busy schedule with the Lions, and Iris's penchant for not accommodating said busy schedule, here I am in Jaxon's penthouse, waiting for Iris to drop Poppy off, so I can take her to the Lions' home game.

I've decided sharing a kid seems like a pain in the butt. Especially when the person you're sharing the child with has no understanding of what being on time actually means.

I check the time on my phone again and wipe down the counter in hopes of feeling useful. She's an hour and half late. Normally, it wouldn't be a huge deal, but Jaxon asked if I was planning to bring Poppy to the game when he gave me the instructions for getting into his penthouse, and there's no way we're going to be able to make it if Iris doesn't get here soon.

Thirty minutes later, I give in and text Jaxon, telling him the crappy news, though I doubt he'll see it since the game has already started, and he always leaves his phone in his office during games.

Reaching for the remote, I turn on the game when the elevator's buzzer sounds. She's here! I skip toward the panel, hit accept, and allow the elevator to come to the penthouse.

I stand at the entrance folding my arms, then tucking my thumbs into the back pockets of my jeans before grabbing my wrist and, yup. It's official. I'm the most awkward person on the planet.

Seconds later, the elevator doors slide open, and Hades barks beside me. "Hades, hush," I order.

With a low grumble, he plops his butt down on the

ground, staring at a very displeased Iris with a car seat on her arm.

Despite working for Jaxon for a couple weeks, Iris and I have barely said two words to each other. Not that I blame her. She didn't hire me. Jax did. But since Jaxon isn't here, it seems she has no choice and is less than thrilled at the prospect of interacting with "the help."

Her irritated gaze flicks over me with enough disdain to make me squirm before her attention lands on Hades. Being the excellent judge of character he usually is, he growls low in his throat but doesn't stand, proving he's more annoyed than anything.

Join the club, buddy.

"Sorry, it's nothing personal," I tell her. "He doesn't like… people."

Her lips purse. "And yet he's around my daughter twenty-four-seven."

Yikes. I didn't think about that. How Hades acting like an asshole might affect Iris's perception of him in general.

Determined to put her mind at ease, I rush out, "Don't worry. He loves Poppy. I can even send you videos of them together so you can see it for yourself. They are so cute."

Ignoring me, Iris sets Poppy's car seat on the kitchen counter, then checks the time on her phone. "Tell Jaxon I need her a day early."

A day early? She wants Poppy a day early after basically dropping her off an entire day late? The woman has to be joking. We're missing Jaxon's game because of her ineptitude. Yeah, her request is problematic on a few levels. Besides, there's no way the timeline will work, regardless of my petti-ness to keep things fair. The Lions have two away games this week, so we won't be back in Lockwood Heights by then. But is it my job to defend Jaxon's time with his daughter, let alone fill his ex in on the potential constraints and unreasonable expectations of her request?

Crap, I don't know.

She starts to turn back to the elevator, but my impulsiveness gets the best of me. "I actually think we'll still be in Houston, so I'm not sure that'll work."

"I'm sure Jaxon will figure it out," Iris retorts. Then she walks into the elevator, barely looking up from her phone as the doors close seconds later.

Welp. So much for defending Jaxon's time with Poppy. I tried.

"Yowza," I mumble under my breath. Shaking off the willies from our interaction, I undo Poppy from her car seat and plant a loud, smacking kiss against her cheek. "Why, hello, Pops. Should we see how your daddy's doing?" I pick her up when the strong smell of poop punches me in the face. How long has she been sitting with a soiled bum? I sigh, deciding not to go down that particular path. It'll only stir the pot and piss me off. "Speaking of yowza," I repeat. "You, my love, need a diaper change."

WHILE THE LIONS' GAME PLAYS IN THE BACKGROUND, WE HANG out reading stories, practicing tummy time, which she's already a pro at, and feeding Hades snacks from the high chair. Yup. It's official. He's a big fan of yogurt melts, and I'm a big fan of watching Poppy drop them on the ground or hang her tiny arm over the edge of the high chair so Hades can steal it directly from her little fingers. And getting paid to play with her confirms my sneaking suspicion that being a nanny is the best job on the planet. Seriously, every time I'm with this little girl only makes me want to be a mom even more. The way Poppy lights up when I make a funny face at her. The way she reaches for me and flaps her little arms at Hades. I'm in heaven.

Or at least, I was until the final buzzer rings out through the speakers, announcing the end of the game.

The Lions lost. One to zero. It was a rough one. With a frown, I turn off the television, my body weighing heavier than moments ago. I can only imagine how frustrated Jaxon must feel. Part of me wants to text him to ask how he's doing and to tell him he's still a badass and he'll get them next time. If he was anyone else, I would. But I know it won't help. Instead, I send the video from earlier of Poppy dropping a yogurt melt on the ground and Hades gobbling it up, hoping it'll brighten his mood. After, I turn on some music, then get to work making dinner while taking dancing breaks every few minutes with a certain little girl who's a big fan of Disney music. I'm not sure how much time passes, but the beef is browned and seasoned, the veggies are cut, and the guacamole is prepped. Satisfied, I wash my hands and pick up Poppy again. Spinning her around, I belt out the lyrics of "Let it Go" as Hades pads across the family room toward a waiting Jaxon.

Shit!

Clutching Poppy to my chest, I say, "And this is why I have a dog. How long have you been here?"

"The elevator opened two seconds ago." He tilts his head. "What are you guys doing?"

"Well, we *were* dancing, and now I'm having a heart attack."

"Of course," he rumbles with a ghost of a smile.

Or maybe I'm imagining it.

I take him in, searching for clues as to how he's handling the loss. His biceps bulge as he keeps his arms crossed over his chest, his shoulder resting against the wall. That same subtle lift of his lips teases me, and his eyes don't look quite as dark as usual. He seems…lighter than the last time—and sober, which is a win.

Determined to not ruin it, I continue our little dance. I sway Poppy back and forth, then let go of her hand and cradle her head, folding at the waist and dipping her like I would if we were in the throes of a tango. When I stand again, I keep her close to my chest, continuing our little dance as Jaxon watches us from just outside the elevator.

"She likes dancing," he murmurs.

I grin. "Mm-hmm. Dancing, cooking, and feeding Hades." I shimmy us toward the kitchen. "Pops and I made tacos."

"Tacos, huh?"

"Mm-hmm," I repeat. "I thought it might be fun for Poppy to try guacamole." I grin. "Are you hungry?"

"Starving." He pushes himself away from the wall and strides toward us, kissing Poppy's forehead before his gaze strays to me, and I know what he's thinking. Whether or not he should do the same to me. Would that be weird? Would it not? We haven't really seen each other since he dropped me off after our date. Now here I am, in his house while holding his daughter.

"Here. Take her," I offer. "I'll dish you up."

I start to hand her over to him, but instead of grabbing her, he wraps his arms around us both, swaying us to the music. And it's…strange. Because in my head, I know it should be strange. But it doesn't feel strange. It feels…really good, actually. Does that make sense? Probably not, but it doesn't stop the feeling from washing over me.

"I thought you were starving," I note.

He nods and dips closer, kissing me with a gentleness I can feel all the way down to my toes. It's so sweet and innocent, it makes me feel like I've been transported to an alternate universe or something. Like this life belongs to someone else.

Someone who's a stay-at-home mom with a baby girl and a white picket fence and a ring on her finger. My eyelids flutter as I force myself to stay in reality. My reality. This reality. One that might not be quite as sweet, yet just as promising. Maybe. Possibly. Hopefully. I clear my throat and wiggle out of his hold, handing him Poppy. "Here. I've been dying to see her reaction."

"To what?" he asks.

"I'll show you." Opening the fridge, I find a small bowl with smashed avocado and a wedge of lime. "I read that babies Poppy's age can try guacamole. Want to see what she thinks?"

Twisting her around so her back is to his front, he gives me better access to feed her. "Hell, yeah. Let's see what you think, Pops."

A baby spoon is already on the counter, so I scoop up a bit of the guacamole, offering it to Poppy. When she opens her mouth, I spoon it in and hold my breath, curious to see her reaction. Her lips bunch and she smacks her tongue against the roof of her mouth, tasting the smashed avocado as if she can't decide whether or not it's a win. The reaction only lasts a second before she wiggles closer, her body jittering with excitement as she reaches for the spoon in my hand. Clearly, someone's enjoying her first hit of Mexican goodness.

Jaxon's low, rumbly laugh mingles with mine as he asks, "You think she likes it?"

"I'll take her reaction as a yes," I quip. "Want to see how she feels about lime?"

Another rumble of amusement rolls through him. "Yeah, let's see it."

Setting the spoon aside, I lift the lime and she opens her mouth again, excited as ever. I glide the wedge against her tongue, barely holding in my enthusiasm. Her nose crinkles, and a shiver races down her spine, pulling another laugh from both of us.

"Okay, so no on the lime," I note. Scooping up another bite of avocado, I offer it to her so she can get rid of the sour flavor as quickly as possible. She takes the bite, settling back in Jaxon's arms like she's the happiest little girl in the world. Then again, it's guacamole. Of course she's the happiest little girl in the world. We stay this way, hanging out in the kitchen while catching up on our time apart, as well as how the drop-off with Iris went, until Poppy has a full belly and a mustache of avocado, refried beans, and applesauce. Jaxon wipes the dinner from Poppy's face, then balances her on his knee at the dinner table as I dish us both up.

After setting a taco salad in front of him, because there's no way he's going to be able to pick up an actual taco shell without Poppy trying to grab at it, I take the seat next to him. "Bon appetit."

"Thank you," he says.

"You're welcome."

"I mean it. Thank you."

Sensing his sincerity, I hesitate. "It's only dinner, but you're welcome."

"And for dealing with Iris. And for the video. I, uh, it was a hard loss, but the video." He looks up from Poppy and meets my gaze. "It was a good reminder of what's important. So, thanks." He leans closer, balancing Poppy, and kisses me again, tasting like cumin and garlic.

I smile against his mouth. "I'm glad I could help."

35
JAXON

I didn't think it was possible. Being more attracted to Rory than I already was. But seeing her dance with Poppy in the middle of my penthouse was a fucking wake-up call. One I'm not sure I wanted or was ready for, but now that I've seen it, felt it, tasted it, it's messed with my head. Made me want things I didn't know I could. Even brought me out of the darkness from the Lions' loss. Add in how good she tasted sprawled out on my bed as I ate her pussy like a starving man after I put Poppy to bed, and I was a fucking goner.

She wanted to reciprocate, but Poppy woke up, saving me from turning her down, and fuck if it wasn't the best decision I've ever made. Not because I don't want her, but sitting across from her father is hard enough now that I know what she tastes like. Feels like.

Fuck.

If she'd actually touched me. Given me her hand, her mouth, her sweet pussy, I'm pretty sure I would've started confessing like a sinner in church as soon as I entered the boardroom.

"Jaxon?" Henry prods.

Shit.

Talk about getting caught with your pants down.

"I'm sorry?" I choke out.

"What are your thoughts on the way Skanchy played last night?" Henry clarifies.

I blink away the view of Rory with her legs spread beneath me and shift forward, scratching my jaw while praying Henry can't see the guilt on my face. "It was, uh, it was his first game, and he's in a tough spot. It isn't easy filling Crowther's position."

"Yeah, but Skanchy?" Hoffman questions from the opposite side of the large conference table. "I thought we agreed—"

"Your grandson needs to go through the proper channels, Hoffman," Henry reminds him. "We've already discussed this." His sharp gaze shoots to me. "Jaxon?"

"Yes?"

"Do you think Skanchy has what it takes, or should we pull someone else up from the AHL until Crowther's back?"

Count on Henry Buchanan to command the boardroom exactly like he does everything else in this world. Over the years, he's reminded me to do the same. And sometimes it's difficult. Riding the line between respect for those around me and not coming off as conceited or entitled while still being a good listener who's open to criticism, other viewpoints, the list goes on. I wonder if he'd be as open to my viewpoint if I told him what his daughter looked like when I made her come in the parking lot a few days ago.

Not the time.

Clearing my throat, I double-down, announcing, "We stick with Skanchy. He's the fastest learner and the best man for the job until Crowther's back."

With a slow nod, Henry turns to one of his assistants. "This meeting is over."

"Yes, sir."

Everyone stands, and I grip the leather coating the armchair to do the same when Henry adds, "Jaxon, stay a minute. I have something else I want to discuss."

My pulse thrums in my ears as I let go of the arms on my chair and rest my elbows on the glass table, unsure what the hell I'm supposed to do. One by one, everyone files out, leaving me alone with Rory's dad. Not Henry, my boss. Not Uncle Henry. But Henry, the father of the girl I like and messed around with recently.

Fingers steepled in front of him, he asks, "Want to tell me what's going on?"

I tilt my head but stay quiet, refusing to show my hand.

"You seem off," he clarifies.

Off. It's a vague answer, but one I can work with.

Choosing my words carefully, I admit, "I'm tired."

To be fair, it's the truth. Apparently, my celibacy has only made my dreams of what Rory would look like bouncing on top of me even more vivid.

Not. The fucking. Time.

"It's no excuse," I add, "But..."

"Don't worry about it. I know what it's like to run on no sleep. How was miniature golf?"

I keep my expression blank, wiping my sweaty palms against my thighs beneath the table. Miniature golf? He knows about miniature golf? "What?"

"When I was with your dad at the gym this morning, he said he saw you," Henry explains. "Seems my daughter's wrangled you into helping her with Crowther?"

Fuck!

"Uh, yeah," I lie. "She did well. Not sure when Crowther's

planning to take her out, since his mom's going through everything, but, uh, she was excited, so…" Again, my voice trails off like my hard-on withered away some time during my wet dream of Rory last night.

"You should ask the team's physical therapist for a massage," Henry decides. "You look tense. Everything going okay with Pops and Iris?"

Relief washes over me at the safer topic of conversation, and I answer, "The usual."

"And Rore?" he prods.

Aaaand, we're back to shitting my pants.

"She treating you all right?" he asks. "Working hard?"

Don't puke, don't puke, don't puke.

I swallow past the bile in my throat and force myself to nod. "Yeah, she's been great. You raised a good one, Mr. Buchanan."

Mr. Buchanan?

What the fuck? I haven't called Henry Mr. Buchanan once in my life, and I blurt that shit out now? What is wrong with me?

"Mr. Buchanan?" Henry repeats, somehow managing to weave his words with amusement and confusion. "Yeah, I'm going to make that massage mandatory. Since when am I Mr. Buchanan to you?"

I shrug. "You know, trying to keep things professional so I don't feel like I'm taking any handouts by being here."

He frowns. "Is this about my comment to Hoffman about his grandson? Jax, you know I wouldn't have offered the coaching position if I didn't think you were qualified. Look at our stats from the season so far. They might not be perfect, but you're doing a hell of a job." He shifts closer. "Which is another thing your father and I discussed this morning."

Dread lines my stomach, though this time it has nothing

to do with Henry's connection to the girl I'm seeing and everything to do with his praise.

"Thanks," I murmur, no matter how hollow it feels. I want nothing more than to have my dad's and Henry's approval. In every aspect of my life, if I'm being honest. I guess we never really grow out of that. Seeking approval from the people we look up to.

Would either of them want to sleep with their boss's daughter?

I doubt it.

The problem is, I can't find the willpower to stop.

"Heard all the grandkids are having a sleepover at your Mom and Dad's," he continues. "Maybe you'll finally get a good night's rest."

Finally.

As if I don't already have her part time. Nah, my exhaustion has little to do with my daughter and a hell of a lot more to do with Henry's. I appreciate my parents' efforts to consider whether or not I have custody when they plan out all our family gatherings, though. The way they always try to include her despite her young age and lack of enthusiasm—aka meltdowns—when I'm not around. Honestly, it's one of the reasons why I said yes. Why I accepted the invitation for a sleepover. The more time she spends with them, the less time she cries in their presence, and the more opportunities they have to cultivate their relationship. Add in a date night with Rory, and I caved, accepting their offer.

"Yeah, It'll be good for her," I reply.

"And you." Tapping his knuckles against the conference table, Henry says, "All right, I'll let you go. But I'm serious about that massage. Understand?"

Numbly, I nod, pushing to my feet. "Uh, yeah. Yeah, sure thing."

"Good," he replies. "And tell my daughter hi for me, okay?

Seems she's never home anymore these days. Guess I have you to blame for that one, don't I?"

He has no idea.

My stomach churns, but I nod again. "I'll be sure to tell her."

Then, I beeline it out of there like my ass is on fire.

36

RORY

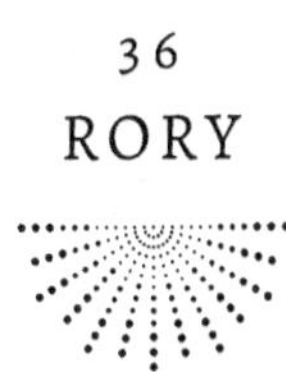

As soon as the elevator opens to Jaxon's penthouse, the warm scent of curry and rice filters through the air. I peek inside the gorgeous space, spotting an array of takeout containers sprawled on the dining table. My mouth waters, and I step off the elevator while Hades gallops in like he owns the place. "Hey."

Setting one of the takeout containers onto the table, Jaxon replies, "Hey."

My forehead wrinkles. Jaxon invited me over for Indian food tonight. However, it seems the man beside me is a stranger compared to the one who had his fingers inside me a few days ago. All it takes is one word. One syllable. And I can tell something's off.

"What's wrong?"

"Nothing."

It's a lie. I don't know how I know, but I do. I've always noticed when Jaxon's lying. Even when I was little. Maybe it's the subtle inflection in his voice. Maybe it's the tension in his movements. Maybe it's the way he's barely looked at me.

"Come take a seat," he offers. His tone is softer, almost

apologetic. It only makes the warning bells clang louder. Without a word, I follow him to the table, and he pulls out my chair, tucking it under me before sitting to my left. As if on auto-pilot, he finishes opening containers, dishing out bird-sized portions onto both plates, barely acknowledging me.

If I was still a kid, I'd push. Demand he tell me what's really going on. If I was the Rory from before my brother's wedding, I'd pretend I'm oblivious to the clear shift in the room. Unfortunately, I'm neither of them anymore, and I'm not sure how to handle this situation.

Pressing my lips together, I reach for Jaxon's hand on the table and run my fingers along his tan skin. "Jax."

His eyes close, and if I didn't know any better, I'd say I slapped him.

"Jaxon," I push. "Look at me."

He does. "Yeah, Squeaks?"

"How was the board meeting?"

"It was good."

Good. That's all he has to say?

"Do you want any rice?" he adds.

Sure. Because carbs fix everything. Okay, they do kind of fix everything, but it's beside the point.

Why is he acting so weird?

"How's my dad?" I ask. Jaxon mentioned he had a board meeting with a bunch of the higher-ups. Maybe work's bothering him?

"He's good," Jaxon says. "Told me to tell you hi."

"Did he also tell you to act like a stone wall, too? Or…?"

He lets out a low chuckle and breathes in a bit more sincerity. "Sorry." He takes another long breath. "Sorry," he repeats. It's the second one that settles my nerves and gives me a glimpse of the *real* Jaxon.

"What's going on?" I ask.

"Nothing," he repeats.

"Wait. I thought we got off Liar's Highway. Should we try again? Maybe merge onto the next exit?" I let him go, lacing my fingers in front of me. "Okay, here we go. Ready for round three? Perfect." Sitting up a little straighter, I say, "Hey, Jax. You seem a little down. What's going on?"

His hand trembles ever so slightly as he reaches for his water, takes a sip, then sets it down. When he looks at me again, the wall's a little lower, and I feel like he can see past whatever's bothering him to really see me. "Hey."

"Hi." I smile, silently urging him to continue.

"The board meeting was good, but, uh, your dad got in my head a little bit."

I nod slowly and pick up my fork. "Okay. Okay, that's normal, I think. Do you want to expand, or let me make assumptions, or…?"

Another cleansing breath slips past his barely-there smile. "I can expand. Uh, let's see. I guess I felt bad."

"Bad," I repeat.

"For touching you behind his back," he clarifies.

I set down my fork and try to understand instead of assuming things I really don't want to. "So, you *don't* want to touch me?"

"Fuck, Rore, I want to touch you more than anything, all right?" He reaches for my hand and squeezes. "Trust me. Watching you fall apart because of me is the hottest, most… fulfilling experience ever. Okay?" He sighs and lets me go. "It's just that…talking to your dad today reminded me of how guilty I feel about it when I do."

Guilty? He feels guilty? And here I thought we were making some kind of headway. Not that we aren't. It's not like he canceled our date tonight, but still. Feeling guilt for being with me or touching me isn't exactly the news a girl wants to hear. Although, he is being honest, which, all things considered, means something. It means a lot. Now, I just need to convince him that his perspective is thoughtful, but...wrong.

Picking at my plate, I tell him, "To be clear, you know you would've had to tell my dad you're not touching me in order to actually go behind his back when you touch me, right?" I pull back, surprised by my sudden epiphany. "Wait, is this why you haven't let me touch you? Because you feel guilty?"

"You've touched me," he argues.

"I mean your dick, Jaxon," I clarify. "You haven't let me touch your *dick*." The words sound so crass, so blunt, I can barely believe I'm saying them, but seriously? He wants to pretend that the innocent places I've touched on his body count in this situation? The guy's delusional at best, and if I have to channel my inner Tatum to make him see how ridiculous he's being, I will.

He shakes his head, though I can't decide if it's because of sheer stubbornness or confusion. "I've told you I'm gonna give you my cock one day—"

"But are you going to let yourself come while you're at it?" I challenge. "Or are you going to pull out and live with blue balls for the rest of your life out of guilt for finding pleasure in your boss's daughter's company, since apparently, that's the only way you see me?"

Jaw hanging off its hinge, he stares at me, dumbfounded. Hell, the man looks like I just told him I have a third eyeball as a belly button or something. "Rory, you know I want you to touch me, and that I want to find..."—he gulps—"pleasure with you."

I drop to my knees and reach for his belt. "Then prove it. Come down my throat."

His molars grind as I struggle with the buckle before his hand descends on mine. "Stop."

I glare up at him. "Jaxon, this relationship has nothing to

do with guilt *or* my dad. This relationship is between me and you."

"I know," he mutters, somehow looking even more tortured than when I first arrived as he stares up at the ceiling like he can't even look at me. "I fucking know, okay?"

Hades boops my cheek with his wet nose, and I shove him away, too distracted by my conversation with Jaxon to give him any attention. "Hades, go lay down," I order. With a huff, he leaves my side and curls up by the couch. Satisfied he won't get in the way, I roll back on my haunches, the fight slipping out of me as I watch Jax struggle. I could offer him a free pass. Could get back on my chair and eat dinner like a good girl. And I would've, too. The Rory from a few weeks ago would've had no issue giving in and letting this go. But me? Well, call me a sucker, but I feel like I deserve more. I deserve a man who isn't going to let his respect for his boss affect his relationship with the woman he's seeing, even if the two are related.

"I know neither of our families has anything to do with this, okay?" He scrubs his hand over his face. "But I respect your dad, and if it was Poppy…"

"If it was Poppy, you'd want her to find someone who treated her well, right?"

He drops his hand to his lap. "Yeah."

"And you've never treated me like anything other than gold."

"You sure?"

"Yes, definitely." I give him a reassuring smile. "And you can still treat me like gold, even if you let me make you come every once in a while." My eyes trail along his chest, landing on the bulge hidden beneath his pants. "Besides, I have a feeling I'm going to like this part, too."

His eyes flash, but he stays quiet, and I know I'm close to

convincing him this isn't a terrible idea. In fact, it might just be a really good one.

"I like you, and I know you like me. You even said so yourself," I remind him, holding his gaze. "How would it feel if all you wanted to do was make me feel good and I said no?"

The same twinge of his jaw appears, but he lets go of my hand over his buckle. Instead of going straight for the belt, I rise onto my knees and start on the top of his shirt, slowly unbuttoning it until his chest comes into view. I run my hands along his bare skin, taking in the slight dusting of hair, the ripple of muscles, and the tan still lingering from this summer. The man looks so incredible, my mouth waters, so I lean forward, kissing him softly.

"Mmm," I hum against him.

Yeah, I'm going to like this a lot. This...access. This opportunity to finally lean into my curiosity of what it would be like to feel him. To touch him. To kiss him. *Everywhere.* Continuing south, I finally reach his pants and unlatch the buckle before undoing the top button. The sound of his zipper echoes in the otherwise silent room as I pull it down, revealing a very large bulge covered by black boxers. Peeking up at him again, I grasp the elastic band, and he lifts his hips, letting me pull them down until all I feel is skin beneath my fingertips. Curiosity and lust unfurl deep inside of me as I finally drag my attention from his dark eyes, down his chest, along the dappling of hair beneath his belly button, and finally, to his erection. It's big. Bigger than I imagined. With a slight curve and a mushroom head, and...

Holy shit, I'm looking at Jaxon Thorne's—

"Rory," Jaxon growls.

I lick my lips and shift on my knees, making space between his parted thighs.

He rasps, "If you don't want—"

"I've been dreaming about this for years, Jax." I peer up at him through my lashes. "Don't ruin it for me, okay?"

With a strained smile, he lifts his brows but doesn't say anything else, leaving the ball, er *balls*, in my court. It's scary. I've never done this before. It's not like I know what I'm doing. And sure, I've seen a video here or there, but being up close and personal with the only dick I've ever actually imagined sucking? Yeah. Yeah, it's a first, and I really don't want to screw it up.

Hands shaking, I reach forward, gently grabbing the base before sliding my palm along his shaft and reaching the head. It jerks in my palm, followed by a low groan echoing from Jaxon.

My attention flicks back up to his face. "You'll tell me if I do anything stupid or awkward or that you don't like, right?"

He chuckles softly, his hands straining against his thighs as if fighting the urge to reach out and take control. "Pretty sure that's impossible, but sure."

"Promise?"

He nods, his lust somehow shifting to adoration as he runs his thumb along my cheekbone. "Promise, Beautiful."

Beautiful.

There's that term of endearment again.

Dipping closer to the beast a few inches from my face, I take a deep breath and try to come up with a game plan of some kind while accidentally blowing on the head.

"Fuck," he grunts.

I peek up again.

"Good fuck," he clarifies. "Torturous fuck, but good fuck. Keep going."

I hold his stare and do it again, blowing softly, then puckering my lips and kissing the head of his cock. Wetness coats my lips, and I dart out my tongue, tasting it.

"Fuck, Rory."

Good fuck, I remind myself.

This time, I lick the slit on top, and his eyes roll back in his head. I do it again, tasting him before swirling the flat of my tongue around the tip like it's an ice cream cone. It's kind of fun. Feeling his eyes on me. Taking in his stilted breathing. The slight twitches.

"Never pegged you for a tease, Rory Buchanan."

"Is that what I am?" I whisper.

When he looks down at me again, I open my mouth and let him sink inside. The same salty flavor hits my taste buds, and my core clenches, surprising the hell out of me. Don't get me wrong. I had a feeling I'd be into this. The idea of giving Jaxon head isn't exactly an unexplored fantasy of mine, but the realization that it's true. That I feel so damn empty and turned on in this moment only makes me want to take him deeper. To see how far I can push him. Rubbing my hands along the base of his dick, I bob my head up and down, using my spit as lube. When he hits the back of my throat, I gag and come up, pulling in a lungful of air.

Okay, there's a point when too far is too far.

Noted.

"Fuck, you okay?" Jaxon asks.

I nod and dive back in, careful not to gag again. It's easier now that I know what to expect and what my limits are. Up and down. Up and down. Pause and swirl. Again and again. Like some kind of rhythmic dance. Faster. Slower. Shallow, then deep. He lets me explore every inch, and I take full advantage, committing it all to memory, my jaw aching, my clit throbbing. It's messy and a little uncoordinated, but he must like it because he won't stop pushing my hair away from my face while cursing under his breath every few seconds. I'm not sure how much time passes, but after a few minutes, his hands find the back of my head and his body grows rigid, proving he's close. My core clenches again, and I moan, determined to see what he tastes like. Every. Last. Drop.

"Rory." I can hear the warning in his voice. The restraint. "Beautiful, I'm close."

I hollow my cheeks, sucking him harder as my own desire reaches a fever pitch. Seriously, one touch and I'm done for. The smell, the taste, the tug of his hands in my hair. It's too much, yet not nearly enough.

Another groan rumbles through Jaxon's chest as his cock tightens even more before it spurts into the back of my throat. I fight the urge to gag from the surprise of it. Realizing what's happening, I swallow it up, licking and sucking until his erection softens and his grip on my hair eases.

"Rory," he rasps.

I raise my head, letting him slip from my mouth and wipe the edge of my lips with the back of my hand, suddenly feeling self-conscious. Maybe I shouldn't be, but that was new and really good, I think? But I don't know. I've never done this before. What happens next?

The thought barely filters through me before Jaxon orders, "Come here." As if I'm a ragdoll, he lifts me up, tugging me into his lap. My legs fall on either side of his hips, and I straddle him at the kitchen table, letting him kiss the shit of me. And maybe it shouldn't be so hot, the idea of him tasting himself on my tongue, but the thought leaves me lightheaded and so damn turned on, I don't know what to do with myself.

"Fuck, Beautiful," he rasps. "Fuck, you have no idea…"

"No idea about what?" I whisper.

"About what you do to me." He presses his forehead to mine. "No fucking clue." Cupping the side of my face, he goes in for another kiss and lifts his hips, proving he's already getting hard again. "Let me make you feel good."

The possibility of everything he can do to make me feel

good rushes over me in the best way possible, so I give him a nod. "Yes, please."

Eyes dancing with mirth, he questions, "You want my mouth or my fingers?"

"I want this." I shift against him again, curious if he feels how hot my pussy is even through my jeans as I lean in for another kiss. He pulls back. Not much. Barely an inch. But it's enough to feed all my insecurities. "Unless you don't want to," I whisper.

"Not why I'm hesitating, Beautiful."

"Then why are you?" I breathe out.

His attention dips to my mouth. "Because this is something you can only give once."

"Pretty sure it's been yours since the beginning."

With a tortured look, he drags his hands down my sides, and cups my ass. "Rore."

"I'm on birth control." I wouldn't be so blunt if I couldn't feel him hardening beneath me. It's clear he wants this. Wants me. Even if it's only for a little while. So, why won't he give in? "And I'm not asking for a marriage proposal," I remind him. "Let me give this to someone who appreciates it. Appreciates me."

His head rolls forward, and he takes another deep breath before kissing me softly. "Trust me, Beautiful. Appreciating you isn't the problem."

"Then what is?"

"Feeling worthy of it." He shakes his head. "Let's go to the bedroom."

37

RORY

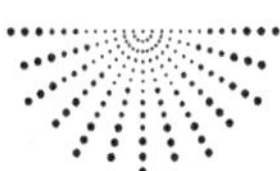

LET'S GO TO THE BEDROOM.

His words play through my mind like a carousel, over and over again, as I force my body to move. To comply. My legs feel like wet noodles, but I climb off his lap, heading toward his room while attempting to stay in reality when a not-so-small part of me is convinced I'm fantasizing the whole thing. I can feel Jaxon's stare as he follows behind me, and with a single step over the threshold, I find myself in his arms. His kisses are soft. Gentle. As they make their way from the corner of my mouth, along my jaw, and down my neck, while his erection presses against my stomach. He's as hard as before, and I press my legs together, grateful for the distraction. The reminder of why we're here and how much I want this. How much I want *him.*

Keeping his hands on my waist, Jaxon closes the door with his foot, locking Hades out of the room in case he gets a little too curious about what's about to go down. Satisfied my dog won't interrupt, Jax guides me until his bed hits the backs of my thighs and he lowers me down. It's soft. The mattress. And the comforter smells like him, just like the other night. I close my eyes, fighting the nerves of what exactly I agreed to in the kitchen now that I'm here. On Jaxon Thorne's bed. Because yeah, I might be one hundred percent positive I'd rather be here than anywhere else in the world, but it doesn't make losing my virginity any less scary.

It's finally going to happen, and with the only person I've ever wanted it to happen with. Seriously, how is this my life? Surreal doesn't even begin to cover the cacophony of emotions ripping through me.

His hands find my white blouse, and he pushes it up, exposing my stomach before scattering kisses between my breasts. Shifting to his left, he blows on the lacy bra, then tugs on the cup, revealing me completely. My heart pounds faster at the contact, and I squeeze my eyes shut, savoring the feel of his mouth on my skin.

"Fuck, Rore." His breath is hot as he kisses my nipple. "Fucking perfect." Shifting to my opposite breast, he does the same. Only this time, he opens his mouth and sucks me softly, his hands dipping lower and undoing the top button of my jeans.

Anticipation flutters through me, and I try to steady my breathing. But this is Jaxon. *The* Jaxon. The man I've dreamed about since...forever. I lift my hips to accommodate his exploration, and he takes full advantage, tugging the rough denim down my legs before hooking his fingers in my underwear and tossing them aside until I'm left bare.

With another heave of his chest, he stares down at me on his bed, taking in every inch as if realizing the same thing. That the woman beneath him is me. Rory. And the connection? The pull? It's strong enough to take my breath away. He shakes his head gently, as if snapping himself out of his revelation, then rifles in his nightstand before retrieving a condom. Setting it on the edge of the bed, he comes back and kneels on the ground, placing his line of sight right between my bare thighs. Now, it's not like I'm not a fan of oral. Trust me. Jaxon's a God with his mouth. But we had an agreement, dammit!

"Jax," I beg. "You said—"

"This is only the appetizer, Beautiful." He grabs my legs and tosses them over his shoulders before grabbing my hips and tugging me to the edge of the bed. And sure, it's kind of hot, but also, he's two inches from my freaking vagina! What if—

His mouth connects with my core, and my body arches off the mattress.

Ooookay, then. Insecurities. Gone.

And when his tongue laps at my center, I know I'm done for. The heat and gentle pressure is the perfect combination. Or maybe it's the edging he's been putting me through since I was on my knees in the kitchen. Then again, I'm not sure it matters. All I know is it's only been thirty seconds, and I'm already close to coming.

"Jaxon," I whimper. "Jaxon, I need—"

He slips his finger inside of me, and my jaw drops. I grip the comforter by my sides, shaking my head back and forth because I'm seriously going to fall apart before we've even had sex if he keeps crooking his finger like that while circling my clit with the tip of his tongue.

Or is that what he wants?

To make me come with his mouth so I don't make him follow through with his promise to take my virginity tonight?

My brows dip as the hazy thought slips past my desperation to come.

"You know," I breathe out, trying to stay focused no matter how impossible it feels when he's kissing my core like this. "You can make me come a dozen times tonight, and I'll still want you to have sex with me, Jaxon Thorne."

He groans his appreciation but doesn't let up, sucking on my folds before spreading me wider with his free hand.

"Not gonna let you off the hook," I add as my eyes roll back in my head and my muscles clench with anticipation.

I'm close. So freaking close I can almost taste it.

"Jax," I whimper. "Jax, you have no idea—"

He pulls away, blowing on my clit and stopping me from coming at the last possible second. The shift and lack of completion hits like a freight train, and I lift my head to glare down at him.

"Seriously?" I cry.

Honestly, I can't decide if I want to smack him upside the head or slam my thighs against his ears so he has no choice but to let me finish if he ever wants to breathe again. Actually, that sounds pretty nice right now.

"Trust me," Jax murmurs, interrupting my plans to smother him with my pussy as he reaches for the condom and rips the foil with his teeth, sliding the rubber onto his erection.

Interest piqued, I wait with bated breath. Because this is it. Me and him. Just like I always hoped.

Climbing on top of me, he leverages his weight to one side as his hand dips between our bodies, causing goosebumps along every inch of me. How? How is he so different? It doesn't make sense, but I'm also so tired of questioning it. Why it's always only ever been *him*. Lining himself with my entrance, he rubs the head of his cock up and down my slit as I tangle my fingers in his hair so I can savor the closeness while also trying not to freak out over what's about to happen. Because yeah, I'm definitely turned on, but I'm a little terrified, too.

"I'll be gentle," he promises.

His words are like a balm, and I stare up at him. The flecks of olive in his eyes. The five o'clock shadow along his jaw. The adoration shining down on me. And suddenly, the fear evaporates. Because he'll be gentle. He said so himself. So, what is there to fear?

"I know you will," I whisper, and I've never been more sure of anything in my entire life.

This. This is why it's always been Jax. Because when life gets scary. When life feels like it's too much. He's the one person I can count on. To put me first. To look out for me. To make me feel seen and heard and understood.

It's always been him.

Achingly slow, Jaxon nudges the head of his erection against my entrance, driving me insane with every minor stretch before pulling out and playing with my clit. He does it again. Pushing himself another sliver deeper then retreating. He's teasing me. Preparing me. And when I'm pretty sure I'm going to go crazy if he doesn't make me come, he thrusts in fully, seating himself inside my body. And then it makes sense. Why he was prepping my body. Making sure I was wet and ready and needy and desperate. Because that? Yeah, that hurt like a bitch. And it doesn't matter how turned on I am, the sharp burn is still enough to make my lungs freeze and my jaw drop.

"I know, Beautiful." He kisses my cheeks and mouth. Every inch of my face while I try to catch my breath at the not-so-little intrusion ripping me in two. "I know." Keeping most of his weight propped on his forearm, he waits for my body to adjust, barely moving a muscle until slowly, it doesn't feel like I'm being ripped to shreds, and I can even wiggle my hips beneath him.

Yeah, it's still tight, but the initial sting of his intrusion is gone. Now, all I feel is…full.

"Hey," he rasps. Pushing my hair away from my forehead, he stares down at me, a question shining in his pretty eyes, though he doesn't voice it aloud. Then again, he doesn't need to. I know what he's asking. What he wants to know. It only confirms my earlier conclusion.

It was always him.

"I'm okay," I promise.

His brows furrow even more. "You sure?"

I nod. "Yeah. Yeah, I'm okay. You can move again."

I can see his reservation. The wrinkled forehead. The twinge in his jaw. But he gives in, drawing circles against my clit with his hand still wedged between us as he slowly pulls out a few inches before gently pushing back inside. The same pleasurable pressure begins building where we're connected, and I wrap my legs around his waist, meeting his thrusts instead of waiting for them like before. And when he picks up his pace, hitting a spot deep inside of me, I swear I can see stars.

"Yes," I whimper. "Yes, yes, yes."

Skin tight, body hot, clit pulsing, I reach the same edge I've teetered on all night. But instead of staying out of reach, I finally tumble over it and free fall. The world spins into oblivion as I come, squeezing him tight as wave after wave of toe-curling pleasure rolls from my core out to my limbs. He follows after, his cock jerking inside of me before the full weight of his body pins me to the mattress.

"Fuck, Rory," he rasps against the shell of my ear. "You have no idea how good you feel. Like you're made for me."

And honestly? A not-so-small part of me is starting to wonder if I really am. Because if I've learned anything over the years? It's that he sure as hell was made for me. Of that, I have zero doubt.

"Let me clean you up," he decides. The mattress dips as he climbs off me, disposes of the condom, and retrieves a warm towel from the bathroom. Without a word, he starts to spread my legs so he can clean me up, but I swat him away and reach for the cloth.

"I can do it—"

"I want to—"

"Yeah, but they're my lady bits." I cross my legs and give him a shy look, hating the way heat floods my face at the prospect of him wiping me clean and seeing all I have going on down there now that our sex drives have settled down.

With a smirk, he folds his arms but keeps the warm, damp towel out of reach. "You're really gonna come between me and my new favorite lady bits? We're good friends. Washing them up is the least I can do to make them feel better."

I quirk my brow, refusing to give in no matter how cute he is when he's playful. "Seriously?"

"What? You don't feel closer to my cock after sucking me off in the kitchen?" he challenges.

"Jaxon!" I squeal.

He kneels on the bed and cups both my thighs. "Let me take care of you."

This time, I let him.

The warmth of the towel feels like heaven as he takes care of me, cleaning me up and making sure I'm okay. It shouldn't surprise me. How sweet and considerate he's being. After all, he's Jaxon Thorne. The man's been kissing my boo-boos and Band-Aiding my ouchies since before I could walk. Even so, it never ceases to amaze me. How thoughtful and caring he is. Once he's finished, he tosses the towel into the hamper, then collapses next to me on the bed.

"There."

"Thank you," I whisper. "Thank you for giving in."

His attention bounces around my face as if I somehow hold all the answers to his many questions and deepest thoughts, though I have no idea what they are. "Pretty sure I'll never be able to say no to you, Beautiful."

"Is that a bad thing?"

He pauses, then shakes his head. "Fuck, I hope not."

Laying down, he tugs me into his side, and I melt against him. "Do you want to stay with me tonight?" he asks.

The question catches me off guard. We've had plenty of sleepovers, but we've also always had Poppy's presence as an excuse. Since she's staying at her grandparents' house tonight, there's no need for me to be here in the morning. Not really. "Do you want me to stay?"

"I did just ask," he counters.

"You know what I mean, Jax." I roll my eyes, fighting the urge to smack his chest. "I don't want you to feel obligated to ask me to sleep over just because we had sex."

"I wouldn't ask you if I didn't want you here. I promise."

My eyes burn, and a lump clogs my throat, though I refuse to let him witness my body's response. Because, whoa, girl. Take a chill pill. He asked you to sleep over, not to marry him.

I hesitate, trying to reel in my stupid emotions before nodding against his warm chest. "I believe you."

"Good. Now, let me ask you again. Will you stay with me tonight?"

Fighting my giddiness—because seriously, how is this my life—I drag my fingers against his bare skin. "I'd love to."

Half-asleep, I roll toward Rory's side of the bed but find the sheets cold. Shit. I pry one lid open, confirming what I already know. She isn't here. Why isn't she here? The sheets pool at my waist as I sit up, scanning my bedroom. It's empty. The bathroom light's off, too, so she didn't slip away to use it.

Unease coats my insides, and I plant my feet on the cold wood floor. After slipping on a pair of boxers, I head toward the hallway. It matches the pitch black bathroom, proving how early it must be, though I didn't think to check the time before beginning my search. When I notice Rory's purse on the kitchen counter, my muscles loosen, and I turn into the family room, finding Rory curled up on one of the chairs closest to the fireplace with Hades sitting at her feet with his head in her lap.

When she feels my presence, she looks up and smiles, though I don't miss the way she keeps running her fingers through Hades' fur. "Morning."

She's here. She didn't leave. She didn't run.

"What time is it?" I rasp. My voice is still rusty from sleep.

"Just after five."

I rub at the corner of my eye. "Why are you up so early?"

"I'm always up this early."

"Always?" With a yawn, I drop my hand to my side. "Rore, it's still dark outside."

"I know." She peeks out one of the large windows as it showcases the lack of sunlight. "I'm sorry if I woke you."

"No worries," I reply. "I'm sorry I didn't wear you out enough last night to sleep in for once."

A quiet laugh escapes her. "You wore me out plenty." Shifting on the chair, she flinches. "Trust me."

Grimacing, I stride a little closer but stop myself from reaching out and touching her completely. "You sore?"

"I'm okay."

"Liar," I argue. "Let me get you some painkillers, or—"

"I'm okay," she repeats. "Seriously."

She isn't, though I can't put my finger on what's bothering her. Not quite. Something tells me it has little to do with her broken hymen, though. "You should come back to bed with me."

She shakes her head. "Can't."

"Why not?"

"It's just…getting to be that time again. You know?"

I frown.

"5:34 a.m." She sobers. "I almost thought I'd sleep through it this time, but…" Her shoulder raises a few inches. "Try telling my brain that, right? I'm awake now, and my OCD is rearing its ugly head, so here I am, trying not to spiral. I wish there was a way to just…ignore it."

Ignore it. The time. I want to ask why she's so obsessed with that particular number. 5:34 a.m. Why it matters. Why she can't sleep. Then, it hits me. Archer's death. It happened before dawn. He was on his way to the airport for an early flight. It must be the reason that particular time is significant.

And I hate that I didn't know. That I didn't notice Rory's odd sleep schedule. We've shared a hotel room several times. I should've noticed. Shouldn't I?

"That's when your parents got the call, isn't it." It isn't a question. It's a fact.

"That's when I looked at the clock after they woke me up to tell me to get dressed so we could go to the hospital," she clarifies. "5:34 a.m." Her sigh is heavy and forced. "When I close my eyes, I can still see the bright green numbers. Haven't slept past that time since. It's like my internal clock knows, you know?" She shrugs again, choosing to stare out the dark window. "Well, my internal clock and my OCD."

"What do you mean?" I ask.

"I know it's not real, but my brain keeps telling me that if I sleep past it, if I'm not awake and alert and waiting for 5:34 a.m., it'll trigger another horrible phone call or something, and even though I know it's not true," she repeats, as if she's already caught in the loop, "my body still decides that having a panic attack is the best way to handle it."

"So, what do you do?"

With a shuddered breath, she glances at the clock on the microwave, her fingers digging deeper into Hades' scruff along his back. "I sit and stare at the clock, trying not to hyperventilate as I relive the longest sixty seconds of my life," —she gulps—"praying the phone won't ring like it did that night."

Understanding washes over me as I stand here, helpless. She fights this every morning? Every. Fucking. Morning. And I had no idea?

I move closer to the unlit fireplace, so I can reacquaint myself with the girl I held the night her brother died. Because let's be honest. I haven't seen her as the Squeaks I once knew since she reappeared for Maverick's wedding. Sometimes, I forget they're one and the same. That the little girl who followed me around is the woman I slept with tonight. Like right now, when I'm caught between feeling helpless and determined to take away her pain and discomfort like I've done a hundred times before. And I have. I have taken her pain and discomfort a hundred times before. So, what's stopping me from doing it again?

Careful not to step on Hades, I hook one arm beneath her knees and the other around her upper back, pick her up, twist around, and plop back onto the chair with Rory cradled in my lap. She's wearing my clothes. A pair of boxers and a T-shirt she must've stolen from my room when she snuck out of bed this morning. The realization soothes my fucking soul and eases the irrational guilt hanging over me from not knowing about this particular compulsion until this morning. "Let me sit with you," I murmur. This time, her sigh is less forced and more content as she rests her head against the crook of my neck.

"Mmm," she hums. "You smell good."

I kiss the top of her head and breathe in deep, appreciating the scent of my cologne clinging to her hair. It might not be as addictive as her natural scent, but the idea of marking her, even in as subtle of a way as my cologne, makes me want to puff out my chest and pound my fists against it.

Mine.

The word feels foreign, yet so fucking natural, I'm not sure how to wrap my head around it. So, I don't. Instead, I focus on the woman in my lap, anxious to help or at least slow down the chaotic loop her mind is stuck in.

"Are you tired?" I ask.

"Exhausted," she admits.

"Close your eyes."

"Jax."

"You don't need to go to sleep," I argue. "You only need to close your eyes." She stays quiet as I slowly run my hands up and down her spine, her body relaxing more and more with every passing minute. I want to tell her nothing bad will happen. That she's safe, and I've got her, and her family's fine, too. But I know it'll only feed her compulsion, making it stronger and more stubborn until she feels like she has no choice but to wake up earlier and earlier in preparation for the time she dreads until sleep is nothing but a luxury.

I'm not sure how much time ticks by when Rory's breathing becomes faster instead of slower. It's as if she can feel the minutes bringing her closer to 5:34 a.m., despite refusing to give in and check the official time.

"Do you remember when I told you I wanted to coach instead of going pro?" I say in hopes of distracting her.

She nods against me, but her breathing is stilted. Forced. "You were so nervous."

"I was," I mutter, lost in the memory. "I was freaking out, Rore."

"I remember." Her words are so quiet I'm surprised I hear her. I can't decide if it's because she's reliving the moment, or if it's because she's too distracted by the time ticking on her internal clock—and the literal one glowing from the microwave in the kitchen—to focus on our conversation.

"Did you know you were the first person I told?" I prod.

"I was?"

"Yeah."

She lifts her head to peek up at me. "Why?"

I hesitate, wondering the same thing. I never thought about it before. Not until recently. "I'm not sure. I guess you felt…safe."

"Safe?"

"I don't know. I guess I knew that…if there was anyone who could accept me and my decisions no matter how illogical they seemed, it was you."

"You're many things, Jaxon Thorne," she whispers. What

little light is in the room makes her round, doe-shaped eyes practically glow. "Illogical isn't one of them."

"Turning your back on something you worked years for felt illogical at the time."

"Maybe," she concedes. "If you'd actually done that."

"What do you mean?"

"Pivoting isn't the same thing as quitting, Jax. You followed your gut and took the road less traveled, and look where it got you."

"Yeah." My attention dips to her mouth. Look where it got me. With a girl who's ten years younger than me sitting on my lap. Am I crazy for wanting her here? For feeling the way I do? "Do you remember what you told me that night?" I ask.

"You mean, after you admitted you were terrified to tell your dad you weren't going to the NHL like you'd both planned for your entire life?"

My eyes thin in a mock glare. "I'm not sure I used the word terrified, but…"

A smirk tugs at the edge of her mouth. "I told you that you were meant for more than following in your dad's footsteps and being a silly hockey player."

"Which is when I told you that if any of our family members heard you call them a silly hockey player, you'd be thrown in time out," I remind her.

"Which is when I told you they could put me in time out for however long they wanted as long as you were happy with your decision, and I stand by it. The question is, are you happy?"

Am I happy? The question catches me off guard.

I'm divorced. I'm a single father. I'm failing at my job, or at least it feels that way. And I'm secretly hooking up with my nanny, who's also my boss's daughter. By all counts, it seems like my life has imploded. But am I happy? Would I want to be anywhere else? With anyone else? The answer leaves my chest tight and my head feeling like it's floating in the clouds.

"Yeah, Beautiful. I think I am."

My fingers dip beneath the stolen T-shirt and glide across her bare skin as I memorize the feel of her, every dip, every inch, before pushing her hair behind her ear. She leans into my touch, and I swear the organ in my chest skips a beat. I check the time on the microwave. "Would you look at that. You made it. It's 5:42 in the morning and no panic attack."

"No panic attack," she confirms. With a deep breath, she lifts her chin and waits for me to kiss her. After I do, she whispers, "Thank you."

"Anytime, Rore."

And fuck, do I mean it.

JAXON

The score taunts me from the board as the time ticks down on the clock. It's the third period, and the score is three to three with forty-four seconds to go. I pace behind the bench, eyes locked on the ice as the boards rattle beneath my feet.

Come on, come on, come on.

Skates cut through the ice, the low hum of fans holding their collective breath throughout the arena as one of the opposing team passes the puck. Reeves intercepts it.

"Get ready!" I bark, stepping to the edge of the bench.

Reeves darts past, juggling the puck left, right, left, right, as the opposing team zeroes in on his movements.

"We're pulling Evans!" I yell.

My goalie catches the signal and darts toward the bench as fast as he can, despite his heavy pads making him drag more than if he was any other player on the ice. Grabbing Skanchy by the collar, I force him to look at me. "You're out there. Run Delta Loop. Got it?"

He nods, eyes blazing. "Get it to Thorne?"

"Every damn time."

I shove him forward, and he hops the boards. It's six on five. An empty net taunts me from our side, shining like a beacon. If this doesn't work, we're fucked. Every inch of me clenches tight, and I try to keep a clear head.

"Come on, come on, come on," I mutter.

Reeves chips the puck off the boards as Skanchy sweeps in, catching the pass and arching around one of the closest defenders. Griffin floats toward the high slot, just like we drew it up. Twenty-eight seconds.

"Let's go!" I yell. "Pick it up! Delta Loop! Let's go!"

Darting into action, they run the play like we practiced. Skanchy to Reeves. Reeves to Skanchy. He passes it between a pair of defenders, and Skanchy swoops in with a quick fake, distracting the opposing team, leaving my baby brother wide open.

The seconds relentlessly tick down on the clock.

Ten. Nine. Eight.

Griffin winds up. The loud crack of his stick hitting the puck sounds like thunder as it connects. I clutch the back of my head, and the rest of my team jumps to their feet, each of us holding our breath.

In the blink of an eye, the siren wails, and the crowd goes wild.

We won.

We fucking won!

Heart pounding, I wipe my forehead with the back of my hand and try to catch my breath. It's not like I was out there, but the adrenaline is still enough to knock me on my ass. That was close. A little too close. But we did it.

We fucking did it.

"Good game, Coach," Evans says.

"Good game," I return, shifting my focus to the scoreboard while the rest of the team congratulates each other, each of them lining up to pat the goalie on the head for an excellent performance.

The post game events are over in a blink, and my body slowly relaxes from the adrenaline and the high from today's win.

"So, when's Crowther coming back?" Evans asks from beside me.

"Hopefully, he'll be at the next game," I answer.

"That'll be good," Reeves interjects. "Maybe we'll score a few more goals with him back on the roster." He rolls his shoulders and glances toward the scoreboard. "Not that the buzzer-beater wasn't a kickass way to end the game, but four to three is way too narrow of a point spread."

"We pulled off the win," Griffin reminds him. "That's all that matters."

"Barely," Everett grunts.

"You saying I should trade you for a younger player?" I quip. "One with a little more stamina, maybe?"

Everett scoffs. "Nah, I'm good. Thanks, though." He stretches his arms over his head. "I'm gonna hit the showers."

"Me, too," Reeves adds. "Good game, Coach."

"Thanks, man," I return while the crowd makes its way out of the arena.

When I realize my baby brother's still hanging out by the bench, I say, "You did good."

"Thanks." He grins, still reeling from the win. "Only so many times a team will buy it, but I'm glad the play worked."

"Me, too."

He smothers a laugh and shakes his head. "Fuck, that was something else."

"Yeah, it was."

Riding the high, he cups the back of his head and turns to me. "Do you ever miss it?"

"Miss what?"

"Being out here." Arms spread wide, he motions to the ice. "In the action."

"Every day," I admit. "Miss it every day."

"Still don't get why you quit."

No one does. No one but Rory. And it doesn't matter how many times I've tried explaining it, my reasoning, people always look at me like I lost my mind. And maybe I did. Even then, I wouldn't change it. Wouldn't trade places with my brother or my dad or anyone else.

"Didn't quit, just pivoted," I offer, using Rory's words from before.

"Guess so." He rests his elbows against the half-wall separating us and stretches out his lower back. "You're right about some of us getting too old for this shit, though."

"Nah, you're still a young buck," I counter dryly.

"Sure, I am." He rolls his eyes. "Not all of us spend our time hanging out at arcades and playing miniature golf."

I drop my head back, trying not to lose my shit as I grumble, "What is it with everyone talking with everyone?"

With a laugh, he slaps his hand against my shoulder. "God forbid you have a family that communicates."

I glare back at him. "Communicates. Gossips. Same difference, right?"

He grins. "Depends on what you consider gossip, 'cause usually that means there's something to hide." His brow kicks up. "She still got a thing for you?"

She. As in, Rory. As in, the woman I went miniature golfing with. Guess it goes to show how many opportunities my brother's had to give me shit for something that happened weeks ago. Keeping my emotions locked down, I say, "What?"

"Finley wanted me to ask. Although, I *am* curious." His gaze narrows as he studies me carefully, waiting for me to show my hand.

If only he knew.

"We're friends," I answer.

"Friends who play miniature golf together."

"Friends who are trying to figure out how to be friends again after everything we've been through," I counter, deciding a half-truth is better than nothing.

My brother cocks his head. "You got a thing for Rore?"

"Griff—"

"It's a simple question, big brother." He shrugs. "Although, now that I think about it, maybe the real question is, why are you avoiding it?"

"Avoiding what?"

"The question," he clarifies.

My eye twitches. "I'm not avoiding anything—"

"So you don't have a thing for Rory?"

Yeah, this asshole's been around Finley way too long. I want to tell him I have a dick, so of course I have a thing for Rory, but the truth is, my attraction to her runs so much deeper than superficial bullshit. Should it, though? Should my attraction for Rory Buchanan run deeper than superficial bullshit? I don't know. I like her. I care about her. I want her to be happy and appreciated. And I keep finding myself searching the stands just to see if she's here with Pops and checking my phone just to see if she's sent me another text or video. But do I have a thing for her? A real, *lasting* thing? Outside of what it feels like to be inside her?

Shit.

I think I do.

Slipping off his helmet, Griffin tucks it under his arm and points out, "Yeah, your silence isn't telling at all."

"She's my nanny," I remind him.

"Who you were seen with when the kid she's supposed to be nannying was at her mom's house."

The asshole makes a good point.

"She wanted me to show her a few things," I argue.

"Like…sexual things? Or—"

"Don't be an ass," I warn.

He raises his free hand in defense. "All right, I'll drop it."

"Will you?" I challenge before motioning to the scoreboard. "Because you're kind of ruining the high from tonight's win."

"Sorry." He drops his hand. "But do you wanna know what else would ruin the high from tonight's win? Crowther stealing her from you once he's back."

My stomach plummets at the idea of Crowther coming anywhere near Rory, but I keep a blank face no matter how much it kills me. "There's nothing to steal." The lie tastes like ass, but I don't know what else to say. Not yet. Not without Rory's permission. Not without Iris finding out and pitching a fit. Not without our families making assumptions and putting even more pressure on whatever's happening between Rory and me than there already is. Besides, it's still new. Way too fucking new to go around announcing our private business to our families all because they're too nosy for their own good.

Isn't it?

"Sure, there's nothing to steal," Griffin retorts. "Just like how there was nothing to steal from Drew when I made a move on Fin."

Drew.

Fuck, I haven't heard that name in years. Drew was Finley's long-distance boyfriend before Griffin drove her across the country to tell him something face-to-face. By the time they made it back to Lockwood Heights, Griffin was all in and somehow managed to steal *and* mend Finley's broken heart in the process.

"What are you trying to say, Griff?" I demand.

"I'm saying you can either shit or get off the pot because

Rory deserves better than being strung along when a good guy like Dodge or Crowther would happily take a chance on her."

He thinks I don't know this? That Rory isn't as close to perfect as a woman can be? He doesn't get it, though. Doesn't understand that I have a daughter to think about. And a career. And Rory herself. Besides, it's only been a little while. Everyone needs to keep their opinions and assumptions to themselves, including whether or not Crowther's a better fit for Rory than I am.

Asshole.

"Some brother you are," I mutter.

"Just sayin'."

"Or Finley's just sayin'," I counter.

His smile grows. "You may have been a hot topic at the Thorne house after the wedding. Add in the miniature golf run-in, and she's convinced you two are sleeping together."

I grit my teeth but keep my mouth shut.

Analyzing my expression, Griffin skates forward. "And if you were, hypothetically, sleeping together, you know none of us would care. Right?"

Yes and no. No one cares until it doesn't work out. Then, it's a shit show. And yeah. Everything wound up fine for Griffin and Fin. Everything even wound up fine for Mav and Lia, but no one likes the reminder of Archer's involvement in their relationship before he died, do they? Because it wasn't so simple before he passed. I know it, and if my relationship with Rory doesn't work out, everyone else will be reminded of it, too.

Scratching my temple, I mutter, "Rory's…"

"All grown up now?" Griffin finishes for me. "Yeah, I know. And so does Crowther." With a grin, he slips off his gloves and shoves them into his helmet. "I'm gonna hit the showers."

He skates away, disappearing into the tunnel and leaving me more on edge than I'd like to admit. He's right about one thing. I haven't talked to Rory about Crowther since I showed up in her parents' backyard and confessed my feelings for her. I figured it wasn't any of my business, and maybe it isn't, but the idea of something happening between them once he's back is more than I can stomach. Then again, so is the idea of telling people I'm sleeping with a girl who's ten years younger than I am and has been in love with me her entire life.

I'm so fucked.

Keeping our extra-curricular activities under wraps has been pretty easy, all things considered. That is, until we step outside of his penthouse and into the real world. Add in being surrounded by the entire Lions roster for today's flight without random strangers acting as a buffer, and I can barely look anyone in the eye. I swear I can still feel him inside of me, despite us having slept together three other times. And yes, I've been counting.

After one too many meltdowns on flights, my dad let the team borrow his private plane since it has a bedroom suite where Poppy can nap without being bothered. Not that she doesn't sleep like a rock, anyway, but Jax appreciated the gesture. I, on the other hand, feel like a thief on the run. Can Reeves or Griffin or Everett tell I'm sleeping with their friend slash coach? Have they figured out that I gave him my virginity and really, really like sex now that I know what all the fuss is about?

Act. Normal, I remind myself. It's not like it's that new. It's been three days. Three blissful days of sleepovers and sex and playing house and basically living out every fantasy I've ever had without a single person knowing except me and Jaxon. Okay, Poppy knows, too, but I think she can keep a secret. Speaking of which, I'm almost disappointed that she's curled up in the bedroom while the rest of the team is in the main area, each in our respective seats. If she was here, I could distract myself, but I guess my phone will have to do.

As I browse social media while attempting to not look like a crazed stalker with all the glances I keep stealing at a certain coach chatting with his brother, a throat clears, so I look up.

"Hey." Eric lifts his chin toward the empty seat beside mine. "Mind if I...?"

"Yeah, of course." I move my carry-on to the floor, nearly taking out my pinky toe in the process. He's been dealing with family stuff for the last couple weeks, and I'm not the only one who's noticed his absence. Truth be told, there've been one or two nail-biters during the last few games, and I have a feeling it has to do with a certain someone missing from the bench.

As Eric collapses into the seat, he asks, "So, how've you been?"

"Pretty sure I should be asking you that question." I place my hand on his forearm, feeling guilty for not having checked in before. I wanted to, but I didn't know what to say. Didn't want him to feel obligated to respond while dealing with everything else. "I heard about your mom. I'm sorry."

"It's all right."

It isn't, but I get it. The need to cover with nonchalance when reality hits too close to home. "How is she?" I ask.

"Good." He smiles, and when I realize it's genuine, a relieved sigh slips out of me. "They caught it early, so the doctors are hopeful it'll be smooth sailing...other than the chemo." He grimaces. "Yeah, that part's a bitch."

"I believe it. That's gotta be rough."

"Yeah, but my mom likes to tell me it's harder for me than it is for her. I think she's full of shit," he clarifies, "but she's handling it like a champ."

"I'm glad she has you."

"Yeah, me, too." That same boyish smile plays at the edge of his lips. "She's the best."

"Seems like it's genetic, then," I reply, unsure what else there is to say. Actually, scratch that. There *isn't* anything to say. Period. It's like when I lost Arch. Sometimes things are just...shitty. If I've learned anything from my own experience, it's that silence can be more genuine than false promises, like, "I'm sure she'll get better soon," or something like that. Instead, I give him a reassuring smile of my own. "Well, it's good to see you. I'm sure the team is glad you're back."

"Yeah." He sighs. "Listen, I want to apologize for ghosting you after the banquet."

"You didn't—"

"I kind of did," he argues. "I was trying to stay focused on the home opener, then I got the call the morning after, and... yeah."

I wave him off. "No worries at all. Pretty sure I'd be a terrible person for holding it against you. So, seriously, you're good. Your focus is where it should be."

"Still." He nudges my shoulder with his. "What do you say I make it up to you after tomorrow's game?"

"Uh. Sure?" My focus slides to Jax for the barest of seconds, despite my best attempt to keep my impulse in check. "I guess it kind of depends on when you're thinking, but..."

My attention flicks to Jax again before I can stop it. He isn't talking to Griffin anymore. Nope. He's watching me.

And thanks to the intensity gleaming in his dark eyes, I grip the edge of the armrest, attempting not to squirm.

Catching on, Eric mutters, "Shit, I didn't even think about you being on the clock, so if your boss says it's—"

"She can't," Jaxon announces. He strides closer and plops down in the seat across from us.

"Oh?" Eric frowns.

"I need her to watch Poppy." Jaxon doesn't bother giving either of us any more of his attention as he pulls out his phone. One of the benefits of flying private with the team is free WiFi, and it seems Jaxon has no issue multitasking despite how rude it makes him look.

Why is he acting so…cold?

"Sorry," he adds. His focus shifts from Crowther to me, then back to his phone like he has better things to do than worry about a girl he's sleeping with making plans with another man.

"Maybe next week, then?" Crowther offers. "You know, when Poppy's with her mom? I'd love to show you the pizza place we talked about—"

My phone buzzes, interrupting him. Well, that's not true. I'm pretty sure he's still talking, but I don't hear a word. Not really. I'm too confused by the random text from a certain someone who's playing with his phone in the seat across from me.

JAXON

I need to fuck you.

What the hell?

I peek up at Jax, but he isn't looking at me. He's looking at his stupid phone.

JAXON

Get up and walk to the bathroom. Now.

Walk to the bathroom? Why?

Before I can type my response, my phone buzzes again.

JAXON

Get. Up.

"There a problem, Squeaks?" he asks, sounding bored and simultaneously interrupting Eric, though I'd almost forgotten he's here.

"N-no problem," I answer.

"You sure?" Eric prods. "You look tense."

Tense? More like intrigued and confused.

"I, uh, I need to use the restroom. I think I'm having some motion sickness issues." I press my hand to my flushed cheeks. "I'll, uh, I'll talk to you later, Eric."

"See you, Rory."

I stand, keeping my pace steady as I head toward the onboard suite where the private bathroom is located. I want to look behind me. To see if he's following. But I don't. Instead, I keep my head held high and my hands loose at my sides like I don't have a care in the world despite Jaxon's text message flashing through my mind like a neon sign.

I need to fuck you.

Stepping inside, I tiptoe past a sleeping Poppy and go to close the bathroom door when it's slapped open. My squeal of surprise catches in my throat before Jax holds his hand against my mouth, silencing me. With his opposite hand on my waist, he twists me around, pushing my spine against the door until every inch of me is caged in.

"Do you have any idea how jealous I am right now, Beautiful?" he growls. "Seeing him ask you out right in front of me?" He bends forward, crowding me and stealing my space as he breathes me in. "Fuck, I wanna kill him."

"You shouldn't have texted me," I whisper.

"And you shouldn't have gotten all flushed and turned on," he argues.

"Well, you'll have to forgive me for getting a little hot and bothered when the guy I'm sleeping with sends me a text saying he wants to fuck me."

His hand locks on my waist, and he grinds against me. "Turn around."

"What?"

He hikes up my sundress and cups my pussy through my soaked underwear before tearing them down my thighs. Once I'm bare from the waist down, he repeats. "Turn. Around."

My breath hitches as I twist in the small space. He kicks out my feet, nudging them further apart like he doesn't have a care in the world. Is he serious? Is he really doing this? Are we really doing this? I peek over my shoulder at him as his hand finds my shoulder, and he folds me in half. The familiar zip of pants echoes through our staggered breathing before the head of his cock nudges against my entrance. "Put your hand on the mirror," he orders. As soon as I do, he thrusts into me, and I jolt forward, grateful for the leverage or else I would've hit my head on the glass.

A familiar burn takes my breath away as I stretch around him. Yup. There it is. Staying fully seated inside me, he nibbles the side of my neck, scraping his teeth against the sensitive flesh as he lets me adjust to him.

"This is mine," he growls.

"Jax."

"You are mine," he grits out.

"Yes." It's nothing but a whimper but is the most true statement I've ever made. Of course, I'm his. I've always been his. And the fact that he's finally owning me the way I've always craved is just the cherry on top of a supremely decadent sundae.

Sensing I'm ready for more, he pulls out, then pushes in again, keeping his pace slow but hard until my fingertips turn white against the mirror. This. This is what I crave. The glimpse of desperation. The need that somehow seems to match my own whenever we're together. He's so good at hiding it. At keeping it locked tight. Until moments like this. When it's only me and him.

"Faster," I beg. "Harder."

He wraps his arm around me and plays with my clit, his fingers dipping a little lower to where we connect.

"You feel so fucking good, Beautiful," he rasps. "So fucking good."

"Keep going," I moan.

I thrash against him as he pushes me higher and higher with every drag of his cock and brush of his fingers.

"Stay quiet," he orders. "Not one fucking sound."

His hand finds my mouth, keeping my moaning in check until sparks erupt and I see stars. My teeth dig into his flesh as I fall apart, coming around him, my body turning to stone before melting into a mess as he jerks inside of me.

Holy shit. Having sex on a plane was the last thing I expected when I boarded this flight. And in my dad's freaking private bathroom? If he ever finds out, he's going to kill me. It doesn't matter how accepting and awesome and open-minded he is as a father. There are some lines that should never be crossed and this is one of them. But also... wow. I've never had a quickie before. Jaxon likes to take his time and leave me begging. But this? This is one for the books. That much, I know.

Slowly, he removes his hand from my mouth, and I lean against the basin, trying to catch my breath while also attempting to wrap my head around the situation. Did we really just do that? As his softening cock slips out of me, cum follows, and my gaze snaps to his in the mirror because, uh, that's new.

"You came inside me," I murmur.

Shit.

We didn't use a condom.

How did we not use a condom?

"Fuck," he mutters. "I came inside you."

"That's what I just said!" I whisper-shout, trying not to panic. "You weren't supposed to do that."

"Yeah, no shit," he returns, but there's a lightness in his tone, softening his words as he looks down, watching his cum drip down my thigh. "Fuck, why is that hot?" Scrubbing his hand over his face, he reaches for the paper towels, wets them in the sink, and cleans me up, being extra gentle as I hiss through my teeth.

"Did I hurt you?" he asks.

Yes. But it's a good hurt. Like sore muscles after a solid workout or something.

Licking my lips, I reply, "I wanted harder. You gave me harder."

With a low chuckle, he leans down and brushes his fingers against my cheek. "I'm sorry I lost control."

"Don't be," I argue as my mind replays exactly what we just did. In an airplane restroom. With his team a few feet away. I bite the inside of my cheek to keep from grinning as my face's temperature rises. "That was...hot."

"Shouldn't have come inside you. Not without your permission. I'm sorry."

"I already told you that you could," I return, referring to the night he took my virginity.

He tosses the used paper towel into the small garbage can, then twists me to face him. "Still." He pecks at my lips. "I'm sorry. It won't happen again. I promise."

Squeezing my thighs together, I admit, "And what if I want it to?"

His brows dip. "You sure?"

I nod.

With a smirk, he entwines our fingers together and kisses my knuckles. "Then I'll make sure it happens again…on one condition."

"And what condition is that?"

"You tell Crowther you're not interested."

My mouth curves up. "He already knows we're just friends. I told him when he dropped me off after the banquet."

Jaxon's gaze narrows. "Are you shitting me?"

"Nope." I kiss him again. "But I really like jealous Jaxon. He can stop by anytime. And I mean *any* time."

With a resounding smack, Jaxon's palm slaps against my ass, and I yelp in surprise before bursting out laughing.

Yup. I like jealous Jaxon a lot.

41

RORY

I still don't know how we did it. How we walked out of that bathroom without looking guilty as hell, but somehow, we managed it. They won two away games and lost the third, but Jaxon didn't freak out like the first game of the season. Part of me wonders if it's because he's found a good coping mechanism—aka burying himself inside of me afterward and finding solace in my body. Or maybe he's growing accustomed to the social pressures of being the head coach and a few losses here and there aren't enough to make him crumble. Then again, I'm not sure it matters.

When we aren't traveling with the team, I've been staying at his home. In his bed. Ever since we slept together. And even though we've been keeping things under wraps in general, the sleepovers have been…eye opening. And really, *really* enjoyable.

Thankfully, Maverick is traveling with Ophelia, so I told my parents I've been staying at their house to keep an eye on things, and they haven't batted an eye. Hades seems to like it here, too. If Jaxon had his own yard on top of the penthouse, I'm pretty sure he'd never want to leave.

Stretching my arms over my head, I move toward Jaxon's side of the mattress, only to find him resting his back against the headboard with a phone in his hands.

"What are you doing?" I ask.

Without tearing his attention from his cell, he answers, "I had an idea."

I rub at my tired eyes. "Okay?"

He clicks a few more times on his screen, then tosses his cell to the end of the bed and gives me his sole focus. "Do you think your parents would be okay watching Hades for a day or two?"

"Probably?" A yawn escapes me. "Why?"

"I want to take you somewhere."

"Okay?" I repeat. I prop my head on my hand, blown away that the man manages to look even more attractive with unkempt hair and no shirt than when he's bossing the Lions around on the ice, and that's saying something.

"Today," he clarifies, oblivious to being checked out. "I want to take you somewhere today."

"Okay?" I repeat for what feels like the hundredth time.

"Gonna need you to pack your bag."

Pack my bag? What is this man talking about? Usually, we travel so much for the Lions that we barely leave his place during any downtime. The idea of him planning an impromptu vacation feels…I don't know, it feels like there's a weight to it. A reason, maybe. Or maybe I'm overthinking things.

Sitting up fully, I let the sheets pool around me. "For how long?"

"It's a short trip. We need to be at the airport in an hour, then we fly home tomorrow night."

An hour? He wants me to be packed and at the airport in

an hour? This man is highly overestimating my abilities right now.

"Don't panic. You'll be fine," he says, as if reading my mind.

"Where are we going?"

"Well," he brushes my hair behind my ear. "I was thinking about our run-in with my parents at the golf course, and how you said that it's hard to date and pretend like everything's normal between us when you're a terrible liar."

With a mock gasp, I smack his chest. "I never said—"

"You did, but it's okay." He kisses the tip of my nose. "It's one of my favorite things about you."

"That I'm a terrible liar?" I challenge.

"Considering who I was married to, yeah." His head dips in a subtle nod. "Yeah, Beautiful. It's one of my favorite things about you."

I can't decide if I should be offended or preen like a peacock at his little admission. I never thought of it that way. Being a terrible liar has only ever been a bad thing, but maybe it has its perks after all, like quieting an overthinker's thoughts. "Well, when you put it that way." I bite the inside of my cheek to keep from smiling like a lovesick lunatic, and he leans in, kissing my forehead. Seriously. What is it with forehead kisses? I'm not sure, but I'm definitely a fan. Basking in his affection, I try to stay on topic and ask, "So, what does my excellent candor have to do with our impromptu trip?"

"Figured it might be nice to go somewhere you don't have to lie." He kisses me again. "You should've seen your face after we hooked up on the flight. I thought for sure my brother was gonna call us out for it."

My brows pull. "What are you saying?"

"Wanna show me around Harden Heights?"

My pulse leaps. "You mean...Harden Heights, as in *the* Harden Heights? Where Tatum and Paxton and—"

"Dodger?" His nose wrinkles as if he's tasted something rancid. "You said he already knows you have a thing for me, which is why he offered to fake date you."

"How did you know he offered—"

His smile stretches. "Told you I know you." As if he can't help himself, he leans in for yet another kiss. "And you already told me Tatum knows about us, too, so what do you say? Will you show me around your college town? Maybe soft launch our relationship? See how it feels?"

Excitement bubbles inside of me as I consider holding his hand and walking down the road. Without fear of being seen or photographed or…anything. Just me and him. In the open. Add in the possibility of hanging out with Tatum and Paxton, and I'm pretty sure I could break out in a happy dance right here, right now.

"Yes," I announce. "Yes, that sounds like an amazing way to end the week."

"Perfect." He kisses me again. "You'd better get dressed and pack, or else we'll miss our flight."

He's right, and sixty minutes to pack and drive to the airport isn't going to be an easy feat. I'm so blown away by his thoughtful gift, I can't help but ask, "How long have you been planning this?"

"Since about an hour before you woke up."

My eyes widen. "An hour? Seriously?"

"I've been thinking about it for a little while, but officially booking things? About an hour, yeah."

His boyish grin tugs at my core, making me want to jump his bones and slip in a quickie before we need to leave. Or at least, I would if the idea of seeing Tatum and showing Jaxon a glimpse of my college days wasn't so damn tempting.

"Okay. I'll get dressed. Wanna let Hades out for me while I call my parents?"

"Sure thing."

~

My parents are awesome. A little oblivious sometimes, but awesome nonetheless. I told them the truth. That I'm going back to Harden Heights for an impromptu trip. I just left out the part where Jaxon's tagging along. They agreed to watch Hades without any reservations, even adding a part about how they'll do the same for their human grandbabies, too. You know, whenever I decide to have any. Bless their souls.

The flight goes by in a flash, and so does our short drive to Paxton's beach house. I've only been here a handful of times, but the view is as breathtaking as I remember. After Paxton unlocks the automatic gate, we drive along the winding path before reaching the driveway.

"Thanks again," Jaxon tells the driver. He reaches for the door handle and lets us out as Tatum squeals from the front door.

"Squeaks!" The pitter patter of bare feet smacking against pavement greets me, and I look up in time to catch a glimpse of dark hair before a pair of arms wrap around my torso, squeezing the daylights out of me.

"Tater Tot," I say between gasps. "Can't. Breathe."

She lets me go and slaps my butt. "Missed you, too, Sweet Cheeks." Her attention catches on Jaxon. "Why, hello, Grandpa." His expression drops, and her grin widens. "Just kidding. Come on. Paxton and I are making lobster rolls."

Threading her arm through mine, she leads me up the steps while Jaxon grabs our luggage. I give him an apologetic look over my shoulder, but he only mouths, "You're good. I got this," before Tatum drags me into the house and Jaxon disappears from sight.

Paxton's house is gorgeous. Floor to ceiling windows give a perfect view of his backyard, which is the beach and ocean.

Add in the winding staircase and insanely tall ceilings, and it's basically like a castle and beach house made a baby. A really gorgeous, really breathtaking baby.

"Tatum!" Paxton calls from the kitchen. "The butter's burning!"

Tatum blanches. "Shit!" She darts into the kitchen and turns off the stove as I follow behind her. When the smell of burnt popcorn hits my nostrils, my mouth spreads into a grin. I kind of love seeing my best friend like this. Playing the domestic partner, when a not-so-small part of me wondered if she'd ever settle down. Period. It's nice. Really nice. Watching her fall into the role of partner, even if it makes me feel a little replaced sometimes. The reminder is as bitter-sweet as the scent permeating the air. She's found her other half, and I can't help but wonder if maybe, down the road, I'll get confirmation that I've found mine, too.

The thought hits harder than I expect, and I glance toward the entrance, finding Jaxon juggling our luggage.

"Hey, Baby," Paxton calls over his shoulder, greeting me.

I motion for Jaxon to join everyone in the kitchen and reply, "Hey, Pax."

"Good news," Paxton adds. "The cold lobster rolls are in the fridge and taste delicious."

"He already stole one as an appetizer," Tate informs me.

"Hey, I gave you half," he reminds her. "And I think we bought more butter if you'll check in the fridge."

Their banter fills the kitchen as I scoot around them and look for extra butter. When I find some behind the eggs, warmth hits my back.

"What'd I miss?" Jaxon asks.

"Burnt butter." I turn and wiggle the newfound cube in my hand. "How are your cooking skills, Mr. Thorne?"

"Depends, but if you're asking if I've ever made a lobster roll, the answer's no."

"It's all right, we hadn't, either," Pax chimes in. "Obviously."

"And we're clearly killing it," Tatum quips. "Now, toss me the butter and take a seat. We want to hear all about how much Jaxon loves my best friend."

My eyes bulge at Tatum's use of the L-word. She did not just say that. To anyone, let alone the man himself. Jaxon doesn't love me. Not yet, anyway, and maybe not ever. We're taking baby steps, dammit! Part of me wants to call her out for making assumptions, but if I do, I'll probably just stumble over my words and look even more like an idiot than I already feel. But seriously? Have you no filter, Tatum?

"I got a better idea," Paxton announces. "Who wants drinks?"

I knew I loved this rockstar.

42

JAXON

All right, Paxton's place is pretty nice. Beer in hand, I watch the fire crackle on the beach as the waves lap at the shore. The lobster rolls—both cold and hot—were delicious, despite it being Paxton's and Tatum's first try making them. They even managed to not burn the butter the second time around.

I sip my drink as Paxton reappears with another six pack, and the girls trail behind after each needing to use the restroom. At the same time. Because some stereotypes are very real, and the girls have no problem embracing them. I have a feeling it's because Tatum wanted a private check-in to see how her best friend's doing navigating the new relationship with her childhood crush.

Oh, to be a fly on the wall for that conversation.

I thought it would be weird. Openly sharing our relationship with another couple. Someone who knew us before. Before I saw Rory as a woman instead of the little girl who would follow me everywhere I went. Surprisingly, it's been refreshing. Not needing to watch my every move. Not needing to tear my attention from her mouth when she laughs. Fuck, I love her laugh.

Her hips sway, and her hair blows in the gentle sea breeze, making her look like a dream as Rory approaches me.

"Hi."

"Hey," I rasp.

"You okay?"

I nod and lift a hand, reaching for her. "Come here."

As my fingers envelop her wrist, I tug her onto the blanket stretched on the sand, then tuck her between my thighs. She melts against me, molding her back to my chest before stealing my beer from my opposite hand and taking a drink.

"Mmm, you're warm." She snuggles against me even more. "So, what game did you decide on, Pax?"

"Game?" I question.

"Blame it on the rockstar," Tatum replies. "Ever since the bachelorette party, Paxton's been obsessed."

"Who am I to *not* embrace traditions?" he returns. "Ghost in the Graveyard was awesome, and now that I know you can get group games on your phone, I figured Heads Up is a winner." He unlocks his phone, opens the app, and tosses it to Rory. "Baby, you wanna go first?"

Baby?

The same flicker of irrational jealousy sparks inside of me, only this time, I'm able to say something about it. "You know, I'm pretty sure that isn't the first time I've heard you call Rory that nickname."

Paxton turns to me and grins. "When I first met the girls, I caught them trying to sneak into one of my concerts. Called her Baby because of her baby face."

"And the fact that she was underage in a twenty-one and older venue," Tatum adds.

"You were a terrible influence on me," Rory points out.

"You're the one who didn't read the fine print," Tatum argues. "And in case you're wondering, I regret nothing." She gives Rory a syrupy sweet grin. "Without me, your life would've been very boring."

"And without me, you probably would've wound up as roadkill on the side of the road."

"Or with a dozen STDs." Tatum winks. "Now enough chit-chat. You go first so I can see the look on your face when we beat you."

"Someone's cocky," Rory notes.

"Confident," Tate quips.

"Whatever." Rory clambers to her feet and moves to the edge of the circle so we can all see the screen. Well, all of us except her. "Are we doing a free for all or teams?" she asks.

"Teams," Tatum decides. "You and Jaxon against me and Pax. Rules are simple, but here's a refresher. Rory, you're not allowed to look at the screen, but you need to use the clues Jaxon gives you to figure out what the word is. Jaxon, your job is to make her say the word by any means necessary without saying the word yourself. To make things harder, you can't do animal sounds, hum tunes, say any part of the word or make her fill in the blank. Make sense?"

I nod.

"Perfect," she continues. "If you want to pass on a word that's too hard, tilt up the phone. Tilt the phone down if you get the answer right. Rory, once you guess the correct word, Jaxon can start giving clues for the next word. The goal is to see how many words your team can guess in sixty-seconds. Got it?"

"Yup." Rory starts the clock, and it counts down from five before the word *frog* shines back at me.

"Finley's greatest fear," I announce.

"Frogs?" Rory answers.

"Yes, next one."

She tilts the phone down, confirming she got the correct answer, and another word flashes on the screen. *Twinkle, Twinkle Little Star.*

Damn. I search for a good clue Rory will understand because humming is off the table. Then it hits me. "Okay, do you remember when you were in kindergarten and you would always mix up the lyrics to this song, and your brothers would make fun of you so—"

Her eyes light up. "So you practiced with me for like two days before making my brothers sit and listen to me sing the entire song, three times, mind you, with the right lyrics so they couldn't tease me anymore." She grins, tilting the phone down and confirming the answer before she's even said it. "Twinkle Twinkle Little Star. Next."

Daisy.

"Your favorite flower."

"Daisies," she answers.

Scar.

"When you were little and obsessed with the Lion King, who would you make Maverick pretend to be?"

Covering her laugh with her hand, she answers, "Scar."

The phone dips toward the ground again as Rory confirms she guessed the word correct, not bothering to ask whether or not she's right.

Ballerina.

"What did you want to be when you were little?" I ask.

"Ballerina?"

"Yes," I answer. "Next."

Green Day.

Shit.

"Uh." *Think, Jax.* "They're one of my favorite punk rock bands in high school. You used to always give me crap because they're old and—"

"Green Day," she rushes out. The phone counts down from five, proving our time is almost up.

"One more," I urge. *Mouse.* "I used to call you Squeaks because you sounded like a—"

"Mouse!"

Buzz.

The timer ends, and Rory clutches at her chest. "Okay, that was stressful. How'd we do?"

Pax and Tatum exchange looks of disgust. "Too fucking good," Paxton announces dryly.

"He's right, we're officially not keeping score because you guys kicked our butts and we haven't even started yet." Tatum laughs and reaches for Paxton's phone. "This is for fun and *only* for fun. We clear?"

"Someone's a poor sport," Rory quips.

Tatum rolls her eyes but ignores her, turning to her boyfriend instead. "Ready, Pax?"

"Bring it on, Birthday Girl."

AFTER WE BEAT TATUM AND PAXTON, THEY WENT ON A WALK along the beach, but Rory opted to stay by the fire since the air is turning colder. I can't complain. Having Rory in my arms and a moment to ourselves feels like the perfect way to end our evening.

I was a little nervous bringing her here. Testing out the waters of how we fit when we're with people who know the dynamics of our families and our history together. Instead of it being awkward, it's felt as natural as breathing. I didn't realize how often I've had to fight it. The pull to touch her. To hold her. To kiss her. Just because I feel like it. Being here has made me realize how easy it is to give in to my instincts instead of holding back.

Finishing my beer, I set the empty bottle in the sand and admit, "I like this place."

"Yeah?" Rory shifts to one side, so I can see her face and she can see mine. Her eyes brighten as she peers around the dark beach, her gaze filling with awe. "Me, too. It's my home away from home, you know?"

Home.

The four letter word causes a twinge under my sternum, though I do my best to ignore it. "So, you still consider Lockwood Heights your home?" I ask.

"I mean…I think so?" She hesitates, and I swear I can see the wheels turning in her pretty little head. "Yeah," she decides. "Yeah, Lockwood Heights will always be my real home. I think I'd forgotten while I was away, but ever since the wedding, it's felt right being there, you know?"

"That's good." I swallow, surprised the words slipped out of me before I could stop them. And she must feel it. The shift. The weight behind such an innocent topic like where you want to be, and whether or not it's in the same city as the guy you're hooking up with.

Peeking up at me, Rory asks, "Is it? Good, I mean."

I scratch my jaw, unsure if she's aware of the tightrope I'm walking. We haven't talked about our future or if we even have one. Maybe we should've before agreeing to sleep with each other, but now that we've already muddied the waters, it's hard to know what comes next, or if either of us even wants something to come next. "I think so. You still planning to come back here after we find a replacement?" I question.

She taps her fingers against the outside of her thigh.

One, two, three. Pause. *One, two, three.* Pause. *One, two, three.*

"I, uh, I guess I'm still deciding," she says.

"Yeah?"

"Yeah." She sounds more sure than she looks. Or maybe it's the rhythmic tap of her fingers calling her bluff. I reach out and thread them with mine, resting our laced hands on my thigh as she stays tucked between them.

"Are you writing a pros and cons list?" I ask, attempting to lighten the mood.

"Noooo," she drags out. "I mean, the whole reason why I initially left Lockwood Heights was because of..." Her shoulder lifts. "And now that it isn't an issue, and Tatum has Pax, and I've realized how much I miss my parents, and the fact that Maverick and Ophelia will be staying in Lockwood Heights, and I'll likely be an aunt within the next couple years, uh," her body expands on a deep breath, "it's starting to feel like the right choice, I guess."

The right choice.

Moving to Lockwood Heights.

I don't miss the fact that I'm not on her list of reasons as to why she's considering moving back. The question is, is it because I don't deserve to be on the list or is it because she doesn't want me to feel any pressure by putting me on it?

The thought ruminates as the waves continue lapping against the shoreline.

"I haven't decided, though, so don't stress," she adds.

"Why would I stress?"

The fire dances in her pretty gaze as she holds my stare, not answering me but not retreating either. She's nervous. And she doesn't want to show her hand. Doesn't want to admit that my opinion on where she lives matters. And maybe it shouldn't. Maybe it doesn't. Maybe I'm jumping to conclusions I have no right to leap to. The old Rory would've caved by now. Would've changed the subject. I can't help but notice the way she's standing her ground, and it's sexy as hell. "Where do you see yourself in five years, Jaxon? Still in Lockwood Heights? Or...?"

"Definitely in Lockwood Heights."

"What else?" she prods.

"Honestly? I'm not sure," I admit. Not because I want to keep an answer from her, but after the last year of my life and everything that's happened, everything that's been taken and given to me, I can't even imagine what my next five years could look like, let alone how I want them to wind up.

"Do you think you'll still be coaching the Lions?" she asks.

"Depends on your dad."

"If you could paint your future any way you wanted and had full control of every scenario," she clarifies. "What would you want?"

I shouldn't be surprised at how quickly she turned the table. How quickly she shifted the attention from her potential plans to move back to Lockwood Heights to me and *my* potential plans. Yet here we are, talking about me instead of focusing on her. She's choosing to play off my decisions, my wants and needs, before revealing her own. It's a cautious move, but considering our history, I understand why. Tugging her back into me, I ask, "And I have full control of this five year plan? Whatever I want? I can be selfish and not think about anyone else?"

She nods. "Pretty sure that's the definition of selfish, but yes."

"Smart-ass," I mutter, giving her an extra squeeze. "Let's see. Iris moves to the opposite side of the world and gives me full custody of Poppy."

"Harsh, but understandable," Rory concedes, her tone thick with mirth. "What else?"

"Poppy's allowed on the bench and never cries during the games or practices."

"Oo, you're shooting for the stars, aren't ya?" She sits up a little more, clearly intrigued. "Go on."

"The Lions give me a billion-dollar raise, and I'm able to have anyone on the team any time I want."

Her body shakes with amusement. "Obviously."

"And…" My pulse jumps as I stare down at the most beautiful woman tucked against me.

Say it, asshole. Tell her what you really want.

"And you're there, too. In Lockwood Heights. At the games. Right next to me on the bench."

"Not in the stands?"

"Too far," I argue.

She tucks her chin, somehow curling into me even more. "Oh?"

"Yeah." My arms tighten around her. "I want you right by my side, Rore. Cheering me on and squeezing my ass to distract me from whatever's happening on the ice."

Her nose scrunches in the most adorable way possible as she tries hiding her smile. "That's kind of difficult if I'm all the way in Harden Heights."

"True." I sigh. "But I told you it was a selfish pipe dream, not necessarily a realistic one."

"I mean, the possibility of getting a billion-dollar bonus is a little on the slim side."

"Unfortunately." I smile. "What about you? Where do you see yourself in five years?"

"Hmm." Her attention falls to the ground. "Let's see. Am I allowed to piggyback off yours?"

"I'll allow it."

"I kind of like the idea of Iris being on a different continent." She grimaces, but I don't miss the levity in her expression. "I also love the idea of you having free access to Poppy whenever you want, although I kind of like the way her bottom lip wobbles when she's about to cry, and how I'm one of the only people who knows how to soothe her, so I think I'll keep the prickliness."

"You sound like Uncle Mack when he describes Aunt Kate."

Rory grins up at me. "True, but it definitely fits your baby girl, too."

"It does," I agree. A familiar ache resurges in my chest at the reminder of Poppy's absence, but I breathe past it, trying to focus on the here and now. "So far, I'm only hearing things about other people. Where do you see your future?"

"Well." She taps her thumb against the back of my hand. "Since we're talking selfish pipe dreams, I want my OCD to be obsolete. That would be nice."

Selfish? The woman doesn't have a selfish bone in her body. She hides it well, though. The effect her OCD has on her. But I know it isn't easy. Battling her obsessive thoughts day in and day out. I can only imagine how much easier her life would be if they were silenced and she could live without them. Fuck, what I wouldn't give to take it away. To carry the burden myself. If only it was so easy.

I kiss the top of her head. "What else?"

"You really want to know?"

"Yeah, Rore. I really do."

"I want to be married," she murmurs with a reverence that shoots straight through me. "And I want two children. Maybe three. At least one boy and girl. Although, I'm not too picky on the gender part."

My mouth lifts. "Of course not."

"And I want Hades to live forever. And I want Archer to come back. And I want a home with a big tree in the front yard and a treehouse in the back for the kids."

"Love a good treehouse," I tell her.

"Right?" Her voice softens. "It would be amazing."

It would. So much so I can almost see it. Rory outside in one of her sundresses with her mini-me on her hip, yelling at her little boy who's playing a pirate from his treehouse and is dropping rocks from the top, pretending they're cannonballs as he battles a fleet of ships. Hell, the picture is so clear, I can't help but want to draw myself beside her with Poppy on my shoulders.

It's a dangerous thought. One I never thought I'd have again. One I never wanted to have again. Not after the fallout with Iris. Rory's always had a way of being the exception, though. Is that what she is in this circumstance as well? Does she want to be?

Pushing past the tightness in my throat, I ask, "And your career?"

We still haven't talked about it. About the deadline we set when she offered to help me out with Poppy. Instead, we've buried our heads in the sand, pretending like it doesn't exist. She's emailed me a few resumes here and there, but I haven't had the stomach to open them, knowing that if I do, it'll mean Rory's quitting. Moving on. And my baby girl will have to rely on someone else—someone who isn't me or the only other person who knows how to dry her tears while I'm on the ice. And damn, if it isn't a hard pill to swallow, even when I know it's inevitable. Or at least, it should be inevitable. Considering Rory's lack of follow up emails, or how they're fewer and farther in between, I can't help but wonder if she's choosing to ignore it, too. Like maybe, just maybe, she's as happy with the arrangement as I am.

"Honestly?" She hesitates. "I don't want to work when my kids are little. I want to be home and be present as much as I can, at least until they're in school, you know? I know I paid a lot of money for my degree, and I love the idea of helping little kids any way I can. But…I don't know. I guess I'm old fashioned." Her shoulder lifts. "We'll see, though. It's not like I need to make any decisions anytime soon, right?"

She did it again. Turned the table. Left the ball in my court. Innocently probing for answers without showing her full hand. And maybe I should be bothered by it. By her lack of transparency when it comes to our relationship. But I *can't.* Because she's never been wishy-washy about her feelings for me. Not in the way I've been with her. And if she needs to continue using ambiguity to protect herself until I can make up my own mind, so be it.

"And where is this treehouse?" I ask.

Rory sits up and peeks over her shoulder to face me again. "Selfishly? In Lockwood Heights. Close to my parents." Indecision shines in her eyes. Or maybe it's not indecision. Maybe it's something else. Something I can't quite pinpoint. "And you. If I get to be selfish, I want to be close to you."

The organ in my chest swells as I drag my fingers along her cheek, watching the dying fire dance across her skin. Go figure. She'd be the one to knock me on my ass. The one to surprise me, even after knowing her all these years. The one to tell me what she really wants despite being able to use the ambiguity I was assuming she would without any fault of her own. Yet here she is, being braver and more direct than I'd ever given her credit. "Wanna be close to you, too, Beautiful," I rasp.

"You do?" Her hushed voice tugs at the organ behind my sternum.

"Yeah. I really do."

And damn, if it isn't the truth.

"So, what does this mean?" she asks.

"It means you're moving to Lockwood Heights."

"And my position as Poppy's nanny?"

"Is yours for however long you want it. I support you, Rore. Completely."

With a soft smile, she whispers, "Thank you."

RORY

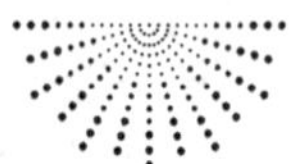

"Woo-hoo!" I shout, cupping my hands around my mouth as Griffin slams one of the Tornados into the glass while one of his teammates swoops in to steal the puck.

"Go! Go! Go!" My mom's cheer mingles with the rest of her friends' from the suite. My dad has the box reserved for every home game, and it gets plenty of use. But this time? This time, it's packed to the brim.

Scooting her glasses along the bridge of her nose, Dylan screams beside me, "Come on, Ollie! You got this! Get over there!"

"Hold me, hold me!" Parker, her youngest, chants.

Without tearing her focus from her husband on the ice, Dylan bends down and scoops up her child, balancing him on her hip before pointing to the flash of black and gold near the blue line while the rest of the kids run around the suite like they own it. "Say, 'go, Daddy, go!'" she tells him.

"Go, Daddy, go! Go, Daddy, go!" the little boy chants.

"Go, Lions, go," I mumble under my breath. My attention drags to Jaxon at the bench. He's yelling something to the team, his hands waving through the air and his hair a disheveled mess as if he's been running his fingers through it for the past hour. I don't blame him. This game has definitely been a nail-biter.

The score is two to three—Lions down by one—with three minutes to go in the second period.

One of the Lions' defenders slaps the puck across the blue line to Crowther, who chips the puck off the board before taking a brutal hit from an opponent. My cringe only lasts two seconds until I'm distracted by Reeves deking left, then darting right around another player as he races for the puck and slaps it toward a waiting Everett, who passes it right back. Around the net Reeves moves, his skates cutting through the ice as my focus slips back to Jaxon. I can't help it. Hell, I've been doing it the whole game.

To be fair, even before we started sleeping together, I was more fascinated by Jaxon's reactions than anyone else's on the ice. He's always been more interesting than the players. More intense. More invested. And that was before. When he actually played instead of coached. Now that he's the one making decisions and commanding his team, it's even hotter. Not sure how it's possible, but it is. My lips part as he paces the bench below, drawing a large circle with his index finger through the air as if to say, *wrap it up, wrap it up! Let's go!*

After a quick pass to Everett, Reeves twists around, racing around a defender to the opposite side of the net where Everett passes it back. The black biscuit cuts across the glassy surface so fast it's hard to keep an eye on it. Hell, it's like a bullet. Winding up, Reeves slaps it toward the corner of the net, and Dylan squeals in excitement. I don't look to see if he makes the shot, though. I'm too distracted by Jaxon's intensity as he watches from the sidelines. Seriously. What is it about men commanding a group like this? I fight the urge to fan myself while the red siren blares, and my family goes wild.

It must've gone in.

"Woo-hoo!" my mom calls. "That's how the Lions do it!"

"PS, amazing assist," Aunt Kate adds as Jaxon wrangles in the team, urging them back to the bench so he can go over the next play.

"What can I say? My husband's hot," Raine quips beside her. "And so is yours, Dylan. Reeves is killing it tonight."

"I know, huh." She shifts Parker to her opposite hip. "Daddy did so good."

"Go, Daddy, go!"

With a grin, Dylan rests her forehead against her little boy's and joins in on his chanting. "Go, Daddy, go. Go, Daddy, go!"

My mom bumps her shoulder with mine. "See how much fun this is?"

I peer up at her and smile. "I think you forget I travel with the team every other week."

"Good point." She loops her arm around my waist and tugs me into her side. "Still. I've missed this. Having you here. Watching you cheer on your team. You used to come to every game."

She's right, I did. We all did. Thanks to my dad owning the Lions, and Mav's and Archer's obsession with hockey, it was an almost daily event. Whether it was peewee or professional, there was always a game, and I was always dragged along to watch. I didn't mind it, though. Actually, I loved it. The cool air. The face paint. The cow bells. The brawls. The memories.

"I've missed it, too," I tell her. "It's been fun coming to more games this season."

"It has," she agrees. "Seems like Jaxon's finally settling into his role, too."

"Mm-hmm." I fight the urge to check him out for the thousandth time, afraid my mom will see right through me. Or maybe she already has. Is that why she's bringing him up? Because she caught me staring like I used to when I was a kid and Jaxon was playing instead of coaching?

"Don't you think, Ash?" my mom prods.

I peek up, finding Aunt Ashlyn on my mom's opposite side. I should be grateful she's here to distract my mom from digging too much, but her presence only adds fuel to the fire. Quietly dating someone's son is one thing. Quietly dating someone's son when they've known you forever and can read you almost as easily as your own mom can? Yeah…that's a bigger issue.

Act. Normal, I silently remind myself. Seriously, with how many times I've had to remind myself of those two simple words since I started sleeping with Jaxon, I might as well have them stamped on my forehead.

Aunt Ash nods. "Yeah, I think Jaxon's finally finding a rhythm with the team." She presses her hand to her heart. "That first game killed me, though."

"Me, too," my mom agrees. "It was rough."

"Right?" Leaning around my mom, Aunt Ash asks, "What do you think, Rore?"

"M-me?" I point to my chest, feeling like a floundering baby duckling. What do I think? Why would Aunt Ash care what I think? Am I that obvious? Did she see me staring at her son like a lovesick puppy? Or am I jumping to conclusions, and I've been hiding it like a champ? And why is she still looking at me like this? Shouldn't she be watching the game or something?

"Yeah," Aunt Ash says. "You're around Jax more than any of us. How do you think he's doing?"

How does she know I'm around Jax more than any of them? Oh, wait. Because it's my job. Right.

Unsure what to say, I tuck my hair behind my ear and try to, you know, act normal. "I think he's…good?"

She glances toward her son below us on the bench. "I hope so. He seems happier."

"He does, doesn't he?" my mom chimes in. "And I mean like, outside of his career. He's finally smiling again." She sighs. "He used to only smile when he was with Pops or after a win."

"Mm-hmm," Aunt Ash agrees. "Now, it's a lot more often, which is great."

"I wonder if he's seeing someone?" my mom muses. "Have you noticed anything, Squeaks?"

"Seeing someone?" I squeak, earning the nickname all over again.

"Yeah." My mom's smile proves she's thinking the same thing before she sobers a bit, explaining, "You know like, is he texting someone or having you stay late to watch Pops so he can go out? Anything like that?"

"N-no, I don't think so."

My mom waves me off. "You're probably right. He must just be happier because he's figuring out work and finding a new rhythm with Iris and Poppy."

"That makes sense," Aunt Ash says. "Speaking of work and Poppy, how's my grandbaby, Rore?"

"She's good," I answer, grateful for the subject change. "Adorable as always."

Her mouth lifts. "She is adorable, isn't she? And when you earn one of her smiles, it makes you feel like a million bucks."

"I'm jealous," my mom interjects. "I've yet to earn one so far."

"You'll get there," Aunt Ash teases before turning back to me. "How's the nanny hunt going, anyway?"

"Nanny hunt?" I choke out.

"Yeah." She frowns, clearly too distracted by our conversation to pay attention to the game unfolding beneath us. "I thought Jax said you were helping him find a long term replacement?"

"Oh. Uh, we actually decided I'm a pretty good fit for the time being, so."

My mom tilts her head. "What?"

My brows crinkle as my eyes drift from one mom to the next. "What?"

"So, you're staying?" Aunt Ash asks.

"I mean…yeah?" It comes out as a question, so I clear my throat and straighten my shoulders. "Yeah, I think I am."

"In Lockwood Heights?" my mom pushes.

I nod, then shake my head, confused by her strange reaction. "Is that a problem?"

"Of course not," she rushes out. "I'm just surprised, is all." She yanks me into a hug before letting me go, giving me a look that makes me feel like I've grown a second head. "You're really staying?"

I can't decide if I'm offended or flattered by her reaction and utter disbelief. "For the time being, yeah."

"Really?" she repeats.

"Unless you don't want me to," I quip.

She rolls her eyes. "You know I want you to. So much so I'm having a hard time believing it's actually happening. We've been wanting you home and in Lockwood Heights since you left. Is that why you've been gone so much? You've been looking for places to stay or something?" My mom turns to Aunt Ash, explaining, "Even when Rory's in town, we barely see her. She's been staying at Maverick's and Ophelia's while they're traveling, but…" She pulls me into another hug. "Ah, I'm so excited. Have you told your dad yet?" Her grip on me tightens. "He's going to be so happy! You have no idea."

"So is Jax, I'm sure," Aunt Ash says. "You're the only person he trusts Poppy with."

Wiggling out of my mom's hold, I ask, "What makes you say that?"

"Because he told us," she answers. "Maybe that's why he's seemed so happy lately." Stealing me from my mom, she gives me a quick squeeze and lets me go. "Being a parent and trusting someone with your child is hard. Especially when you're divorced and there's tension there, you know? He doesn't even have Poppy's mom to rely on. Not really. Add in Poppy's affinity for only liking particular people, and he was a mess. Trying to be a good father and do what's best for his daughter, while also being the breadwinner and building *and* maintaining the career he wants." She shrugs. "Honestly, I think you coming back to Lockwood Heights has been the best thing for him. And the fact that you're staying?" Her voice fills with awe. "I don't know. It's like you're the missing puzzle piece in Jaxon's life. So, thank you. For looking out for my baby boy."

Aaaand why do I suddenly feel like crying?

With the sleeve of my oversized Lions jersey, I pat the corner of my eye while biting the inside of my cheek to keep the tears at bay, but it's really hard. Like, really hard. Because Jaxon has always felt like the missing puzzle piece in my life. The idea of me being the same for him is…it's a lot. More than I'd ever hoped for. And yeah, it's not like Jaxon has officially told me this, but coming from his mom? Someone who knows him better than most? It means a lot to me. I just hope she's right.

"Rory's always looked out for Jax," my mom points out.

"Very true," Aunt Ash agrees. "Same way he's always looked out for you. Speaking of which." She brightens. "How was your miniature golf date with Crowther a few weeks ago? Were you able to use what Jax showed you?"

My eyes widen. "Oh. Uh, it didn't end up happening after Eric got the news about his mom, but, uh," I frown, "we decided we're better off as friends, anyway, so…"

"You and Crowther?" Aunt Ash asks.

Ignoring the golfball lodged in my throat, I force myself to nod. "Mm-hmm."

"Mmm, gotcha." She clicks her tongue against the roof of her mouth. "Probably for the best. I'm still rooting for you, though. You're a catch. You'll find someone awesome."

"Mm-hmm," I repeat as my fingers find the denim of my jeans.

One, two, three. Pause. *One, two, three.* Pause. *One, two, three.*

"Did you see that?" Raine shouts, her nose practically pressed to the glass. "They scored again!"

And just like that, everyone's attention is back on the game, and I can finally breathe again.

For now, anyway.

JAXON

"Y ou did amazing!" Rory gushes as soon as we reach my office. After the win, the team showered, I gave a quick speech, then we went to the conference area to answer reporters and give my two cents on the game. By all counts, I should be exhausted. But finding Rory in my office waiting to congratulate me is enough to renew my energy.

"Thanks." I wrap my arms around her waist and pull her close.

"Um, excuse me, sir." Her body goes rigid. Peeking over her shoulder at the glass windows, she challenges, "You sure this is a good idea?"

Despite the closed blinds, I understand where she's coming from, but I'm too elated by the win to give a shit. Honestly, even without the W, part of me thinks I still wouldn't give a shit. The more time I spend with Rory, the quieter my reservations become.

"Anyone who's still in the building knows to leave me alone when my office door is closed." I lean in and peck her lips. "We're good."

Relaxing into my hold, she drags her hands along my pecs before wrapping them around my neck. "Well, if that's the case." Her chin lifts and she rises onto her tiptoes, closing a bit of the gap between us before I do the rest of the work and meet her halfway, kissing her gently.

Fuck, I missed her. I saw her before the game and stole a few glances up to the box where she was watching me during it. She even slept in my bed last night, but none of these facts eased the weight of her absence. How the hell did I survive the past ten years or so?

Dragging my tongue along the seam of her lips, I kiss her deeper, riding the high of today's win as my cock hardens against her stomach. I wasn't lying before. The locker room's empty, and anyone still in the facility knows not to bother me when my office door is closed. I slide my hands lower, cupping her ass and pulling her into me. Maybe we could—

My phone buzzes on the desk behind us.

Ignoring it, I slip my hands beneath the hem of her oversized Lions jersey, dragging my fingers along her spine.

The phone buzzes again.

She tears her mouth from mine. "You gonna answer it?"

"I'll call them back later." My hands trail down to her ass again as I dive in for another kiss. Brushing her tongue against mine, she sucks me deeper, and the feeling shoots straight to my cock. Apparently, we're on the same page. Thank fuck. I grab the backs of her thighs and lift her up, setting her on the desk.

"Mmm," she hums. Threading her fingers through my hair, she kisses me harder, opening her mouth and letting me steal another taste of her.

My phone buzzes again, and she pulls away, arching her brow.

With a groan, I rest my forehead against her shoulder, blindly reach around her back, and find my vibrating cell on the edge of my desk. When I read the name shining back at me, I groan all over again. "It's Iris."

"Does she usually call when she has Poppy?"

"Sometimes."

"Answer it," Rory pushes.

And even though I don't love Iris cock blocking me, the fact that Rory understands the position I'm in and why I'll always answer my ex's calls even if it kills me only makes me fall for her more. I lean in for one more kiss, then slide my thumb across my screen.

Bringing it to my ear, I mutter, "Hey, Iris."

"Oh, Jax," she cries.

My spine turns into a steel rod. "What's going on? Is Poppy all right?"

"Poppy's fine." She sniffs, and my body sags.

"Fuck, Iris. Don't do that to me—"

"I'm so sorry, Jaxon. I'm so, so sorry."

"What?" I shift my cell to my opposite ear. "Why are you apologizing?"

"Because…because I screwed up."

I can feel Rory's gaze on the side of my face, so I lift my forefinger, silently requesting she give me a minute. Her nod is immediate, and I say into my cell, "Iris, are you okay?"

"No, I'm not okay." She hiccups.

"What happened?"

"He cheated on me." Another sob echoes through my cell. "He cheated on me, Jaxon. Can you believe it?"

He. As in, Chris. Chris cheated on her. The same guy she cheated on me with. And now she's calling me to chat about it? The irony isn't lost on me. I could rub her nose in it. Remind her how karma's a bitch, and what goes around, comes around and all that. But instead of feeling any kind of humor or elation at the situation, all I feel is pity. With a sigh, I mutter, "I'm really sorry to hear that, Iris."

She sniffs again. "Thank you."

Silence follows, and I glance at Rory, mouthing, sorry.

"I saw the game," Iris adds. "You did great, baby."

My brows tug downward.

Baby? Why the fuck is she calling me baby?

"Uh, thanks?" I clear my throat. "You're sure Poppy's okay?"

"Yes, Poppy's fine. She's sucking on the little stuffed bunny you got her. That was really sweet of you, by the way."

Sweet? Since when am I sweet?

Scrubbing my hand over my face, I grumble, "I'm glad she likes it. I'll, uh, I'll talk to you later, okay?"

"Wait."

My head falls forward, but I dig deep, searching for patience. Not because she deserves it, but because she's the mother of my baby, and my life is a hell of a lot easier when I'm not on her shit list, which apparently I'm not anymore? Because she caught Chris cheating on her? Seriously, the woman is delusional.

"What is it, Iris?"

"Do you ever...do you ever think about what our life would be like if I hadn't..." She lets out a long breath. "If I hadn't slept with Chris?"

"Iris, I gotta go-—"

"You're not gonna answer me?"

"Can we talk about this later?" I snap. Not that I want to. Ever. But if it'll get me off this call, I'll say whatever she wants to hear.

"Sure, sure. Whatever you...whatever you need, baby."

There it is again. *Baby.*

I scrub my hand over my face, suddenly exhausted. "I'll talk to you later." Ending the call, I drop my cell back onto my desk. "Sorry about that."

"What'd she say?" Rory asks. Her voice is quiet. Hell, it's

nothing but a whisper. And even though I can tell she's trying to act nonchalant and shit, she's a terrible actress. Clearly, she overheard the conversation. And clearly, she wants to talk about it. Maybe to see if I'm telling the truth. Maybe to see if I'm actually considering going back. Then again, I'm not sure it matters.

Rubbing my hands along her thighs, I answer, "She told me Chris cheated on her."

Her lips part, though I don't know if her surprise is from my response or my candor. "Oh."

"Yeah."

She nods slowly but doesn't say anything else. She wants to, though. I can see it. Taste it. Feel it. Her reservations and unease. I guess I don't blame her. If the roles were reversed, I'd be on edge, too.

Cupping her face, I force her to look at me. "I don't love Iris anymore."

"I know, but…"

"But what about Poppy?" I finish for her. "Poppy's better off with her parents not living together. Trust me."

"You say that like it's a fact."

"It is a fact."

"Yeah, but—"

"No buts," I argue.

"Let me finish."

My jaw locks, but I keep my mouth shut, and drop my hands, slipping more between her thighs as she stays seated on my desk. Instead of touching me back, she leans back on her hands, adding some space between us and killing me in the process. Even then, she doesn't speak.

"You said to let you finish," I gently push.

Avoiding my gaze, she grumbles, "My selfishness is keeping me from saying it."

With a low laugh, I reach up and grab her face again. "I want you, Rory Buchanan. You and only you."

"And Poppy?"

"Okay, I want my Poppy, too, but choosing you doesn't impact my relationship with my daughter."

Whatever concern I'd been hoping to erase remains present. "Isn't that a little debatable in this circumstance?"

I lift a shoulder. "Maybe, if we're talking about technicalities. But I look at it this way. She can have a miserable father one hundred percent of the time, or a happy father and happy mother fifty percent of the time."

"But Iris isn't happy," Rory argues. "Which she just informed you of on the phone."

"Iris is Iris," I remind her. "I give her a week before she's right back to where she was yesterday, convinced I'm a worthless piece of shit who can't do anything right."

"Yeah, but what if—"

"You know you're trying to do the same thing my mom did when she found out about me, right?" I ask. "My birth mom? Eleanor? She approached my dad after telling him about my existence. Then, my mom, Ashlyn, who was my dad's girlfriend at the time, tried to play the martyr. Tried to sacrifice her happiness for the well-being of my dad and me. But what she didn't understand, or what took her a while to understand," I clarify, "is that she was actually sacrificing my dad's happiness, too, and mine. Because a life without one of the women who raised me, someone I call *Mom*, it's…" I hesitate, taking a second to consider what my childhood would've looked like without Ashlyn in the picture, and a burn hits my eyes. "Damn, Rore. I can't even imagine how much I would've missed out on without her. I wouldn't have Griff or Dylan. I wouldn't have been able to travel to London with my mom. I wouldn't have had you." The realization hits harder than I expect, and I lean in, kissing her softly. "If my dad had caved to either of my moms' requests. If he had chosen to break it off with Ashlyn and marry Eleanor, I wouldn't have had you. Not when you were born. And not now." I kiss her again. "So, don't. Okay? Don't question my feelings or my decision. If you decide you don't want to be with me, then do it for you. Don't do it for anyone else, all right?"

I start to drop my hands from the sides of her face, but she reaches up, grasping my wrists and keeping me in place.

"I do," she whispers. "I do want to be with you."

My pulse stalls as I take her in. Vulnerable and hesitant and so damn fragile, I want to scoop her up and protect her. From the world. My ex. Everything. As long as we're together. "Promise?" I rasp.

She nods. "More than you'll ever know, Jaxon Thorne."

Relief washes over me, and I press my forehead to hers, praying she can sense my sincerity the same way I can feel hers. "Good. Because I want to be with you, too."

She hesitates, as if letting my confession ruminate, testing to see whether or not she buys it.

"I mean it, Rore," I push.

"I believe you," she whispers. Lifting her chin, she kisses me softly, then lets out a slow breath. "Can I ask you something, though?"

"Anything."

"I know it's not any of my business, but...what happened? Between you and her?"

Wrinkles crease my forehead as I consider her question. "You already know she cheated."

"I mean before that," she clarifies. "You had to have loved her to propose, Jaxon. I guess I just...I don't get it. She's..."

"The worst?" I offer.

A quiet, almost sad laugh escapes her as she lifts a shoulder. "If you always thought that, you wouldn't have married her."

Unease fills my gut. It's a question I've asked myself a hundred times, if not more. Why did I marry Iris? The longer we were together, the clearer it became that whatever we felt for each other wasn't love, more of a convolution of obligation and complacency. She was gorgeous. Independent. She didn't need me the way other women did, and at the time, I was grateful. Grateful I could focus on work and meeting my own unrealistic standards both on and off the ice. Grateful I didn't have to shield calls or worry about offending her if I stayed late at work to watch a few more tapes. What I didn't understand was that this was the problem. This was the part where I fucked up. Because if you love someone, you want to be with them. You want to skip work and stay in bed. You want to call and let them know you're on your way because you've been counting down the minutes to when you'll see them again. When you can hold them. And kiss them.

Fuck, I was a terrible husband. Iris knew it, and so do I.

So, how the hell do I admit it to the woman in front of me?

"Rore..."

"Tell me. Please?"

Ignoring my shame, I tell her the truth. "I was a workaholic. I was so focused on my career that I didn't put in the time with my wife to build a strong marriage."

"And what about her?" Rory challenges. "Did she put in the time to build a strong marriage?"

My brows pull. "Why are you giving me an out?"

"Because you deserve it, and I want the truth." That same mixture of vulnerability and hesitancy shines in her pretty blue eyes, only this time, there's understanding, too, though I'm not sure I deserve it. "You're a little too good at taking responsibility, Jaxon."

"I don't know what you want me to say," I mutter. "That she wasn't always like this?" I scrub my hand over my face. "I don't know if it's true. I look back and…I don't know. She was there. And we'd been together for so long that people started asking when I was going to propose, and on paper, it made sense. Taking things to the next level." I frown. "I still remember my wedding day. Seeing her walk down the aisle toward me. And I was confused. Why I didn't feel…lighter. Instead, all I felt was anxious. Like I was making a mistake. But the thing is, I didn't know what other choice there was." Blinking away the memory, I sigh. "Until I saw you again. We talked, and I…I felt it. The connection I'd been missing. The connection I never felt with any of the girls I'd dated before meeting Iris, let alone Iris herself." I pause, lost in the realization. "I didn't want to believe it, Rore. Didn't want to think about all the wasted time. But I can't regret marrying Iris," I add. "Without her, I wouldn't have Pops, and…without her, I'm not sure I'd have you, either." A wrinkle forms between my brows. "I think you've always been my endgame, Rory Buchanan. And I'm sorry if that scares you, but—"

"It doesn't." She slams her mouth against mine, tangling her fingers along the hair at my nape and kissing me with every piece of her. Every fucking ounce. And there it is. The light, heady feeling I'd never experienced before. The one I always wanted but didn't think was out there. Not for me.

When she finally pulls away, she rests her forehead against mine, letting our breath mingle as we each search for oxygen.

"I think I love you, Rory Buchanan," I rasp. "Think I've always loved you. First, it was platonic, and now…now it's very different, and I know it's taken me a while to wrap my head around the shift, but…I love you, Rory."

Her lashes flutter. "You have no idea how many nights

I've spent thinking about those three words, and what it would be like to hear you say them."

"Not gonna say it back?" I tease.

But instead of joining in, instead of laughing it off or making light of my admission, her lips bunch on one side, and her eyes well with tears.

"Hey." I grip both sides of her face, dragging my fingers along her cheeks. "Hey, don't cry, Beautiful. Don't cry."

"It's just…you love me."

"You know I do."

"I know, but…but I never thought you'd say it."

"I love you." I kiss her cheek. "I love you." My mouth brushes against her opposite cheek. "I love you."

"I love you, too." Her bottom lip wobbles all over again, so I kiss her there, as well, and she dips her head, a pathetic, yet adorably Rory-esque laugh spilling out of her.

And damn, if they aren't the sweetest four words I've ever heard.

RORY

Propping my feet on Jaxon's coffee table, I pop another piece of popcorn into my mouth as Jaxon excuses himself to the bathroom. He has the next two days off, and we're planning to take full advantage. Don't get me wrong. I love traveling with the team and going to games, but when he has downtime, it's like I get to play house and see how I fit in his daily routine. So far? It's been pretty close to perfect. Add in that I finally get to see Poppy again, and I'm on cloud nine.

Seriously, sharing a child sucks, and she isn't even mine, so when Iris texted Jaxon earlier today, asking if she could swing by and drop Poppy off earlier than normal, we popped popcorn and binge-watched a few episodes of *Gilmore Girls* to help pass the time quicker. That's how excited we both are to see the little nugget.

When a buzz from the elevator sounds a minute later, I jump to my feet, practically skipping toward the panel and accepting the request for someone to enter Jaxon's floor so I can see my little Pops. Seconds later, the doors glide open, and I find Iris with Poppy tucked in her car seat and out like a light.

"Hey, here's—oh." Iris jerks back. "What are you doing here?"

Like a fish, my mouth gapes open as I take in her skin-tight, blood-red dress and the full display of cleavage. Seriously. The woman's breasts are the size of watermelons, and I've never been more jealous of anyone in my entire life. But also, why the hell are those things out? Does she have a date or something? And with who, since Chris just broke up with her. It's been a few days since the random phone call I eavesdropped on in Jaxon's office, but even then…wait.

Is she dressed like this for him? For Jax?

Something curdles in my stomach, and I fight the urge to vomit all over her six-inch heels. This is why she came over early. Why she asked if Jaxon was busy on his night off. She's trying to seduce him. And here I am. The other woman—and wet blanket—she has no idea exists.

"Did you hear what I said?" Iris demands.

My eye twitches as I attempt to focus on what she's saying instead of how awkward this exchange really is. Forcing my eyes to her face instead of her boobs, I say, "I'm sorry, what?"

"I said, what are you doing here?" She says the words slowly, like she's talking to an idiot.

Then again, considering how I'm acting, maybe I am one?

I shake off the thought and clear my throat. "I, uh, I'm here to watch Poppy?"

Hades growls at my side, and I wave him off, trying not to hyperventilate or pass out from full-blown shame. "Hades, go lie down."

Nose wrinkled in disgust, Iris stares at my dog like she just tasted something sour. "Where's Jaxon?"

Hooking my thumb toward the bathroom, I start, "He's—"

"Hey, Iris," Jaxon jogs from the hallway. "Sorry, I was in the bathroom. Where's my Pops?" When he reaches us, he lowers his voice to a whisper, realizing Poppy's still asleep in the car seat. "Here, I got her."

Iris passes her off, her expression as harsh as before he arrived. "What's she doing in your house?"

Jaxon's eyes slide to me, and I have no doubt his confused expression matches my own. "Rory?"

"No, the mailman." She scoffs. "Yes, I mean Rory. What. Is. She. Doing. Here?"

He frowns, as confused as I was until I pieced together the boobs, tight dress, and strange texts. "Is there a problem, Iris?"

"Are you fucking the nanny?"

My jaw drops, and I swear I would've been less shocked if she'd backhanded me. I mean, yeah, he kind of is fucking the nanny, but he's been fucking me for a while now, and she's never noticed or called me out like this, so what the hell is her problem?

"Ooookay," Jaxon drags out. He hands me Poppy's car seat and steps between me and his ex, creating a physical barrier with his broad shoulders and steely-eyed face. "Not sure what I missed when I was in the bathroom, but—"

"Why. Is. She. Here?" Iris demands.

"Lower your voice," he warns. "We don't wanna wake Poppy up."

"Then you better start talking," Iris snaps.

"I'm here to watch Poppy," I whisper-shout, refusing to let the woman pretend like I'm not standing three feet away from her. "Because that's my *job*."

Her body stiffens even more as she glares at me from around Jaxon's torso.

Raising his hands into the air, Jaxon gives me a quick look over his shoulder, then sighs. "I have to work tonight, and when you said you wanted to drop Poppy off an hour early, I asked Rory to come over to keep an eye on her until I'm finished. That's why she's here." He sighs again and takes Iris's arm. "Let me…let me walk you out. Okay?"

The elevator doors slide closed behind them, and I shake my head, reeling from the interaction. Did that really just happen? Like, what the hell?

Refusing to be caught standing frozen in Jaxon's penthouse, I carefully undo Poppy's straps, then lift her from the car seat. After double checking that everything's where it needs to be and she's as safe as possible, I set her in her crib and close the door behind me. A few minutes later, he returns, finding me on the couch.

"Hey." There it is. That unsure syllable. He adds, "Where's Poppy?"

"Still asleep." I stare at my lap. "I moved her to her crib. I read somewhere that it isn't safe to let them sleep in the car seat if they don't need to."

"Thanks," he murmurs. The floor creaks as he moves closer to me. "You okay?"

I look up at him. "What did you say to her?"

"I told her she's not allowed to talk to you like that."

I nod, digesting his words.

"I also told her she has no say in who I am or am not allowed to see."

My eyes bulge. "What?"

"I didn't say we're seeing each other," he clarifies. "Only that she's not allowed to have any say in it." The cushion dips as he sits beside me. "She came over wanting to get back together and was pissed you were here because then she couldn't make a move like she wanted to. I informed her it's never gonna happen. Not now. Not in a million years."

It should make me feel better. His conversation with Iris. The ground rules and expectations he set. And maybe it does? Honestly, I don't know. I don't know how to feel. Or how to act. Or what to say.

"You didn't answer me," he points out. "Are you okay?"

I shrug, unsure how to answer.

"Did you want me to tell her? About us? Because I will. Fuck, Rore. I'll call her right now and—"

"No." I shake my head. "No, I get why you didn't. And honestly, I don't want her to have any say in how we handle our relationship or when we decide to tell people. I just... wow." I shake my head again, forcing the numbness to wear off. "She's..."

"I know." He presses his forehead to my temple. "Trust me, I know."

"I just...I don't understand what you saw in her."

"I ask myself the same question all the time, believe me." His brows knit. "She's manipulative. Arrogant. Stubborn. Honestly, I was a little relieved when she cheated so I could leave her without feeling like I was tearing my family apart. Fuck, I've never said that out loud, but..."

I turn toward him, surprised by the self-hatred in his confession. "You didn't tear your family apart, Jaxon."

"Not sure about that, but thanks."

"I'm serious," I push. Reaching for his hand, I place it in my lap, hoping the innocent touch will quiet any lingering— and likely toxic—thoughts that I know are still spiraling through his cluttered replay of tonight's event. "Besides, I figured it out."

"What?"

"Why you married her."

He pulls back, surprised. "Oh?"

"Mm-hmm." My mouth spreads into a grin. "She has really nice boobs."

His breath of laughter kisses my cheeks as he shakes his head. "Personally, I prefer them like yours."

I snort. "Sure you do—"

"I'm serious." Grabbing the back of my neck, he tugs me toward him, his eyes falling to my mouth. "No one has made me feel the way you do. And I mean that in a very dirty, very literal way." He dips closer, sliding his fingers through my hair and kissing me. It's soft at first. Slow. A little tentative, like he can't decide whether or not I'm mad at him for not exposing our relationship. For not claiming me publicly.

The thing is, I'm not sure I want him to. Not out of force. Willingly, sure. I'm more than ready to take that step, but we aren't on my schedule. And we sure as hell aren't on Iris's, either.

Squeezing my eyes shut, I open up to him, wrapping my fingers around his forearm and shifting closer, craving his touch more than my next breath. With a quiet groan, he slides his tongue into my mouth, deepening the kiss and dragging it against me. Seconds later, he grabs my hips and picks me up, urging me to straddle him. Silly man. He doesn't have to ask me twice. Twisting my fingers through his short strands, I play with the hair along the nape of his neck, making myself comfortable in his lap. He's already hard. It isn't surprising, but it does quiet my insecurities. He wants me. He *still* wants me. Even after seeing Iris looking drop dead gorgeous in her dress with her boobs on full display. And that reminder? It's exactly what I need.

"Do you feel me, Beautiful?" He shifts beneath me as if to make sure I'm aware of exactly what he's referring to. "What you do to me?"

I nod and kiss him again, rubbing myself against him without any shame or embarrassment. And I kind of love that part. That I don't need to be reserved around him. He makes me feel...cherished and confident in a way I didn't even think was possible. It's like with every single interaction we share, he puts another piece of me back together again. A piece I swore was shattered forever after spending so much time convincing myself that the rejection I felt during our first interaction was all I ever deserved. Now it's nothing more than a blip from my past. And this? This is what I deserve. Me. And Jax. And intimacy. And orgasms. Lots and lots of orgasms.

Tearing his mouth from mine, he moves lower, kissing my throat and chest before stretching the fabric of my T-shirt down. With a laugh, I point out, "Pretty sure you take it off by lifting it over my head, not pulling it down."

"You think you're smart, huh?" He holds my gaze hostage as he grips the hem of my shirt and slowly tugs it up and over my head, leaving me in my bra and jeans. "Give me these perfect tits."

I arch my back, rolling my hips against him as he drags the cup of my bra down, then takes me in his mouth. Swirling the tip of his tongue along my nipple, I gasp. Blown away by what the heat of his mouth does and how it feels directly connected to my empty core.

"Need you," I breathe out. "Need you right—"

Hades lifts his head from the floor, hearing something I don't. I stop moving to listen.

There it is. Poppy's whimpers.

My head rolls forward, and I squeeze my eyes shut. "She's awake," I announce.

"She's awake," he confirms. He bends down and kisses my nipple again, blowing softly before tucking my bra back into place, grabbing my waist, and setting me on the cushion beside him.

"That was just mean," I point out, catching my T-shirt as he tosses it to me.

"You're not the one who's gonna be walking around with blue balls for the rest of the night."

"Girls can have blue balls," I argue.

"Can they?"

"I have no idea, but it doesn't mean you're the only one who's a little disappointed they didn't get a solid orgasm out of this."

"I'll make it up to you." He kisses me again, as deep and needy as before. "Now, put your shirt on. I'm gonna get Pops."

I rumple the fabric, slipping my shirt over my head just in time to see Jaxon disappear into the bedroom. *And* he's a good father? Seriously. How is that man so freaking attractive? I bite the bottom of my lip to keep from groaning.

So. Freaking. Perfect.

He returns ten seconds later with Pops in his arms, and you would think it would help the libido, but nope. Watching a sexy man dote on his baby girl is gasoline to an already lit flame.

Yup. I'm a goner.

But what a way to go.

"Knock, knock," a sweet, feminine voice calls.

I look up from the computer in my office, finding Rory in the doorway with my baby on her hip and her dog at her feet. It's been a few days since our encounter with Iris, and I'm still blown away she isn't pissed at me for keeping Iris in the dark about us. She was right, though. Iris shouldn't have any say in the timeline of my relationship with Rory. It doesn't mean I'm not in awe of the way she handled it. Even when Poppy woke up and cock-blocked us, Rory shrugged it off without any issues, but I did make it up to her after Poppy went to bed. Fuck, if I close my eyes, I can still taste her pussy on my tongue.

My cock jerks at the memory, and when our eyes lock from across my office, Rory smiles. "Hey."

"Hey." I push to my feet and stride toward her. "What are you doing here?"

"We were at the park and figured we'd pop in to say hi." Rory looks down at my daughter in her arms. "Isn't that right, baby girl?"

Hades bumps his nose against my thigh, and I bend down,

giving him a quick scratch before glancing around the empty locker room. Satisfied we're alone, I tug Rory into me, creating a Poppy sandwich. Rory's laugh tinkles through the air as she smiles up at me, making my pulse skip a beat in the process. Damn. How did I get so lucky? Unable to help myself, I kiss her softly, watching the way her eyes soften. Then, I drop a kiss on Poppy's forehead. My lips lift when her scent fills my nostrils. "She smells like sunshine."

"Gotta soak up what's left of the warm weather," Rory returns. "Where's the team?"

"Already on the ice."

She nods. "Makes sense."

"You staying for the game?" I ask as Hades pads around my office, sniffing anything and everything and probably searching for a few crumbs from one of my late-night dinners spent behind the desk.

"Depends on how tired this little girl is." Rory looks down at Poppy. "What do you think, girlfriend? You gonna stay happy and watch your daddy's game? Hmm?"

With a grin, Poppy coos and reaches for Rory's face, making my heart fucking melt in the process. I still can't get over it. The way they are together. How much they love each other. How much easier my life is knowing they love each other.

Oblivious, Rory peeks up at me and nibbles on Poppy's fingers. "I think your odds are good. She's still pretty smiley, even though she's exhausted—"

"I love you."

She pulls back slightly, like I've knocked her off guard. "I love you, too." Her eyes bounce around my face. "You okay?"

I nod. "Yeah."

"You sure?"

"Yeah," I repeat. "Just…happy."

Confusion swirls in her pretty blue eyes, telling me more

than she knows. And to be honest, I'm confused, too. By the depth of my feelings for her. But when I see her with Poppy, the way she openly adores my daughter and treats her like she's her own, it's something I can't even describe. Something I want to bottle up and keep forever. Something addictive and scary as fuck because the idea of losing it, losing this kind of connection and acceptance... I'm not sure what I would do. I also don't want to scare her off by telling her all of this. Especially when I need to be on the ice in ten minutes. Hell, I should be out there right now, but I can't make myself walk away.

"I'm really glad you stopped by," I rasp, hoping it'll settle her nerves and erase the crinkle between her brows. It does.

"Me, too," she murmurs with a smile that's so fucking sweet I swear I can taste it.

"Do you want to hang out in here while I go over a few more plays?" I offer.

She takes in the empty office, then shakes her head. "No, no, we don't want to intrude. We just wanted to stop by and say hi. We'll see you after the game, though. Either here or at home. Depends on this girl." She bounces Poppy on her hip. "Isn't that right, Pops?"

I ignore my disappointment knowing Rory's making the right choice. "Okay." I kiss her again, feeling like a damn addict, and she exhales against my mouth, leaning into me.

"Careful," she breathes out. "If you keep kissing me like this, I might not let you leave the office."

"Is that a promise?" I nip at her bottom lip.

With a laugh, she wiggles out of my hold, retreats a few steps, and grabs Poppy's wrist, waving it gently. "Say, 'Bye, Daddy!'"

"Bye, baby girl." I follow Rory's movements into the open locker room, grateful it's empty. Cupping the back of Poppy's head, I brush my lips against her forehead before giving Rory another slow kiss on her mouth. "Bye, Beautiful."

"Good luck, Jaxon." She raises her head, letting me kiss her one more time like she can't help herself, either, then steps back. With a short whistle, she adds, "Hades, let's go."

The sound of heavy footsteps echo from my office as Hades bounds out of the space toward Rory.

"Good boy." Her attention flicks from Hades and back to me. "Bye, Jax."

"Bye, Beautiful."

Hiding her grin against Poppy's forehead, she holds my gaze for one more tempting second, then turns away, leaving me.

IT'S A HELL OF A GAME, AND WE MANAGE TO TAKE THE W. SIX to four. Poppy only makes it to the second period, or at least, that's what Rory's text says. I don't blame her for taking Poppy home so she could get some solid rest in her crib, but it doesn't make me any less anxious to get home to my girls as quickly as possible.

Pulling out my phone, I send Rory a quick text.

ME

Just finished the last interviews. Want me to grab dinner?

Rory's response is almost instant.

RORY

Sure! I'm good with whatever as long as it's quick. I miss you :)

Knock, knock.

The quiet vibration of knuckles against my open door

steals my attention, and I almost drop my phone before recovering at the last second. Arms crossed, Macklin leans against the doorjamb of my office, inspecting me.

Setting my phone face down on the desk, I close my laptop and motion to the chair across from me. "Hey, come on in."

His movements are slow as he moves closer before perching on the edge of the seat.

"What's up?" I ask.

His deep inhale makes his nostrils flare, but he stays quiet.

"You good?" I ask.

"Depends. You gonna tell me what's going on?"

Blindsided, I lean back in my seat, my mind reeling. Mack's a laid-back guy. Always has been. Never one to be impulsive or say shit he doesn't mean. He's consistent. Dependable. And doesn't rock the boat or make assumptions. It's why the underlying tone catches me off guard and leaves me on edge. "Not sure what you're referring to," I finally say.

His eyes thin. "Sure, you don't."

Refusing to cower under his scrutiny, I tilt my head. "If you've got something to say, say it, Mack. Is this about the team? The way I'm running things?"

"I saw you," he clarifies. His razor-sharp gaze somehow manages to sharpen even more as he folds his arms, daring me to deny it.

First Iris, now Mack? It's like we're playing with fire.

I could ask him for specifics. I could deny it altogether. What he did or didn't see. And if I didn't care about Rory the way I do, maybe I would. But it's not like we haven't been careless. Our late night rendezvous. Our early walks to get coffee. Our meet-ups in my office. Honestly, it's a miracle Mack waited this long to approach me about it. And even though my body buzzes with adrenaline, and my fight or flight instincts are threatening to kick in, there's an ember of relief, too. That maybe it's finally out in the open. Or at least, it can be, depending on how I play this. A not-so-small part of me wishes Rory could be here. To help make the decision. About whether or not she's ready to publicly launch our relationship or if she'd rather keep it hidden and safe for a little while longer. Or maybe I'm the one who wants to keep our relationship hidden and *safe* for a little while longer. Fuck, I don't even know anymore.

"It was in your office," Mack clarifies, as if I'm stupid enough to deny it. "I saw you with Rory. Tell me what's going on."

Giving in, I thread my fingers in front of me and mutter, "We're waiting to make things public."

"Why?"

It's a good question. One I've asked myself more times than I can count since kissing Rory the first time.

"Her dad's not gonna be happy if he finds out," Mack adds.

If?

I cock my head, not bothering to hide my confusion.

"It's not my job to say anything, but it *is* yours," he explains. "I'll tell you this much, though. If I found out Griffin was hiding his relationship with Finley for over a month, I'd be pissed."

To be fair, I'm pretty sure he *was* keeping his relationship with Finley under wraps for at least a month before they came clean, but I bite my tongue to keep from throwing my brother under the bus.

The bastard owes me.

Keeping my fingers laced, I cup the back of my head, letting my attention graze the ceiling as defeat washes over me. "I know—"

"Do you?" he challenges. "Because Rory deserves more than being a dirty little secret."

Dirty little secret? The thought alone is enough to make my blood boil. "You think I don't know that?" I demand.

"Do you care about her?"

"Of course, I care about her," I retort. "I love her, Mack."

"Does she know that?"

"Yes."

"Then what's the problem?"

It's another good question. I scrub my hand over my face. "We were…waiting."

"For what?"

"I don't know?" The lack of confidence leaves a bitter taste in my mouth, and I try swallowing past it. "To…to make sure, I guess."

"To make sure it's real?" he asks.

I nod. "Yeah."

"Well, since you just told me you love her, I'm gonna guess it is, right?"

"Yeah," I repeat. "But…"

"But what?"

The muscle beneath my eye pulses as I hold his gaze. "If I come clean to Henry, it means I come clean to everyone."

"And?"

"And that includes Iris," I say while hating how much control my ex has over me, even now. Even after drawing the line in the sand with her the other night. Because I can say whatever the hell I want, but it isn't only me who will have to deal with the fallout. Am I so wrong for wanting to shield Rory from it? From Iris's wrath?

Understanding swallows his frustration, and Mack sighs, resting his forearms on his knees in the quiet office. "All right, that's the first reasonable excuse I'll accept for keeping things quiet."

My mouth lifts. "Glad I've earned your approval."

"Not approving of your decision, only understanding the reason behind it," he clarifies. "Rory still deserves more than what she's getting."

"I know, but you don't understand—"

"I understand better than most, Jax." He glances over his shoulder, confirming we're still alone as he drops his voice low. "Or have you forgotten you're not the only one with an ex who has a penchant for friction and a lack of acceptance?"

Well, shit.

He's right. If anyone gets it, it's him. Rumor has it, his ex, Summer, threw a massive fit when she found out he was dating Kate.

If Iris gave me an ultimatum, what would I do? Would I let my daughter go? Not a chance. But would I let Rory go, either? The thought alone makes my fists clench, and a shudder of unease rolls down my spine. Poppy's my world. She's my baby. My everything. But Iris would never put me in that position.

Would she?

She couldn't. Not legally, anyway. Not without forcing me to take a paternity test, which would put her monthly child support checks on the line, and she's too greedy for that. Add in Iris lying during mediation about when she started sleeping with Chris, and I'm pretty sure the odds of her requesting a paternity test are close to zero. The real question is whether or not Rory's ready to put up with Iris's shit. Because that much is inevitable. And I'm so exhausted from the fighting. But let's say she does play nice and doesn't threaten to take my daughter from me. Iris still won't be happy. Pretty sure she's incapable. Doesn't Rory deserve more than that? Dealing with a shitty ex all because I share a daughter with her? Then again, isn't it Rory's decision in the first place?

Shit. I don't know anymore. Not really.

I want to protect her from it all. My past. My baggage. Not because she isn't strong enough to handle it, but because they're my mistakes. Mine. Then again, so is she. She's mine. If she'll have me. The familiar mind-fuck swirls through my brain, digging into every tiny crevice until my thoughts are so consumed, it takes me a second to feel Macklin's curious stare.

"Seems you have a lot to think about," he notes.

"Not that it's new," I clarify with a sigh. "But you're right. She does deserve better."

"She does. So the question is, what are you gonna do about it?"

47

RORY

"Are you sure you want to go out tonight?" I ask as I lean closer to the mirror and dab on some lip gloss. After the game, he sent me a text, saying he was picking up dinner. Instead, he showed up with a little black dress and a reservation at a local restaurant. Not that I'm complaining. Doing anything with Jaxon and Poppy is a win in my book, but still. "What if someone sees us together? I mean, I know we have Poppy as a buffer, but it's a little harder to write off our motives considering this dress." I twist the cap back on the makeup and motion to the dress in question. It's gorgeous and fits me perfectly, highlighting my curves and showing just enough skin to look sexy without making me feel uncomfortable. Honestly, the choice is evidence of how well the man knows me, and when I tried it on a few minutes ago, my stupid heart pitter-pattered like a lovesick puppy.

Leaning against the doorjamb with Poppy on his hip, Jaxon watches my reflection. "Don't worry. I took care of it."

"Are you sure you don't want takeout or something?"

"In that dress?" His chuckle is low and throaty. "Not even

close." He strides toward me and kisses my cheek, careful not to step on Hades lounging on the tile at my feet. "You look way too good to be hidden in this penthouse."

"Maybe, but outside of this penthouse is Lockwood Heights and way too many family and friends," I remind him.

"It's a risk I'm willing to take. The question is, are you?"

My brows furrow as the buzzer to the elevator sounds from the front. "Who is it?"

With a shrug, Jaxon stays quiet and moves aside, giving me room to go see for myself. Curious, I stride into the hallway toward the panel near the kitchen, confirming that whoever's requesting access to the penthouse can come up, since it's clear Jaxon knows their identity.

Thirty seconds later, the elevator opens. When I recognize the culprit, my lips part, and my breath stalls. "Oh." Hades' bark cuts through the awkward silence, and I show him my palm. "Hades, hush." Leaving less than an inch of space between us, my grumpy beast plops his butt on the ground but doesn't take his eyes off one of the last people I would've expected to see. I clear my throat. "Uh. Hey, Uncle Mack." I peek over my shoulder in hopes of Jaxon being close so he can save me from an awkward conversation. Not that Uncle Mack is awkward. It's just…what the hell am I supposed to say if he asks about my outfit? It's not exactly my regular nanny attire.

"You look nice," he says.

I smooth down the front of my dress, avoiding his gaze. "Thank you. Uh, Jax is…"

"Hey, Uncle Mack," Jaxon greets from behind me. "Thanks for coming."

With a frown, I glance at Jax. Did he plan this?

"We'll only be gone for a couple hours," Jaxon continues.

"I'm not worried. Take your time," Macklin answers.

Dumbfounded, I turn back to Uncle Mack. Why is he

acting like me being in a sexy black dress for an evening out with Jaxon is the norm?

Reading my expression, he smiles. "Don't worry, Squeaks. I already know."

"Know?"

Seriously, what is happening?

"Cornered Jax after the game earlier today." Grinning, Uncle Macklin drops his voice low. "Told him to keep you in the dark as payback. But don't worry. Your secret's safe with me."

Secret? How does he know about our secret? I thought we were hiding it well, or at least, *relatively* well.

Weren't we?

I want to ask what he's talking about, but I can't convince my tongue to work, let alone my vocal cords. Instead, I stand there in stunned silence.

He knows?

He knows.

Shit.

What does this mean? And is Jaxon okay with it? I mean, he seems okay with it, but making assumptions is the last thing I was raised to do. What if he's not okay with it? I don't know. I don't know, but I'm really confused, and if Uncle Mack wanted to knock me off kilter and dish me up some solid payback for keeping him—and the rest of the family— in the dark, he's nailing it.

The big butthead.

Giving Jax his attention, Macklin claps his meaty hands and reaches for Poppy. "How's our Pops doin'?"

"She's good," Jaxon answers. "Just had a bottle. Should be ready for bed in a few minutes. And don't mind Hades. He'll hang outside her bedroom door as soon as you put Pops in her crib."

"Wait, are you babysitting?" I ask.

"Figured you could use a night off," Macklin explains.

A night off? Why would I—the *nanny*—need a night off? Oh, because our secret's safe with him. Right. How could I forget?

Closing my gaping mouth, I ask, "What if she starts crying?"

"I know how to handle a baby," he reminds me. "Raised a few of them and everything."

"Well, yeah, but Poppy…" I cringe as Jaxon hands her off to Macklin and she starts fussing right away.

With a low laugh, Macklin starts shifting on his feet, swaying from side to side as he pats her back softly. He's completely unbothered and in his element in a way only a good parent can be. "I'm aware Pops has her favorites. Don't worry. She'll calm down."

And maybe she will, but the unproven assumption doesn't ease my anxiety. Quite the opposite, in fact. Panic rises in my chest as her bottom lip wobbles. As her tiny face scrunches and her skin reddens with every squeal of anguish. I've never liked seeing a baby sad, but Poppy? This is torture. Digging my fingernails into my palms, I challenge, "And if she doesn't calm down?"

Mack looks down at the bag hanging by his side that I hadn't noticed before now. "Just invested in some noise-canceling headphones, and she's set to go to sleep in a few minutes. I'll be fine. And so will she," he promises. "Besides, if she doesn't calm down in fifteen, I have both your numbers, remember?"

He gives me a look that somehow rides the line between amusement, confidence, and a sprinkling of patience, though I don't know if it's because I'm fighting back on the proposition of a night off or if it's because he's channeling his inner monk in hopes of feeding the same energy to the baby in his arms.

Regardless, the man makes a good point. He does have our numbers, and it's not like we're going far. We could be back in ten minutes. Five, if we go somewhere close by. Even so, Macklin could have a thousand good points, and none of them would ease my growing anxiousness. I stare at Poppy on his hip. The way she leans away from him. The way she throws her head back. The way she flails her arms. It's soul-crushing. Helpless, I tap my fingers against my outer thigh.

One, two, three. Pause. *One, two, three.* Pause. *One, two, three.* Pause.

Hades bumps his nose against the side of my knee, snapping me out of my spiral, or at least attempting to.

Turning to Jax, I beg, "Jax."

"She'll be okay." His confidence surprises me, though it probably shouldn't. He's Poppy's dad. He knows her better than anyone. And this isn't his first rodeo, either. Not when it comes to knowing what's best for Poppy and what she can and can't handle.

"Go," Uncle Mack urges.

On shaky legs, I reach for my purse on the kitchen counter, sliding it onto my shoulder while trying to ignore Poppy's wails no matter how much it kills me.

Dodging her flapping arms, Jaxon kisses her on the forehead. "Love you, Pops. We'll be home soon. I promise."

Tears well in my eyes as I fight the urge to grab Poppy from Mack and never let go, even when I'm pretty sure I've never felt more torn in my entire life. How do parents do this? How do they leave their babies? How do they shut off the voice inside their head screaming at them to pull them close and never let them go? But the worst part? The worst part is that I don't know if it's my OCD rearing its ugly head or if the instinct is real and shouldn't be ignored. And what if it *is* real and I *do* ignore it? I'd never forgive myself. And it's not that I don't trust Uncle Macklin. I do. I trust him as much as I would my own dad, but still. This is...this is torture. And what if—

A warm hand touches my lower back, and I glance up at Jaxon.

"She's okay," he murmurs.

She's okay.

She's okay, she's okay, she's okay.

Holding onto his words like they're a lifeline, I shove my irrational fears aside and lift my quivering hand to drag it over Poppy's wispy blonde hair before leaning in for a quick kiss. "Love you, Pops." A lump forms in my throat, but I swallow past it. "Like your daddy said, we'll be...we'll be home soon, okay?" *Breathe.* "I promise."

Jaxon reaches for my hand, tugging us into the waiting elevator. Once the door closes behind us, he leans against the rail, and I tuck my arms around me, digging my fingers into my bare skin to keep from giving into my compulsion and tapping against my thigh. Even then, it doesn't stop the carousel of thoughts circling through me. What if they're on the balcony and Macklin trips and she falls over the edge? What if she finds something on the ground and chokes on it? What if he forgets she's there and trips over her, breaking her or arm or leg? What if he steps on her head? I know it would be an accident, but—

Stop!

"I can't decide if what I just did in there was a mistake or not," Jaxon announces.

"Hmm?" I look up, finding his attention on me.

He gives me a sad but reassuring smile. "You know I always love taking you on dates, but you look about as excited as a woman on her deathbed. You okay?" He moves closer and brushes a stray tear from my cheek, spreading the moisture between his thumb and forefinger as if inspecting it. "I'll take this as a no."

Batting his hand away, I sniffle pathetically. "I just…I hate to see her sad."

"Me, too." His focus moves to the closed elevator door, and I realize he hasn't pushed the button to the main floor yet. "Do you want us to bring her?" he asks. "I kind of wanted to talk to you about something and figured a night off might be good, but we can go in—"

"No, no, no," I rush out, no matter how appealing the idea of bringing her with us is. "Honestly, I know it's good for her." I wipe at my cheeks and let out a slow breath, trying to get my shit together. "To be exposed to new people and have a positive time, even if it sucks to see her sad in the beginning. And I know it's good for me too. It's just…the OCD is OCD-ing, and"—I force out all the air from my lungs in a short, sharp breath—"wow. I'm good. I'm good. I swear. I'm good. And I can't go back in there. Not until after dinner. If I do, it'll only feed my OCD and"—I take another quick but deep breath—"I'm good."

"Come here." As if he can't handle witnessing my own mini-meltdown, he pulls me into his chest and rubs his hand along my spine. "I'm sorry that triggered you."

"It's okay. I just can't give in."

"We won't," he promises. "Although, it's nice to see how much you care about her."

I blindly smack his butt, offended he'd even think about assuming anything different. "Of course I care about her—"

"I know." I can hear the smile in his voice. "It makes this even easier."

With a frown, I wiggle out of his hold, unsure if I heard him correctly or if I missed something thanks to being distracted by the memory of Poppy's little cries. "Makes what easier?" I ask.

"Come on. We'll talk at the restaurant."

"Jaxon—"

"You know what? You're right." He wraps his arm around my waist again, tugging me into him and kissing the shit out of me until my head spins and my legs grow weak. It's hot and minty and so damn commanding, I can't help but wonder if he's trying to brand me with his lips. Then again, I wouldn't complain. I've always been his. Or maybe he's trying to distract me. It's definitely working. I open my mouth wider, and he takes full advantage, slipping his tongue into me, so I suck on it the same way I would his—

He pulls away from me. "Careful, or we won't make it to dinner."

"Is that a bad thing?" I blink slowly, trying to get a handle on my libido after being blindsided by the hot as hell kiss, only to find Jaxon staring at his phone.

Really? He's looking at his freaking phone after a kiss like that? I fight the urge to smack him all over again.

"What do you think of this one?" he asks.

"Huh?"

"This one." He shows me his phone. And there, front and center, is a photo of Jaxon Thorne kissing me with the ravenous hunger of a starving man in the middle of an empty elevator. The reflection on all sides only amplifies the view, showing the viewer every angle of the kiss, while making my knees weak all over again. "I think you look gorgeous, but we can take a few more." A smirk tugs at the corner of his kiss-able mouth as he cocks his head. "I'm game if you are."

What is he talking about?

"The photo's fine," I reply, "but…what are you going to do with it?"

"I'm gonna send it to the family."

My heart lodges in my throat. "What did you say?"

"I said, I'm gonna send it to the family." He hesitates. "As long as you're okay with it."

Send it to the family? Does this mean he's ready to

announce our relationship? To finally fill everyone in on what we've been doing right under their noses? "Why would you…"

"Because I'm tired of hiding this, Beautiful." His expression is so damn genuine and contagious, my stomach squeezes in response. Holding my gaze, he bends around me and pushes the button to the first floor, lingering in my space in a way that has no right to be as hot as it is. "Aside from Pops, you're the best thing that's ever happened to me," he says. "And it's not that I didn't see it. It's that I was scared that if I gave it too much attention, I'd jinx it or something, and I'd lose you. But it isn't fair to hide this from anyone, let alone the people you care about. You're the person I want to be with, Rory Buchanan. And the fact I've been too scared to make this public is on me, not you."

He wants to make this public. He wants to make his relationship with me public. The realization makes me want to laugh and cry all at once. Happy tears. But tears, nonetheless. Then again, would either of us expect anything different?

"To be fair, I'm pretty sure I'm the one who suggested we take things easy and keep it quiet," I point out.

He gives me another peck. "So, it's your fault, huh?"

"Let's call it a mutual decision."

"All right, it was mutual," he concedes dryly. "So, what do you say we *mutually* make another decision?"

My gaze narrows in suspicion. "Depends on what it is."

Wiggling his phone back and forth, he showcases our kiss shining back at me as the elevator reaches the main floor. "Can I send this to the family? Tell everyone about us?"

I want to say yes. I want to say hell yes. There's only one problem. One really annoying, not-so-little problem ruining this entire moment. I feel my smile droop, and I look down at my shoes as I walk into the building's main lobby.

Jaxon's grasp is gentle as he reaches for my wrist, stopping me in the main area. "Rory, what's wrong?"

What's wrong? He wants to know what's wrong? I really don't want to ruin a perfect moment, a moment I've been waiting to unfold for as long as I can remember. But I also know there's no avoiding it. Literally.

"What about Iris?" It's not that I don't like her, it's only… Yeah, I don't like her. She's kind of awful.

Whatever enthusiasm he'd been sporting seems to retreat ever so slightly as he tilts his head. "We already talked about this."

I hold his gaze, letting him read my stare instead of wasting my breath because…seriously? He can say whatever he wants. Put on whatever front he wants. He can live in la-la land for the rest of his existence. And none of those things will change our reality. If Iris finds out we're together, she's going to react, and it won't be in a good way, especially after Jaxon lied to her about him fucking the nanny, as she so eloquently put it, just a little while ago.

Reading me like a book, he pushes, "Rory, Iris has no say in regards to who I date."

"Yeah, but…" My voice trails off as my attention falls anywhere and everywhere except on the gorgeous man in front of me.

With a gentleness I've come to expect, Jaxon touches my chin and tilts my head up, encouraging me to look at him. "I can handle Iris. The question is…are you ready to put up with her?"

Am I ready to put up with her? I don't think anyone's ready to put up with someone like her. But if it means Jaxon and I take this to the next level and tell our families, then…I think it's worth the inconvenience. Isn't it? This is Jaxon, for Pete's sake. My Jaxon. *The* Jaxon. The guy I've dreamed about for decades. The guy I would give up anything for. The guy I would move across the country for. So what if he has a crappy ex who's never going away? Right?

"You're hesitating," Jaxon notes. "Does that mean you're not ready to put up with Iris?"

"I think I can handle her." My mouth lifts. "But only because you're really good in bed."

He laughs and tucks his phone back into his pocket. "Perfect. I'll send the picture after dinner then."

"Why after?"

"Because we should probably tell your parents first." He touches my lower back again, and leads me onto the street. "Speaking of which, they're waiting for us at Butter and Grace."

"What?"

"I told your parents to meet us there."

"Oh." The air whooshes from my lungs as I wrap my head around the turn of events.

We're going to dinner. With my parents. Who, at this point in time, have no idea I'm dating Jaxon Thorne. Perfect. Absolutely perfect.

What could go wrong?

48

JAXON

I've never been one to feel nervous. Not really. Even the spiral after the first game of the season wasn't based on nerves but rather from crumbling under the pressure of holding myself to unrealistic standards. I know this.

And I also know that if Poppy came to me and told me she was dating someone—had been dating someone—who'd already fucked up one relationship and had kept his feelings for my daughter from me instead of coming clean and being open, I'd be… Well, let's say I'd be less than enthusiastic about the whole thing.

I tug at the collar of my button-up with my free hand, keeping my opposite on Rory's waist as we approach the hostess table.

"Hello, we have a reservation under Thorne," I announce.

The hostess smiles. "Yes, of course. The rest of your party is already seated. Follow me."

When we reach the table, I fight the urge to remove my hand from Rory's side as Henry stares at the location like it's Pandora's box. Maybe it is.

"My baby!" Mia gushes. She pushes to her feet and cuts

off Henry's pinpoint stare, tugging her daughter into a hug. "I missed you!"

"Missed you, too!" Rory says. "What are you doing here?"

"Your employer requested our presence for the evening." She gives me a curious look over Rory's shoulder. It's even heavier than Henry's stare from seconds ago. Not angry or judgmental, just…heavy, as if she's warning me to tread wisely. Then, in an instant, it disappears, and she lets her daughter go, giving Rory a smile. "Take a seat. We ordered a few appetizers to nibble on. Hope that's okay?"

"Oo, thank you," Rory returns. "I'm starving."

I pull out her chair and help her sit down before doing the same to my own. The cheesy scent of artichoke dip turns my stomach as I grab my cloth napkin and place it on my lap. Part of me wants to take control. To announce why we're here and what Rory means to me. The other part? Call me a fool, but the other part wants to let Henry have a minute to digest what I'm pretty sure he already knows. The question is, for how long?

"So," Mia starts. "I heard my daughter accepted a full-time position."

"Mm-hmm," Rory returns as she scoops a piece of pita bread into the dip. "We figured, why fix what isn't broken, right?"

"Not broken, huh?" Henry interjects. His expression is locked down, but I know what he's doing. He's probing. Baiting us. To catch us in a lie or to come clean.

Why do you think I brought you here, Henry?

So much for giving him a minute to process shit. I guess it's now or…*now.*

Clearing my throat, I announce, "Rory and I are dating."

"Oh?" Mia returns. If she's surprised, she doesn't show it. Or maybe she's finally mastered Henry's poker face. Sure enough, he's sporting the same one, refusing to give me the slightest clue as to what he's thinking.

Reaching beneath the table, I grab Rory's knee and squeeze, stealing her strength and silent support. "We reconnected at Maverick's wedding and wanted to see how things played out before announcing it to everyone."

"At the wedding, huh?" Henry says. "What about Dodge and Crowther?"

Twisting the linen napkin in front of her, Rory peeks at her dad. "I think we all know there's only ever been one guy for me."

Damn, if it doesn't make my chest swell with pride. And guilt. For taking so long to reciprocate, even if it was the right thing to do.

"And you?" Henry challenges, giving me his attention. "Is she the only girl for you?"

My chin dips. "Yes, sir."

"For how long?"

"Dad," Rory whines.

I squeeze her thigh beneath the table. "For as long as she'll have me."

"Does this mean you're not house sitting for your brother anymore?" Mia interjects.

Rory has the decency to blush as she chews her bite of flatbread and artichoke dip. At least she doesn't choke on it. Swallowing, she weakly offers, "Surprise?"

"What about your career?" Henry pushes.

"Nannying can't be a career?" Rory tosses back at him.

Henry doesn't budge. "You know what I mean, Squeaks."

"Rory's career is independent of our relationship," I explain. "I'd love it if she watched Poppy while I'm working, but if she decides she wants to pursue child psychology or anything else for that matter, we'll make it work. Whatever she needs."

"As long as she stays in Lockwood Heights?" Henry's same indecipherable expression gleams back at me.

"It'd be more convenient," I acknowledge dryly, "but we're in this for the long haul, and I'll make anything work."

"We both will," Rory adds. She dips some more flatbread into the artichoke dip as if she's trying to act normal despite her knee bouncing beneath the table. "Like I said. Jaxon's it for me, and let's be honest, staying in Lockwood Heights makes life easier for Jaxon with Poppy and the Lions—"

"And you?" Henry challenges, pinning me with his stare.

"Henry," Mia warns. "I know we agreed to let you play hardball, but you're walking on thin ice."

"Two minutes."

"I've given you two minutes," she reminds him, refusing to back down.

"Give me one more." His gaze cuts to her. "*Please.*"

Please. Henry Buchanan doesn't say please to anyone. He doesn't need to. His attention cuts to his wife, and the two volley back and forth in a silent conversation only two people in love and who've been together for decades can. With tight lips, brow knits, and cocked heads. Finally, Mia settles back in her seat, giving her husband the floor while proving exactly how much she trusts him.

Satisfied he has his wife's approval for at least sixty more seconds, Henry turns to me and Rory again. "Let me be clear. I'm not saying I don't support this relationship." He hesitates, giving me a glimpse of the Uncle Henry I was raised with as he gives his daughter a reassuring smile before sobering. "I'm saying I need to know where you land on Jaxon's priority list, since we all know he's been at the top of yours since you were only a kid."

"Dad," Rory scolds. "Really? We're going to bring up my childhood crush right now?" Red blooms across her cheeks, and her body curls in on herself as if she's ashamed her dad just aired out her deepest, darkest secret. The fact that she's loved me for as long as we all remember.

"Let your dad finish, baby," Mia murmurs. "We care about you, and need to know—"

"If Jaxon's feelings for me are real?" Rory snaps.

Henry sighs. "We know they're real, Squeaks."

"Then what's the problem?" She wipes the crumbs from her fingers and folds her arms, clearly over tonight's appetizer, thanks to the conversation. "I love him, and he loves me, and I know you want me to be happy, and he makes me happy, so I'm a little confused as to why you're grilling him instead of congratulating me on my first real and pretty freaking healthy relationship."

Another look is exchanged between Rory's parents before Mia reaches for Rory's hand while I continue clinging to her opposite one.

"Baby, he's your only relationship," Mia says, gently. "Your only person. Ever. And it isn't a bad thing. Honestly, Jaxon's the luckiest man in the world, okay? We just want to make sure he's aware of it, too."

"That he's my only relationship?" Rory grumbles. "Gee, thanks. You guys are super supportive—"

"Rore, it's okay," I interject.

Because suddenly, it makes sense. The real reason behind their reservations. I've hurt their daughter before. Ruined her. And even though it was the right choice at the time, it couldn't have been easy for them. Seeing their daughter fall apart and run away, leaving them feeling helpless as parents. If the roles were reversed, I'd feel the same way. Hesitant. Restrained.

Keeping this in mind, I say, "To be clear, I am the luckiest guy in the world. I know you think that because we took things slow and kept our relationship private that you're afraid I'm not willing to stick around if and when things get tough. Because they will," I clarify, "It's part of life. I know I have a shit-ton of baggage, more than anyone, let alone your daughter, should have to help carry. I know Rory deserves the world and more. I also know I love her. Have loved her for as long as I can remember. I mean it. And that platonic love—and *only* platonic love—" I emphasize, "shifted into something more when we reconnected at Maverick's wedding. It turned into something deeper. And I know it's scary. Trusting someone to look after someone they care about. Trust me. I've thought about what I would do if Poppy showed up with an asshole like me. But I promise you," I turn to Rory, holding her gaze, "I promise you," I reiterate, "I will always put you first, and the feelings I have won't go away. I don't want them to," I add honestly. "I've already lived a life without you in it, and I refuse to do it again. Even if it means giving up my job or moving across the country. Even if it means putting up with a pissed off ex who loves making my life miserable." I turn back to Henry. "I love your daughter, and one day, I hope you accept it."

The same intensity I've grown accustomed to during Lions meetings glares back at me, making my pulse ratchet as I hold Henry's stare from across the table, refusing to back down or cave under his scrutiny.

"I love her," I repeat. "I do."

"I believe you," Henry decides. "Only needed to hear you say it."

"Then it looks like we need champagne," Mia announces. She orders a bottle from the waitress, and within minutes, glasses with amber liquid are set in front of us.

Raising hers into the air, Mia says, "To Jaxon and Rory. The couple we had pegged long before any of us shipped Finley and Griffin or Maverick and Ophelia." She grins.

"What?" Rory gasps, lowering her half-raised glass as she registers her mom's words. "You had us pegged?"

"Of course we did," Mia laughs. "I mean, it was a little touch and go with the whole Jaxon-decided-to-get-married and all, but after he announced the divorce earlier this year, *and* we knew you'd be coming back to town for Mav's wedding, I had no doubt you two would wind up together." Her eyes cut to Henry. "By the way, you owe me big because that was a lot longer than sixty-seconds." Her attention drifts to me. "I'm sorry we had to put you through the wringer. Trust me. It wasn't fun for us, either, but we needed to be sure."

"I get it." My mouth curves up. "And I'm glad I passed."

"With flying colors," she promises.

"Hold up," Rory interjects. "You're saying you had us pegged before anyone else?"

"Of course we did," Mia returns. "Baby, a love like this doesn't go away, and it's not something you can fight, either. You just needed to be patient until the timing was right."

"She's sugarcoating it," Henry clarifies. "But we know Jax is a good guy, and after watching you grow up and holding onto your feelings for him despite your best effort to let him go, we knew he was the only person who could ever really make you happy."

Rory's bottom lip juts out like she's fighting back tears and she reaches across the table, squeezing both her parents' hands. "I love you."

"Love you, too, Squeaks," Mia returns.

"Love you, Rore." Henry raises his glass into the air with his free hand. "To Jaxon and Rory."

"To Jaxon and Rory," Mia repeats.

Peeking over at me, Rory raises her glass. "To you and me."

"You and me." I clink my glass against hers then lean in for a kiss, sealing my promise for everyone around us to witness.

This is it. No more running. No more hiding. I brace myself for an onslaught of trepidation or second guesses. But instead, all I feel is…peace. And damn, if it isn't the most cathartic feeling ever.

"Love you, Beautiful," I murmur against her lips.

"Love you."

JAXON

"You sure about this?" Rory asks. "I mean, I know my parents are one thing, but…" She peeks up at the house I once shared with Iris before giving it to her in the divorce. I follow Rory's gaze, taking in the red brick, trimmed lawn, and black door. If I close my eyes, I can still feel the hot sun beating me down on me as I painted it a few years ago. So many memories, yet I don't miss it at all. Strange.

Turning off the ignition, I grunt, "Might as well get it over with. I think Iris will take it better if she finds out from us."

She hesitates and picks at her T-shirt. "That's probably true."

"Why don't you stay in the car, and I'll take Poppy inside? She might handle it better if it's only me."

Not that she'll handle it well in general, I silently add, but the more I can shield Rory from Iris's wrath, the better. And maybe, in a week or two, she'll have calmed down and things won't be so shitty. Maybe.

"Whatever you think," Rory offers. "I'm here to support you, so…"

I bend over the center console and kiss her softly. "I'll be quick, I promise."

Climbing out, I grab Poppy's car seat from the back and hook it on my arm, then make my way up the steps and knock on Iris's door. With a creak, it opens seconds later.

"Hey." Iris leans against the doorjamb in a lacy white tank top, her nipples saying hello through the thin material, and a pair of my old boxers. Where the hell did she get those?

"Hey, Iris." I ignore her inappropriate outfit choice and hold her gaze, determined to get through this as painlessly as possible.

"You look nice," she compliments.

"Thanks."

Moving aside, she opens the door a little wider. "Why don't you come in? I can make you some coffee."

"Can't." I clear my throat and scratch my jaw. "Listen, we need to talk."

"Which is why I suggested you come inside," she teases. "You know I don't bite. Usually." Her laugh grinds on me as she turns around and strides toward the kitchen, her hips swaying seductively with every step. Seriously. How the hell did I not see through her bullshit before we married? I need to get this over with.

With a quick look over my shoulder, I find Rory staring at me from the passenger seat. *Sorry*, I mouth to her before stepping inside and closing the door behind me.

"Iris?" I call. "We need to talk."

"Bring Poppy in here and set her on the table." Her voice echoes from the kitchen at the back of the house, and I bite back my annoyance, following Iris's instructions as she pours two cups of coffee.

She offers one to me. "Here, just the way you like it."

"Thanks." I set the coffee down without bothering to take a drink. "Listen, I—"

"Do you remember when we had sex on this table?" Her hand runs along the solid oak before she takes a seat in one of the chairs. "I miss that. The way you knew how to make me scream—"

"Not here to reminisce about our past, Iris."

"Of course not," she agrees. "You're totally right. I'm just so glad you're here, and we have a chance to actually talk. I know I was distracted with Chris, and you've been busy at work, which you're totally killing it, by the way, and—"

"Iris—"

"Do you ever think about us, Jax?"

Pinching the bridge of my nose, I mutter, "We've already had this conversation."

"I know, but you never seem to answer."

"No, I don't think about us," I reply bluntly. "And if you want me to be honest, I stopped thinking about us long before I ever found out about you and Chris."

Her expression falls, and my guilt rises with it. Okay, maybe that was too far. I don't want to be a dick. She's the mother of my child. But can't she see how exhausting she is? How uncomfortable I am?

"How can you say that?" she whispers.

"I'm sorry."

Her breath is shuddered at best as she stands from the table. "So am I, Jaxon. I'm so sorry."

I look down at my feet. "I know."

"Why don't you sit down? I'm so tired of fighting. I want to just…talk, you know? I want to talk and reconnect, and…I don't know."

"I'm not here to make small talk, Iris."

She moves closer, touching my chest and making my skin crawl. "Then what are you here for?"

I grab her wrist and lower it, careful not to hurt her while also standing my ground. "To tell you I lied to you."

Her breath hitches. "What?"

"I said I lied to you. When you dropped off Poppy last week, you asked if I was sleeping with Rory, and—"

"How could you?"

I shake my head. "I don't owe you anything, Iris. We're not together, and we haven't been together for a long—"

"You're right," she rushes out. "And that's my fault, okay? It's my fault we got divorced in the first place. I was just lonely, and it doesn't matter. What matters is that I forgive you as long as it doesn't—"

"Not asking for your forgiveness." I let her wrist go and take a step back. "I'm informing you that I'm dating Rory, and that I see a real future with her. That's it. I wanted to apologize for lying to you, clear the air, and let you know so you don't hear it from someone else."

Staring up at me, her eyes bouncing around my face as if searching for answers, she whispers, "You're serious."

"Yes."

Her nose wrinkles. "But she's the nanny."

"Yes."

"And a child."

I shake my head again, feeling the beginning of a migraine at the base of my skull. "She's not a child—"

"You sure about that?" she challenges. "Because she looks like a child and probably acts like one, too."

"Iris." I grit my teeth, trying my fucking hardest not to stoop to her level, no matter how difficult she's making it. And yes, she's making it really fucking difficult. "My warning last week is as true today as it was then. You are not allowed to attack Rory, call her names, or speak to her without the respect she deserves. Do you understand?"

"That you're a fucking asshole?" She folds her arms, pressing her tits together while doing an emotional one-eighty like she used to when we were married. "Yes, I'm aware."

Guess this means you don't wanna get back together, right? I almost say, but I bite my tongue, knowing the asshole comment won't get me anywhere. If anything, she'll wind up using it for ammunition in a future fight. Besides, there's nothing left to say. I've done my job, said my peace, and now it's time to walk away.

Twisting the car seat toward me, I drag my fingers along Poppy's and murmur, "Love you, Pops. I'll see you next week." I glance up at Iris. "See you next week, Iris."

She stomps her foot like a petulant child. "I'm not done having this conversation—"

"Have a good day."

"Jaxon—"

Ignoring her, I turn on my heel, get the hell out of dodge, and climb into the driver's side of my truck.

My body feels like it's hooked up to a live wire. It surges with adrenaline and frustration as I syphon the last of my energy, forcing myself to calm the hell down. I should be familiar with this feeling by now. This anger and annoyance. I lived with it for years. Instead, all it brings is flashbacks and bitter memories I'd rather keep buried.

"Everything okay?" Rory whispers. "Are *you* okay?"

I can feel her stare on the side of my face as easily as I can taste her discomfort and concern. The combination shines the brightest of lights on how different she is compared to the woman I was married to for years. The fact that she cares. That she doesn't make assumptions or jump to conclusions instead of waiting for me to speak my mind, allowing me to gather my thoughts and inspect my own emotions before announcing them to the world. It's so refreshing I feel like I can finally breathe again.

Facing her, I say, "I fucking love you."

Her mouth twitches, her amusement cutting through her confusion. "What?"

"I said, I fucking love you." I reach toward her and grab her face, pulling her into me and kissing the shit out of her. "With you, it's so…" I shake my head, analyzing her. "Easy, Rory. It's so easy with you." My brows pull, and I try to find a way to make her understand. "Thank you. For making my life easier. For supporting me and loving me and not shoving my nose in shit or making me feel like I've lost my mind. You have no idea how much it means to me."

"Life is hard enough without me adding to it," she whispers. "And I love you, too. You know, just in case you're wondering."

"Jaxon!" I squeal. He boops my nose with the tip of his vanilla ice cream cone one more time for good measure. "Seriously?"

Way too proud of himself, he laughs, licking the ice cream in his hand as the monkeys squawk around us while I wipe the cold, sticky milk from my nose, giving Jaxon a mock glare.

"You know I owe you now," I tell him.

"Do you?"

"Mm-hmm." I bump his hip with mine, shoving him to the side as I take over pushing Poppy's stroller. "Come on, Pops. Let's go see which monkey looks the most like your dad."

"Ha, ha, very funny!" Jaxon calls from behind us.

My mouth spreads into a grin.

It's been a few weeks since we told everyone about us, and the freedom it's brought is out of this world. We even went to Sunday brunch with everyone a few days ago, and no one batted an eye. If anything, they took turns making jokes about what took us so long.

I loved it.

Iris has decided I don't exist and only talks to Jaxon. Not that it's very different from the way she handled everything before Jaxon told her we're officially dating, but I won't complain. Things are…happy. And steady. And so freaking perfect I could cry.

Jaxon doesn't need to be at the arena for a few more hours, so we decided to take full advantage of the free time by going to the local zoo. It's nice to soak up what's left of the fresh, unseasonably warm air, and the snack isn't bad, either, even if some of it did end up on my nose.

Ever since we came out to my parents, Jaxon's been… different. More open, I guess? It's like he's finally embraced our relationship fully, and it's been incredible. Or maybe the transition really happened in Harden Heights. When we talked about dreams and what we want out of life, realizing the other person played a role in our future, even if we were scared to fully embrace it at the time.

Not anymore, though. And it's scary and exciting and every other emotion a girl like me can feel with a guy like Jaxon. When we reach the apes, I park the stroller in front of the glass, then squat down beside Poppy, pointing out the great, big silverback near the back of the space.

"That's the one, right Pops? The one who looks like daddy?"

Jaxon squats on Poppy's opposite side. "Don't listen to her, baby. Your dad is a lion, not an ape."

I give him the side-eye. "Maybe a buffoon who gets *eaten* by a lion."

His laugh cuts me off. "You think you're cute, don't you?"

Batting my lashes, I grin back at him. "The cutest—"

"Excuse me," someone interrupts.

I look behind me, my eyes widening when I notice someone from the zoo standing behind us. Feeling like I just got caught doing something I shouldn't, I start to stand, an apology rolling off my tongue like it's the most natural thing in the world. "Oh, I am so sorry. Are we in the way?"

"Not at all." The stranger lifts his camera. "I take photos for the zoo's website. Do you mind if I take a few photos of your adorable family?"

Family?

He thinks we're a family?

"Oh. Uh." I turn to Jaxon and shrug, unsure what to say.

"Sure, we'd love to," Jaxon offers. "What do you need from us?"

"Perfect!" the photographer says. "Let's see…" His attention shifts from Jax, to Poppy, to me. "Mom, if you want to hold your daughter instead of having her in the stroller, that would be great."

Like a bolt of lightning striking out of nowhere, my body jolts in surprise. The photographer using the term family was one thing, but Mom? The assumption steals the breath from my lungs, catching me off guard. And maybe it shouldn't. I'm sure from the outside looking in, we appear to be the picture perfect family. But the truth is a lot messier than that, isn't it? I look at Jax, curious if he heard the photographer's comment. How does he feel? Does it bother him? Someone making an assumption like this? We're not wearing rings, but there are plenty of families without the binding agreement of marriage. Does it scare him? Should it scare him?

Jaxon rounds the stroller and slips his hand around my waist. "Hey, Mama, you good?"

So, he did hear.

And he was okay with it. So much so, he isn't even kindly correcting the photographer. He's leaning into it. And I don't know why, but it kind of makes me want to cry.

"Yeah," I breathe out. I wipe beneath my nose with the back of my hand, then sneak a peek at the photographer.

He must think I'm a wacko.

"Sorry, let me just…" I undo Poppy's buckle, pull her out of the stroller, and prop her on my hip.

"Perfect," the photographer announces. "Let's have you stand right over here." He motions to the right side of the glass. "Mom, twist Baby around so she's facing me. Dad, put your arm around Mom. And then everyone look at the camera."

We follow his instructions, posing for the photo as the photographer uses a squeaky toy to convince Poppy to look at the camera. Fiddling with the buttons on his device, the photographer snaps a few more pictures, then lowers the camera and smiles. "These are great. Thank you so much!"

"Anytime," Jaxon returns. He kisses the top of Poppy's head, then kisses mine as the worker leaves the ape area in search of another family to photograph. "You can stop looking like a deer in the headlights now."

I grimace. "Was I that bad?"

"A little." His chuckle softens the blow of his words. "You okay?"

"Yeah, he just caught me off guard, I guess."

"Me, too," Jax admits. "Not sure why, though."

I twist around so we're facing the exhibit, and Poppy kicks her feet, leaning forward to press her hands to the glass as the gorilla strides closer to us.

Distracted, I ask, "What do you mean?"

"I mean, you look like Poppy's mom. The blonde hair. The way you hold her. Talk to her. Make her smile." He shrugs. "It makes sense he'd assume you're her mom."

The easy way he says it, like we're talking about the weather or something, makes me pause.

"Are you okay with it?" I ask.

"Are *you* okay with it?" he tosses back at me, but there's a lightness in his words that eases the knot inside of me.

Shifting Poppy to my opposite hip, I argue, "You answer first."

His mouth lifts. "Of course I'm okay with it."

"You're sure?"

"Shit, Rore." He shakes his head and moves closer, wrapping his arms around me and his baby girl until we're in a makeshift group hug in the middle of the apes building. "Do you know how happy that made me? Hearing him call you Mom? It makes me think…" He shakes his head again as if he's in disbelief. "It makes me think that we can do this for real. You, me, and Pops."

"You, me, and Pops," I repeat.

"Yeah."

"And that's what you want?"

I don't know why I push it. Maybe I shouldn't. But I can't help myself. I love Poppy more than anything in the world. I would literally die for her. But being her mom? Slipping into that position, even if it's part-time? Let alone knowing it's what Jaxon might want, too? It's scary. The good scary. The life-altering scary. The kind of scary that feels a hell of a lot like my childhood crush on the man in front of me.

He tilts his head. "Are you still questioning my feelings for you, Beautiful?"

"Not in general," I argue, looking down at Poppy in my arms. "Just in…*this* way. The mom-role way. The non-employment way."

With a subtle curve of his mouth, he leans in for a kiss, dragging his cheek along Poppy's soft hair as he holds my gaze. "I want it more than you can even imagine."

"Hey," I announce, balancing my cell between my shoulder and ear as I flick on the bath water.

"Hey, Beautiful," Jaxon returns. "What's up?"

"Nothing much. I know we talked about coming tonight, but I think I'm going to stay home with Pops. Are you okay with that?"

"Yeah, is everything all right?"

"Yeah, everything's great. I think she's just fighting a bug." I sit her in the lukewarm water as Hades plops on the cool tile beside us. "She has a little fever, but I just gave her some medicine, and we're taking a bath right now."

He hesitates. "Poor girl. Can I get you guys anything?"

"No, you're good." I shift my cell to my opposite ear, careful to keep an eye on her on the off chance she loses her balance. "Focus on the game, and we'll talk after, okay? We'll just hang out, and you can give her big kisses when you get home."

"You sure?"

"She's okay, Jax," I reassure him. "I got her."

"I know you do. Guess this is just dad guilt. I wish I was there."

"You're an amazing dad," I remind him. "Focus on the game. I'll focus on Pops."

"Thanks, Rore." A beat of silence passes as if he can't decide whether or not to take my suggestion before he gives in. "Don't know what I'd do without you. I'll see you tonight."

"We'll be here."

OKAY, SO SHE'S NOT DOING SO GREAT. THE POOR THING WAILS even louder as I walk from one edge of the room to the next. She won't eat. Won't sleep. Won't quiet down.

"I know, baby girl." I gently rub my hand up and down her spine. "I know." My lips brush against her forehead, and I frown. She's still warm. Too warm. My worry grows like a bad idea, but what I hate most is that I can't figure out if it's rooted in reality or if my OCD is blowing things out of proportion. Keeping her pressed to my chest, I head to the medicine cabinet to grab the thermometers. There are two. One you swipe along the forehead, and one that's old school and should be slipped under the tongue or placed under the armpit...or used rectally, but I'm not that mean. I grab them both, then head to the bedroom and lay Pops down. She's already stripped down to a white onesie after I noticed her rising temperature an hour ago. It was ninety-nine point nine degrees at the time, and after giving her some medicine, I figured she'd be fine and could get some rest. Jokes on me. She hasn't stopped squirming and crying since. Swiping her forehead with the thermometer, it beeps seconds later, and I read the screen.

No, that can't be right.

My frown deepens, and I lift her arm, tucking the other

thermometer under her armpit in hopes of getting a better idea of exactly how warm she's grown since I talked to her daddy on the phone before the game. Poppy arches her little body on the mattress, uncomfortable and frustrated.

"I know, baby," I repeat, holding the thermometer in place despite her best protests.

With every never-ending second that passes, my anxiety ratchets higher and higher. What if she's not okay? What if I did something or *do* something wrong? What if—

The thermometer beeps, and I blink back the ache in my eyes, staring at the small display on the older gadget.

One hundred and three point two.

It's point-one degrees higher than the other reading, proving both stupid devices to be accurate despite my deepest hopes. Yeah, this is bad. This is really bad.

I pick Poppy up again, heading back to the kitchen. Nausea churns inside of me as I grab a different medication from the cabinet. Hands shaking, I measure the proper amount in the syringe, then administer the cherry-flavored Ibuprofen. Nearly half of it spills out of the side of her mouth as she jerks away from me, pawing at the syringe like it's a vial of poison. I don't want to give her too much, but if she doesn't have enough, will it even do anything?

Shit.

I pull my phone from my back pocket and call Jaxon. It goes to voicemail, like I knew it would. He turns off his phone or leaves it in his office, but if I can't get ahold of Jaxon, who the hell am I supposed to call? I click Jaxon's name again. "Pick up, Jax. Pick up."

"Hey, this is Jaxon Thorne, I'm sorry I missed your call—"

I hit end and squeeze my eyes shut, trying to block out Poppy's cries so I can think clearly and come up with a game plan, but my brain is too foggy. Too frazzled. I tap my thumb against the edge of my cell.

One, two, three. Pause. *One, two, three.* Pause. *One, two, three.*

Is this my fault? Did I forget to sanitize her hands after the zoo earlier? I thought I did, but what if I didn't? What if I let her touch something she shouldn't have, and—

Stop!

"Feeding my OCD is not the way to handle this," I mutter under my breath. Poppy flaps her arms and arches her back in discomfort, demanding my attention. "It's okay, baby." My hand runs up and down her spine again as I try to figure out what to do. "It's okay."

Searching for Iris's contact information, I hit the call button and bring it to my ear, but it doesn't even ring before a familiar, robotic voice comes through the speaker.

"The number you have called cannot be completed as dialed."

I hang up and try again, only to receive the same response.

Seriously?

Unsure what else to do, I dial my mom as my body trembles with fear.

On the third ring, it connects. "Hey, babe—"

"Mom?" My voice cracks, though I doubt she can hear me over Poppy's soul-shattering screams.

"What's wrong?" The light, airy tone from seconds before evaporates. "Is Poppy okay?"

"Pops." I squeeze my eyes shut and sway from left to right, despite knowing it won't help. Nothing has. Hades lets out a small whimper at my feet and paws at my knee. I think he can feel it, too, thanks to his time in service dog school before he failed out. Something's wrong. She needs help. *More* help. More than I can give. "Fever," I add, trying to focus instead of getting lost in what-ifs. "She has a fever."

"Okay, breathe," my mom orders. "Did you take her temperature?"

"Yes. Twice, er, three times," I clarify. "Once before her bath, and twice just a minute ago." I take a deep breath, praying the oxygen will help me think clearly and stop the panic from taking over completely. "She's really hot, Mom."

"Okay. Henry," she addresses my dad. They're probably in the suite at the arena surrounded by friends and colleagues. I bet the last thing they expected was a call from me. I bet this call is like a bucket of ice water on their entire evening. Not that it matters. We all know where my family's priorities lie, but it doesn't ease the guilt. Am I over-reacting? Is this my OCD clouding my judgment? I don't freaking know! I brush my lips against Poppy's forehead again. She's burning up.

Breathe.

As my mom relays everything, I shift my weight from side to side, trying to calm the hell down since I know my anxiety isn't doing Poppy any favors. But it's hard. Really hard. What if—

"Okay, your dad is sending someone to fill in for Jax on the bench."

"That's good," I breathe out while Hades paces at my feet. "That's really good."

"Yeah. Then your dad and I are going to come pick you guys up and take you to the hospital, all right? Everyone else will meet us there."

Like a punch to the gut, I register her words. *Your dad and I are going to come pick you guys up and take you to the hospital.* Hospital. And not just any hospital. But *the* hospital. The one I promised never to enter again. The one I went to when I was a kid. The one where I had to say goodbye to my big brother. The one where I was blindsided and left so damn broken. The idea is enough to bring me to my knees and make me want to vomit.

"Mom," my voice cracks all over again, and a tear slides down my cheek.

"I know, baby," she murmurs, letting her words hang in the air as if they have the power to overcome my soul-crushing fear.

And I know she wants to understand it. To fully grasp exactly how crippling this situation is. Add in the 'h' word, and I can barely see straight, let alone create an actionable to-do list that'll get me and a helpless and very sick baby to the one place I vowed to never go to again. What if she catches something even worse? What if she never comes home? What if they have to hook her up to the same cords and machines in the same room where my brother slipped away? The familiar beep-beep that haunts my dreams manages to cut through Poppy's screams, leaving me cold as ice. I slide to the floor, keeping the distraught baby close to my chest, my muscles cramping and tingles spreading through my limbs.

"It's going to be okay," my mom promises. "It will."

"Give me the phone," a low voice demands before my dad's voice cuts through the speaker. "Hey, Squeaks."

"Hi, Dad," I choke out.

"Hey, baby girl. We're gonna be right there, okay?"

Poppy fidgets in my arms, her cries threatening to drown out my dad's strong voice as Hades nuzzles himself against my cheek and lets out a quiet whimper. He's worried. And so am I. But being paralyzed by fear isn't going to get me anywhere. It'll only slow things down. And time is the only resource I have any real control over. Isn't it?

"You're not alone," my dad promises. "You're not alone. But you need to—"

"I don't want you to come pick me up."

"Rore—"

"It'll only waste time," I clarify. Hades leans his weight against my side, and I close my eyes, threading my fingers through his thick fur while balancing an angry Poppy with my opposite hand. "I'll meet you there."

"What?"

"I can drive, Dad—"

"I know, but—"

"I'll meet you at the hospital. I have to go." I disconnect the call and press my forehead to Poppy's peach fuzz. God, she feels even hotter. If we don't get there soon, she could seize. Thanks to Finley and Aunt Kate having epilepsy, I'm aware a seizure is the last thing anyone would want Poppy to experience. So even though it kills me, even though I could puke at the thought alone, I push to my feet, cradling a very distraught Poppy against me. "I got you, Pops," I promise, despite the acid lining my throat. I swallow past it and grab my keys from the counter. "I got you."

Fear is a funny thing. The way it can fog your mind, yet makes your focus so lasered in it's hard to see anything else. The chair in the corner of the room is stiff, and the fabric feels scratchy, but thanks to my dizziness, I keep my butt planted where it is. On that stupid chair. They took Poppy to a different room so they could start an IV. You'd think I'd feel better now. Knowing her safety is in the right hands. It doesn't help. I need to see her. To know she's okay.

Please be okay.

My hands are still shaking. I doubt they'll stop anytime soon. After arriving at the hospital, I tried calling Iris a dozen more times, but the call would never go through. It only feeds my anxiety. The doctor reassured me I did the right thing, and Poppy's in good hands. They're just trying to get the fever down.

It doesn't make things any easier. I feel absolutely helpless.

"Here she is," the nurse informs me, carrying a tiny Poppy over to me. My gaze catches on the IV in her arm as she hiccups and reaches for me. Flashbacks of Archer in a room so similar to this, with tubes and machines and my fear.

Not the time, I silently remind myself. *She isn't Archer.*

Wiping the tears from my face, I take Poppy from the nurse, careful not to jostle her too much. "Thank you."

"You're welcome," she returns. "She did great, and her fever's already coming down. The IV will also keep her a little cooler, since the fluids are cold, and now we just wait for the antibiotics to do their job." She reaches for a tissue and hands it to me. "Here."

"Thanks," I choke out, taking it from her before dabbing at my face with my free hand while balancing Poppy on my lap.

"I'll be right back to check in, okay?"

I nod, unable to speak as Poppy's exhausted body melts against me. She's so tiny. So delicate and fragile in her little onesie. Another wave of grief filters through me, and I sniffle, dropping a kiss to her velvety soft hair. "Love you, Pops. Love you so freaking"—I hiccup—"much." My eyes feel as dry as sandpaper from all my stupid crying, but I can't convince my tear ducts to stop.

She's okay.

Jaxon arrives a few minutes later with our parents in tow. When he sees me, he rushes closer, and he swallows me in a hug, careful not to squish a sleeping Poppy in my lap as I stay seated on the same scratchy chair. And it's funny. The power in a simple hug. I swear it has the power to fix anything. I squeeze my eyes shut, grateful for it in a way he'll never fully understand. It's like I can finally pass the baton. Like I can finally let go and allow him to take over. Like I can finally acknowledge the crippling fear I've been pushing aside in an attempt to be strong enough for her. For our little Pops.

"I got you," he rasps. "I got you."

Nuzzling closer into his chest, I take a deep breath, letting his familiar scent ground me.

It's going to be okay. He's got me. He's got Pops. Everything is going to be okay.

"How is she?" he asks.

"She's okay." I let him go, and my parents take his place, giving me and Pops a quick squeeze before Aunt Ashlyn and Uncle Colt do the same.

"They had to start an IV, but the fever's down, and they've given her a round of antibiotics," I tell them, replaying everything that's happened since we arrived so I can pass on as much information as possible. But it's been a whirlwind of chaos, and I have no doubt I'm missing a lot. "I'm sure the nurses will be in again any second and can give you all the details. It feels like they've barely left the room."

At that moment, a gentle *knock, knock* sounds from the hall, and the same nurse who's been helping Poppy steps into the room. "Hey, it looks like everyone made it."

"Hello." Jaxon's long legs bring him closer to the nurse as he strides across the room and offers his hand for her to shake. "I'm Jax, Poppy's dad. How is she?"

"She's doing really well, all things considered. She has an ear infection, which can be really scary, but it's completely normal for something like this to cause a fever, especially in kids Poppy's age." She tacks on a reassuring smile. "We've been keeping a close eye on her, and the fever broke, which was our main concern. She's very lucky to have you two," she continues. "And the good news is, she's going to make a full recovery."

A full recovery.

She's going to make a full recovery.

I hang on to the prognosis, praying it'll calm my still-racing heart.

"Thank you," we all say.

"Anytime. I'll be back to check on Poppy again in a few."

As she leaves, there's a shout from the hallway. "Where the hell is my daughter?"

Jaxon and I share a look of confusion before he strides to the doorway and peers out. "Iris!" he calls. "We're in here!"

The angry click-clack of heels jars me as she marches into the room but stops short when she sees me holding Poppy. "Get your fucking hands off my child."

Jaxon steps in front of her. "Whoa, Iris."

"Don't *whoa, Iris* me," she snaps.

Aunt Ashlyn shifts around them, keeping a wide berth as she moves toward me. "Hey, why don't I…"

With a jerky nod, I hand over a sleeping Poppy, then wipe my hands on my jeans, suddenly feeling more out of place than if I were dropped on Mars with a knapsack and a "see ya later." I should give them some privacy. Some space. Some…something. On shaky legs, I step toward the door, but Jaxon stops me.

"Rory, wait—"

"Get the hell out of here," Iris snaps.

My body freezes in place, and I honestly don't know what to do. I've never done well with confrontation. Never done well with yelling in general, actually. Add in the death glare from Jaxon's ex, my already frazzled brain, and my more than depleted emotions, and I'm pretty sure all I want to do is crawl into a hole, bawl my eyes out, and disappear entirely.

"Iris, the nurse just filled us in," Jaxon says in an attempt to placate her. "Poppy's okay."

Ignoring him, Iris reaches for me, her long, manicured nails digging into my wrist as she tries to physically remove me from the room by dragging me toward the door. I yank my arm away from her and shove her back, my body moving on instinct.

"What the hell?" I screech.

"You—"

"What the fuck are you doing?" Jaxon snarls. He pushes me behind him, using his body as a physical barrier.

Still not bothering to acknowledge the man between us, Iris seethes at me, "This is your fault!"

I rub at my bruised forearm, confused more than angry. "What are you talking—"

"What did you do to her? What did you do?" she shouts.

"It wasn't her fault," Jaxon growls. "Now, I'm gonna need you to calm the hell down, Iris."

"Don't you dare tell me what to do!" She shoves against his chest, but he doesn't budge. "Do you know how I found out my daughter was in the hospital, Jaxon? I had to hear it from the announcers while I was watching your game! Are you kidding me?"

Glancing over his shoulder at me, Jaxon asks, "You didn't call her?"

The blood drains from my face as I realize how awful this must look. "I tried—"

"Bullshit!" Iris sneers.

"I called you at least a dozen times," I argue, defending myself. "But none of them would go through."

"Bull. Shit!" she repeats, as if all rationality has clearly left the building. "You're trying to take my place! You're hurting her! You're—"

"Iris!" Jaxon snaps. "If you don't lower your voice, you're going to wake up our daughter, and after everything she's been through, I think we can all agree that's the last thing she needs. This isn't about you. Now, you need to calm down because if you don't, they'll make you leave."

Tears gather in her eyes, and the fight seeps out of her. "I can't believe you would choose to be with someone who doesn't even think to reach out to the mother of your child when she's in need." She peers around Jaxon and shakes her head. "Get out of here. You've done enough."

Jaxon's head falls forward, but before he can even turn to me, I press my hand against his lower back. "It's okay," I whisper. "I'll, uh, I'll be in the waiting room."

"We'll wait with her," my parents announce as I make my way toward the hallway and into the empty waiting area.

Covering my mouth with my hand, I try to steady my breathing, but it's so. Freaking. Hard. Maybe it's the combination of everything from tonight. Maybe it's the combination from everything over the past few months. Honestly, I don't know, but I'm not sure I can do this. I'm not sure *how* to do this.

"Hey." My dad wraps his arms around me. "It's okay, Squeaks. It's okay—"

"I swear I called her, Dad. I swear—"

"I know, baby. I know." He squeezes me tighter as I fall apart even more.

"I just, I don't understand how someone can hate me so much, you know?" I cry, still in shock. "Like, I understand that I'm around her daughter, and that I'm in a relationship with her ex, and that she has to put up with me, but why does she have to be so...mean?"

"I don't know, Rore," he mutters. "I don't fucking know, but she's lucky I'm not calling our lawyers right now to have her charged with assault for that move in there."

"Maybe we can ask Ash if she has any suggestions? Or Kate," my mom offers beside us. "I know your Aunt Kate has to put up with your Uncle Mack's ex every once in a while."

It's only half-true. Miley and Hazel were teenagers when Aunt Kate came into the picture, so she never had to deal with Macklin's ex. Not really. A run-in here and there is so much different from weekly drop-offs and pick-ups. So, even though

I know my parents are trying to help, it doesn't work. It only makes me feel more hopeless and overwhelmed. My teeth dig into my wobbling bottom lip in hopes of stopping the tears from streaming down my face, but I'm a mess. A big. Fat. Mess.

"Want my two cents?" Colt asks.

I turn to face him, surprised he followed us into the hallway instead of staying with his wife, granddaughter, and son. Hands tucked in his pockets, he moseys toward me, looking so much like Jaxon, it makes me want to cry even harder.

"Hey, Uncle Colt." I sniff. "And I'm pretty sure I can use all the help I can get, so, yes. I'd love your two cents."

"Nah, you're doing great, sweetheart." He moves closer to our little circle in the waiting area. "But not all exes are the same. It seems Jax got the short end of the stick on this one, which means you did, too."

"Not helping," my dad grumbles beside me.

"Just saying it like it is, Henry." Colt squeezes my shoulder. "Eleanor was easy. She was willing to work with us. Willing to accept Ashlyn after realizing she wasn't the one for me. Willing to share her little boy and the title of mom because she knew it was best for him in the long run." He glances behind him, making sure we're relatively alone. "I have a feeling Iris doesn't agree with that sentiment."

"Me, too." I sniff. "And just to be clear, it's not that I want to replace her, but if she could just hate me a little less—"

"I know." He steps closer. "Trust me, I know. You don't need to defend yourself. Ash and I were the evil in-laws, so we know what it's like to be on Iris's shit list." He pauses. "And maybe it'll get better. Maybe I'm being an asshole for not giving Iris the benefit of the doubt, but..." He squeezes the back of his neck. "I guess I just want you to know that I've been where Jax is, and it isn't a picnic even under the best of circumstances. Add Iris to the equation and...he needs you. Needs you more than he knows. And I know that's a selfish take on everything. He's my son, so I know I'm biased. I know you'll have to put up with name calling and being blamed for shit you didn't do. And I know that isn't fair," he adds, his eyes flicking to my dad's for the briefest of seconds before returning to me. "It isn't. But, uh, stick with him, all right? It's in our darkest moments when us Thorne boys like to beat ourselves up the most."

He's right. And boy do those Thorne men like to beat themselves up and take blame for things that are out of their control. The reminder manages to quiet the chaos inside of me, bringing with it a fresh, yet somehow familiar perspective. Because if that was rough for me, I can only imagine how hard it was for Jaxon.

"I'm not going anywhere," I promise. "As long as Jaxon believes me and doesn't buy her lies, I'll be right by his side."

"That's my girl." He pulls me into a side hug. "You'll get through this." And for some reason I can't explain, his promise makes me feel a little bit lighter.

As soon as Rory leaves, Iris collapses against me, wrapping her arms around my neck and sobbing like the world's been ripped from her. In a way, I guess it has. She has every right to be frustrated. I should've called when I left the arena, but the only thing I could think about was getting to Poppy. I guess I assumed Iris would be here when I arrived.

"Sh, sh, sh," I murmur. "She's okay, Iris. She's okay."

With a soft sniffle, Iris lifts her head and peeks at my mom, still holding a resting Poppy.

"I'm sorry I didn't call when I found out," I tell her. "I should've, and that's on me."

"You're right," she says. "You should've." Her expression hardens and she shoots her gaze toward the hallway. "And your nanny should've, too."

My nanny.

Of course, she'd call her that instead of using her name. Hell, even the term girlfriend is better than painting her as a nameless, faceless nanny I have no connection with. The urge to correct Iris sits like a shot of whiskey on my tongue, burning the shit out of me, but I swallow it back, picking my battles.

"Rory did call you," I tell her.

Her attention cuts to me. "You really believe that bitch?"

My nostrils flare, but I don't take the bait. Because I know her. And I know she's deflecting, trying to shine a light on everyone but herself. Instead, I call out her bullshit. "You blocked her, am I right?"

"I didn't—"

"Then show me your phone and prove it."

Determined, my ex starts to pull her phone from her purse before the blood drains from her face. Yeah…I called it. She blocked Rory. I'm not surprised. It was her go-to when we were together. She gets pissed and blocks someone under the guise of protecting her inner peace, then leaves herself to fume alone at the fact that the person never reaches out to apologize for upsetting her in the first place. Round and round she goes, fucking up her own life then blaming it on anyone and everyone else. The reminder drains me more than she understands.

I pinch the bridge of my nose, unsure where to go from here. Because this is what I was afraid of. Rory being caught in the crosshairs. Iris taking the target off my back and placing it on Rory's instead. Why wouldn't she? There's a new player. A new person to blame. To hate. Even when Rory's the last person to deserve it.

Glancing at my mom in the corner of the room, I ask, "Hey, can you give us a minute?"

"Yeah, of course." She carefully sets Poppy down on the hospital bed in the center of the room, then tiptoes into the hall, giving me and Iris some privacy.

Looks like it's time to lay some ground rules. And this time, I'll make sure she understands the severity of what will happen if she breaks them.

"Listen," I start, "I know you're frustrated, and I know you probably forgot you blocked Rory and that she had no way to get ahold of you, but coming in here and putting your hands on someone I love is not okay. Do you understand me?"

She doesn't answer, choosing to stare at my forehead instead.

My upper lip curls. "Do. You. Understand?"

"Fine."

The clipped syllable gets on my nerves, but I force myself to let it go. "Good. You're also going to apologize because not only did you grab her, you also painted her to be someone she isn't. Someone who's dishonest and spiteful when she's the furthest thing from it." Iris scoffs, and my short fingernails dig into my palms. "You don't have to like her, Iris. But you will respect her. Do you want to know why?"

Her glare cuts to me.

"Because if you don't, I'm gonna take a paternity test, and you're going to risk all those payments you receive every month for child support, despite us splitting custody fifty-fifty. Do you understand?"

It's the last thing I'd ever want to threaten. The last thing I'd ever want to admit out loud. That my baby girl might only be mine by proxy and not by blood. The possibility is enough to make bile coat my mouth, but I keep my expression locked down, refusing to show my hand or how few cards I actually hold because if Iris knew me at all, she'd know I'd never abandon my daughter like this. Not for anything. But if a precarious bluff will make Rory's life a little easier, then it's worth saying. Isn't it?

"Are you threatening me?" Iris demands.

"I'm calling you out on your infidelity, and what it means if you don't stay in your lane."

"Stay in my lane?" She scoffs. "Says the man who fell for

his *nanny*? Couldn't even be creative and hit on a player's girlfriend or something?"

"Not all of us are into cheating, Iris."

She shakes her head. "You were the one ignoring me—"

"Our marriage is over," I interrupt, refusing to let her point fingers and refute any blame for our failed relationship, let alone change the subject after what just happened in this very room. "Now, I'm only going to say this one more time." I move forward. "You do not have to like Rory, but you will respect her. Do you understand?"

"And if I don't, you'll lose your daughter?" She laughs. "You really want to play that game?"

Praying she doesn't call my bluff, I answer, "I think you're focusing on the wrong things, Iris. Sure, I'll lose a narcissistic ex who lied during mediation. But what about you? What will you lose?" I scratch my temple. "Fifty-percent of your free time. That's gone for sure." I snap my fingers. "Actually, a hundred percent. Because you'll have to get a job since those alimony checks won't include child support anymore."

"You're forgetting something," she sneers. "Whoever Poppy's father is will still have to pay—"

"Child support is based on the father's income. It's not a flat fee. You know that, right?"

"So?" She stands even taller, too stubborn to connect the dots or be logical for once in her life.

I tap my finger against my chin. "No offense, but I think you forget that I know Chris's family. If he had any money, there's no way in hell you would've kept the house. You would've sold it and moved in with him." I tsk. "But that didn't happen, did it? That's right. Because he doesn't have any money. And he sure as shit doesn't have enough to support your lifestyle while also taking care of Poppy fifty-percent of the time. That's not how it works."

"That's how it works with us," she argues, raising her chin

another inch as if she has any ground to stand on. "You forget I won in the divorce, Jaxon. *Me.*"

"You think you won in the divorce, Iris?" A low, laugh rumbles through me. "I gave you everything you wanted. You didn't earn any of it." I shake my head, replaying the late night phone calls with my mom, Eleanor, who was also my lawyer during the divorce. "Did you know my mom was screaming at me to give her free reign during mediation because she knew she could take everything from you? But I couldn't do it. Do you wanna know why, Iris?"

She gulps but stays quiet.

Good.

"Because I felt sorry for you. I felt sorry for being the husband I was." I hesitate, losing a bit of my bravado. "And that's the truth, Iris. You deserved better, but so did I, and I think I forgot that part during our divorce. I was so busy taking responsibility for my actions, I forgot to give you the chance to do the same." Bending closer, I warn, "But if you keep fucking with Rory, that guilt will disappear real fast, and I have no problem taking this back to court and showing everyone who you really are." I pull away. "Or don't. You know? It's like you said, I have so much to lose."

Iris's throat constricts on a swallow, and I know she's searching for an out. For a way to fuck me over. For a way to regain the upper hand. Problem is, there isn't one. Not without her risking financial ruin. I know it, and now, she does, too.

Finally, she nods, giving in. "Fine."

"Fine, what?"

"Fine, I'll give your little girlfriend the respect she deserves."

"Good." I move away another step, giving her more space. "Keep an eye on our daughter. I'll be back in a minute."

The hospital is quiet as I stride into the main area, finding

Rory in the waiting room. Her fingers tap against her outer thigh, her feet taking her from one end of the space to the other when she catches my approach.

With tears streaming down her cheeks, she blurts out, "Jaxon, I swear—"

I pull her into my arms, squeezing her against me. "I know, Beautiful. I know."

"You don't understand—"

"I do." My lips brush against her forehead. "Trust me. I know how Iris operates. You did nothing wrong."

"Yeah, but I…" Tears cling to her lashes as she peeks up at me. "I thought you were mad at me or that you thought I was trying to manipulate you into believing me or…"

"That I thought you were like her?" I question.

Another tear rolls down her cheek as her head bobs up and down.

"Fuck, Rore. You have no idea how little you're like her, and I think I always knew it," I rasp, scrubbing my hand over my face. "Maybe that was the point back then. The reason why I dated her. Why I proposed. Because I knew I could never have you." I cup her cheeks with my hands, making sure I have her full attention. "Even then, I couldn't help myself. The way I always compared her to you even when we were married. I didn't see it then. How I couldn't open up to her. How I couldn't talk to her. How I couldn't let my guard down, not without risking her throwing it back in my face a day, or a week, or a year later. You're nothing like her, do you understand?"

She squeezes her eyes shut, unable to look up at me. "Are you sure?"

"Never been more sure of anything in my life." I lean in and kiss her damp cheeks. "I love you, Beautiful."

"I love you, too," she whispers. "So much."

5 4
JAXON

We're able to take Poppy home a while later, though Iris left shortly after our showdown in the hospital room. The Lions lost, and even though my phone's blowing up, not a single message is about the score or how it might affect the team's stats. No. Everyone wants to know how Poppy's doing. If she's okay. If they can bring anything or help out.

Sometimes, I forget.

The family I'm lucky enough to have. Some by blood. Others by circumstance. They're one and the same.

Exhausted, I carry Poppy into the house, then change her bum before putting her in her crib to get some rest, since Rory already gave her a bottle on the car ride home. Poppy goes down without a fight, falling asleep before her head can even hit the firm mattress. When I get back to the family room, I find it empty.

"Hades?" I call. "Rore?"

Nothing.

I collapse on the couch in the family room and pull out

my phone so I can call Rory to find out where she is when the time on my cell distracts me.

Shit.

The elevator opens. Squatting next to Hades, Rory removes his leash, and he bounds into the family room, jumping onto the cushion beside me.

Scratching behind his ear, I cautiously say, "Hey."

"Hey," Rory returns.

I zero in on her hand, curious to see if she's tapping away on her thigh, but there's no shaky movements.

"Where'd you go?" I prod.

"Figured Hades could use a quick walk and a bathroom break before I sit down and never get back up again," she explains. Rummaging through the fridge, she adds, "Hey, are you hungry?"

"Nah, I'm good. Too exhausted to be hungry."

She finds something to snack on, then grabs a spoon from the drawer and sways into the family room before curling up on the cushion beside me."You're missing out. It's strawberry." She pulls the lid off the yogurt, her eyes gleaming with enthusiasm.

Is she really okay?

Digging her spoon into the cup, she pulls out a massive bite, but instead of putting it into her mouth, she brings it closer to me.

"Rore, I'm really not—"

Yogurt smears against my nose, and I jerk back, wiping it away. "What was that for?"

"Told you I owed you." She smirks and shoves the bite into her mouth.

With a low laugh, I wrap my arm around her shoulder and tug her into my side. "Smart-ass."

"Mm-hmm," she hums around another bite of yogurt as

Hades lifts his head. "Give me a minute," she tells him. "I'll let you lick the cup once I'm done."

I'd tease her for assuming he understands what she's saying even though he's a dog, but he lowers his head back to the cushion, proving she might be onto something. "You spoil him," I point out.

"I totally do, and I regret nothing." She scoops up another bite, devouring half the serving in under a minute.

"You really were hungry," I realize.

"You have no idea." She licks the edge of her mouth, cleaning up a small splotch of yogurt. "I was too stressed about Poppy's fever to eat any actual dinner, but now that we're finally home, and I know she's safe, I feel like I can kind of breathe."

Home.

She called this place home.

Warmth spreads through my ribcage as I watch her finish the yogurt with one final scoop.

She sets the empty container on the ground. "Here you go, buddy."

Hades jumps off the couch without having to be told twice and starts licking the container clean.

A soft smile plays at the edge of Rory's lips as she watches him, and I can't help but lean in to kiss her. I've always loved this about her. The way she's always thinking of others. The way she finds joy in making others happy. The way she looks outside of herself. Fuck, I love this girl.

When I pull away, her smile widens. "What was that for?"

"Just love you."

"Love you, too."

"Come here." I pull her into my lap until she's straddling me and kiss her forehead, anxious to touch her. To make sure she's still here and hasn't given up on me, even after all the shit we went through tonight. "How are you?"

"Tired."

"What else?"

She shrugs. "Just tired."

Tired? That's it? That's all she has to say?

"Did you, uh, did you see what time it is?" I push. I don't know if I'm shooting myself in the foot by bringing it up, but I can't help myself. She thinks I don't notice the way she still wakes up every morning, but I do. And she can hide it all she wants, battle it all she wants, but I know how much of an effect early mornings bother her. Knowing it somehow slipped past her today is huge.

With a frown, Rory shakes her head, and I show her my phone.

Lips parted, she breathes in a sharp breath of air but stays quiet.

5:48 a.m.

She missed it. Or made it? I'm not sure which term is more fitting.

Her gaze flicks to mine. "I didn't notice," she whispers. "I didn't...the hospital kind of sucked up all the time, and I didn't notice."

"Rore, that's amazing," I point out. "This is a huge win. How are you feeling?"

"Torn." She hesitates. "And elated? And confused." Her smile wavers before she focuses on me. "Jax, I haven't not stared at the clock and counted down the seconds to 5:34 in the morning since the accident." Another long pause hangs between us while she tries to wrap her head around the monstrosity of this moment. "And I know it's a good thing, that it slipped past my radar, but...holy shit." A tear slips past her defenses, rolling down her cheek before she wipes it away. "I can't decide if I feel hopeful about this or..." She gives me a watery but relieved smile. "Jaxon, I made it past 5:34."

"I know, Beautiful." I pull her against me. "I know."

A relieved laugh bubbles out of her as she sits up again and touches her cheeks to cool her heated skin.

"You're killing it," I say, encouraging her. "Kicking OCD in the ass."

"Is that what I'm doing?" she challenges. "Because it feels like I'm floundering around most of the time."

"Nothing wrong with a little floundering." I grab her hands, lowering them from her face. "Speaking of OCD and wins. You went to the hospital today.," I remind her. "You. The girl who would've rather lived with a dislocated shoulder for the rest of her life than step one foot inside a hospital went straight into that building today with her head held high. That's huge."

She tucks her hair behind her ear, fighting back tears as if just now feeling the gravity of today's events. "I mean…it's Poppy. She needed me to put on my big girl pants, so I did."

"Which is huge," I repeat. "Because there's no way it wasn't hard for you, but you still did it. Rore, that's amazing."

Mouth bunching on one side, she gives a half-assed nod. "I'm just glad she's okay."

"Me, too."

"I was thinking about it, though. And…" Her fingers dance along my T-shirt. "Even with today's win with the time and the hospital, I think…I think I should go back to therapy."

"Yeah?"

"Yeah." She hesitates. "When I first started watching Poppy, I could tell I was having more intrusive thoughts. And I thought I was okay, but I think…" Her lashes flutter as if she's fighting a battle only she can see. "I think it would be good to kind of get a tune-up, you know?"

"Yeah, I think it's great." I hold her waist and kiss her, grateful for her honesty. "Can I do anything to help?"

Her smile is genuine when she shakes her head, seemingly present again. "I'm good. Thank you, though."

"Okay." I drag my hand along her spine, loving the way she melts into me more and more with every sweep of my touch. "How's your arm? I know Iris grabbed you—"

"I'm fine. Honestly, she's lucky I didn't deck her." She smirks before hiding it behind her hand as if she feels guilty for finding the interaction amusing. "Shoving her back was like a reflex. I kind of feel bad, though. Should I apologize?"

"The last thing you should do is apologize," I grumble. "You're too nice for your own good."

"Well, someone's gotta be, right?" she quips. "By the way, I talked to your dad."

"Oh?"

"Yeah, while you were in the room with Iris. He said something to me." She snuggles in closer to my chest. "Something about you."

"What'd he say?"

"That you need me."

"I do need you."

"And that I should stick by your side."

"That'd be nice," I agree.

Her mouth lifts, but she stays quiet, studying me, and I don't miss the mirth in her pretty gaze. It's like she knows a secret. One I'm dying for her to share.

"What is it?" I ask.

"It's just…" Her smile widens. "I found it a little ironic, is all."

"Why?"

"That he thinks I'm even capable of *not* sticking by your side." A quiet laugh escapes her. "Considering our past, I mean…"

Our past. As in, her long-standing crush. I guess it is a little comical. The idea of Rory getting bored of me or cutting ties after everything we've been through. She even moved out of Lockwood Heights to escape her feelings, and look where it got her. Right back where she belongs. With me.

"Maybe he's afraid you'll finally gain some common sense," I argue.

"Nah." She waves me off. "That ship sailed a long time ago."

"Oh, really?" I say, not bothering to hide my laughter.

"Yup. You're stuck with me, Mr. Thorne."

"Good. Then, it looks like you're stuck with me, future Mrs. Thorne."

Her eyes widen. "Future Mrs. Thorne, huh?"

"Yeah." I kiss her softly, surprised by the lack of fear that accompanies those words. Future Mrs. Thorne. Fuck, they've never sounded better, and considering the swell of regret I felt the last time I toyed with those words, it shocks the hell out of me. But maybe that's the point. The reason why Maverick and Ophelia had no issue moving up their wedding date. Because they knew what real love was supposed to feel like. The same way I know I'm never letting Rory go. Ever.

Leaning back, Rory murmurs, "You know, I like the sound of that."

"Thought you might."

"Mm-hmm." She tilts her head to the side, giving me better access to her throat as I skate my lips across her sensitive skin. "Now, I can dig out all those older binders and use them again."

"Huh?"

"Since they all say Mrs. Thorne on them," she teases. "Wait, am I a psychic or…?"

I roll my eyes and kiss her again. "Smart-ass."

Smiling against my mouth, she wraps her arms around

my neck and presses herself against me. "And you wouldn't have it any other way."

She's right. I wouldn't. In fact, I wouldn't change a thing. Life is funny that way. The way it winds, taking unexpected turns. Some good. Some bad. But none that are regrettable. Not for me, at least. Because if they were, I wouldn't find myself here. With the love of my life in my lap. Her dog at our feet. And my little girl in the room next to us.

Fuck. Henry and Mia were right. I really am the luckiest guy in the world.

And I'll spend the rest of my life making sure Rory knows it, too.

The End

EPILOGUE

RORY

A few years later

I t's funny. How Jaxon constantly accommodating Iris's unreasonable schedule slowly transitioned the fifty-fifty split to be closer to ninety-ten. And after a few years of unsteady schedules and a little girl who looks more and more like her daddy every day, Jaxon finally took Iris to court for full custody.

We won.

We. Freaking. Won.

The memory alone is enough to bring tears to my eyes. Or maybe it's the hormones.

Resting one hand on my swollen belly, I shield my eyes from the sun and call out, "Hey, you two! Lunch is ready!"

"Just a sec!" Jaxon's head pops out from behind a thick branch, and he grins. "I think the black's gonna look awesome."

"Look, Mom! Black!" Poppy chimes in. Black paint is smeared across her shirt and part of her cheek as she stands on the large platform ten feet off the ground. Thankfully, there are railings, and she isn't allowed in the treehouse unaccompanied, but the girl's obsessed. And I mean *obsessed*. She raises a paint brush into the air, wielding it like a sword. "Argh! I'm a pirate!"

"You are definitely a pirate," I agree with a breath of amusement. But seriously. How is she so cute? "And pirates eat grilled cheese sandwiches. Tell your daddy it's time to eat, will ya?"

Her eyes light up, and she turns to Jax. "Grilled cheese, Daddy! Grilled cheese!"

"All right, all right. We're coming. Let me go first, okay?" Once he's down a few rungs, she joins him on the ladder and slowly, they climb down together before Jax moves out of the way so she can land on the grass with a quiet thump.

As she rushes inside, he approaches me with his usual sexy swagger. "Hey, Beautiful."

"Hi."

Invading my space, he brushes his lips against mine in a toe-curling kiss. "Thanks for making lunch."

"Don't thank me yet," I reply. "I left your sandwich on the burner while I was changing Declan's bum, and it got a little burned. Speaking of…" I grimace. "I left Declan inside with some apple sauce. How much do you want to bet it's smeared all over the wall?"

"Don't worry. I'm sure Hades will lick it up." Wrapping his arm around my waist, he kisses my cheek and guides me inside.

Sure enough, Hades is on his hind legs, leveraging himself against the wall and licking what's left of the smeared apple sauce from the window next to the high chair.

"Hades, off," I scold, and I swear, if it was possible to roll his eyes, he would. Tail swishing, he pushes away from the wall, collapsing onto all four legs before sitting next to Poppy at the kitchen table. With a smile, she drops him the crust of her sandwich, and he gobbles it up like he hasn't been fed in days. "Why do we even buy dog food?" I ask Jax.

He shrugs. "It's the thought that counts."

"Of course, it is." Slipping his sandwich from the warm pan and onto a plate, I offer it to him. "Eat up."

He bounces his eyebrows up and down. "Don't tempt me."

Biting the inside of my cheek, I shake my head and try not to blush. But, seriously?

"I forgot to ask, how was therapy?" Jax adds.

"It was good. The usual."

"Anything I can do?"

It's the same question every time. And every time, it leaves me swooning. I love all the research he's put into being a father and a coach and a husband. How he manages to make me feel seen and appreciated, offering help while also not overstepping his bounds. It's a fine line, and he masters it more and more every day.

"Nope," I answer. "Just keep being awesome."

"Fine, but only if you take a bite of this sandwich to see how burned it is." He offers me a bite, and I take a quarter of the sandwich just to prove how big of a baby he is. I make it two chews before spitting it into a napkin.

"Okay, that's awful."

With a laugh, he wraps his arm around my neck and kisses me, refusing to let me get away unscathed.

"Is everyone still coming over tonight?" I ask.

"Yeah. Everett's bringing burgers and asked to use the smoker."

My stomach rumbles at the thought. "That sounds incredible!"

"Fin's bringing Mama Taylor's cookies, too."

I pretend to swoon. "My hero."

"You're lucky you and Ophelia both have the same pregnancy cravings," Jaxon teases. "Apparently, she begged Fin to bring them."

"Ah, then she's the one who's my hero," I quip. "I don't know what they put in those cookies, but…" I fan myself as Poppy chimes in.

"I want a cookie! I want a cookie! *Please* can I have a cookie?"

"You can have a cookie," I reply. "But only if you promise to be nice to your cousins, okay? Make sure you share the treehouse and follow all the rules. Deal?"

She rolls her eyes, sassy as ever before offering her cute little hand for me to shake. "Deal."

As I take it, sealing our negotiations with a handshake, the front door opens, and in walks the chaos.

A slew of children tumble in, racing through the house and to the backyard without so much as a hello. Then again, compared to all their cousins, Aunt Rory is chopped liver.

"You guys are early!" I call as the front door swings open again, revealing the rest of the crew.

"Sorry, not sorry," Finley says. "We left the house early to see if Ashie would nap in the car, but nope."

"Can't blame the girl. She just wants to keep up with her older siblings," Griffin adds. "Speaking of which, hey, baby sister."

Adjusting her glasses, Dylan gives him a quick squeeze. "Hey, big brother. How's—"

I block out their little reunion, popping my head through the sliding glass door, so I can warn the kids about Poppy's and Jaxon's afternoon project. "Paint's still wet on the treehouse, so no going up there! Okay, guys?"

"Good luck," Reeves quips from behind me. "Poppy's been bragging about the pirate treehouse to the boys for the past two weeks."

I rest my hand on my hip like a woman who means business and face him fully. "Yeah, well, I'm not replacing anyone's clothes, so…"

"Shit." Reeves darts out the back. "Boys—"

"Hey, Squeaks." Maverick steals a quick hug from me. "How are you feeling?"

"I'm great. Baby's wiggly as ever." I palm my massive belly. "How's Lia?"

"Ready for her due date," he says dryly. "I'm sure you are, too."

"You have no idea." I groan. "I'm jealous Ophelia's due before me."

"We'll see. You look ready pop, so—"

I smack his shoulder. "Hey!"

"Mav, will you check on AJ?" Ophelia interrupts. "He thinks he's a big boy and wants to keep up with everyone, but—"

"I got it, Goose." Leaning in, my brother gives Ophelia a quick kiss, then traipses into the backyard. "Hear that, AJ?" he says, addressing his little boy, Archer Junior. "No climbing on the treehouse without daddy's help, all right, buddy?"

Pax and Tatum walk in next, each of them balancing a toddler in one arm and a side dish in the other.

"Tater Tot!" I call.

My best friend swoops in for a side hug, careful not to bump our pregnant bellies together like a pair of cymbals. "Get over here, Lia!" she yells to her sister. "Pregnant ladies unite!"

Squeezing through the crowded kitchen, Ophelia wraps her arms around us, already munching on a cookie while creating a small, bumbling circle of pregnant ladies, as everyone else catches up around us.

And it's so…surreal. I'm still not sure how I got so lucky. How I wound up with this life. With these babies. And this husband. And this family. And these friends. And this house.

It even has a white picket fence and a treehouse in the back, just like I dreamed about. Don't get me wrong. It's far from perfect, and I still have OCD. I also know Hades won't be around forever, and Jaxon didn't get that billion-dollar raise he joked about, despite earning his upgraded status of son-in-law after marrying the owner's daughter. But life doesn't have to be perfect to be worth living. It's allowed to have its ups and downs, as long as you surround yourself with people who are willing to take the ride with you.

We're happy. I'm happy. And I wouldn't have it any other way.

Read the hijacked Epilogue here

ALSO BY KELSIE RAE

Kelsie Rae tries to keep her books formatted with an updated list of her releases, but every once in a while she falls behind.

If you'd like to check out a complete list of her up-to-date published books, visit her website at www.shopauthorkelsierae.com/

Or you can join her newsletter to hear about her latest releases, get exclusive content, and participate in fun giveaways.

Interested in reading more by Kelsie Rae?

The Little Things Series

(Steamy Don't Let Me Next Generation Series)

(Steamy Contemporary Romance Standalone Series)

A Little Complicated - Maverick and Ophelia's Story

A Little Tempting - Reeves and Dylan's Story

A Little Jaded - Everett and Raine's Story

A Little Secret - Griffin's and Finley's Story

A Little Broken - Tatum and Paxton's Story

A Little Crush - Jaxon and Rory's Story

Harden Heights Series

(Steamy Contemporary Romance Standalone Series)

Coming late 2025

Jagger's Story

Ford's Story

Hawke's Story

Roman's Story

Don't Let Me Series

(Steamy Contemporary Romance Standalone Series)

Don't Let Me Fall - Colt and Ashlyn's Story

Don't Let Me Go - Blakely and Theo's Story

Don't Let Me Break - Kate and Macklin's Story

Let Me Love You - A Don't Let Me Sequel

Don't Let Me Down - Mia and Henry's Story

Wrecked Roommates Series

(Steamy Contemporary Romance Standalone Series)

Model Behavior - River and Reese's Story

Forbidden Lyrics - Gibson and Dove's Story

Messy Strokes - Milo and Maddie's Story

Risky Business - Jake and Evie's Story

Broken Instrument - Fender and Hadley's Story

Signature Sweethearts Series

(Sweet Contemporary Romance Standalone Series)

Taking the Chance

Taking the Backseat (novella)

Taking the Job

Taking the Leap

Get Baked Sweethearts Series

(Sweet Contemporary Romance Standalone Series)

Off Limits

Stand Off

Hands Off

Hired Hottie (A *Steamy* Get Baked Sweethearts Spin-Off)

Swenson Sweethearts Series

(Sweet Contemporary Romance Standalone Series)

Finding You

Fooling You

Hating You

Cruising with You (A *Steamy* Swenson Sweethearts Novella)

Crush (A *Steamy* Swenson Sweethearts Spin-Off)

Advantage Play Series

(Steamy Romantic Suspense/Mafia Series)

Wild Card

Little Bird

Bitter Queen

Black Jack

Royal Flush (novella)

Stand Alones

Fifty-Fifty

Sign up for Kelsie's newsletter to receive exclusive content, including the first two chapters of every new book two weeks before its release date!

Dear Reader,

I want to thank you guys from the bottom of my heart for taking a chance on *A Little Crush*, and for giving me the opportunity to share this story with you. I cannot believe we're finally wrapping up the Little Things series and leaving Lockwood Heights when I've spent so much time creating a world I absolutely adore. Yup, it's definitely a bittersweet moment.

Don't worry, we'll still see plenty more familiar faces in future stories, but this still feels like the end of an era. Thank you for joining me on this journey and for loving my characters as much as I do. I couldn't do this without you, and no, I'm not just saying that. :)

As always, I would also be very grateful if you could take the time to leave a review. It's amazing how such a little thing like a review can be such a huge help to an author! (Seriously. It has the power to make or break a book's success.)

Thank you so much!!!

-Kelsie

ABOUT THE AUTHOR

Kelsie is a sucker for a love story with all the feels. When she's not chasing words for her next book, you will probably find her reading or, more likely, hanging out with her husband and playing with her three kiddos who love to drive her crazy.

She adores photography, baking, her two pups, and her cat who thinks she's a dog. Now that she's actively pursuing her writing dreams, she's set her sights on someday finding the self-discipline to not binge-watch an entire series on Netflix in one sitting.

If you'd like to connect with Kelsie, subscribe to her Patreon. Patrons receive a wide range of goodies including:

- Exclusive sneak peeks of works-in-progress
- ebook releases one week early
- Signed paperbacks on all new releases
- Exclusive special edition hardbacks
- So much more

You can also sign up for her newsletter, or join Kelsie Rae's Reader Group to stay up to date on new releases and her crazy publishing journey.